IMMORTAL
CURSED

BY M JACKSON

This is a work of fiction, names, characters, and places may exist, but are used in a fictious manner at the expense of the author's imagination. Any resemblance to actual persons, living or dead, or events are entirely coincidental.

Copyright © 2022 by Mark Jackson (M Jackson)
Instagram: mjacksonauthor

All rights reserved. No part of this book may be reproduced or used in any manner without written permission of the copyright owner except for the use of quotations in a book review.

First digital edition November 2022.
First paperback edition December 2022.
New cover paperback edition July 2023.

Supporting book design Heather Phillips and Simon Jackson

ISBN 978-1-3999-3647-7 (eBook)
ISBN 979-8-3660-0405-3 (Paperback)

Digital release by
Amazon Kindle

Paperback published by Amazon Kindle Publishing

Table of Contents

From the Author *4*
Prologue: Egyptian Rulers *5*
Waking up *9*
Pennyview *20*
Out of the house *32*
Instinct awakened *46*
Lakebrook High School *64*
The Titans *78*
At the mall *90*
Party at the Walker house *101*
Miracle blood *119*
A date? *150*
Supernatural hunters *166*
Mr Callahan *193*
Lone Mountain *204*
Montage *229*
Falling out *250*
Resolutions *276*
Acknowledgements *313*

From the Author

First of all, thank you for purchasing this book. This is my first book.

I started planning this story over a couple years ago, where I had dipped into writing more over the holidays when I possibly could, it had developed vastly in size and story.

This passing year was the ultimate decision to get this story out there in some capacity, or let it wither away and be forgotten about as a save file backed up on some device. So, the decision was made to spend countless hours outside of my main career to get it finished and I have enjoyed doing it.

It felt like the first year of the main character, Arthur, was a sensible place to stop for the end of this book, from the story that I had planned. However, the chapters I have planned reaches far beyond the timeline of this book to wherever Arthur will end up.

So, I hope you enjoy the beginning of Arthur's story as he begins his new life within his strange unfamiliar surroundings. All of the difficulties he may come across and situations he will need to solve.

Prologue: Egyptian Rulers

The spell Immortalis :
"A state where the human body has returned to life and is ultimately indestructible by any mortal concepts or actions."

2600BC Ancient Egypt

Many Egyptian leaders adored the thought of being an immortal ruler; to rule the throne for the infinite years beyond.

Many rulers claimed methods of how to cheat death in history. Secretly, this was because the Egyptian rulers feared what would happen beyond life and to leave behind what kingdom they had built in their time. Many of those feared the God Osiris, who takes many forms and different names in cultures. Osiris would be stood at the gates into the afterlife and would be waiting to rightfully claim those souls who were passing into his realm.

Those eccentric Egyptian rulers sought out methods to cheat the God Osiris, many succumbed to failure.

A method was discovered to craft a spell which cheated the God Osiris from taking their soul and to live forever and rule, the spell that became known as *Immortalis*.

A particularly cunning Pharaoh named Sneferu first successfully crafted a spell of said immortality. The crafted spell would be cast upon a body before death, either timely or untimely. The body would rest in a dead state, which will resurrect within days and will be frozen genetically in an instant.

Superhuman strength would grow by the day within the body's muscle tissue and structure, becoming indestructible. The target of the spell cannot be killed by the injuries that would be deemed fatal to the mortal human.

Regeneration speed of the body's cells reproduce at a faster rate to fix any damage caused to the body as though it had never occurred in the first place. The occupant that had been cast with this spell will not age a second after the moment of their reawakening.

After the succession of the Pharaoh Sneferu's immortality, the group of spell casters who helped craft the spell disappeared, secretly at the orders of the Pharoah himself. The Pharaoh Sneferu disappeared himself from the throne many years on leaving his kingdom behind, rumour had it, hiding by other names.

Untranslatable hieroglyphics have been discovered since time had passed, which archaeologists were unable to translate the true story.

Supernatural speculators insist that the Pharaoh went mad after decades of immortality and watching those who he loved around him, die of old age. Another speculation was greed, the Pharaoh Sneferu wanted to be the only unique being in the universe, this speculation matched up with the disappearance of the original spell casters who helped craft the spell.

It is still unclear in modern times on what really happened on Sneferu's immortal journey and where it had ended.

1200AD – Onwards, The Middle Ages

The spell was never documented accurately by the great Pharoah himself, or any known casters that had assisted him. All of the other copies from the spell casters vanished back in 2600BC along with their disappearance. Only some hieroglyphics left, dated many years later of Pharoah Sneferu's rule would vaguely summarise a location.

A curious Italian archaeologist accidently discovered one final copy of a scroll that was hidden away, breaking a false wall within one of homes of the original spell casters. Many tried to translate the scroll back in Rome, passed from historian to historian.

Eventually being passed onto a curator, the scroll was sold on as an artifact, a collectible transferred from museum to museum. The scroll became famous for its dated age and discovery rather than the content it bestowed. Lost even further within passing and translation of many civilisations throughout the ages, as kings were conquered, and new powers ruled.

Many religious and conspiracy groups, some who believed to be of supernatural powers tried to replicate the spell for its trait of immortality, trying to claim themselves as a higher being within a well-kept society. In an attempt of the spell many voluntary deaths followed from the failed attempts.

With the rare knowledge of the spell moving across the European continent, more specifically in Paris, France. A secretive, small settlement of incredibly funded witches and warlocks linked to the great House of Capet, bestowed with great wisdom and supernatural favour could reproduce the spell for righteous use of justice.

These witches were famously made known to be the Sorcières de la Justice *(Witches of Justice)* for the art of how they carried out this spell. As the spell became known to be the meaning of an enchantment, the enchantment of everlasting life. The witches correctly replicated the spell upon one of their own, with sheer precision and favour, only to discover that their supernatural magical abilities had been stripped from them.

With that discovery of the potential immortal power the spell became something worse, a curse. The Witches of Justice became a political group of assassins within the Parisian culture. Casting the spell, now reclaimed a curse; would cast this curse to any unrighteous person fitting of a devastating crime. The Witches of Justice were a shadow organisation to undermine the ruling parliament courts of Paris; if justice were not served for the heinous crimes displayed by a criminal, the criminal would be a target of this group.

The criminal would be firstly cursed to be an occupant of the immortality spell unwittingly, then murdered and buried. The criminal would then awaken from the curse within a coffin far under the ground, rumoured to be a hidden space located deep in the catacombs underneath Paris. Starved of oxygen the criminal would pass out continuously and never gain full consciousness or control of his or her own body, the only feeling would be pain. Infinite pain.

With many years passing as the cursed ones were moved around and buried deeper within the catacombs of Paris, with no oxygen for half of a century the immortal beings would simply decay to a point of withering for an eternity.

The Witches of Justice were poetic killers of their time, it was an art emerged from deserved cruelty. The witches prestigiously handed down their knowledge to those specially chosen to commit their existence to the Witches of Justice.

These witches still exist on today in smaller numbers mainly throughout the European mainland.

"A spell so gloriously crafted and well enchanted to become a curse, to rot and wither for the infinite years of man."

Waking up

This story starts with Arthur, a normal young man of his time at the age of nineteen. He had an average build, with the scruffy look of someone who rarely kept up with his appearance. Strong blue eyes with a hint of yellow near the pupil that sat at the focus of attention when spoken to, if he ever held his head up high long enough to withstand a long conversation. With a simple fashion sense of someone who favoured basic clothing that involved wearing only solid colours at a time and wasn't too vibrant or costly.

He attended a university in England that involved business and management, studying three hours far away from the family home, which made it impossible at times to return. The days would turn to weeks and those weeks would turn into months, before Arthur had any time to stop and breathe, half a year would have passed. Arthur was always busy with studying, working, and living.

Friends meant a lot to Arthur; with a small modest group of friends he could turn to. Both, at home and at the university. The two groups of friends from the university and home life were vast of character and style, they were all a unique bunch. Friends were like a second family to Arthur, sticking together throughout the hard and the toughest of times. Family was just as important; Arthur had a medium sized family, which consisted of a mother and a father, an older brother and younger sister. Who he would visit when he could.

It was nearing the winter season; the skies grew darker and the days passed quicker. Arthur was driving through the dark southbound of a motorway that began high up in the north of England, further up the country to where his family home was. The roads were dimly lit and slippery from the ice that set, which caused warnings for extra caution out on the road.

Suddenly the vehicle in front abruptly lit up its break lights, with breaking force the vehicle came to a stop. Arthur pushed his feet down all the way on the brake pedal, the car clambered to a halt with what friction it had, his grip intensified on the steering wheel as his car came closer. Both of the cars came to such a close stop, an inch's stretch away from colliding with each other.
   It was a lucky escape Arthur thought, considering the outcome of what could've happened, for a moment there was time to breathe and process the catastrophic event that could've occurred. Whilst sat in his moment of relief, a glimmer of light began to grow from the back of his car, it was a glow ever so faintly becoming brighter and brighter.
   Seconds had only passed and as soon as he could comprehend, a heavy goods transport lorry had tried its best, but it was too late to stop. Too late for Arthur to react and try and escape through the car door. The breaks were not enough of the lorry, the road flawed with ice allowed a presumptuous slide of this hulking unstoppable beast. With all the might of that transport lorry with its haulage, seemed to come rushing through both vehicles inevitable to stop.
   That was the end, or so we thought.
   Waking up from what seemingly was a dark sleep. A light began to appear, it was blurry at first. More focus came to Arthur's eyes and the lights grew to three masses of a blur, three dim light spots. A deep gasp of air, which filled his lungs that ignited the senses back into Arthur's body and unexpectedly back to the living realm. Arthur's thought process was slow, to his understanding he began to contemplate the lights above were just ceiling lights, not lights from an after-world where he'd ended up. Coldness was the first feeling he felt return. He felt the coldness in the air, gather all around his limbs, lingering closely over his body.

To Arthur's realisation, he lay there barely covered, upon this cold metallic slab with a small thin white sheet covering up towards his chest.

Confusion of his own existence was the next thought that came to mind. He began moving his neck as that was all Arthur felt he could move, from this looking down first at his torso. He noticed his body was all scarred and stitched together; such horror filled him within, rediscovering the pit of his stomach. Then it struck; memories came flooding back of his last moments from what seemed from another lifetime ago. His mind began to work itself more, questions struck him next but with no answer or inkling of what to do. Trying to examine the room around him with his eyesight still poorly returning at the corners of his eyes.

Everything he looked at around the room through the corners of his eyes, was encased with darkness that sat creeping at the sides. As the blur began to thin away there were only one certain answer at this moment within his unexpected resurrection.

The furnishings around all so bland and cold in design, the lighting that illuminated was so clinical as it engulfed the entire room hand in hand with the cold. It was quickly figured out to be known that this was a morgue.

As Arthur tried to wriggle some life back into his limbs, the task was difficult. He was unsure if any limbs were left to move, stretching his neck further he could see just about his hand. Starting from finger to thumb underneath the sheet he wriggled, from the hand to the wrist and within this short amount of time feeling and movement returned, at most he could see it moving. He dragged himself like a bag of unwilling body parts to hang off the end of this cold metallic slab.

There was a noise. The doors across the room took the attention of Arthur in the next moment, dim grey paint with a metallic doorframe around and the small window blacked out.

The rattle of the handle became the immediate focus of his concern. Arthur's heart began to race, trying to keep up from all of the questions that surrounded his thoughts. Fear flooded through him. The entire situation is completely unusual but to add on top of that, a member of the staff was about to come into the room where he, had come back to life.

They would see at this very moment sitting, a seemingly limp naked man with his decency half covered. Who ultimately from the making out of his stitches, should not be alive, Arthur had no answers for those questions.

The doors broke open with some force almost taking the hinges off, a gust of wind also followed through with such force throwing the papers loose off the cabinets amuck to the floors.

There walked in haste was a human as the doors slammed shut from such an invisible pushing force, a girl it seemed from what the returning eyesight could make out. The girl was not scared neither was she lost; she seemed to have some urgent agenda and clearly didn't work here.

She sped towards Arthur with such stepping pace and only one question to ask, "Can you move?"

An accent. She was an American, the first thing evident, that accent was incredibly different comparing it to his own and others around him.

Arthur replied with a murmur, a grunt of some sort.

It seems the muscles in his throat had not redeveloped and the use of his vocals had not yet returned. A struggled shake of the head to assume *no* would suffice.

As the girl leaned closer, she became clearer to see. The next thing Arthur noticed was her blonde hair that reflected from the lights within the room. Helpless with no idea of how to react or even attempt to say, the girl placed her hand behind Arthur's arm. With a struggle she hoisted his awkwardly stiff body, with her other arm pulling his thighs towards the edge, off the metal bed.

Barely clutching onto the sheet that covered his resurrected body, to keep what dignity he had left. It came clear to Arthur that she was in a rush, for what he wondered about. Besides the fact that she was stealing a potential dead body and didn't belong here.

A sound took away the girl's attention on Arthur as she now snapped her sight to the doors of which she just barged through. Someone else was trying to get in through that very door over the other side of the room. Slowly she raised her hand in the air as if to sign stop and waited.

The door began to open, she vigorously pushed her hand through the air and following that motion those heavy doors slammed shut with an almighty force.

Arthur began to feel startled, what was this girl doing he thought.

She grasped her hand in a fist and acted out to crunch something imaginary in the air, following that sharp action, the lights in the room all burst from their sockets. The room was complete with darkness with a touch of an occasional spark of an exposed wire.

With Arthur's arm over her shoulder assisting him out of this unusual situation, each stumbling step became sturdier regaining use of his legs. This girl must've been in a hurry with the force she was hurling Arthur with.

The clanking sound of the fire escape doors opening followed by the bright light distorting Arthur's vision once more. Blind whiteness surrounded his vision as his eyes were adjusting to the daylight, forcing himself to squint, to find any familiarity where his footing is. It took a while for Arthur's vision to return, but as soon as he could see at a short distance the girl pushed Arthur into the back seats of a car.

"Wait here until I return, don't move!" she instructed firmly. "I've got some cleaning up to do."

Arthur waited obediently in the car and adjusted his bearings, stretching every muscle and limb possible.

Questions and nothing but questions seemed to creep up inside Arthur's mind. With his thoughts suddenly returning and being able to recall of those events that happened up to realising his fate of the accident.

Arthur didn't know what he was coming up against, this once average life, lived young man who attempted his mediocre at best. He was average, never made a fuss and never did his best either, only enough to get along without a worry. Being startled turned to fear, which led to horror, which somewhat paralysed him.

What did she want from him.

Arthur moved his barely working fingers towards the release of the door, he pulled it, nothing.

It was locked.

All Arthur could think about was escaping whatever strange reason this girl wanted him. As he began to frantically pull, there was no escape unless he tried to get out through one of the front doors.

He launched himself over the gap between the two front seats, his chest rested on the shoulder of the seat.

It was too late; he couldn't escape either way. His body just wouldn't allow it.

The girl reappeared out of the fire escape door, seemingly much calmer now than moments ago. Arthur sunk into the backseat of the car pushing his back as far into the edge of the interior as it could go.

His eyes were locked onto her as she moved closer to the car, desperately observing any signs she gave off.

She was walking at a normal pace, there seemed to be no urgency.

What had happened? Did she just kill them all? Arthur thought to himself.

She opened the driver's door and sat into the seat, calmly adjusting the rear-view mirror to examine herself, before directing it towards Arthur. She glanced for only a second and switched on the engine returning her gaze back to the rear-view mirror as the car began to reverse. Arthur's eyes caught hers, it seemed as though she was analysing him whilst hiding some judgement.

With that stare, Arthur's mouth slowly appeared to open with the opening of a question. She cut him off coldly.

"I won't answer any questions just yet, relax for now." the stranger snapped, "You will just have to trust me for the meantime. We just need to get you out of here."

That response held the questions momentarily off within Arthur, sitting there with sinking curiosity.

He couldn't wait much longer as the car began to move down the road. A question blurted from his lips, that was a matter of urgency. "How did you do that in the morgue?"

The girl's eyes sharply moved back and forth to the rear-view mirror as she continued to drive in the car, her eyes shot straight back to his with a reply so bold.

"My name's Hannah, and I can cast spells, magic you know?" she began to state, "I am a witch, not one of those fake talk to the dead ones, a supernatural one."

A witch?! What does that even mean, Arthur's thoughts bounced within his head.

That answer made Arthur quiet for most of the journey with questions erupting within his mind, it was difficult to not ask questions, worried she may be able to cast a spell on him. So many assumptions and just trying to assimilate what had happened and to what will happen, Arthur continued to stay quiet in the backseat.

Arthur was searching around his surroundings through the car windows, trying to catch the outside of any familiarity of where he was.

Hannah noticed by the rear-view mirror and spoke, "Are you trying to find where you are right now? Because it's on the sat nav here at the front." she pointed towards the centre of the car screen.

"Oh… I see." Arthur replied, feeling slightly like an idiot.

As the conversation began to dribble through the awkward silenced atmosphere of the car. Arthur began to understand what type of person she was; she was intelligent, incredibly sharp to react to anything but also with seemingly impulsive tendencies.

Hannah began to reveal details about who she was, as Arthur smoothly tried to pry more and more, coming to an understanding that she adored talking about herself. He began to figure out that she seemingly has a high standard in expectations of anything and anyone. Hannah explained that she loves to be the centre of attention back at the house and enjoys attending any type of event, to one day become a powerful personality, presumably giving her this full-on approach.

Hannah had blonde hair with shades of almost gold within it, pale skin that made her look cold. A soft rosy makeup set blushed her cheeks as the focus attracted any notice to her eyeliner, it seemed like she takes her time with her appearance; and looked after herself. Her brown eyes which may seem like the look of innocence but deep down, it was insinuated that those eyes could be something fearsome beneath if she were pushed easily, especially now what he had experienced at the morgue. From what Arthur had gathered as she held him up earlier to escape, she was similar height to him, possibly a slight bit shorter in difference but still she was a dainty thing. It was impressive that she could move him.

The two had been in the car for more than an hour, Arthur began to catch the signs that were repeating over and over and the familiarity that he'd been there before. It became obvious that the two were heading to Stansted Airport as the signs became more frequent. Arthur questioned Hannah, who confirmed where they were heading to.

"But I don't have my passport, no clothes and anything?" Arthur sharply soon added.

She was confident in her response, "All you'll have to do is not look suspicious and make a scene, I have some clothes that will fit in the trunk."

Arthur's family came to mind, "What about my family?!" he quickly questioned her.

She paused for a moment, "All of your family think you're dead. Sorry." she added, not lingering a second more.

Arthur felt massively uneasy, as the two began to park the car and walk through the airport.

It was true, it wasn't obvious until it was finally spoken out loud, everyone thinks Arthur is dead. Gone forever.

Hannah, keeping her voice down, trying to reassure Arthur, "They won't know you're missing as your funeral will be a closed coffin when they bury you."

A whispering hiss erupted from Arthur's curiosity, "They're missing a body! What did you do back at the morgue, you went back in? How will that solve anything?"

Hannah let out a sly grin, "Witchy power, I can cast a spell to fool people, to believe what I tell them is true or to command them to do anything I wish… So, I told them to weigh up the coffin to make it seem like it had a body in it. I will use the same spell to get you through the security." she was firm in her explanation.

Arthur started to feel less uneasy as the two began their way through the airport. Going through the motions of getting through every checkpoint in there; with some supernatural way she convinced every staff member who the two communicated with.

Hannah paid for both tickets on the spot at the desk, the clerk had seemed to have entered a mysterious passport number on the airplane ticket once Arthur analysed it.

The only other big obstacle was the physical passport checking before stepping onto the plane. Hannah went first; she smoothly stepped forward and with a mumbling of an enchantment to the woman, it was Arthur's turn for checking his passport. After stepping ahead by one step slowly at a time his heart jumped, with a thrilling feeling of getting so far without getting caught. He had no passport to show.

The sound of Hannah's voice made him jump before she had crossed the check line. "Oh Arthur, I still have your passport here!" turning around and rummaging through her bag, handing him a passport.

Slowly Arthur reached for the passport with great curiosity, how did she have his passport!?

Arthur opened it to the portrait page.

It was Hannah's passport.

At that very moment Arthur felt an overwhelming sense of lunacy, was this just a strange sick game?

Hannah looked pale in person but in this passport, her picture in this could be mistaken for a ghost, barely seen from the background. Thinking of how pale she was in the photo; Arthur became pale himself with the fear now finally creeping back up at the pit of his stomach.

With every step forward to the woman at the gate it felt as though his heart dropped lower within him, weighing him down. Arm propped forward handing the passport to the woman at the gate, finger keeping apart the pages to easily show her as quick as possible.

The woman raised her hand to take the passport, Arthur felt a sweat break out at the back of his neck. She began to stare at the page blankly with no emotion, Arthur had no idea what to think or feel, he only felt the churning of emotions all mixing around inside of him. The churning began to become fiercer, battling against the vomit from all of the commotion.

What happens if Hannah just left? She couldn't she needs that passport to land, or does she? What would happen to him?

All these thoughts bouncing from the adrenaline fed his excitement and shrank the fear.

"Here you go, please move forward." the woman instructed.

He was frozen in place at her instruction. Arthur was dazed with what just had happened, with a clenched face to hold a grin of a madman as the woman handed back the passport. Looking forward Hannah was waiting for him with such a vibrant smile; Arthur began to trust her and what her capabilities could do.

The two walked down the boarding corridor, deep down with a smirk Hannah knew it would always work. Arthur could see she was filled with confidence, and she loved it.

The flight went fast, understanding from Hannah that they were on route to the state called Oregon in the United States, specifically to a small town named Lakebrook.

Hannah suggested to Arthur to get some sleep, as the time difference will catch up with them. "We have a busy schedule ahead when we get there, you'll need that rest." she suggested.

Arthur tried to sleep; it was either the awful seats that stopped him from sleeping, or the excitement of what was to follow; the thoughts of those he had left behind didn't seem to arise near any surface of his thoughts.

Pennyview

The sun seemed to shine brighter over this side of the world, the heat was more prominent as Arthur made his way down the steps of the plane. As the two travelled through the airport, Arthur saw a sign to where they had landed, Salem Municipal Airport. Arthur stereotypically put two together, Salem and witches. He giggled to himself.

Hannah noticed the giggle, "Hm? Something funny? she asked, turning around, and stopping.

Arthur had a short look of surprise, caught off guard, "Oh no. Nothing." he quickly guarded.

Hannah gave a strange look, before continuing, "I've parked somewhere over here." she mentioned, facing outwards to the parking lot.

Walking through the rows of vehicles, a long grey car gleamed with pride as it sat there, waiting patiently for Hannah to return.

"Here it is!" she announced out loud as she then began to fumble around in her bag, looking for the keys to the car.

As she unlocked the car, Arthur walked around to the opposite side and lifted the door handle to the passenger side, sliding himself into the seat. Hannah sat in the driving seat and took a deep breath of relief; happy she was finally home on her side of the world.

She switched on the engine and began to drive the car out of the parking lot. Leaving the airport behind, the drive seemed to linger on the busy roads. The roads began to become bumpy; pine trees began to gather at the sides of the road. The trees began to get taller allowing a large amount of shade to cover the route ahead.

Arthur was silent throughout the journey, taking in the new world around him in. He was drawn to this new world, stuck to the passenger window. The road signs that named different routes began to appear; the signs drew frequently repeating the location Lakebrook on them. A giant billboard loomed up towards the sky, which announced the population and the infamously heard tag line of the town.

"Welcome to the great town of Lakebrook, home of the Lakebrook Giants – the best football team in the west!"

Arthur somewhat gathered a large amount of excitement at the sight of this humble, yet modest welcome sign, completely forgetting what had happened within the last twenty-four hours. As the car moved in through the outskirts of this town called Lakebrook, the suburbs were breath taking. Arthur had never seen any houses like these before, except in the movies. The grass was a healthy, vibrant green, the sizes of the houses changed intermittently from small to enormous. The wooden panelled fronts of the houses were all well looked after and freshly painted, they were grand at a first glance, astonishingly impressing those who walked up to the front doors.

Hannah took a turn with the car, the street seemed wider than the others. A seemingly wealthier part of the suburbs where the tallest of houses challenged each other by height, the pointy towers they had and the size of their gardens.

As Arthur pointed the towers out to Hannah, she corrected him, the small towers attached into these houses were called cupolas.

The gardens grew bigger and bigger as the houses were pushed further back into the distance, particularly followed by a majestic road that hid behind wide tall gates and walls.

Excitement was not in short supply for Arthur with the thought of new discoveries ahead. The car began to slow down and calmly cruise along the sidewalk where a tall black cast-iron Victorian fence guarded the house behind it, scaring off any visitors who simply laid eyes upon the house. The car finally came to a halt further down from the cast-iron fencing, a similar gate appeared, much lower than the one previous.

"Here we are! The Pennyview Boarding House where you will be staying." informed Hannah, tapping at her phone which activated the gate to open.

She began to drive slowly up the driveway's entrance, as a clearing through the trees appeared Arthur noticed something impressive. There stood a grand, white Victorian house with a black shale roofing with each tile rounded at the bottom. Low black wrought iron fencing seemed to guide Hannah's car towards an area to where a few cars were parked, outside a double garage separate from the house.

Arthur pushed the car door open and as it swayed, the brightness of the day flooded his vision, all of the colours that surrounded him seemed more intense. Hannah made her way out of her side and stood in front of the car and stopped for a second.

"Come on." she ordered, as Arthur took a moment to absorb his surroundings.

Arthur followed a few steps behind her down the side path which led towards the front garden, rich flowerbeds filled with a spray of red and white flowers.

Two older women stood atop of the front garden's path, one on the right wore a more welcoming facial expression. They were both stood close together, the seemingly cheerful one held the other's arm. They were expectedly awaiting the return of the two.

Hannah picked up her pace as she pulled out the car keys and placed them in one of the woman's hands.

She turned around with a grin on her face, "Here he is, ready to be sacrificed to the monster in the basement. All fresh and still alive!" she paused for a moment, taking joy in the look of confusion mixed with fear on Arthur's face. "Just kidding! I'll see you inside, I'll let the others know you are here!" she added.

The woman who appeared to smile at Arthur, stepped closer carefully treading over the lawn, trying not to damage it. She reached out with an open hand to offer a handshake to Arthur.

"Welcome to Pennyview Boarding House, home to the secret witches of Lakebrook. I'm Myra, and you are?" as she smiled shaking Arthur's hand firmly.

"A-Arthur." he just about managed to spit out, another witch, these all must be witches he gathered from that welcome.

The other woman then stepped forward, the expression on her face grew a half-smile, she raised her hand to Arthur's and proceed to welcome him.

"My name is Ethel, I'm Myra's wife. I can imagine you have lots to ask us, but for now we would like you to adjust, to settle in. Have a look around the house and meet the others." she spoke, warming up the tone of her voice. "Hannah will show you around, and your room."

Arthur began to make his way towards the front door, the two older women watched him as he walked towards the house. The entrance into the house was through a magnificent door; red as it firmly stood shining away in the daylight. The door was already open where Hannah was waiting on him, to give a welcome tour around the house.

As Arthur stepped up a short staircase towards the red door, he noticed a golden plaque to the side of the doorframe, engraved with black writing. It read the name of the house, "Pennyview Boarding House"

Hannah opened the door a bit further, revealing the inside of the house, "Come on in!" she cheerfully announced.

The main foyer was grand in width as it was in height, the walls that surround it covered with the shades of a white and a light grey damask design, halfway down the walls the design was split by the wooden panelling that was painted white to compliment the furnishings.

Tall arched glass windows covered the front of the house that were facing outwards to the lawn. Arthur could vividly imagine the light peering in from these on a fantastic summer's day. Arthur took a step forward as he gawped around his surroundings.

As he took that first step, he noticed the floor was hard. The floor, a tiled white marble glistened from the light that flowed from those tall arched windows.

Hannah guided Arthur down the foyer, through the hallway she began to explain aspects of the house to Arthur. Arthur peering into other rooms as he walked by, paid no attention, his visual curiosity seemed to deafen him. The kitchen opened out to a wide space, a similar theme of whites and grey seemed to join this room from the rest of the house.

What stood out most was the chequered black and white tiles that flooded the floorspace. An island of black counter tops filled the centre of the room, immaculately clean, showing off the sparkling surface. These counters surrounded half the edges of the kitchen. A floating metal hanging rack stacked of rustic copper pots hung from the centre of the ceiling, vintage in design of the twisted metalwork of the hanging frame.

There were a few doors here, a door hid in the corner of the kitchen; it was slightly open where a couple of stairs could be seen descending downwards narrowly. The only presumption for this would be an entrance the basement under the house.

Another door at the side of the kitchen took the two into a strange room. A scent of lavender and sage forced its way into Arthur's nostrils. This room was entirely different to the few areas he had just been, it was narrow with its stone paved tiled floor and half-wall windows that allowed the room to be colder than the rest. A pair of lights dangled from beams across the glass ceiling which focused on dimly lighting the centre of the room. There was an enormous wooden table that sat amid in the centre, it was cluttered with various odd stems of plants, bowls that kept various petals and other items within them and a range of old looking books. Smaller wooden tables surrounded the outsides of the room which were also cluttered with various coloured flowers, giving off a mixture of strong scents.

Hannah stood by the table in the middle of the room placing her hands on her hips, "This room is our herbalism room, where Ethel spends a lot of her time nurturing the plants which help make potions, charms and medicines." she educated Arthur.

Heading back through the kitchen towards the opposite side, the rooms linked by an open archway which led to the dining room. That similar theme crept up again, no real colours, just shades of black and white seemed to dominate.

Arthur took a step into the dining room, his foot felt differently on the floor this time, looking down to see what the difference was. He noticed the floor was not marble, nor stone in this room. It was wooden. A wooden slatted floor but still, to no surprise, it was painted white. His eyes moved up off the floor, a chandelier crowned the dining room with glass and gold. Another enormous table stood at the centre of attention for this room, the dining table accompanied by fitting dining chairs that gathered in great numbers around it. What then took the attention of Arthur was another girl who sat at the head of the table attentively absorbed in her mobile phone.

"That's Kimberly, sometimes she can be fun. She is a witch here to." Hannah introduced her.

"Surprise, surprise, we're all witches here…" Kimberly announced in a sarcastic tone as she looked up. A look of shock masked her face. "A male… and a *witch*?! A *warlock*?!" she presumed, her pitch getting higher at the end of her sentence allowing some expectation of excitement.

Arthur shuffled his hands ever so slightly, feeling awkward to break the news. "I'm not a witch, sorry to disappoint. I'm just a guy who died and came back to life magically." he raised his eyebrows for a second.

Hannah added to Arthur's sentence, "Yeah, he is the one who Myra sensed as some interruption casting some new spell or something. Whatever Arthur is it drew her towards his magical existence."

Now that Hannah had mentioned that about Arthur, everything seemed to get a bit more interesting to him. The more he thought about it, the more curious he became and wanted to know exactly what had happened to him.

Was his death just a one off, could he die again?

Kimberly hopped to her feet, "I'm going to get Peter. He's going to be *so* excited now that there's another guy here." she sung excitedly, pacing fast out of view from the two.

As the two head through the back of the dining room it led to another small room with a couple of wicker armchairs. These were sat in front of two wooden French doors that lead onto the back porch of the house. The French door gracefully held open along with the netting flowing ever so slowly through the gentle breeze. Leading out to stand on the back porch a set of small wooden stairs and bannisters separated the house from the grass.

Onlooking the back garden the grass proudly lay a vibrant green and it seemed to stretch on forever. A fountain glimmering in the light of day stood halfway in the middle of the garden with a winding path of stepping-stones that took the eye into the distance of the garden. At the very back of the garden there seemed to be some tall hedges with an opening, it looked like the beginning of a maze, not a big maze but a modest one.

Arthur became curious to where he was staying in the house, hoping it wasn't anywhere in the basement. "Where am I going to stay?" he asked.

Hannah jumped at the question, "Follow me." she was excited to show him his room.

Arthur followed Hannah back to the foyer at the start of the house, now beginning to climb the grand curving staircase.

They stopped on the first floor just across from the landing where the staircase ended. There seemed to be a communal seating area which looked over the banister of the stairs. Four two seated sofas gathered round a glass coffee table. An enormous rug captured the collection of furniture and confined it to its corners. The space was big enough to almost be called a living room itself. Next to this communal seating area there was a hallway which enclosed the door of Arthur's room, it was waiting to be explored. The door was already open, welcoming its new resident.

Hannah stopped at the opposite of the open door in the hallway "Here it is, your room." she raised her arm, open handed, gesturing Arthur in.

Arthur's now-new room bellowed with its space and with every crack and corner spotless.

Immaculate.

The floor was similar to the one in the dining room, Arthur could almost sneak out at night watching a couple of the floorboards to avoid making a creak. A metal framed bed, with the bars that stood along it vertically. A simple white, wooden wardrobe and a dresser that looked like it had sat there for at least a hundred years. One white bedside table with a lonely lamp sat on top with a black base and a glass lampshade of an upturned flower and finally a writing desk sat by the large bedroom window, accompanied by a chair.

Minimalist, this room screamed to Arthur.

The entire rooms within this house were all similar in design, spotless and two-toned Arthur summarised.

Hannah left, giving Arthur time to collect his thoughts, and let him settle into his new surroundings.

Arthur sat on his new bed, the change in life was daunting as it seemed hard to simply just forget his previous life. As exciting as it was it became harder to swallow, as thoughts of his loved ones, the pain they will feel having to bury him. The whole situation seemed to be a lot to simply accept, but

Arthur knew he had to adjust. There was no going back and nothing he could do. Even with so much left behind a new future was waiting for him, a strange new future with a lot of discoveries. New places and new people.

Only a short moment of time passed when Hannah had returned, she stood at the open doorway and tapped at the doorframe to gain Arthur's attention as he still sat there on the bed. She announced that the residents within Pennyview were all waiting downstairs to introduce themselves.

The two walked down the stairs as Ethel stood at the bottom of the last step waiting on the two to take them through to the dining room. As Ethel guided them into the dining room there was a silence in the air as each of the residents were already in the room. They were all waiting, watching and presumably making early judgments as Arthur entered the room.

Ethel began to introduce Arthur, just as he glanced around the room, avoiding any long eye contact between any other of the residents. What became obvious to him were the number of female residents that lived here. To what Arthur understood that witches seemed to be predominantly female. Just by looking at each of the girls, each one of them seemed a different personality.

Suddenly, someone different caught Arthur's eye. It was a boy, standing behind Kimberly, which was a surprising change to see. This boy would probably be the only male friend Arthur could speak to, or even hang out with, at least for now he thought.

Arthur's chain of thought broke as soon as Ethel brought in the introductions to those around the room. Arthur trying to remember the names of everybody introduced.

Ethel came around to introducing the boy, "This is Peter, he is a friend of Kimberly." she said before being interrupted.

"Boyfriend!" Kimberly added.

Ethel continued after a short glare at Kimberly, "Erm yes and I am sure it is reassuring to see a male presence in this household."

Peter raised a thumb in Arthur's direction, "Nice to see another dude here! It's boring being around these girls all the time." Peter announced warmly and bravely over the table.

Myra added to Peter's introduction, "Peter is human, so play gently with him, he knows all about this house and who we are. We trust him completely… and Arthur is somewhat special, magical, we think anyway… at this time"

So far? Arthur thought. This returning to life could be just a one off? This news discomforted him, but he wasn't planning on dying anytime soon.

After the introductions, Arthur scrambled at trying to remember a few of the names. As many of the residents vacated the dining room and began to carry on with their day.

Pennyview boarding house was quiet at times, the odd anomaly would be a spell that would shake the house, as the witches would be practicing at the teachings of Myra or Ethel.

For the beginning of Arthur's stay, he was observed by the witches to see if there were any changes in his magical essence that surrounded him.

Running some strange misunderstood tests with various trinkets. Secretly he believed that these observations were only to check if he were a threat to the witches in this house.

Understanding a gathering of this many witches is rare, Arthur began to understand there were dangerous stranger forces out there, which would take joy in wiping the whole household out of any magic.

Day to day life soon became stale for Arthur living in the house, he was limited of where he could go.

Some rooms were off limits to Arthur, but what interested him the most was outside of the boarding house; thirsting for the outside world he wanted to discover more. In this great and vast country, he wanted to explore what life is like out there. Occasionally Ethel would let him join the group that would shop for the household groceries, following her around and helping with the bags. This was not enough for the sake of his new life; it was as though he was being trapped.

One sunny day which could only be observed from either any front window or the back garden of Pennyview house. The suburban streets gleamed with the sun whilst younger children played, and others strolled past. It was only then until Arthur overheard Hannah talking about a big party that would be happening later in the evening a couple blocks away.

It had been ages since Arthur had been to a social event.

Hannah was trying to convince Kimberly to go as there were students from a place called Lakebrook State University going. It was going to be big from how Hannah had exaggerated it. From the response of Kimberly, it seemed she was uninterested, she was not interested in meeting guys or drinking opposite of what Hannah was enthusing. This was a chance, a chance for Arthur to escape the somewhat becoming dull lifestyle.

This couldn't just be his life, he needed to get out he thought. Walking in the room trying not to sound like he was listening to the previous part of that conversation, "A party! Where? It would be great to get out of this house." Arthur questioned casually.

"You know you're stuck here Arthur, anyway you might cramp our style to look for cute guys." Hannah lightly rejected his wish.

Arthur tried not to show any desperation. "Come on, let me come with you. It's so boring, it feels like I may have been better off in that coffin underground. I won't even talk to you or hang about with you if that's the case."

Hannah's face showed no interest in his offer.

Arthur knew he had to pull the low blow, it was a level of desperation he wasn't happy with, "I'll tell Myra that you're off out on a hunt for strange older guys. You know she'll flip from that news." he didn't feel great even saying it out loud, but desperation took Arthur for a slight turn.

The look on Hannah's face became scorned, she wasn't that easily threatened. "You can tell her if you like, but I am pretty sure I could put a spell on you to make you sleep for the next week." she abruptly fired back.

At that point something ticked over in Hannah's mind, as though a switch had just been turned on. For somewhat a second Hannah may have just felt sorry for Arthur. "If you beg, on your knees and ask. You can come. But! Only if you keep a low profile and don't be uncool." she demanded.

This was the golden chance for a hint of that freedom to get out of the house. Arthur mentally jumped for joy.

With no shame, down on both of his knees Arthur collapsed, as he began to form his hands together with a grin that he battled holding in.

"Please, will you let me come with you to the party, I beg you and promise to not cramp your style." Arthur continued to beg, holding the immense amount of excitement releasing within him.

Out of the house

With the summer sun that began to lower over the houses drawing long shadows across the street, bringing an end to the glorious sunny day. The streets had been filled with those passing through and enjoying the day. The fun had not yet ended; in a matter of fact, it had not yet even begun for Arthur. It was almost time, time to get out of the house and sneak off quietly into the evening, off to the party many blocks away.

As Hannah left through the front door with Kimberly without any mention of a curfew or boundaries, all dressed up to impress, the girls began to make their way down the front lawn's path. Slowly getting smaller and smaller into the distance, to finally disappear into Hannah's car. Arthur had made up his bed, piling up the centre with covers and clothes to make it look like it was occupied; no one would check, but it was the thrill. Arthur's challenge was tiptoeing through the inevitable creaky floorboards of the house trying not to alert any attention towards his movements. He crept his way successfully through to the back of the house, passing through the kitchen and out of a door at the back. Slipping through the garden gate, which was situated at the side of the house, partially hidden by the tall hedges that kept the privacy of the grounds. As he quickly shuffled, closer towards the street; he began to stride, faster and swifter with a spring in each step. There he disappeared, just as the other two did into the back seat of the car that was waiting nearby, crawling at the street's curb. Peter in the front; directed to be the designated driver, which arose an interesting question whether if he were allowed to drive Hannah's car. Regardless he was ready and driving them on their way.

On the journey towards the party Arthur could only presume from what the television shows would dictate how an American high school party would be like. The imagination of the music thumping, the latest pop music that was the next big thing with no clue how the lyrics even went. There was always a group of teens that seem to be having a great time, beer flowing with the mass of steel kegs littered in every room. A table full of colourful bottled spirits, some in different languages and some not even known to mankind. The group knew they were getting closer to their destination as Hannah guided Peter from her phone, the loud thumping music became clearer with the chants and screams of the revelling guests littered around the street. The area seemed to be some type of university housing.

    As the group parked up by the curb a slight bit further down from the house, Hannah took little time to waste, taking Kimberly by the hand and marching her towards the house.

    Peter sat there, switched off the ignition and spent a moment to enjoy the silence, preparing himself. He took a deep breath and exhaled slowly "Here we go, this is going to be one hell of a long night." he expressed.

    Arthur and Peter made their way up the lawn following after the girls, beer bottles and cans, scattered around everywhere presuming all of them were from just the party this evening.

    Arthur looked up at the house and he could see it was busy from room to room. "This is an actual *rager*." he spoke, forgetting to close his mouth shut afterwards.

    Arthur had been to parties at university, but none this huge, where it was looking like absolute mayhem.

    The two, following in behind from the girls through the front door, made their way to the kitchen where the work surfaces were littered with alcohol, any types of alcohol, all sizes, and strengths.

    Peter dunked his carrier bag of alcohol on the countertop. He held out a can of beer, "Start her up with a beer, Coors?"

offering Arthur a can. "Or whatever piss they offer at these college parties" he finished with.

Arthur picked up a slight touch of bitterness within Peter's voice, it was soon understood that Peter had not been to college. He began to work, where he watched his friends leave his area and head to whatever prosperous future they had aimed for.

Kimberly suddenly had a reversed feeling towards this party compared to yesterday, she was suddenly all up for the excitement. Arthur could see how them two got along, they were opposites to each other. Peter was the calm one, grounded and socially welcoming, compared to Kimberly, she would be the loud one. Always pointing out things and talking about another's business like it were her own.

The girls were finding anything to drink, anything with a sweet taste seemed to be the popular choice. Arthur would watch the conversation pass between the two girls whilst standing with them, they could almost forget he was even there. Peter would occasionally chip in, involving Arthur to any conversation. It was clear from Hannah that she was after someone, that someone being a Lakebrook State collegiate.

As the atmosphere was indefinitely exciting, the group decided to head outside so Hannah could scope the area out there. She consistently announced that they needed to be older and more mature than Peter and Arthur. Even though Arthur was only slightly older than her by a year, Peter a few years from what was figured out. Peter would glance at Arthur throughout the party as though he were trying to communicate telepathically, signalling that this were a normal thing he brushed off.

Arthur began drinking fast to ensure the reach of that buzz from intoxication, now he had the chance. Searching among the ranges of drinks on the countertops, Arthur looked for a drink that didn't taste like a Coors. There was a miniature keg that seemed to be something else. Taking a red cup from the stack, Arthur began to use the tap to fill his cup. Gripping it firmly in his hand he examined the drink, trying to guess what beer it was.

Arthur raised his cup and peered into it, as he took a sip, "Yup, that's still Coors." he said softly, unimpressed to himself.

He turned around to head back in the direction where he had left the other three outside.

There was a clash in bodies, ending up with spilled beer splattered up his shirt and some, over the floor and stranger.

He had bumped into someone.

Arthur was quick to apologise, "Sorry man, my bad I've lost my friends." quickly sounding apologetic, not trying to cause any trouble.

A look of surprise overwhelmed the strangers face, he wasn't annoyed. "It's cool, no point crying over spilled beer, right?" he paused for a moment, looking Arthur up and down. "British? I've never seen you around here before, are you new?" Asked the stranger holding back a hint of surprise in the tone of his voice.

Arthur thought to himself, this boy seemed nice, normally fights happen in the movies when beer is spilled at a party like this.

"Yea, only recently moved into the area." Arthur replied to his question.

The stranger nodded away in approval of Arthur's answer. "If you're lost you can join us for a bit until you find your friends." offered the stranger.

"Uh, yeah! Sure." Arthur wasn't sure he should be socialising with anyone else, but it would make a great difference from being around the girls for once.

The stranger continued to ask another question excitedly, "Hey! Do you go to any school around here?"

Arthur hadn't even thought about that, he hadn't thought about any types of universities or colleges. "Umm, I don't go to any school." he replied.

Arthur's answer seemed to disappoint the overwhelmingly nice stranger, "Ah man! Pick Lakebrook High School, it's a decent school. Home of the Titans." suggested the stranger. "That's what they say anyway."

High school? Arthur thought to himself, this guy goes to high school. Not the university here?

Did this stranger just confuse Arthur for someone his age?

Understandably that Lakebrook was a big place, but not that big. Only two high schools existed in the town, so there weren't many options, even if Arthur did want to regress his school years.

As Arthur and the stranger walked through the house party, the stranger finally introduced himself.

His name was Daniel Bayer, the friendly guy that Arthur had bumped into five minutes ago. Long darkish blonde hair draped down to his shoulders, a slim build of an average boy of that age. A mucky green t-shirt that somewhat had an 80's print of a band that Arthur had never heard and presumably Daniel didn't even know of, if asked. The classic ripped blue jeans at the knees tattered from the time when they were most likely bought, or never replaced. But overall, Daniel seemed like a pleasant person.

The two walked past crowds who were having a great time, into another busy room within the house, which seemed to be a second living room of this university house.

There was a big sofa, there sat, sprawled as many teenagers as possible that could possibly fit on the thing. Daniel walked closer to the sofa; Arthur soon realised that this was his group of friends.

Daniel formally introduced Arthur to the group he was with, on the very edge of the sofa – on the arm. Sat Laura Tisdale, a young timid girl, with such bright, illuminating blue eyes and her light platinum blonde hair tied back in a ponytail; a flick of a fringe covered over the right side of her face. She was a petite type of girl who was just somewhat seemingly short.

Sat to her left, who had sunk right into the pit of the sofa's cushions was Jade Green, dark olive tanned skin, who was thin, copper coloured hair ran down the side of her face down to her chest. When you caught her eyes at the right angle, a hint of green could be seen. Jade looked cheerfully quiet at a distance, but that look was only from the surface, deep down Jade was the life of any group with a level of self-importance Arthur soon gathered from his first impressions.

Sat to the left of Jade was another boy, Abel Bodie, an ethnicity of an Indian boy. He was skinny like a rake; this was obvious with the fashion of wearing skinny jeans and tight-fitting tops. Abel had a matt black, clumpy mop of a haircut, a fringe that you could chew as it was grown so long.

Next to Abel was a boy of an Asian ethnicity this boy seemed to be the best of friends with Abel, Cheng Lee. Cheng was a cheerful type of guy, who had little to talk about when it came to larger groups, but directly loved talking about tv shows and other sci-fi favourites. Cheng was as short as Laura almost was, he was the smallest boy of the group with his jet-black hair with a little too much gel in it. Cheng had a simple fashion sense by the looks of things with a basic white shirt and black skinny jeans with the signature Converse shoes. Arthur began to wonder who wore it first between Abel and Cheng.

The final member of the group who sat on the very last arm of this sofa was another girl, she had long platinum blonde hair, with the same blue eyes matching what Laura had. This began the presumption that the two girls were sisters.

Arthur was right.

Her name was Ellie Tisdale, she seemed to have the most fashion sense of the group, on par with Jade.

She wore a blue denim jacket with a half cropped white top this was complimented by three-quarter length blue skinny jeans. Ellie was taller than her sister, even though the two were non-identical twins but shared the same age. Ellie seemed to have more of an interest in things like, bands, boys, and clothes, talking to no ends about that with Jade.

Arthur sat on the coffee table opposite Laura and Jade whereas Daniel sat on the other end of the it in front of Ellie and Cheng. Questions bombarded the newcomer Arthur, asking questions about England and London itself, as though every British person should be fluent in the country's history and London especially.

The group seemed to give off a warming welcome to Arthur, like how friendly Daniel was to him moments ago. They were all describing more about their daily lives and events that had happened at Lakebrook High School.

They started to ask Arthur further into his life here in the United States, asking how long he were staying for and how did he end up here.

Avoiding the truthful topic of how Arthur had realistically got there, an improvised script of details on how Arthur had got to the States arose in an instant. Somewhat believable to, unless it was the alcohol helping to fool them.

Arthur caught the occasional glances of those around him, especially Laura, who kept a close-lipped smile. Arthur tried to avoid looking at her too much in case he gave off a creepy feeling. There was something about her that captivated Arthur that he couldn't quite put his finger on. She was hilarious with her conversation and the way she spoke there was a sound of attractive confidence within her voice, or it could be down to the fact, that she was the first girl to look at Arthur and smile.

At this point Arthur had lost his original group for about an hour now, looking around the room for any signs of what the time was. The party continued to thrive and had no signs of stopping until the hours of the sunrise. The new group he had sat with seemed to enjoy asking questions, getting Arthur to speak, secretly adoring his accent as though he were the newest strange animal at the zoo.

Daniel offered to get refills for the group, Arthur thought this would be the best time to offer and see if he could find the others. The two had moved their way through the party, returning to the kitchen, they began to collect up what drinks were left on the counter.

"So have you thought about which high school you would apply to?" Daniel had asked, confirming the belief that Arthur was the same age to him.

At this very point Arthur had realised that all those new friends he had just met believed he were the same age. It could be a new start for Arthur, maybe he could extend on this false age, only by a year or so, and try to experience this style of American high school with another chance at a different path rather than the branch of business studies.

Arthur decided to dangerously dream a little, "You mentioned you were at Lakebrook High School, right? as you said that is just around the corner and it sounds ideal." Arthur answered, allowing himself to enjoy just the thought of it.

Peter came rushing into the kitchen, his eyes rushed around, identifying every living person within the immediate area.

"Arthur!" he shouted in a matter of urgency. "There you are man; I need you we have a situation!"

Arthur with urgency rushed out the room with Peter, leaving Daniel behind.

All that came to mind was the girls, drunk beyond movement and that Peter needed help carrying them back.

As the two rushed upstairs, following Peter through one of the doors next to the landing. There was a tall, stocky jock in his Lakebrook State varsity colours gripping tight to both of Hannah's wrists as Kimberly tried to pry them apart. Hannah was beyond having drinks anymore, it was clear she had drunk too much by the look on her face.

The sight of this taking place sent a strange sense through Arthur, as though a crack opened at the back of his neck, a rush went through his head of what may have been the lack of oxygen. The sight of Hannah being in danger ignited something throughout him, he owed it to her, keeping her safe as she was the one who saved him from being buried alive.

Headfirst Arthur wedged away the jock with surprisingly minimal effort, as the jock stumbled, Arthur had raised a clenched fist and without thinking it through. He followed it through connecting with the jock's face. It was as though something powerful had taken over him in that moment, Arthur had no willpower to have any say in restraining himself.

The drunken jock composed himself, stumbling to gain his stance after taking a nasty hit, he raised his fists high.

Arthur thought he didn't want to fight, but his body acted in a way of another response, preparing his stance to go full on into this fight no matter what the outcome would be.

Peter stood at Arthur's side, ready to help. "Are we doing this bro!" he asked rhetorically in retaliation.

Hannah was sat, slouched on the bed as Kimberly was trying to pull her up off it. Hannah, looked up with a moment of clarity, standing up she wobbled over towards Arthur and Peter. Placing her hand on Arthur's shoulder and gently squeezing it, trying to prop herself upright.

Everyone in the room all paused watching her movement.

The grip of Hannah seemed to halt and settle the aggression within Arthur. She rose her other hand past Arthur's eyeline, he could see her pointing at the jock standing opposite. With the flick of her wrist the jock was struck by an almighty invisible force, flung carelessly into the wall behind him. Smacking the back of his head as he collided with it, dropping to the floor, and lowering his head unconscious.

Kimberly's jaw dropped as she stood there, slowly walking over to Hannah, the shock of what had happened sobered her for those few seconds.

It was clear this was an unusual situation and Hannah had just used her magic, which Arthur knew well enough already that the head witches would be mad if they knew.

They needed to leave.

"Right, this party is over for us guys, we're off now." Peter announced sternly, he clearly had enough and took authority over the group.

Arthur lifted Hannah's arm over his neck to sway her to the exit of the room and Peter took Kimberly by the hand and began to guide her out through the door, towards the staircase landing.

Looking around, it seemed as though no one knew what had happened within that bedroom upstairs, all that was left were a deservedly unconscious jock.

The four made their way down the stairs, Arthur propping up Hannah and helping her down with every step. As the four walked past the room where the kind Daniel Bayer was and his group, Arthur peered in to check if they were all still there.

Daniel caught the sight of him and looked shocked trying to understand what was going on. He proceeded to give a thumbs up with an odd expression on his face, reacting to Arthur helping a girl.

Arthur waved awkwardly whilst keeping Hannah upright.

They walked outside and up to the car down the street with some difficulty, the fresh air seemed to help control Hannah a bit more, the further they walked.

Peter got in the driver's seat and switched on the engine, waiting for Arthur to sit Hannah in her seat before he could run around the car and find his.

Unexpectedly the four managed to get into the house very slyly, making little noise as possible. It seemed to be a miracle to Arthur, but he was assured that coming home drunk was well rehearsed from the past in Peter's experience.

"In a bit." was all that Peter said, before disappearing off down one of the corridors to Kimberly's room.

Arthur guided Hannah to her bedroom, planning to put her to bed before he would return to his own. Turning down the other corridor and around the corner of another, he found Hannah's room.

Hannah's room was different compared to Arthurs; he'd never been in here before. He just knew what door she slept behind. The desk in her room was cluttered with what could only be spell books, notes, and other trinkets scattered over the top. It was apparent the colour purple was her favourite as that was the only colour added to the whiteness of the room.

Arthur sat her down on the edge of her bed and managed pull the covers over, allowing him to easily get her into bed. She was out like a light as soon as he pulled the covers up. Arthur walked into her bathroom and looked for a glass, filling it with water and lightly placing it on her bedside table.

Before he left, Arthur was curious at what items a witch would keep. He walked over to Hannah's desk peering at the objects on the desk. Curiously flicking through the pages in a few of the books on the desk, some in English and some in an odd language.

He felt great, it had been a good night overall for him at least. He met some new strangers and dreamed a life outside of the house, if only it were for a moment.

After a few moments of being nosy, wondering what witches do keep around, he began to gingerly step over the floorboards, unsure which ones would creak loudly. A few steps away from escaping through her bedroom door, Arthur was unlucky, the floorboard creak was loud. He quickly looked back over his shoulder to Hannah and listened out to see if he woke any other member of the house.

He waited, pausing all movement.

"Thanks." Hannah muttered out loud before turning on to her side and drifting back to sleep.

Arthur smiled, making it out into the corridor in front of Hannah's open door, turning his head left and right he noticed it was still all quiet. There was an eerie silence all around the boarding house, now he noticed it.

It was as though the whole building was still but listening to every movement within it.

Arthur looked back into Hannah's room; she looked peacefully sound asleep. How has this surreal lead of events got him to this position, living thousands of miles away from his real home where he had been declared officially dead and helping a witch similar to his age into bed.

Arthur walked back down the corridor making his way towards his room, finding Peter sat in one of the armchairs in the communal area. Peter had a beer in his hand, and another sat on the coffee table unopened.

Arthur thought that beer might be for him. He walked over and sat in the chair opposite Peter. Peter was clearly taking in the moment to relax, away from all of the drama that had just happened. Arthur sat down grasping the bottle and raising it with a short nod, thanking Peter for bringing him one. He then sank into the armchair to fully unwind, joining Peter in the silence of relief.

Peter looked at Arthur and widened his eyes, making an explosion sound, in sync with the gesture of his hands. "What a night huh?" he exclaimed, being glad it was over.

Arthur hadn't really hung out with them; he had been occupied with the others. "I got distracted by that group, but how was the rest of the night?" he asked politely.

Peter held the bottle between his fingertips, balancing it on the arm of the armchair, "You know, same shit really. Hannah drinking too much, and boom, drama happens. Dragging

Kimberly into it." he said as though this didn't surprise him at all, it wasn't the first time.

Arthur let out a nervous laugh, "Luckily I missed out then ay?" taking a sip from his own beer.

"That punch though on the big guy!" Peter laughed. "Brave stuff man."

There was a long silence for a seemingly short amount of time, the echo of the clock downstairs ticking seemed to fill the air.

"You know, Kimberly said something strange to me the other day... about you." Peter pointed out, breaking the silence.

Arthur leaned forwards from his armchair and looked directly at Peter, as though those words seemed to finally sober him and catch his full attention.

"She said that there is a weird feeling around you, like a dense aura." Peter continued. "I don't feel it, but I'm only human and I get to live the simple life." he sneered, growing a smile.

This puzzled Arthur as he was listening, he wasn't quite sure if he was joking or something he should take seriously, with the smile on Peter's face.

"But what do we know? Peter continued, "You were tracked from far, far away by the great witch Myra... You came back from the dead, so who knows what is going on anyway dude." he stated without any worry, taking a chug of the beer.

Arthur felt at ease with Peter, he seemed to present that calm vibe, it seemed to rub off on others.

Peter began to ask Arthur about his life back in England mainly, Arthur didn't ask too many questions in return, he was tired and almost sick of answering questions about England for the night. Arthur understood that Peter lived with his parents still, but never spent any time at his family home. Understanding that the life back there was too normal, and

Peter often questioned, who settles for normal given the option.

    The two parted, Peter heading back to Kimberly's room and Arthur to his, through the overwhelming silence of the house. It had become the early hours of the morning and sunrise wasn't far away. What Peter had said played on Arthur's mind as he made his way undressing and getting into his bed. In the midst of his thoughts the silence of the boarding house would still creep in, reminding him to try and fall asleep.

Instinct awakened

Days passed by after Arthur had been able to escape to the party that he had to beg pathetically to go to. There was a brief chat about what had happened about that night over breakfast the following day, but no one mentioned the use of magic, or even the intoxicated jock. It was brushed aside as though that never happened in the first place, Arthur knew Myra or Ethel would have been the reason, if any of those two found out. They would be in serious trouble; permission was needed to use magic out of the house, not for aggressive reasons.

It was one early morning that followed the repetitive days within Pennyview, where a house meeting was called early, earlier than breakfast.

Myra and Ethel were both at the head of the large dining table within the dining room. Myra more relaxed and sat in the dining chair, whilst Ethel stood rigid and tense with her hands firmly planted on the table.

All of the Pennyview residents were sat around the table waiting in suspense on what the news could be, most still half asleep.

"There have been tensions with another witching institute in the outskirts of the county." Ethel began to announce.

She continued to explain that Myra and herself were going to head away for the night to meet with those head witches of the coven.

As Ethel explained the purpose of the meeting, to hopefully start building a friendship with the other coven, she became tense the longer she spoke. Myra placed her hand on Ethels, squeezing it gently in affection and reminding her to calm.

Ethel finished with, "In no circumstance are any of you allowed to leave the house."

Myra placed her index finger directly down on the table, pushing it ever so slightly bending the tip. "In no circumstance do you leave the house! Or! Tell anyone that we aren't here. If anyone were to know we've left this house at this very moment," with a calming breath she paused for a second to continue, "be vulnerable to anything! Do you all understand?!" Myra ordered around to the room, breaking character from her usual calm self and glaring militantly for confirmation at each resident.

This did indeed collect everyone's attention in the room with a collection of nodding heads and muttering of verbal agreements. Arthur could see straight away that Hannah had that look, it was a look of planning an escape by the sheer look of concentration in her face. There was a strange feeling among the rest of the boarding house throughout the rest of that morning. With a high level of suspense in the air predicting that something may happen, but no one knew what.

Before midday, Myra and Ethel began to make their way to wherever the meeting would be and wouldn't be back until the early hours of the morning. It was clear they had no intentions of staying overnight, away from Pennyview.

The entirety of the boarding house was all sat in the pristine living room that faced outwards to the main street, the room opposite the dining entrance. Arthur had never seen so many of the residents all together in the same room since the first time he'd arrived and outside of a meeting.

There was Hannah, Kimberly, Peter, Charelle, Jean, Melissa, and himself, Arthur was happy at the thought of just about remembering the names of them all. Alongside them was the housekeeper who worked quietly in the background of the house, and either was spelled to forget who they were in the house or was paid a handsome amount.

The first person to break the casual atmosphere unsurprisingly was Hannah, with taking charge of her daily plans.

"Off to the mall it is!" she announced openly.

A shock of excitement rolled over Arthur; he'd never been to a mall in America so far. With only the chance to drive to grocery stores, this had to be an opportunity worth jumping for.

There was a disagreement not everyone was ecstatic about the idea of leaving Pennyview house, especially after being warned not to. A small select few of the boarding house decided to take on Hannah's invite to the mall, including Arthur himself.

The group consisted of, Hannah, Kimberly, Peter, Charelle, and Arthur. Kimberly claiming the passenger seat in Hannah's car meaning that the rest of the group were sat in the back. The newest one to join the group in their outing was Charelle.

Charelle was another one of the witches in the boarding house, she was similar to Hannah in personality and age. Charelle had flawless brown skin, with purposely knotted hair that she would flick occasionally to get any point across and always wore pastel colours. She was similar to Hannah, that even Arthur could see with his short time so far in the house, that they clashed a lot and bickered. With their fashion-acceptable clothing, make up and boys, if the two were ever on the same page it would be a horrible match for the rest of the house.

Arthur thought the only true reason that the two girls never spent any time together is that they both wanted to be the centre of attention, which meant that neither of them could be together at the same time.

At the start of the journey in the car, the group were all discussing what they were looking for at the mall. It seemed the most common purpose of the trip was to buy new clothes and whatever sweets or rubbish they could find, understanding that it was just going to be one of those horrible trips to endure. Arthur felt lucky to be seeing outside of the boarding house walls once more. He liked the house, but there is a limit of being stuck inside it for too long and the borderline of going insane.

It was something he definitely didn't want his new life to be like and that was picked up by the others throughout his short time at Pennyview.

Kimberly turned her head around in the passenger chair looking at Arthur, "So what are you after at the mall?" she asked him.

Arthur had no money, even being at the house for many weeks, he'd never needed it. So, purchasing anything was out of the answer.

"I'm just happy to see what a mall looks like, you know. Get out of the house and all that." he replied, comparing himself shortly after to a tourist.

At least Peter was on this outing, he had gotten on well with him, especially since the house party. At least they could both endure the painful trip together.

As Hannah drove through the streets Arthur had noticed that the group began driving into an area where the buildings got a little taller and closer together. Hannah interrupted Arthur's observations that focused outside of the car.

"This is a bit more of a tour for you Arthur, as you haven't really seen the sights." she explained.

It was nice that she thought about Arthur for a split second, which he then became unsure if she was being sarcastic or not.

"There are sights in this quiet town?" Peter questioned back sarcastically, peering his head trying to search out through the car window.

Hannah informed Arthur that they were driving past the centre of the town, as part of the short sight-seeing tour. This then took a few turns into a less dense neighbourhood, finding the mall was very easy as there were signposts everywhere. As the group turned past a stop sign leading out to a busier road, Hannah indicated the car and they sat in traffic, patiently waiting for the lights to turn. Arthur tilted his head to where she was intending to go, in that direction there was a vast sea of cars, all parked up. The cars gleamed and flickered from the sunlight bouncing off every shiny surface blinding anyone who looked. It didn't take Hannah long to park at all, there were plenty of spaces dotted throughout.

A long, wide path filled with the cheerful strangers graciously lead up towards the entrance of the mall. Planters that sat in their twos repeated every few metres down the wide path. The tall glass doors which held constantly ajar and above them, held the sign of the building, "*Lakebrook Mall – The place to be est 1850."*

"Here we are! My second home!" Charelle exclaimed in genuine excitement.

The group began heading towards the tall glass doors of the mall, up the graciously wide path. With each step, this excitement in Arthur grew, alongside in his expectations rising. Was this mall going to be all that he had expected, or would it be a bust for him. As he entered the mall, there was the dim music playing in the very background, smothered by the busy sounds of footsteps and chatter. It was busy, filled with the incomprehensible voices and steps of many strangers, who were going about their day. It was absolutely vibrant with colour, lights, and signs were everywhere offering names, to discounts to the fleeting customers. Small stalls seemed to fill the odd spaces throughout the mall with bits of make-up, sweets, and phone accessories.

Being here, being at the mall excited Arthur intensely, it had definitely matched up to his expectations. A sudden strike of realisation hit from what he had thought about briefly on the journey here, Arthur had no money, no bank account and not even any ID.

Turning to Hannah he tried to whisper, "Hannah, I don't have any money."

Surprisingly Hannah had a good idea prepared to solve this problem, understanding that Arthur was stuck with them in the boarding house and never had gotten the chance to set up anything like that. She led him to some sort of local bank in the mall and opened another bank account in her name. An account that Arthur could use, but of course with no overdraft limits, she stated carefully.

"There, when that card arrives you can use it and Myra can sort out some allowance. But for now, you can borrow fifty dollars." Hannah offered. "Pay me back another time." she smiled.

Arthur was unsettled by the generosity that Hannah had showed him within the last half hour, however he dialled it down to her secretly remembering him that night at the party and helping her. The only next step for Arthur was how to earn money to pay her back.

As the rest of the group waited outside the bank, they were joined by Arthur and Hannah and explored around the mall going up to the first floor. This was a good time for Arthur to ask Peter about his past a bit more, considering the last time they spoke, Peter mainly asked Arthur about his.

The particularly interesting part was how Peter, a normal human being, got himself involved up within a boarding house full of witches with how he met Kimberly. To Arthur's surprise he found out that Peter was from another city hours away and had met Kimberly through a day visit out there. Joking around the fact that it was love at first sight, it really was an adorable story deep down.

The group were diving in and out of various clothing shops as the two boys continued to follow, bonding and ignoring all the girls. Arthur soon came to understanding that Peter hadn't had much in the other city, he graduated high school and held a rather dull job. There was a sense of relief when Peter mentioned his life now, even though strange, he was much happier.

The expression in his face shared a smile as he explained, "So, what's your plan?" Peter asked, "You know, what's next for you?"

That was in fact the question Arthur tried to avoid, as he had no clue or choice whatsoever in this matter. Staring off into the crowd below on the ground floor, following them with his eyes, Arthur had to think for a moment on what he was going to say.

"Hey! Look, it's that guy from the party!" a voice was heard from the side.

Arthur turned around to the voice and stared at the group of strangers trying to work out who it was.

The awful, dreaded band t-shirt was a sign, it was that guy... from the party the other week. He was waving at Arthur, with two others at his side. With a slow raise of hand, Arthur motionlessly raised it trying to recall this guy's name.

The group of strangers walked towards Arthur and Peter, "How's it going? Arthur, right?" the familiar stranger asked.

Arthur gathered his memory together in his mind trying to recall their names, "Daniel? Yeah. All good." he replied, pointing to the other two, "Ermm, Abel? Aaand Cheng?" he guessed.

The two nodded.

"Well remembered." said the lad who was Abel.

"Have you joined a school yet?" Daniel asked.

Arthur suddenly remembered the name of the school he and the others spoke about at that house party and that thought crossed through his mind once again.

"Heh, school?" Peter commented with a giggle.

"Not yet, but it was Lakebrook right?" Arthur asked, getting the idea that this could be a good move.

"Yeah, exactly!" Daniel said excitedly.

Cutting off any more of the conversation Abel butted in, "We gotta go, the girls are waiting for us at the cinema." Abel reminded them.

"Oh! Yeah, we gotta go. Catch you later." Daniel said his goodbye, "Lakebrook High, remember!" he called out as they walked away.

In that odd moment of bumping into those three, Arthur like the thought, daring to dream some more. Lakebrook High School might be a good idea or at least a starting point.

Arthur turned towards Peter, "Go to high school, start over again and pick something different I think."

Peter wore a very confused look on his face, "You wanna go through high school again? he asked.

Arthur nodded, confirming his plan, "Yeah I think so."

The dream was going to high school, but the real question was how he could get there, he would need to ask for permission. That permission he figured never came easily from the heads of the house Myra, and Ethel.

The continuous visits to many different shops came finally to an end, although as horrible as the experience was, Arthur did find himself a few new shirts spending some of the money Hannah had given him.

The group were making their way through the giant car park outside the mall, Hannah had continued her bright plans once they had made it home back to Pennyview.

The plan had a main intention to drink, play music out loud and eat the rubbish they had bought. Hannah shared her main focus was to get the group to mix cocktails once they had gotten back to Pennyview.

Arthur and the group all agreed that the plan was a great one, what harm would it do, they would all be back at the house in no time. The only small doubt that held back Arthur was how the trouble started with Hannah drinking last time.

As the group made it back to the house and parked up. Inside, Kimberly found a website on her tablet computer with the ingredients and steps to mixing cocktails.

Arthur had no intention of making any cocktails but offered being a tester for them, which could be a bonus, especially winding down after a day with the girls shopping.

After a few trials of mixing cocktails and loud music playing in the kitchen, it was clear that none of the girls measured the spirits going into the mixtures, the cocktails were strong.

It didn't take long for the strength of the spirits to get through Arthur's head, and the others also. He just remembered the evening going very fast into the night.

Arthur could just about recall making his way into his room, before falling face first onto his bed. It was only after midnight into the morning that he gained little clarity, through the drunken slumber and tossing the sheets around, there was a noise.

A rather blunt smacking noise, as though something were bludgeoning something, somewhere was all that was concluded through his cloudy, hungover mind. With every blunt hit Arthur's senses became a little sharper, then the sound became more comprehendible to Arthur. Each hit woke Arthur up from the deep, drunken sleep.

The blunt noise became overwhelmed with the screams of some of the girls in the house. The banging of something on a door, something very blunt. The alerted screams of the residents in the house sobered Arthur up enough, rising to his feet, searing with a sharp headache from being pulled into action.

Something inside him had forcefully switched his senses on, from sobering up, to fear, then to a heightened level of alertness.

Arthur who had arose to his feet pacing step by step across the wooden floor of his room, slightly slipping on the bedside rug, as he regained the sturdiness of his legs. He pierced through the door of his bedroom to quickly look down the corridor and tried to understand where the noise was coming from. Leaping down the corridor to where he presumed the noise came from and down the stairwell, it was still unclear what was happening.

Arthur walked through the house, quickly scanning into the rooms for any sign of any residents. As he came to the kitchen doorway, he found them. The girls and Peter were all around the kitchen counter, close together as though they were huddling in a pack.

Arthur looked at them confused, not grasping what was happening. There was another bang on the glass pane of the door, which drew the attention from him and the others to the door that led to the outside of the house.

There was collective scream from the group huddled around the kitchen counter, Arthur stared at the door with intense examination. There was another bang, an object pierced the door and stalled there for a moment. Glass shattered and dropped to the floor whilst the object was stuck in the frame that held the pattern of the glass. A head of an axe stuck, wriggling its way back out, from what Arthur could just make out from his angle.

"What is that?" screamed Kimberly.

Whoever it was, retracted the axe head out of the door, preparing for another strike.

"I'll hold it off from coming in!" Hannah called out to the rest. Raising her hand to cast a spell, she flicked her hand whilst muttering the words she needed. "It's... It's not working, I can't cast a spell?" disappointment stuck her.

Kimberly shakily raised her hand to cast a spell in repeat of what Hannah was trying, not entirely believing her, she tried. Nothing happened from the certain look of fear in Kimberly's face.

At this point it was clear that this thing was impervious to magic. The girls began to step back a little, shuffling to any door furthest away from whatever it was.

A crunch of glass was sharply heard, as a hand pierced though, fiddling at the door's handle. The hand unlocked the door, giving it a push, it came to a halt. There was another chain lock higher up. The hand began to search for that final lock as it dragged its hand upwards ignoring the cutting teeth of broken glass. It was a rather unusual looking hand with a dull colour of blue and grey joint with the torn flesh from the glass, at an instant it was clear that this thing wasn't like any normal human.

Arthur sternly stared as though he were taken in a trance at the unhuman hand fiddling around trying to find the door chain, the forceful rattling of the door held suspense ready to burst at its hinges.

All other sound for Arthur went muffled as all he could focus on was the hand at the door, his heart began to beat forcefully, becoming faster in its pace.

The group began to clear out of the kitchen in absolute fear, with the movement of the others, the voices around Arthur became clearer. Arthur snapped out of his trance and back to realisation when Peter grabbed his arm, trying to drag him out of the kitchen.

"Come on bro, we can't just stand here, we gotta hide!" Peter's voice quaked, tugging at him.

As Arthur's mind returned Peter had managed to drag him through the hallway, finding themselves at the front door in the foyer.

Charelle began to tug at the front door, it had been locked and bolted shut. As she began to frantically move her fingers at the locks, she froze. The sound of the kitchen door breaking placed a great amount of terror in her.

That sound of the door giving way and cracking open stopped Arthur from moving. Something inside him, something mysterious was drawing him straight back into this trance taking over the actions of his body. Peter forcefully tugged at Arthur once more, trying to move him with any ounce of strength he had. Arthur was immovable in his stance; it was clear there was no chance of Peter moving Arthur whilst he was in this mentally overwhelming state that controlled him.

"God dammit man!" Peter shrieked, turning his head to the others, who were halfway at up the stairs. "He isn't moving!" he called out, tugging in desperation at Arthur's arm.

Peter grunted in aggravation as he left all efforts from trying to pull Arthur back into the situation, he began to run up the stairs.

It was Hannah's turn to try.

Hannah bounded down each step, to see if she could grab Arthur. She moved into Arthur's eyesight, analysing him briefly, it was clear she could see no one was home. Hannah began to pull at both of Arthur's hands, screaming at him to move.

The footsteps of the intruder began to stomp heavily as it came from the kitchen tiles onto the wooden flooring of the hallway.

There it stood, some creature that used to be a human and had died long ago. Broken down and rotting away at the surface of its skin. Clothes that barely hung on, faded, and torn. The fetid smell of the pungent intruder quickly filled the noses through the foyer.

The sight of the intruder that stood down the hall from Arthur's eyeline brought back that instinct, the one that took over Arthur when Hannah was in trouble at the house party. Something incomprehensible had fully taken over Arthur, and this time it felt like he had fallen deeper into the back of his mind.

The undead being began to step forward slowly, as it dragged the axe along the floorboards, flicking onto the tiles in the foyer scratching and chipping away.

Hannah became desperate with her options of trying to move Arthur. She grabbed his face with her hands and stared into his eyes, trying to break the line of sight that seemed to captivate him.

Hannah stepped backwards slowly letting go of Arthur completely, the colour had drained out of her face. Her mouth was open in shock as her eye contact stayed firmly on Arthurs.

She could see that something had changed inside him, the blue in his eyes had disappeared completely. His iris had turned into a never ending black. The white that surrounded, had turned into a blood red. The eyes made it clear that something sinister had taken over.

The possessed being that still looked like Arthur, stared back vacantly into Hannah's eyes.

"Arthur..." was all that Hannah muttered through the fear that prominently took over her.

She took a few more steps backwards, unsure of how to react to whatever had happened to Arthur. She carefully kept eye contact with him, noticing his eyes followed hers.

A side table sat by the staircase; Hannah had forgotten about it being behind her. Still moving away, she caught the table with the back of her leg. Slipping on the floor, sitting there on her bottom.

The undead being began pick up the pace shuffling forwards towards the two, taking the opportunity that Hannah was on the floor. It began to drag the axe from the floor and raise it above its head, it was getting ready to strike.

Hannah screamed, cowering her head in her hands helpless, overwhelmed by fear.

Hannah's scream cut through Arthur. His eyes widened, they fixed towards the intruder poised in the foyer. As the axe began to drop down on Hannah, Arthur's body moved with a burst of speed and pushed his hands at the handle of the axe, wrestling the intruder from dropping it any lower. The two stumbled back and forth struggling for overall power.

Arthur's uncontrollable body pushed the intruder to the wall as hard as he could, with the intruder returning the force back, twisting Arthur's grip towards the banister. The being pushed with some mighty force, a crack was heard from the banister resulting from the sheer pressure of Arthur being crushed into it. The two wrangled for power frantically as the undead began to snap away at Arthur, trying to bite at his face.

Arthur ferociously pushed back, raising his left arm forcing the being away from him. The being dropped the axe as it stumbled backward. Arthur rushed towards the being pushing himself off the banister, drawing his fist by his side ready to hit. As he struck the undead being's face, some rotten skin had broken off, sticking to Arthur's knuckle.

The intruder turned its head, aligned straight back at Arthur, it stood there as though it felt nothing from that strike. It spent no time waiting to retaliate and grabbed Arthur's throat, lifting him with ease off the floor. Arthur's feet scampered trying to keep himself from being choked as the being paced him towards the front door, it was no use, the being had control over Arthur's movement. It tossed Arthur away, flinging him into the front door. Arthur heavily hit the back of his head, losing consciousness momentarily as he slumped down to sitting on the floor. The darkness of his vision flickered as his eyes tried to repeatedly stay open, he could make out that Hannah was shuffling on the floor away from it and the rest of the group were at the very top of the stairs peering down in horror.

A scraping noise of the axe being picked up was all that Arthur could focus on, the being ignored Hannah and proceeded to walk slowly past her towards Arthur, ready to finish him off.

As Arthur tried to keep his eyes open, his consciousness began to take over, he could only think for himself. Recollecting the moments before, he felt scared, as the being raised the axe preparing to deliver another strike. Arthur's mind was screaming inside to act, but his body still wasn't under his control.

The axe came plummeting down on Arthur, but his thoughts didn't connect quickly to the actions of his body. The movement returned too late, he held his hands up to stop the axe from hitting him and had managed to grab the neck of the axe.

Too late, he was too slow, the axe had sunk into his chest.

Arthur let out a deep roar of pain as it echoed in the foyer, the blood began to trickle down his body. The instinct inside him snapped back over for control, pushing Arthur's consciousness further back into the corner of his mind. Rising from his knee, Arthur pushed back at the being whilst the axe was still deeply caved into him.

The two twisted around fighting for a steady stance, both clutching at the axe. The intruder barged Arthur pushing him back, allowing it to keep hold of the axe, ripping it out of his chest. With another swing of the axe, it flicked Arthur's blood in the air at the highest point held up. Gliding it down the air into Arthur's torso once more.

Screams of the others cut through the air, witnessing the end of Arthur. The intruder held the axe in place and pushed it further into Arthur, as more blood began to trickle. Arthur weakly gripped at the axe, feeling all life release within him. The undead being showed no pleasure or any emotion at all as it was ending Arthur's life. It released the axe from Arthur's torso, blood began to flow fast and freely from the second wound it had just split open. The being stared at Arthur as he sunk to his knees as his blood began to pool around him on the white tiles. The dead being continued to stare at Arthur as though it were awaiting to confirm that he wasn't getting up again, so it could return to its purpose of ending all life within Pennyview.

Arthur's eyes closed as he hunched lower on his knees, accepting the feeling of life, escaping from his body.

The being, satisfied with its work, slowly turned to Hannah gripping the axe tightly as it dripped Arthur's blood onto the tiles as it approached her.

It fixated its gaze towards her and made an ear curling growl. Hannah let out a scream of fear, it was her turn next.

The fear filled scream of Hannah electrified Arthur throughout every nerve in his body, a strange burst of energy exploded within him. Arthur could feel his consciousness slip back in, taking control of the final moments he had left. For that final action, opening his eyes he sprung towards the being as it faced Hannah. Whatever it was inside Arthur let out a painful roar from somewhere deep within.

As Arthur sprung, he firmly gripped either side of the being's head with each hand. His fingers began to sink under the skin of this undead being, pushing deeper into gripping its head. Arthur twisted left and right with his hands, pulling the being down backwards, he twisted the head separate, tearing it from the body. The being's hand dropped the axe and Arthur dropped the body to fall on the floor, limp.

Arthur lost balance and fell from his knee to flat on his back, dropping the being's head at his side. Whatever it was inside of him seemed to step back and let his consciousness fully return. Everything was dull to Arthur, his hearing, his vision, and his touch. All numb. Arthur wanted to talk, but nothing was moving, nothing was making a sound.

At this point he knew he were dying as a greyness began to crawl in at the corners of his vision, something similar to when he woke up at the morgue. A dark grey shadow of a figure appeared closer, presumably Hannah shouting and being distressed. Hannah's shadow reached at him, clutching at him, she was holding his head up. The others gathered around as everything went from grey to black.

Whatever was sent to that house, was meant for the witches. To only kill the witches. The only misjudgement was whoever sent the undead being, didn't know that Arthur was in that house.

The blackness seemed to go on forever, but there was something strange. Something still ticked in Arthur's mind. There were no thoughts and no movement… all there was, was a sense.

A sense of existence.

It was not the end, even anywhere near the end.

Time passed filled with the darkness.

The first thing to return was sounds, dull sounds began to process through Arthur's mind. His mind couldn't comprehend the sounds yet, he knew that there was just a noise. A stream of consciousness came flowing back, Arthur's ability to think again began to return, backtracking previous events he could feel his eyes move around in the darkness replaying these events.

Remembering what had happened, the first sense to return was fear, Arthur understood that he had died and tried to remember how. But no clear recollection could recall the steps before death, only the understanding that he had died.

Was this it? He thought. The end?

Something built up inside of his body, the sense of feeling was returning. It was as though his body was exploding with new life, each nerve ending electrifying with life, senses of touch returning. He could feel that he was lying down, he was stiff and needed to move.

Next, he understood a need for something and needed that something fast.

He needed air.

He inhaled gasping, trying to keep up with how quickly he filled his lungs. Arthur shot sitting up and opened his eyes.

Screams filled the air around where Arthur was, his eyes were now open as he looked in the direction of the screams. But his vision had not yet returned. Greys were the shades that he could first see, outlining the shapes around him. The grasp of a hand was felt over Arthur's face, a gust of air brushed passed him as the hand quickly pulled a cover off him.

All the colours came back to him as he awkwardly moved his neck around the room, understanding who the screams were.

The room was dimly lit, he could see at the edges of the room that there were potted tiny plants. He knew this was the herbalism room and began to focus to the figures standing at his feet as he was laid on the table, in the middle of this dimly lit room.

Around him was Myra grasping the sheet that just covered him and Ethel staring blankly at him. Ethel's mouth gaped open, wider as he twisted and turned his neck to glance freely with ease around the room.

A few residents of the house were gathered around the table that he laid on. Hannah, Peter, and Kimberly all pale.

There was an exchange of glances from Arthur and the others.

"What are you?" questioned Myra, the only one who dared speak first in the room.

Lakebrook High School

Over the next few days that followed in the house, it was very quiet, as though everyone were too cautious to move or even make a noise. Presumably under a thorough scolding from Ethel or Myra after disobeying their rules.

Arthur had been strictly instructed to stay within his bedroom, he wasn't allowed to leave unless he was called for. It was like the beginning when Arthur had just joined the house.

The days started off in Arthur's room with the door closed, he felt like he had done something wrong, but was unsure of what that exactly was. Only a few days had passed where Arthur became hungry for any type of socialisation, Peter would be the only one who would stop in the doorway of his room and talk to him.

Arthur cunningly left the bedroom door open to catch passing residents, but there was little need to be down his hallway of the house. There was a clear understanding in the air with many of the witches not eager to talk to Arthur as instructed by the Ethel. Alongside Peter dropping past, Hannah was the only other one to have a loose conversation or two towards him.

He was often called to the herbalism room for tests, magical and traditional, which were unclear to him. He would sit upon the table in the room where the air would seem to stand still. If he moved, he would feel the still, cold air brisk against his skin.

Myra and Ethel would do a series of things to Arthur, involving cutting him, taking his blood, observing his wounds, and feeding him different drinks which he could only presume that they were an assortment of mixed concoctions. They didn't speak much at first as they trialled and tested him, they seemed somewhat cautious of themselves, unsure with what they're dealing with.

It came to an understanding that a lot of magic would not work on Arthur, something about him, in him that would be immune to any type of magic that the witches cast at him. Not even the most powerful witch of this coven, Myra could lay a magical spell, curse, or enchantment on him.

Many formal meetings and passing discussions continued throughout the days, all presuming what Arthur may be, could be or shouldn't be.

Arthur was dismissed every day, or even twice a day after the testing had been completed for that moment in time.

He would close the herbalism door behind softly and linger… every time he had the chance. To try and catch snippets of discussion, hoping he'd find a clue to what was really happening. Most of the mutter after Arthur had left was just an insight to what had happened to him during the next test but. The word that he often seemed to hear was *titan*, which was an odd word to use for something supernatural. This was normally followed by a strong disagreement by Myra behind closed doors.

The word titan, played on Arthur, it's all he had to go on after days of being experimented on. He knew the word titan was related to Greek mythology. A titan came before the gods and was an almighty being, Arthur looked at himself in the mirror back in his room.

No chance.

As he looked into the mirror at himself, he knew something else was deep down inside of him. That thing, that took over his actions and Arthur knew he needed to be control it.

As Ethel and Myra consistently expressed the main concerns for the house was that magic could not affect Arthur meaning that he could be turned into a potential threat if things got out of hand.

Four days passed, until the awkward tiptoeing had been completely thrown upside down, upon a house meeting over the grand dining table.

The house was asked to meet twenty minutes before dinner in the evening, an unusual time in the day. As the house all sat around the table, nervous glances passed around. Arthur would catch some of the witches of the house glance away as he would try to catch their eye. His eyes met Peters, Peter retained eye contact and winked, with a slight smile, slowly nodding pleasantly.

All that sat at the head of the table was the white oak French chair, with floral carvings that proceeded from the top towards the bottom, empty awaiting for an important figure to fill it.

Footsteps became heard, louder down the hall, from the herbalism room as Myra and Ethel made a stride towards the head of the table. Myra lowered herself to sit down in the empty chair at the end, Ethel stood at her side. There was a continued moment of the silence, Ethel placed her hand on Myra's shoulder, giving her some confidence to start.

"Ethel and I" Myra began, "Have decided that Arthur is something different in this supernatural world, which is impervious to magic of any kind that we immediately know… After a lot of discussing. We only have one question for you Arthur."

There was definitely some uncertainty in Myra's voice, it was clear to him. With his hands, one cupped in his clenched fist, Arthur diverted his focus from his hands and then looked upon Myra, to Ethel, then back again to show he was paying attention.

Ethel didn't hesitate a moment for an answer, "It seems that no magic that we cast can affect you. This means that you are very dangerous towards us Arthur. The real question is, are you a threat to us?" scorning her eyebrow in severity, as she questioned him.

At that moment Hannah could see that the question was already answered, her facial expression changed from surprise to an annoyed look, lowering her eyebrows. She stared at Ethel, then back to Arthur and back to Ethel.

"What sort of question is that!" Hannah interrupted. "If he were a threat, why would he have saved us from that undead thing?! Which I may remind you is currently deep in our backyard." she firmly stated.

Myra instantly stood up from the chair, placing both hands firmly on the table. "Let him answer for himself Hannah!" her voice shut the room down for any more interruptions.

Hannah sunk ever so slightly back into her chair, from the fierce reminder of who is in charge in this house.

Arthur looked at Hannah with a faint smile. His eyes moved back towards the head of the table, where Myra regained her calm and lowered herself into her chair once more.

Arthur swallowed and began to nod. "I'm not a threat towards you, any of you." he mentioned, looking at the others around the room, mending any unsure thoughts with a confident look. "You all have given me another chance by finding me, which makes me grateful. I just don't know who I am at the moment." Arthur didn't stumble with his words, allowing the honesty to be clear in his answer.

At that very point, the invisible tension that had held the house up tight vanished. It seemed everyone in that room felt the tense atmosphere fall away. Understandably that no one in that room had seen a body come back to life by itself from an immense cause of death.

Over dramatically Myra sighed in relief, "We would appreciate it if you were to, in a sense look over us like you have already been doing so, unasked."

Ethel placed her hand on Myra's and gently squeezed it, smiling from the corner of her lips. Ethel turned her look towards Arthur. "Stay in this house and watch over us, we would gladly appreciate that." she stated, as she opened up with a big smile. Happy with the outcome.

It was a different feeling for Arthur, suddenly feeling more trapped, as though the house may turn into some sort of imprisonment to him. This was the chance where he could bargain for something he wanted. Scrambling his thoughts for something he could wager for, the words echoed in his mind, Lakebrook High... something that Daniel boy had mentioned a short while back.

"I want to go to high school; If I have this second chance at a life, I want to be able to direct it in a way I would feel to discover myself." Arthur bargained for, trying to not sound desperate or pathetic.

Kimberly's eyes lit up. "That's a great idea!"

Myra turned to Ethel for a supported answer, Ethel had no response but raised her eyes and glanced to Myra as though to throw the weighting responsibility of the answer to her.

"I think that's fair." Hannah interrupted. "He's already saved us once and I think it's a great idea to get out and about."

Peter abruptly stood up from his seated position, "I agree! He's gotta be brave or stupid to go through high school again." Peter looks at Arthur and nods, thumping his chest gently "I got you bro."

The conversation seemed to loosen a little, during dinner. The entire house seemed to return to their normal selves. It was agreed upon that Arthur would go to Lakebrook High School on the condition that Hannah would attend as a new student also. It was made clear that it would be pretty hard for Arthur to register due to the fact that he had no proof of identification or citizenship and needed magical intervention from the house overall.

The following days involved Hannah preparing Arthur for his orientation day, this meant that a new wardrobe was needed. Involving the favourite thing Hannah loved most of all, shopping – *the mall*. She was in charge of the preparations. But in all fairness Arthur wouldn't refuse due to the fact that the house was going to pay, he had a fairly small wardrobe and it got him back out of the house.

Hannah led the shopping tour, Kimberly and Peter also joined along. Kimberly was already a current student at Lakebrook High, she was awfully keen for advising and giving Arthur pointers on the many stereotypes, rights, and wrongs of the American high schooler. Giving the specifications of which stereotype likes what, and where to sit at lunch and who to sit with, which conclusively led to Kimberly asking Hannah and Arthur to join her group of friends.

All Arthur could think about was how he didn't want to spend time with those from the boarding house as much as he did, outside of the boarding house. He had planned to make a wider range of friends.

As the group were at a clothing store, Arthur was trying on a piling amount of clothes prepared for him. He was in the changing room; the light illuminated every corner of the small space. As he was trying on a clustered range of many shirts, he caught a glimpse of himself in the mirror, maybe it was the lighting that particularly lit up the focus of his body. He paused in horror, from what was visible was horrendous, even though he had died, leaving his mortal life weeks ago.

Scars.

Scars were all around his body, matching up from slice to slice, from where the metallic wreckage must've ripped through him from the car accident.

The look of himself hit Arthur with a strong level of realisation, what was he doing?

How could he just jump into a new life, new school, try to make new friends with a monstrous body like that, what about getting changed for sports class? How would he explain the cause of this atrocity of an aftermath?

Arthur's mind wrestled back and forth between tempting to scrap the whole plan and live indoors forever confined to the walls of Pennyview, but then the thought of getting another chance persuaded him otherwise. After all, they seem to be fading.

At least that's what he hoped, settling his mind.

A fair amount of time seemed to have past, Arthur was just staring at his body, following the scars meet and where they end, it must've been for quite some time.

Hannah interrupted his trance "Are you alright in there?" popping her head through the curtains, "Oh…"

This question brought Arthur back, the braveness returned throughout him and the sheer excitement of starting that new life returned. He looked himself in the eyes through the mirror in the dressing room.

Putting on a brave front, "Yeah, I think so, I was just looking at all of those scars on my body, I never really noticed them until now…" Arthur replied, his voice lingered softer near the end.

Hannah walked in, letting the curtain drop to a close behind her. Standing a few feet away from Arthur, her eyes scoured all over his body, she rubbed her fingers over some of the scars. It was clear she was trying to think of something to say that would make Arthur feel somewhat better. "You know, I'm sure we can figure this out, we can ask Ethel back home." she offered, growing with confidence in belief of her answer.

Arthur wondered if the head witches back at Pennyview could really do anything about it, regardless it seemed that they were going to eventually fade away.

He continued to believe.

The day before school grew closer, time had seemed to go ever so fast for Arthur. Up until the one point of the night before his first day. He lay there, awake, staring at the bland ceiling of his room. Unable to fall asleep from the anxiety that curled inside of him which seemed like it was never going to settle.

The start to the first day of Lakebrook High School was slowly ticking down minute by minute as he stared at the clock from across his bed and towards the window. Glimpsing at the night sky through his curtains.

Ethel had agreed to enrol him and Hannah under her guardianship which would make it easier for the two of them, which seemed to settle any doubt or worry that she may have had.

The alarm clock buzzed, a sharp awakening for Arthur which caused him to rise to his feet incredibly fast. It was incredibly early compared to what he was used to, he now had a purpose for the day. With little sleep gained throughout the anxious night, he was ready, in fact he was more than ready for his first day of high school. Arthur got changed quickly and found himself at the kitchen counter, sitting upon the stool by it with an empty school bag beside him. An arrangement of food was laid out across the surface, Kimberly, sat opposite, had already tucked into her breakfast. Hannah, still yet nowhere to be seen.

Kimberly began conversation, "So are you excited for your first day? You'll love it!" she seemed over energetic for this time of the morning.

Arthur, trying to keep his voice steady replied, "Yeah, I am ready! I Wonder what it will be like."

"It'll be great! Luckily you and Hannah will be in the same year, so you'll have someone to hang around with… including me! But you don't usually see juniors hang out with sophomores."

Arthur was confused by these terms, "What is a sophomore?" he scratched his head, taking a bite out of some toast, straight from pile on the serving plate.

Kimberly began to educate Arthur on the entire American school year naming system, sophomore is the year before junior and junior was the year before senior, which was the final year of high school. Kimberly began to verbally drift off into explaining buildings and spaces of the school, up to the point where Hannah thankfully had made an appearance.

Kimberly paused in her ramble, "Finally!" she announced loudly over the counter. "We've got five minutes until we need to get the bus, Ethel isn't here to give us a lift. But she's already phoned in. They're expecting you at the front desk."

The thought of a bus threw a disgusted look over Hannah, it was clear in her face, "Bus? I'm driving, we aren't getting the school bus. It's our first day, we're driving in." she protested, which inevitably meant she was offering a lift in.

The drive to Lakebrook High School was exciting, Arthur was sat in the back of the car whilst Kimberly sat in the front.

The excitement built up as they passed through the inner city, the tall buildings seemed to become less frequent as the car began to go through a residential area. There was a wide-open space that started to appear on the right, Hannah began to slow down the car.

"Here it is!" Kimberly confirmed.

Hannah indicated, turning the car into the school's car parking lot. Finding a space to park, the car came to a stop, there was a few cars that filled up the spaces already. Not as many as Arthur thought, but then again not many would drive to school besides the seniors he assumed.

It was lively, it was noisy, the buildings seemed to be endless, flooding over the grounds. Curiosity struck to what each building may teach, as Arthur would begin to guess at what Kimberly had already mentioned.

As the gang stepped out of the car, Arthur followed Kimberly's directions, taking in as much as he could. The fear of what Arthur may have felt from the other day at the mall, had disappeared, at least for now.

The experience of adventure, an exciting new path had begun, Arthur now had more free choice than being trapped within those walls of the boarding house. This direction now meant a chance to meet new friends who he could essentially pick, another to choose what subjects he wanted to take a new interest to. It was a new beginning, and he was in charge. It was a little strange that he was older, but that was quickly was beaten to the back of his mind.

As the group walked down the wide main path towards the high school's main doors, the left side held a three-tiered fountain which had jets streaming graciously out from the top. To the right, a weathered bronze statue of some confederate statesman with one of those civil war outfits on, stood ever so proudly. There was action going on everywhere, students skateboarding up the main path, either trying to be careless or cool. Students were tossing an American football to and forth between themselves on the grass further off the main path. Some students were scattered, sat in all different places, on the grass or the concrete benches that lead up to the main doors.

As the group went through the double doors into the main foyer of the school, Kimberly stated, "You guys will need to go to the main desk, that's where they would be expecting you."

Looking around the foyer, the floor was that plasticky tiled, yellow and red. The walls were a dull yellow. These were the standard colours of a high school Arthur thought. It was a space where students all gathered and passed through before disappearing off into the corridors that sunk deeper into the grounds, in the centre of the foyer were some dark red chairs.

"There it is, that's where you need to go." Kimberly said, pointing over with a cheerful expression. Even though it was pretty obvious with a sign marking the front desk reception.

As Hannah and Arthur walked up towards the desk, a middle-aged lady was typing away, off in her own importance of clattering on the keyboard.

Hannah stood for a moment, to be ignored by her. "Hello?" she said impatiently, gaining her attention.

The receptionist's eyes slowly crept up over the screen of her computer. Peeking over the rim of her glasses at Hannah. "Can I help you?" her voice gurgled away, sounding bothered.

Arthur, leaned in with one arm on the counter, "We're here for our induction day?" he said proudly, hoping his charm would help.

The receptionist's eyes searched around for a moment, she was possibly translating what he had just said, from the British accent Arthur had delivered.

"Do you mean, new student orientation day?" as she questioned, staring blankly at the two.

Hannah took over, "Yes, that's it."

"Excellent. Let me check on here first." the receptionist began to click away at the computer whilst the two stood, waiting on her, taking her time.

"You must be Arthur and Hannah? It says here on the screen. Oh, here it is on a sticky note also." the receptionist chuckled to herself, as the two nodded.

"The student rep will be down from class shortly, so please take a seat and fill out these forms here." the receptionist instructed, placing some clipboards with paperwork and pens on top of the counter.

As the two took a clipboard each, looking back at the dark red seats, situated in the centre of the main foyer. Arthur began to step closer to the seating.

"Not there, over here. I don't want to sit in the middle." Hannah urged, walking to some seats out the way at the side.

As they sat, in between two doors which seemed to be offices of some sort. Arthur couldn't help but glance up over the clipboard. He noticed others glancing back as though they were observing the new, strange fresh addition to the school.

A girl stood out in the open, searching around the room with her eyes and approached the two of them, they were engrossed in the multiples of questions that they had to scribble through.

The girl, unnoticed stood in front of the two. Her voice stood out, "Hey, it's you! That British guy from the party the other week." she said out loud.

The two looked up, Hannah clueless. Arthur began to recollect the girl who stood in front of them, the olive-skinned girl, with the copper hair. Arthur scrambled his thoughts together to try and remember her name.

"Adam? Was it?" the girl questioned first, awaiting his answer.

"Close. Arthur, aand you're… Jade! Right?" Arthur paused before picking one of the names in his head.

"That's right, the accent also, I forgot about that until I just saw you." Jade smiled.

"What's your name?" Jade aimed at Hannah.

"Hannah." she replied bluntly.

"Right, well, I am here for your tour around the school and to give you your timetables and your registration classes." Jade explained, "So, shall we begin?"

The two followed Jade around as she explained the many areas of the school, one of those who had not been to a normal school since learning of her magical abilities at a young age and the other in an entirely new school environment.

The tour started with the main foyer where the two had entered, just prior. The main foyer split into two different corridors, each longed further down and stairs that lead to the classrooms on the upper floor.

The bell for class had rung and students began rushing about to wherever they needed to be. The three continued moving around the grounds, Lakebrook noticeably had a massive cafeteria, the rows seemed to stretch on for miles all accompanied by red and yellow seating iconising the school's colours.

Jade could sense some nervousness from Arthur as she continued to explain areas of the school. Hannah, unmoved with all of the new surroundings.

Jade directed towards Arthur, "In the movies, it matters where you sit in the cafeteria on the first day, that is all true, it matters. If you sit in the wrong place on the first day, it'll be horrendous for the rest of the year." she lied, awaiting the expression on Arthur's face to crumble. "I'm kidding!" she added, laughing away at his expense.

That was a short burst of anxiety for Arthur, but soon came to realise that Hannah and him, were both in it together. Even though Hannah was a confident person overall, he knew she would be fine.

The tour covered many areas of Lakebrook High School, leading out towards the outsides of the grounds to a massive open field, filled with energy and life. Athletics were in full swing with a class dotted around the green field, all focusing on separate physical activities.

The busiest groups were practising track, some American football, and a group of cheerleaders. It all looked so strange as Arthur looked at each of those groups, this was something that never happened back home when he was in school at this age.

Hannah leaned over, catching the moment Arthur was looking at the cheerleaders. "Huh, look at those cheerleaders, I think that's something that I have always wanted to try." she leaned into him nudging ever so slightly, as she stated her interest.

The entire fact that this was a new start for Arthur didn't really click until this moment, with his newly gained skills of strength and quicker reactions he could follow up a hobby in track running. The two continued to follow Jade around the outsides of the field as she continued to explain more about the school.

Arthur's concentration was abruptly cut off, as a ball landed near his feet.

He analysed it, an American football, it was a light brown ball shaped similar to a rugby ball with white crossed lining over a section in the middle of it.

"Hey, you mind passing it back over here?" came a voice from a distance.

Arthur looked up to see a familiar face. It was that Daniel guy from the party that he had attended to the other week and bumped into again at the mall. It was the guy that had the poor taste in music shirts with the long hair.

"Oh, it's you! Hey man! Touring around?! Welcome! Throw it back could ya?" Daniel shouted mildly across the field.

Picking the American football up Arthur positioned the ball in his hand and returned the ball. Misjudging his power, Arthur threw it back. The return of the ball cut through the air with such velocity, Daniel received the ball with grunt taking a step back to compensate not falling off his feet.

Arthur instantly realised that he probably should've put less power in the return than he'd imagined it would need, something he needed to work on being new to whatever he was, and being around humans.

"That was an insane throw man." Daniel shouted back over. "Catch us around when you can!" he added.

"Thanks… I guess." Arthur quietly responded.

Hannah and Jade both looked at Arthur, Jade confused with the power he had returned the ball, where Hannah had more of a concerned look.

The tour continued.

The Titans

After the tour, the two had settled into their classes, gaining bearings to how the school system worked, he shared some classes with Hannah but not all of them.

Hannah seemed to make easier conversation to the other students than Arthur had done. Many students were more interested in the different accent Arthur had, rather than much else.

Arthur presumed that he and Hannah were to sit together for lunch was a false presumption to make.

Hannah who was understood for being rather outgoing had already made herself known to a small group of girls, who had invited her to sit with them at lunch, coincidently were part of the cheerleading squad. She had made her moves wisely on her first day of school.

Lunch was the high point of the day, where the stress of decisions seemed to matter, but it was only high school. Arthur was older, he was beyond all of that pressure, or so he thought with Jade's comment from the tour in the morning creeping in.

Arthur queued up with his tray, to select food from the counter. Walking out of the queue this was it, this was the moment he needed to decide where to sit. Glancing left to right, looking for where to sit and who with. It was tense.

There were clear groups of friends all sitting at the tables, some split into two groups at either end of them.

Arthur had to decide, he was standing there doing nothing with the tray held out in his hands. Where was he going to sit?

The tense pressure was growing by the second.

So, tense that Arthur bottled the thought of sitting with strangers and found a seating place where he was alone. His mind mimicked himself for not having the courage to sit with strangers on his first day of school, telling himself how pathetic he was being for his age.

Staring down at his plate with not even a smartphone to keep him company with endless searching on the web. His food was his only company. If anything it made him look more pathetic.

A couple of lads stood by Arthur, looking down at him.

Arthur, peering down, he peeled his eyes away from his food to see who was standing over him.

It was Daniel and the other guy, Abel. They were both stood waiting to grab Arthur's attention with their lunch trays in hand.

Arthur looked up, Abel had a cheeky grin on his face, whereas Daniel smiled.

"You wanna sit with us?" Daniel offered.

Abel jumped in, "Unless you want to stay here and hang out with all your friends?" it was clear he had prepared that line with how proud he looked.

Arthur tried not to physically express his relief of finding someone to sit with on the first day, with a smile escaping Arthur nodded, "Yeah, sure!"

Following the two, with them firing questions to compare what food was like in school from another country, insulting the food they ate from the cafeteria here. The group stopped to the end of a table further into the corner of the cafeteria, the table already accompanied by a group of students. Some faces not known to Arthur but others familiar to those who Arthur had met at the house party the other week, Cheng, Laura, and Ellie.

Further introductions and reintroductions occurred for Arthur to remember those he had met the while back and to the new faces sat there, Chase and Kay. Who was soon introduced.

Arthur sat there oddly chipping into the conversation, trying to make an effort to be liked, but not seeming too eager.

He didn't want to be a people pleaser as a first impression or seem needy for acceptance. The group were comparing what classes Arthur had with them, which seemed a decent way to welcome him into the new school. This was great so that Arthur had someone to help him find his room throughout the first few days.

The focus of the group struck its attention to Arthur from a question that Daniel had asked, "That throw earlier on the field was insane, have you thought about trying out for the Titans, the football team here?" he awaited Arthur's answer as though it would big a major revelation.

Arthur thought for a second, "I could do, but I haven't got a clue about how it all works and who plays where?" he asked. "I was thinking of getting into track and field. Was it?" adding the alternative option to the topic.

"You don't need to run track! You'll be fine, you seemed to have a great arm there and we can go to the tryouts together." Daniel explained, further informing that tryouts for the team were tomorrow after-school.

"Yeah, Daniels always been a *tryout* and never a Titan." Abel joked, digging at the hidden desperation of Daniel's efforts.

Jade, the girl who gave Arthur and Hannah the tour earlier came to the table and casually sat down.

The group all welcomed her, Arthur had forgotten that she was a part of the group sat around the cafeteria table and had met at the party. She was more of a social butterfly here in this setting.

"Are you still throwing a party on the weekend Kay?" Jade asked.

"Of course! I'll send a message to the group chat later letting you know the times and stuff..." Kay then explained.

Another of the girls spoke, it was Laura, "Oh wait, Arthur? We need to add you to the group chat, so you can come along." she responded looking from Jade to Kay, and then to Arthur.

Arthur was silent, looking back down to his tray of food, trying to think of an excuse to why he doesn't own a phone at all... not owning a phone and being in his teens is *the* sign of a weirdo.

"Oh yeah, but it's broken at the moment. I need to get a new one at some point." Arthur came up with that excuse on the spot.

"I'm off to the mall at like 10AM Saturday if you're down Arthur, you can get a new phone then and I'll get you added and stuff?" Daniel offered.

Arthur thought this sounded like a decent plan and agreed to take up the offer, without thinking. The only issue he had was his bank account that Hannah had helped set up earlier would actually work and to know how much money he needed.

Lunch came to an end, the day seemed to draw closer to returning back to Pennyview Boarding House.

During the drive home Kimberly asked them both on how their first day had gone, Arthur had a great experience being back in school altogether, expressing his excitement for the next day. He had completely forgotten about any other issues he had around him, being able to start out again.

The next day came fast and tryouts for the Titans was at the end of the day. Throughout the day Arthur shared a few subjects with different members of the group, where he had the chance to talk to Daniel and ask what was expected in the tryouts.

It was in the locker room, many of the attendants were getting ready into the kit. It all seemed intense as Arthur wondered how to wear some of the borrowed kit. The coach of the team who was also the physical ed teacher, followed by a few other staff walked in.

"Alright listen up!" he was fired up and ready to get things moving. "I'm Mr Decker, you can call me Coach Decker. You're here for the second tryouts of the year, if any of you here aren't in it one hundred percent, the door is there for you to head home. I only want the fiercest and most willing to apply for the Titans."

Silence filled the room if that didn't set the bar high, before things haven't even started, who knew what did.

Arthur turned to Daniel, "Second tryouts?" he questioned.

"Yeah, they host tryouts three times a year, I couldn't get in on the first tryouts, but I'm gonna get in this time." Daniel explained, enthusing his dedication.

As the fresh candidates for the Titan tryouts walked out onto the field, stood there opposite them by the side of the coaches were a few current members of the team all in the school famous, red, and yellow Titans gear.

Bleachers sat at either side of the pitch, with a track that encircled it all. Floodlights hung high around the corners of the pitch, switched on ready for the start of the early evening tryouts.

Coach Decker began his introductions. "These are my first-string boys, Chad Johnson, centre position, a Senior and also captain of the Titans, he is the Titan's right arm".

Chad, a bulkier ginger lad stood with a smirk on his face, the smirk of someone who is in power and living the high school dream.

"Andrew Carver, my quarterback, a junior who is the Titan's left arm." Coach Decker continued.

Andrew was a dark-skinned lad with a face of thunder, passion, and his intense eyes scanned the fresh tryouts.

"These fine lads of the Titans will be assisting me on who gets into the team and who does not." Coach Decker stated.

The group of stragglers made their way onto the field, where the practicing teams were picked. Arthur and Daniel had made it onto Chad's group where the aspiring Titans began running suicide drills with Chad pitching in moments of motivational lines. Keeping up with the pace.

Chad's group began to warm up with throwing and kicking practices towards the field goal on their end of the pitch. Arthur had to keep in mind his power and not to overthrow inhumanly or kick a great distance.

Arthur stopped to look around for a short moment, he could see that the coaches and the Titans were scoping out all of them who were on the field. Some coaches making notes on their clipboards.

Just as Arthur began to practice a throw towards a player at the field goal, his new group of friends cheered his name from the bleachers followed by Daniels.

Taking Arthur's attention by surprise, he lost slight control of his power and threw the ball with such strength, clearing off over the goal with force that gained the attention of Chad.

Chad strode over, "What arm was that?! You're the new British kid in school, right?" he fired without hesitation at Arthur's answer for the first question.

"Uhh, yeah I am, was that a good throw?" Arthur replied.

"It was insane, do you work out?" Chad questioned

Arthur to be quick on his feet, had obviously not worked out at all, for a very long time. "I did a fair bit back in England yeah." he lied.

"Nice!" was all that Chad said, before walking off to continue his observations.

Arthur walked back to Daniel, who was at the edge of the pitch with the group at the bleachers. Abel, Ellie, and Laura had decided to surprise them by watching the tryouts.

The whistle blew, it was time for a practice match. Chad's team versus Andrew's team. Gathering around each of the teams' captains, choosing who would play which position on the field and discuss tactics. Arthur pretended to understand what half of the tactics were.

"British, you're our quarterback." Chad pointed at him.

Arthur eagerly nodded, cluelessly.

"All you have to do is throw it to our wide receiver as soon as you get the ball." Chad pointed out for him.

Daniel was chosen to be the teams tight end, to make sure the wide receiver can receive the ball more smoothly without being tackled.

The whistle blew again, the teams lined up in their given positions. Andrew and his opposing team all lined up to be stood in their defensive positions. There was a moment of silence, Arthur could feel the tension for the rest of the group, he just about felt it himself. The whistle blew once more and the call outs began from Chad, it was *go* time!

Others in the field prepared their stances, getting ready for whatever was about to come. Chad, the centre, snapped the ball back up to Arthur who was remembering to play as the quarterback. As Arthur rose from his position eyeing out the wide receiver, looking far to the side he drew back his arm, ball in grip raising his arm. He fired the ball from an overhand throw, cutting through the air nicely into the hands of a wide receiver. Arthur stood back after his throw and watched the play take place in front of him, the wide receiver gaining yards with the mighty throw that he had thrown. Arthur stood there still, amazed at what was unfolding from a simple throw. There was so much movement taking place, as his eyes followed the wide receiver, the player was caught up by the defending team and tackled down to the ground.

Coach Decker blew the whistle in prep for the next play. "That's an arm and a half right there kid, keep that up." Coach praised Arthur.

Chad's team fired away with a few more plays, getting the ball to the other side of the pitch. Coach Decker's whistle was blown, it was time to swap around and become the defending team. The team hustled together with Chad giving positions left, right, and centre, he informed Arthur that he was to play an end position this time.

This should be easy for Arthur, he thought, with his new developed strength. All he had to concentrate on was not completely disabling or breaking any limbs of the attacking player.

The groups positioned themselves, Arthur prepared his stance, trying to mimic those around him on the front-line of this defence. Arthur glanced behind over to Daniel who was currently further afield taking the role as a cornerback. It would be up to Daniel to chase down any plays that involved the wide receiver from what Arthur picked up.

The whistle blew, it was time again. The opposing team's front-line player, the tackle was bounding towards Arthur. Arthur glimpsed through his helmet as he predicted where the players hands were going to counter a push back.

A giant thud emerged, with the right amount of power Arthur had managed to block the player, pushing at his chest forcing him to fall back onto the ground. He turned around to notice that the wide receiver had made it past Daniel, with ease.

It didn't look good for Chad's team.

The opposing team were gaining yards, but what did that mean?

Were the whole defending team not going to get through to the tryouts, or would it be individual performance.

Another play was set up, the attacking team had gained some yards on the football field. The defending team set up their positions further back down the field.

This happened once more, this time Chad was keeping a close eye on Daniel, Chad decided to call a team hustle. Explaining that he needed some fast feet as a cornerback, subtly hinting that Daniel was being outpaced drastically. Arthur knew that he could do it, but he stayed silent, he didn't want to take anything away from Daniel's efforts on joining the team.

"I'll swap out with Arthur." Daniel offered, I'm sure he's much faster than me. I can hold the line."

Arthur reluctantly nodded as Chad confirmed the swap.

The group made their way into positions, it was time to continue the struggle of a defence that the entire team were putting on.

The whistle blew, the calls were made. Arthur eyed every inch of movement, a wave of strong focus and determination rolled through him.

"Crap." Arthur muttered to himself, as he watched the opposite team's quarterback launch the ball to the other side of the field.

The opposing team's play was planned to be on the opposite side of the field this time. Chad's team did better at defending, but still lost a few yards.

The teams were set again in position.

This was it, Arthur felt it! It was going to come his way this time.

He prepared himself.

Watching the ball intensely, with the switch of hands from the opposing team. It made its way to the quarterback; it was thrown through the air making its way to his side of the field. Looking away to the wide receiver on the other team, he could see him getting lined up to receive a throw. Arthur watched closely, whilst he began to prepare himself to get closer to the player who was getting ready to receive the ball. The ball was thrown into the arms of the wide receiver, it was caught perfectly. Arthur leapt towards him in giant bounds, gaining on him quicker.

There was a thud.

It was a clean, it was a tackle, the ball flopped to the ground. The whistle was blown.

Arthur had successfully stopped the opposing team from gaining much space, if any at all.

The tryouts continued back and forth for most of the evening, there was a certain enjoyment for Arthur who had never really been good at any types of sport at all in his past. Arthur began to feel relaxed and forgot about everything else around him, only needed for his ability in the game. The evening of the tryouts had come to an end. The group was getting changed out of the football gear, Arthur was proud of himself. Feeling as though he picked up the basics somewhat quickly, he looked over to Daniel.

Daniel didn't seem pleased and energetic as he was earlier.

Coach Decker, Chad, Andrew, and a few other coaches were all deliberating in the office by the dressing room. Peeping through the office window at some of the players.

The staff and helping players of the Titans emerged from the doorway of the office.

"Alright! Listen up! It was tough, but we've come to a decision who is in and who hasn't made it." Coach Decker announced to the dressing room.

Arthur phased out every sound that was around him, at this very moment his hearing only focused on the names rolling out of Decker's mouth.

Then, the moment happened. Arthur heard his own name… Returning to his surroundings he looked at Daniel, Daniel seemed sombre with his expression. Tracking back, rushing to remember through the names that had just been announced, Daniel's name had not been mentioned.

It was time to head home back to the boarding house, Daniel was quiet as the two walked out of the dressing room towards the front of the school. Arthur knew he had to say something to help the situation in any way possible, Arthur felt somewhat responsible for taking a spot in the team.

"I'll get you on the team, somehow, I will." Arthur stated as an offer hoping to console Daniel. He contemplated swapping places on the team, knowing that Daniel had tried hard to be a part of the Lakebrook Titans.

"It's alright, I'll try to do a bit harder next time when the third tryouts come around. Anyway, how are you getting home?" Daniel responded.

Arthur looked around, unsure, had no idea how he was getting home that evening responding with a similar thought.

"Oh, you know what, I don't really know. No one really knows that I need picking up… I guess they thought I would get the bus or something anyway." he presumed, starting to feel a little worried on the bus routes to get back to Pennyview.

Daniel kindly offered Arthur a lift home, walking into the car park where Daniel's Mother was waiting. A giant Ford pickup truck awaited, with a tiny woman cheerfully waving at the direction of the two.

As Arthur climbed into the truck, the backseats were small. He felt cramped compared to the luxury of space Daniel and his Mother had in the front.

Introducing Arthur to his Mother, there was some small talk of when he started, what classes he had the same as Daniel. She was friendly, it was clear Daniel had gotten some of his welcoming traits from her.

Then the question of direction happened. "Where am I dropping you off Arthur?" asked Daniel's Mother.

Arthur had no clue.

He tried to remember some of the directions home, with just the name of the street where the boarding house was on. "Upper heights?" he called out from the back.

Many minutes passed of searching on Daniel's phone, the location of Arthur's residence, Pennyview Boarding House.

Shortly with direction they had found it, "This is alright, just here thank you." Arthur instructed, as they stopped outside Pennyview.

"Wow, you live here do you Arthur? It's a lovely place." Daniel's mother mentioned.

"Yeah, it's real nice man." Daniel added.

"Ah-yeah, I do live here with many others though. It's a busy place." Arthur pointed out. Making his way out of the car thanking them both for the lift back.

Daniel rolled down the window "I'll catch you tomorrow at the mall, remember 10AM outside the Coffee House." he reminded.

"Got it, will see you there." Arthur replied nodding. Arthur hadn't forgotten, he was excited to hang out on the weekend with someone different for once.

Arthur opened the gate which led on to the long path through the front yard up to the doors of Pennyview. He didn't have a key to the front door, he had always come home with Hannah or someone else when they had returned. Standing at the front door, Arthur wondered if he should knock or just walk in. Being late he already knew that he would be in trouble regardless.

He decided to walk in, stealthily.

Taking the chance of being sneakier, Arthur opened the front door's handle, twisting it slowly. Peering round the door he managed to guide his way around it, without needing to open the door any wider than needed for him to slope through.

Walking through the house to his room, he began to climb the staircase, did any of them even remember him speaking about tryouts?

"Did ya make it in or na?" Peter surprised Arthur, sitting down in one of the chairs in the landing. "Kimberly told me earlier."

Slightly startled by Peter, "Yeah first time and all." Arthur proudly exclaimed.

"Great stuff! You stink, go shower the girls will be finished with whatever witchy stuff they're doing, and it'll be dinner." Peter jokingly instructed.

At the mall

It was Saturday morning, his alarm clock reminded him of the time, time to get up. Arthur rose in his bed switching the alarm off, he sat up for a minute, it seemed like a tough week starting a new school and trying to fit in. But that peak moment of anxiety had luckily passed with Arthur finding a group of people to hang out with. Especially outside of school.

After scrubbing himself clean in the shower and preparing to meet the rest of the group at the mall, Arthur prepared his clothes. It was a weird feeling trying to impress a group of new people, even though they were a few years younger than him. It was as though he had forgotten what stage he was at in life. Arthur had been to university; he knew how to meet new people and seem like a complete normal human being, even if he were only there for a year.

But that wasn't the case for Arthur, trying to revaluate where he was at in this new second chance of his.

After finally getting ready, Arthur made his way downstairs finding himself at the kitchen counter, a few others of the house were up and about. Arthur had found Kimberly's tablet left on the side and used it to research the bus routes to get to the mall, she wouldn't have minded as she left it about all the time.

Hannah walked past retrieving the coffee pot from the kitchen counter at the side of the room, her eyes looking over what Arthur was up to. Silently tapping away and typing on the local map.

"Are you planning to head off somewhere today?" she pried with a hidden interest.

"Yeah, I need to meet those new friends from school at the mall. I'm going to look at getting a phone today, with some of the money you all gave me on that account and what Myra had given me." Arthur justified himself, answering as though she was challenging him for a reason to get out the house.

"Hey! No need for your life story." Hannah laughed.

Hannah continued to peer over, as she walked to him. Placing her finger on the tablet she rotated it on the counter to her view. "You're planning to get the bus?" she then nosily asked with a touch of judgement.

Looking puzzled Arthur looked up at her and responded. "Well yeah it'll be good to know the times and routes anyway for around here." he reasoned.

Hannah slid the tablet back round to Arthur and took a sip of her coffee. She leaned in closer to him, placing her hand on the lock button, shutting the screen off.

"Hmmm! I suppose I can take you, that'll give me an excuse to buy something new and see these losers you're meeting. Come on, grab whatever you need to and let's go." Hannah offered without a moment to hesitate.

Arthur scoffed up his toast and checked his belongings before he left, he only needed the bank account card Hannah had set up weeks back.

In the car on the journey towards the mall, Arthur didn't know how to feel or what to say. He didn't expect her to offer a lift, but then again, this is Hannah and an opportunity to shop.

Arthur decided to ask Hannah how she had gotten on at school and settled in, it was all he could think of to get a conversation rolling.

Hannah seemed to quickly get bored of the school talk, directing back a question at Arthur, "What kind of phone are you going to get?"

Arthur thought to himself, "Erm I'm not so sure, I'll probably look for a cheap Android phone or something." was all that he could think of saying.

"Are you getting a contract?" she quickly questioned further, like she had already prepared to ask.

"Erm probably get credit, you know, pay as you go? As I don't know how well I would be able to get a contract, with having no ID or any credit rating." Arthur explained.

Hannah's face dropped in horror, "Wow, pay as you go? Really?! Okay. Okay." she was disgusted at the thought and composed herself for a moment, keeping an eye on the traffic. "I will get you a number under my name so you can just pay me that every month, we can sort it later, just go get a phone of some sort." she generously offered.

Arthur was terribly confused, "What's wrong with pay as you go?"

Hannah laughed at the question "Oh you're seriously asking. It's just embarrassing." she continued, "Anything or anyone that is linked to me at school can't be embarrassing and pay as you go is. Imagine if anyone found out you couldn't reply because your phone ran out of *credit*." she shivered in disgust.

Arthur soon picked up that Hannah's aim was to just be in one of the popular crowds at school, it wasn't a surprise at all. Pretty predictable considering who she was.

But he agreed with Hannah that it was slightly embarrassing, but that was all that he could possibly do. However, he did wonder why Hannah was being ever so generous to helping Arthur and he found that answer.

She loved to shop, and she loved to look good physically and socially. Either way, this felt like Arthur had to owe her something in the future which wasn't a settling thought.

The two arrived at the mall, Hannah picked an adequate parking spot which didn't require too much walking, but just enough to make an impression that she wasn't lazy. From what Arthur remembered from the conversation at school, the group were to meet in the food court area of the mall, where the Coffee House stall was.

The two walked up the main path to the front entrance of Lakebrook Mall, even though Arthur had been here before, the still-new experience of American malls had not worn off from him.

"So where are you meeting them?" asked Hannah.

"The food court, Daniel said." Arthur answered.

"Okay, do you remember where that is?" she added.

Arthur confirmed, remembering, but Hannah persisted to walk him some of the way there. Not out of the kindness of her own heart it seemed, but maybe to show off her presence to Arthur's new group of friends.

As the two got closer to the food court, Arthur could see the stall called Coffee House, some of them were already there. Daniel sat at a table chatting to Abel who was sat next to him. Laura sat opposite with her sister Ellie who comfortably sat on the table, with her feet rested on the chair. They were both looking at their phones, showing whatever it was on their screens to each other and giggling.

Jade was there, strangely with Chad. The same Chad that Arthur had to impress to join the Lakebrook Titans, why was Chad there?

Walking closer, he noticed Chad was holding Jade's hand. It all made sense.

"Right, see you later loser. Meet at the car at two for a lift home." Hannah announced just as she began to part ways, not having to interact with any of his new friends.

Getting closer to the group, that were all sat around, Laura looked up from her phone with a smile at Arthur's approach and waved.

"Hey Arthur, how's it going?" Laura welcomed him vibrantly.

This took the attention of the group, stopping what they were doing to greet him.

"We're just waiting on Kay and Cheng. Then we can all do whatever." Daniel explained, as they waited around.

It was Chad's cue to leave, Chad kissed Jade on the cheek before letting go of her hand, presuming this was the signal that he was heading off.

Almost leaving without a word, Chad looks towards Arthur as he passed him, with a slight nod and a response, "Sup Arthur?" rhetorically. As though Arthur was the only other one worthy of acknowledgement, but barely at best.

The girls began to talk to Jade and question her about her boyfriend being the captain of the Titans. Understanding that the relationship must be relatively new, as Chad would never be the type of character to hang around with some of the group, or at least that's what Arthur had seen from the outside.

Once the rest had arrived, the group began to go from store to store, looking at clothes, chatting, buying slushies, and gossiping about other students within the school. An occasional question would be returned to Arthur asking him what various things were like back home for him.

Arthur enjoyed listening to them, not understanding who they were talking about, but it was entertaining getting to know what they all were like.

Then there it dawned, the shop sign that shone the brightest, Macy's, it looked like a nightmare from back home, a department store.

As Arthur pointed out this type of store to the ones back home. The thoughts of back home seemed to erupt in his mind, as back home wasn't home anymore. In no reality could he return *home* being declared as officially dead.

Whilst the group were all waiting around as the girls tried on some clothes, the guys were sat around waiting in the chairs by the dressing rooms.

"Congrats on getting into the Titans man, I must admit I am jealous. I've been trying ages." Daniel pointed out, realising he had never congratulated Arthur since it was announced.

Arthur thanked him and returned the question, "How long have you been trying to get into the Titans for?"

Daniel replied, "Probably for the better half of a year now, but they would rarely take on sophomores when I started. I can never seem to make the cut."

Arthur thought to himself, that it may not be a judgement of sporting skill at all, but popularity. Daniel wasn't good at American football, but he wasn't the worst. Daniel didn't look like the sporting type, with longish hair and the fashion sense of a kid who hangs around in his basement for long periods of time. That might be the reason he didn't get on the team.

Arthur began to learn a bit about some of the boys in the group, Daniel had come from a medically career driven household, both of his parents were doctors of some sort.

Cheng who wore plain clothes similar to Abel without the punky touch, was from a Chinese family background where studying and grades come first, it amazed Arthur as it sounded like he barely was allowed to be out, even today.

Abel had a religious Indian background but didn't act like that was a part of his current life, he was the alternative one of the group, who wore studded bracelets, a leather jacket like he was from a punk era. Black natural hair with a long fringe, something like Arthur would've had years ago at that similar age.

The group seemed great to Arthur, they were all just out to have a good time and were not worried about much in the slightest, this was something Arthur once cherished before leaving for university. They weren't popular, but that was ideal. Being around them helped Arthur relax and move a step closer towards feeling normal, as normal could be for him.

After visiting from store to store the group found themselves at a familiar store to Arthur had seen in England, H&M. Not to a complete shock but Arthur had noticed that the clothes were pretty much the same over here as they were from back home. Walking through the men's isle to get to the shoes, Jade stopped for a moment and pulled out a ridiculous, bright purple zip-up jacket. H&M always had a good talent for hiding fantastic monstrosities like that.

"Guys, who's brave enough to try this on?" Jade challenged aiming it at the group of boys holding it in front of her.

Glances to each other exchanged, no one would dare be brave enough to volunteer. Arthur thought this could be a moment to be brave, but why was his heart thumping. Someone in the group asked one of the boys to try something on, it's not a big deal. Or is it? He thought.

As he tried to gain the courage to say he will try it on and take one for the boys' team.

Laura jumped in with an idea, "Arthur should try it on! Initiation for the new addition to our gang." she thought it was a brilliant one.

In that split second that felt like a dauntless amount of time, the group awaiting the response of Arthur. Arthur looked around the group, the only thing that really caught him out was the way Laura was smiling, as though she enjoyed offering him up as the centre of embarrassment.

"Okay, sure." Arthur nodded, knowing he needed to accept it. It was only a jacket anyway.

They all sat gathered outside the changing room awaiting Arthur to reveal the horrible masterpiece that had been found for him.

Inside, Arthur was staring at the mirror with the purple jacket hung up, where polo shirt had been magically added from the journey across the shop floor. What had he become, seemingly playing dress up for a group of people.

Arthur began to lift his top and a cold sweat crawled across the back of his head, his scars.

He'd forgotten.

As he peeled away his top further up his body, more scars. How had he forgotten about those scars from that fatal deathly accident in the middle of this brave excitement of dressing up. In this very moment it all seemed silent, the sound around him seemed to fade away as he examined his torso and taking in what he had now looked like.

There was something different, something odd. He tilted his head analysing himself. He had muscles where they weren't previously before, different twists and turns that he couldn't remember even having. Now to think of it those new twists and turns of his body weren't there before he had been killed by the strange creature that attacked Pennyview.

He'd avoided looking at his body in the mirror back at Pennyview since the last time he noticed. He felt noticeably stronger in that moment, Arthur took a deep breath and realised that he felt healthier, clearer inside.

But no matter how much healthier he seemed Arthur could notice the scars, "Wait a second." he muttered to himself, pausing.

He noticed as he tried to follow the scars, some of them seemed to clear up. They were beginning to fade, but it was unclear how long it would take, or if they all would fade completely. He hadn't asked Myra or Ethel, as he didn't want to bring up anything about them and have to sit there topless to be experimented on.

Jade peeked in uninvited, only for a slight moment wondering what was up. "Everything alright in here Arthur?" she asked.

Startling Arthur and catching him off guard from his thoughts, as quick as possible he tried to cover himself up, holding his shirt in front of his body. Jade's eyes moved from Arthur to the mirror, looking at his back through the reflection.

"Yeah, all fine, one minute." Arthur responded, starting off a little high pitched than normal.

She dismissed herself quickly, it was possible that she had noticed.

He could almost imagine hearing them whispering about what Jade had just seen. Arthur had to get this over and done with, moments later, a deep breath. He appeared from the curtains.

With a motivational entrance of cheering and clapping from the group. Jade walked towards Arthur and placed her hands on his shoulders, brushing away something imaginary, grasping at the jacket's lapels and slightly pulling on them to neaten his appearance.

"Looking good there Arthur, shame about the colour though." Jade joked full well knowing that was her choosing.

Laura added her thoughts on the jacket, "I dunno, maybe a darker purple might look good on him."

Arthur's attention switched to Laura, he noticed she had that attractive warm smile.

Midday passed quickly, where the group were all sat back at the food court. Arthur needed to get a phone; he had almost forgotten through the fun he'd been having with them all.

"Oh, I forgot! I need to get a new phone and meet Hannah at the car." Arthur mentioned to the group. Arthur had under half an hour left before it was two o'clock. "Where is the closest phone store?" he asked them all out loud.

Laura jumped at the question, "Verizon is just down that way, I'll take you if you like?"

Arthur nodded with a smile, "That would be great, thank you." it would be interesting to spend a short while with Laura.

"Arthur, remember you're welcome to come to the party later." Kay mentioned, informing Laura to add the details of the party later that night on Arthur's phone.

As Laura walked, leading Arthur to the Verizon store, she asked a question, "How has your stay in the States been for you so far?" barely holding eye contact with him. She seemed different, more nervous now that it was just the two of them.

Arthur swallowed some confidence, he felt nervous, but unsure why, "It's been great, I'm still getting used to a lot of new things, but it's been great hanging out with you all today. It was something that I had missed since the move, but I hadn't really realised I missed it until now." he opened up.

Laura looked pleased from what Arthur had said as a smile drew over her face, "Here we are."

She stopped as the two were at the entrance of the store, it looked like any other phone store that he knew.

Looking through the store's selection, Arthur was finding it difficult to find a phone that didn't have a contract. As he read a handful of the models displayed, looking for the one that was easy to buy outright.

"So why aren't you getting a phone contract? Even a cheap one?" Laura asked.

"Well, Hannah said she would get me a contract and all I had to do was get a mobile phone." Arthur explained whilst looking through the few options he had left.

"And is Hannah your sister or…?" Laura began to ask reluctantly.

"Nope, just someone I live with at the house." Arthur replied.

A moment of silence lingered for a second waiting for the next question that never came. Arthur knew her next question in mind was to ask if Hannah and him were involved in some way, he had a feeling that was something she didn't have the courage to ask.

"Yeah, she's been a good friend so far with helping me starting a life here. Kimberly and Peter at the house also have been great." Arthur added, clearing up any answer she may have wanted.

The two continued to look through the phones on display, pointing out various ones that seemed to be pricey.

"Here's one. What about this? It doesn't look too bad." Laura asked, finding a cheaper alternative.

Arthur looked at the phone, time was certainly ticking down for his ride home and he couldn't be picky. He agreed with the one that Laura had chosen. He didn't really need a good phone, something that could just do the basics of calling, messaging, and browsing.

After purchasing the phone, Arthur took it out the box and began to set it up, handing it to Laura as she wrote the notes of the party later that evening.

"I put my number in the phone for you, send me a message when you get your sim in it." Laura offered, "I'll get you added to the group chat also."

Arthur thanked her for helping him and said their goodbyes before making it back towards the car, with only a few minutes to spare before Hannah's deadline.

Walking up towards the car Hannah was waiting, leaning against it. "I would've left without you, if you weren't careful." she joked, as Arthur opened the passenger door.

On the drive back to the house in the car, Hannah shared the events her day, to which clothes or cosmetics she had purchased and how fantastic she would look in them at school. Arthur eagerly waited for her to ask him about how he got on with his new friends.

She never asked.

"Oh yeah here you go, a sim card, it's in that bag just behind my seat." Hannah pointing out the sim packet that she had bought for him.

"Awh, is that all you bought me?" Arthur joked.

Hannah laughed in her reply, "You'd be so lucky. Be grateful with what you've gotten already off me." she pointed out.

Party at the Walker house

It was later that Saturday evening. Arthur was getting ready for the party at Kay Walker's house, deciding from the few clothes he had obtained so far on his transition into a new life. A notification on Arthur's phone had pinged, causing him to walk over to it, as it charged by the bedside table.

Unlocking it appeared a message from Laura, "Can't wait to see everyone later! Should be good! X"

Presumably this must have been a message to a lot of her contacts considering it said everyone. Arthur responding to her message, "Catch you later! She still hadn't replied to his message earlier confirming his number.

After calling for a ride through an app on his new phone awaiting the arrival of the car, Arthur lingered in the foyer at the bottom of the stairs, Ethel had conveniently walked out from the living room to offer some wise words.

"Understandably you want to go out and have fun, I get that trust me. But don't reveal anything that you don't want others to know." she slyly warned him with some words of advice, tapping at the side of her head twice with a slow wink.

Arthur looked up towards Ethel and nodded.

"If you know what I mean." she added.

Arthur took on board her hidden warning, "Understood, don't worry." he confirmed.

Ethel continued to walk past Arthur into the other room down into the hallway. He would never dream of revealing what he had become or was. Overall, he didn't understand it entirely himself, but he knew Ethel was speaking on behalf of the residents at Pennyview regardless.

After getting into the taxi, he found himself at the front door of Kay's house, holding an eight pack of some beer that was discovered from the Pennyview pantry, possibly Peters or for the guests that they never had over. It was noisy, surprising noisy for someone who had been guessed as the quiet one, in the same group as him at the mall earlier. It wasn't just the music that gave off the noise, but voices could be heard. At this point it was probably easier to just open the front door and walk in.

As he walked through Kay's front door it truly looked like a house party, it was impressive. Decorations covered various corners, balloons were up high and down low. A wide lounge area to the right room, a massive dining set sat in the left room and straight ahead where a hallway aside by the stairs upwards. The dining table was spread with a game that Arthur had recognised from back at his time at university, beer pong.

This was where most of the athletes of the school were found if they turned up, and predictably so, some of the Lakebrook Titans were there playing.

In the lounge, the TV was on linked to the music that was playing through the surround sound within the room, no one Arthur knew was within sight.

Did Kay really know this many people? He thought scanning them around him to find the others.

He would have to explore further into Kay's house to find the others, the corridor would be the best decision next to follow the kitchen and if failing. The garden would be next on the list.

Weaving down the corridor guests were hanging out chatting and drinking. As Arthur found the kitchen and lay his pack of beer on the table, there was an assortment of many different alcoholic drinks to be found. Impressive considering that many of those at this house party were under the age to even purchase it in the first place.

Finally, a face familiar to Arthur, it was Abel.

"Yo Art." Abel greeted him, taking him to where the rest of the gang were all hanging out in the back of the garden.

As Arthur walked towards the group there was an enthusiastic hello from them all, one that stood out was a tipsy Jade.

They've all clearly been here a while before Arthur and have had a few to drink already it looked like.

He sat down next to Daniel who was knocking back a bottle of Bud Light, tapping his drink against his. The group spoke for a while, and Arthur enjoyed listening to the others make fun of everything and anything, especially Abel. It was great. It had seemed to have been a long time since Arthur had sat down and had a drink with people at a somewhat calm and social level; that were also normal humans.

Individuals were back and forth returning from the kitchen to resupply any drinks needed. It appeared the group had moved towards playing twenty questions, and Arthur, being the newest and strangest edition to the group became the frequent target. It was fine, at least the questions about England had finally subsided. Arthur didn't mind answering any questions, carefully of course in line with Ethels words of wisdom. He knew that this would only be a phase being the newest, and part of the acceptance process of any friend group.

Many different members of the group would ask questions about "How was school lessons over there?" or "Who were your friends and what did you get up to?" knowingly Arthur wouldn't give off his real home city and gave the name of another, in place of his answers. Hiding any chance of those searching him up on a rare occasion.

Arthur began to notice that if Laura asked a question towards him, Jade would have some verbal remark as though she were trying to take the focus away off her. It was clear that Jade had too much to drink, in her state she seemed to purposely overshadow even the other girls around them.

Jade began the personal questions, getting closer to Arthur's personal background.

"So, what about girls? Or guys? Have you ever kissed a girl, or guy?" Jade began to become forward, sitting at the end of her chair.

Arthur of course responded with confirmation, but that didn't seem to satisfy Jade's curiosity, it was clear in her facial expression.

She pried further. "Have you ever been with someone, had sex?" she finally asked with a look of suspense, not holding back at all with that question.

Arthur of course had, he was older and were at a different environment back home. He couldn't lie, entirely that is. "Yes of course I have." Arthur responded firmly, trying to brush it off as no big deal.

It was a big deal for those of their age.

With that response he could feel the group see him in a slightly different light, unsure if it was a positive or negative one.

His eyes darted around gathering all the facial expressions of them around him. "Things are maybe different back over there, with stuff like that?" Arthur tried to unnecessarily excuse his answer.

A booming voice cut through the strange tension in the group, walking from the house, it was good timing to take a break from being on the spot.

A few looked over, Arthur looked over.

"Hey hey! How's the gang Jade?" it was Chad. It was a few drinks in Chad, who had possibly played and won beer pong many times over already.

His movement to joining the gang and taking a seat next to Jade was not the most subtle, it was clear he had been having a great night as he dumped himself in a chair.

He reached his arm around Jade and pulled her in as she sat close. It looked as though Jade wasn't herself for a moment, not as relaxed as she was earlier, more tense. Something must be up with the two and it must be something recently since midday.

Conversation seemed to be forceful for the next few minutes, as Chad would mock any sociable topic that came up. Disrupting the enjoyment of the group.

"Too bad about not getting into the team Daniel, maybe try *next* year." Chad stated, giving off a manner that he shouldn't bother for the third and final tryouts of this year.

Daniel didn't fully respond; he slumped back in his chair and took a sip. Clearly still sore at not being able to get onto the team.

One of the football team came over, Andrew Carver, the quarterback of Chad's team. "Beer pong time bro, we're taking on the losers from the basketball team." he aimed at Chad specifically.

Thank goodness, he was going all that Arthur thought, the atmosphere had changed entirely with his presence.

Chad leaned into Jade and gave her a kiss on the cheek, he just about managed to stand up from his chair. He turned back around to the face Arthur, "British, coming with?" he asked.

Arthur couldn't understand what Chad meant, "Coming with?" he questioned back.

"You're part of the team now, you gotta join in." Chad slurring the final few of his words.

Arthur looked around and could see that the confusion wasn't just on him, it was clear with the rest of the group. He looked from person to person in the group, waiting for any of them to oppose him going, saving him.

Everyone was silent.

What hit Arthur that moment in time was the look on Daniel, he looked upset, but it was clear he was trying to put on a cheerful look. Something that Daniel had worked on a while for, just seen and taken by someone new in such a short amount of time. Arthur felt guilt, Daniel had been the most welcoming to him and he couldn't simply turn down Chad as it would look like a sign of weakness to him.

Arthur looked at Chad firmly, "I'll take Dan with me? Right?"

Chad looked confused; Andrew looked confused.

"Why?" Andrew questioned.

"Well, he's pretty good at beer pong and at football also." Arthur challenged.

Daniels eyes lit up raising his head off the floor, he wanted to include Daniel and felt that this was the right timing to bring him in.

"No chance! He isn't part of the team!" Chad continued to oppose.

Arthur thought quick, and to think quick was to bargain. "Okay, how about this. Daniel and I, against you two? If we win you allow Daniel into the team. You win, I'll leave the team." Arthur offered.

"What's you leaving the team really bargaining for us?" Andrew pointed out. "You owned in the tryouts."

Arthur had nothing left to offer in return, he had nothing of value. A brilliant idea hit, "I will buy you beer for the rest of the year, every week." It was a costly offer as a loss, but Arthur felt confident.

High pitched noises came from Chad and Andrew excited at the offer.

Daniel mentioned instantly at backing down because of his offer, but Arthur had no plans of the sort. Arthur thought he could win, if he had the skills to play in the tryouts as good as he could. Arthur could use his experience and his skills for winning a simple game of beer pong.

"Deal." Chad confirmed with such a confidence that a loss was never going to be on the table for him.

Andrew foolishly believed in Chad, sharing the confidence from him.

The pairs made their way to the dining room where some of the others here were still playing at the table. Arthur and Daniel's group followed behind.

Chad announced the game as loud as he could with the stakes at play. This sounded like a bigger deal to him, than what it really was.

The players mucking about on the table stopped and began to reset the game, setting the cups out ready as the four began to pour beer into them, flocks of teens began to gather.

Everything was ready.

It was the moment to begin, from the flip of a coin, who goes first. Arthur knew from how he had played, if the coin flipped in your favour, your team offered the opponents first throw. It allowed them to get the first observation of your opponents, at the risk of going second.

Daniel questioned Arthur with allowing them to go first.

"It's okay, shows confidence. Are you any good at throwing a ping pong ball into a cup?" Arthur stated, these kids had no clue what was coming for them.

"I've never really played this before, I mean, how hard could it be?" Daniel replied, keeping his voice ever so slightly down.

Chad didn't turn down the offer to go first, "Whatever gets me closer to winning that beer! Wahoo!" he laughed obnoxiously whilst holding the ping pong ball up level with his shoulder height.

The first throw of the game and… it sank! It was in. Arthur felt a little hit with his own confidence.

"Another go! Alright!" Chad announced as Andrew high fived him.

Picking another ping pong ball out of the bowl, raising it to the same level and release.

Plop.

In.

Okay, it was fine, clearly Chad had a lot of practice and warmed up earlier in the night.

Another round of celebration and Chad began his third throw, Arthur and Daniel were still waiting to even get a chance at the opposite side of the table.

Chad plucked a ball, held it up ready to throw.

Pop! Off the cup's rim it bounced and off the table, there was some hope yet.

Arthur wanted to win but considered letting Daniel have the first throw, he wanted the focus to be on him. It would also allow him to judge how much effort he would need to support Daniel.

Daniel picked up a ball out of the bowl, rolling it between his fingers and thumb.

"Nice and easy, not too hard, let it float through the air." Arthur offered guiding words of advice, starting to become invested in the game.

Daniel raising the ball to his eye level, pulling his arm back to flick it from his fingers.

Pop! It'd bounced off the rim of Chad and Andrew's cup. Close, but not a bad shot for someone who had never really played before. This still didn't fill Arthur with confidence, he knew he may have to play dirty.

It was Andrew's turn, ball in the air, to head height and release.

Plop.

It was in, Arthur and Daniel, down seven to ten.

Andrew with his big ego let out a smug line, "You guys got nothing on us, haha." he high fived Chad. "This will be an easy one."

Andrew picked up another ball, pretending to do a few release shots to pump his ego up as well as the crowd that had gathered from other rooms in the house.

Releasing the ball... a complete miss. Over the top line of cups and straight onto the floor.

A sigh was heard amongst the crowd.

A sly grin cracked through Arthur's lips, Andrew wasn't all that, and it was his turn now. He muttered with confidence, "I've got this." turning to Daniel and reaffirming that confidence with a nod.

Arthur picked up the ball, it was light between his fingers and thumb. He had to focus and somewhat channel whatever it was inside him that helped throw an American football across the field. Obviously, he didn't need to clear the house with the ball, he needed a minor fraction of that. Arthur felt the flimsiness of the plastic ping pong ball, squeezing it, feeling the pressure of it push back.

Arthur raised it up to his eye level, he'd done this thousands of times before, now he could throw it with a little extra accuracy.

He took a deep breath, trying to tap into his inner self.

The focus rushed over him, something ever so small released within him before releasing the ball from his grip. It soared across the air which seemed to take forever in Arthur's eyes. It was perfect, it had the right projection, it had the correct power!

It was… in!

Gripping his fist in celebration before turning to Daniel to high five. It was clear that the confidence of the sporty duo across had been dinted and Arthur had another throw to go.

It was a perfect shot. If he could do the same and sink another, that would be great. Plucking another ball out of the bowl, Arthur drew his arm high, just like last time and threw.

It was in, perfect just as planned.

Arthur and Daniel's group behind let out another cheer, this time with a bit more enthusiasm. Showing there was a chance, but mentally this was a shock to Chad and Andrew. Two was enough to show confidence, rather than one being a fluke. Arthur could get a third one in a row, he knew he could, whatever this thing was inside him it helped. But he couldn't get a third one in, as much as he would've liked to humiliate the two, a low profile really was what Arthur needed for now. Even if it were a silly beer pong game that he seemed to be over invested in.

He drew his third shot and threw missing the side of the cups by an inch, bouncing off the table's surface.

A sense of relief drew all over Chad and Andrew. It was Chad's turn to pick a ball from the already halfway empty bowl.

He raised his hand, he'd practiced that movement perfectly, he released.

Plop.

Chad had scored a fourth for his team and missed his second attempt afterwards.

It was still on; the game wasn't too far gone.

It was like this for a few turns between the pairs, Daniel had even begun to improve and sink a few cups himself. Arthur knew he had to gradually work on evening out the score before it became dangerously down to a few cups left on both sides.

It came down to the final shot for Chad's team, with Andrew's turn to take the shot. It was amazing that the guy could still throw with how much beer he had consumed, in fact most of them around the table, especially Chad who should've been passed out ages ago.

The ball released from Andrew's grip, seemingly going higher than planned but it still sunk the cup.

It was almost over.

It was sudden death, Arthur or Daniel had to take a shot to stay in the game, miss and that's it, over. No team dream for Daniel and a free yearly beer supply from Arthur's pockets.

Daniel looked at Arthur, trying to keep focused with his eyes straight, he'd had enough to drink.

"You gotta take it man, I don't think I can." Daniel mustered out of his mouth, swaying back and forth.

Arthur nodded, he seemed to be more sober than the rest of them. He could still feel the effect of the alcohol, but not as much as if he would normally.

Picking out one of the balls that had been wiped and placed back in the bowl. Clenching the ball ever so slightly in his fist, he looked around the room, the crowd gathered had somewhat paused the party to watch this momentous game.

Arthur threw the defending shot. There was a moment of suspense felt from the crowd, all eyes were on the ball as it soared through the air.

It was in followed by a large groan from the opposing team, another chance to win the game for him and Daniel.

It was Arthur's turn to throw, repeating what he had been executing most of the night, it was time for one more throw and time to win.

Picking another ball from the bowl, rising it to his eye level he took a deep breath. He doubted himself at the back of his mind, the pressure was mounting.

He released.

It was in, the group cheered ecstatically behind them.

All eyes were on Chad and Andrew, who were having a discussion between the two, who were to take the sudden death shot to keep in the game.

Andrew was appointed, which may have been the most sensible decision of the two. Responsibility had been forced upon Andrew as he held his ball; this was important for him. He needed to prove to Chad that he was worth his respect being a junior.

He threw the ball, and in that moment, Arthur could see the change in Andrew's expression that the throw had not gone to plan. A sobering look of shock appeared all over his face, knowing he had messed up. With the ball skimming the far back of the cup's rim, it missed and hit the table just behind the cup.

There was a massive cheer and screaming going on within the house, the captain of the Titans and the leading quarterback had been defeated at their own game.

Arthur and Daniel turned around to face their group, cheering and celebrating with the others.

"Oh man! Whatta game! That was great!" Chad loudly announced whilst walking over to the two. He took the remaining cup on Arthur and Daniel's side and began to chug away at it. "Arthur, you are something, something else. It's good to have you on the Titans." he stated, firmly planting the empty cup on the table.

"Good game Chad, Andrew." Arthur modestly replied.

Chad then directed his look upon Daniel, "Alright, you're on the team, but you gotta sort this whole…" Chad gesturing his arms and fingers pointing in a circling motion. "Geeky look, look the part for a football player and play better."

Andrew stood further behind from Chad; his ego was clearly bruised. He had a look of hidden hatred at them, embarrassing him in front of those all around.

The crowd began to disperse back into rooms of the house, some of the party began to set up another game for themselves.

The party resumed, flowing back into the other rooms.

It was getting past midnight with Arthur and some of his new friends, they were all sat in the lounge relaxing indoors and the party had died down to a smaller crowd.

Chad's team of football players who attended made their way out of the front door loudly to continue the party elsewhere, without Chad, Kay was lucky that they weren't going to be her problem anymore. The front door closed. Chad stormed down the stairs, an angry looked covered his face as he opened the door to join the rest of his crew.

Arthur was sat there on the sofa with most of the guys, looking over to Daniel, he was drunk, very drunk. Laura came over with Ellie and slumped herself down closely on the sofa next to Arthur, Ellie sitting on the arm of the sofa next to Daniel, keeping her distance in case he was to vomit.

"Kay has offered to us about staying over in the other bedrooms." Ellie mentioned to the guys, "So it'll just be you guys getting home tonight or staying here on the couch."

Abel was the first to respond with needing to get home himself, the question was then directed to Arthur. Arthur looked at both girls then to Abel, then back to Daniel. He had to get Daniel home; he was in no fit state for anything.

Laura edged a bit closer towards Arthur on the sofa, her body touching Arthurs, knocking her leg gently against his, playing it off unintentionally. Arthur could hang out with Laura if he stayed, they could start to bond more now that the party had now became quieter. He couldn't, he needed to get Daniel home. Even though it was cute, clearly, she had gained some courage through drinking and possibly had a small crush on him.

Arthur had no romance on his mind at all with what he is, even though he felt somewhat differently towards Laura. He couldn't lead her on.

"I would like to... but I think I need to get Daniel home; he looks like he needs to go." Arthur said cutting any potential further connection between Laura and him.

The girls agreed and began to get up and start saying their goodbyes. Arthur came to understand that Abel and Daniel didn't live too far from Kay's house. Offering to walk them both home as hailing a ride might be too dangerous if Daniel were at a vomiting point. As the three gathered on Kay's front yard, preparing to walk down the path.

Daniel felt his pockets, frantically searching. "Um. I think I've left... Phone in there." he just about managed to splutter out.

Arthur propped him up against Abel and headed back into the house to grab it. Opening the front door and looking right into the living room, there it lay on the table, just as the drunken teen had left it. As quick Arthur grabbed Daniel's phone, he turned around to face back to the door. Jade was there by the door, at the bottom of the stairs. She looked strange, not sober at all with the looks of an aftermath from an argument. It would explain why Chad was not out of the door at the same time as his friends, they must've had some sort of disagreement.

Arthur looked at her as he went towards the front door, "Are you okay?" he kindly asked.

"Boys are just dicks, aren't they? he just wants to go out and get up to stupid shit with his friends." was the complaint she began to reveal.

Arthur had to console her quickly, knowing the other two were waiting outside for him, "Some guys are just new to not knowing how to act, especially after a few drinks." it was a small white lie; Chad was always going to be an alcohol fuelled dick. Arthur had presumed that from the first time he had met him. "Anyway, I'm sure things will be sorted out. He's just going out to get drunk as the party's not over for him. He'll feel like an ass tomorrow and apologise." he finished with. Hoping that would console Jade, only if for a minute as he could escape back to the other two.

Jade looked at Arthur for a moment, she placed her hand flat on Arthur's chest. "You seem like you're older than the other boys in our year. Thank you." she mentioned before cracking a smile through her teary face.

A small sweat broke over Arthur on what she mentioned about age, his eyes looked towards the corner.

Jade leaned in.

She kissed him.

It was a shocking moment for Arthur, there was no quick response, he was frozen in place.

He pulled away announcing his leave, "Uhm, I gotta go, see you later Jade." barely sticking around to finish his sentence, he had already opened and stepped through the front door.

After closing the front door behind him he looked down the front path for the others. He took a deep breath, Arthur didn't think about it, he didn't want to. Forcing the thought of that kiss out of his mind, he exhaled. Heading straight towards the guys where Daniel was still propped up against Abel, waiting to finally start walking home. Handing the phone to Daniel, Abel reached out and took it, stuffing it in Daniel's pocket.

Abel and Arthur spoke most of the way to the first house. Daniel just being able to drag up his feet and follow along before they stopped outside; it was Abel's house. Just before leaving Abel's front garden, Arthur confirmed where Daniel lived and began to make his way to his to drop him off. It was a quiet walk with the two at a slow pace, trying not to let Daniel trip up over himself, Arthur's arm around his waist. The fresh air and walk home seemed to do him a little better than what he was when they left Kay's party.

"Thanks Arthur." Daniel murmured.

"That's alright Dan." Arthur replied, thinking that there wasn't far left to go.

"No no no." Daniel repeated, still not being able to speak clearly, "For helping me out a bunch, you've been a good friend since you got here." he tried to explain in once sentence as best as he could.

Arthur smiled, in that minute the silly guilt had washed away, knowing that he had got Daniel on the Titans and he was happy. "I know what you mean. It's all good buddy, now let's get you home and I'll get a ride back." he explained to Daniel, still propping him along with his arm around him.

The two carried on, through the darkness where spots of light illuminated from the streetlights along the sidewalk. The two were on the street to Daniel's house.

"Here we are Dan, it's your stop. You all good getting in?" Arthur questioned, who seemed better, the fresh air and walk must've helped a little bit. He could just about walk on his own, using the walls around him, anyway.

"Arthur do you wanna crash at mine? My parents won't mind at all." Daniel offered kindly.

Arthur paused and thought about it, he'd realised this was a moment where he had made a friend which offered some sense of certainty in his new life so far.

"Yeah, you know what. Sure." Arthur answered, whilst unlocking his phone and sending a message to Hannah that he was going to crash at Daniels. Just to make sure someone in the house knew that nothing bad had happened, if they discovered his bed was empty in the late morning.

The two entered Daniel's house and made it halfway up the stairs, Arthur prepared himself in case Daniel fell backwards on him.

The light flicked on. It was man standing on the landing above, it was Daniel's father. The two squinted from the sudden light, Arthur tried to make out who it was.

"How are we doing there boys?" Daniel's father asked with an expression of concern yet enjoyment in how awful Daniel looked.

Arthur felt obliged to introduce himself, "Hi Mr Bayer, I'm Arthur, Daniels friend from school, just bringing him back from Kay's house."

Daniel's father just laughed, "I figured you're Arthur with that accent, Daniel mentioned a new kid in class. I just thought I'd see the state he'd got himself into. It doesn't disappoint!" he continued to laugh to himself, "You're welcome to stay the night anyway Arthur." Daniel's father offered.

Daniel's father seemed very nice, considering he was from a medical career from what he had been told, which required long strenuous working hours and discipline. He seemed fairly okay with Daniel drinking and coming home in such a state. Both of Daniel's parents seemed to be very welcoming and friendly.

They made it into Daniel's room where he collapsed onto his bed, falling asleep shortly after he had landed. Arthur had made a bed up on the floor of a spare duvet and various throw pillows he managed to pry off around Daniel, it'll be fine for one night.

Arthur laid there, looking around Daniel's room. It was a typical teenager's room, with band posters dotted around the place. Shelves were full of some nerdy figures and a few trophies from some time ago in Daniel's youth for something. A computer desk stood with Daniel's laptop on it with a few books stacked by the side. It was certainly something that Arthur's room wasn't at Pennyview, there was personality to the entire room.

Arthur closed his eyes, trying to relax his body. Taking in the night of what had happened, that kiss finally crept its way back into Arthur's head. Many questions in Arthur's head arose, it was such a mess, she was with Chad and just drunk. What would happen if Chad found out, what about his place in the team?

What about Laura?

Wait.

What about Laura? His mind echoed again.

Arthur doesn't have time for any of this romance, even the messy kind, he must work out what his plans are for this strange supernatural new life he had begun. These questions and events caused Arthur to predict the different futures and what possibilities he could go down.

There was a snort.

His rapid streams of predictive futures were interrupted as they began to spiral off uncontrollably.

"Hey Arthur… Could you help us… with my look, like Chad said?" Daniel could just about put together before drifting back off to sleep, snoring softly.

What had Arthur become, a high schooler pretending to be a younger age. Hanging out in a witch house. Also, alongside the events of being declared dead in another country, but not actually dead. Superhuman strength and accuracy with throwing either an American football or a ping pong ball and now also a seventeen-year old's fashion advisor.

    Arthur focused on closing his eyes, what he had become bought a smile.

    He drifted off to sleep.

Miracle blood

The next week passed by and chatter about the party followed, it was a great party from what was heard around the school. There was no mention about any kiss or argument whatsoever.

It was midweek at Lakebrook High School and football practice was at full swing with a noticeably high energy. There was a moment where Arthur was sitting back on the bench, whilst the other half of the team were practicing plays on the field. His half for practice should be running drills, but Arthur was sat on the bench observing the practice at play. He didn't need to practice on his agility having some type of supernatural ability. Using the time to reflect what had happened over the weekend, it's all he'd been doing.

The kiss from Jade was the most confusing and an out of nowhere occurrence. There was a fear that the kiss could fall into conversation at any moment, making the fragile beginning Arthur had set up, crash. All that could be summed up from it was Jade being very intoxicated and upset, it was nothing and simply a blip of a bad decision. They had spoken at school the last few days, but only in passing of brief conversation in class or at the cafeteria table together. Arthur secretly hoped that Jade had forgotten about the kiss, so he didn't have to bring it up and defend himself from Chad.

Letting his mind rest, simply summing up that Jade had forgotten the kiss entirely. It was time to focus on the next issue that cropped into his mind.

Now, Laura on the other hand was a completely different story, she had messaged a few times over the weekend. She had been welcoming and a great person to talk to, Arthur had a peculiar feeling for her which he tried to push aside. He had been reluctant in his replies considering all the complications he had going on.

Arthur planned to hopefully stick to school to pass through the time, get some grades, and then work out what he would next be doing with his life, that *normal-ish* life.

For now, all that Arthur began to know was how to play American football, it was his only lead in life through a new hobby which he had begun to enjoy unexpectedly; Arthur never saw himself liking any particular sport in his previous life, especially American football.

The whistle blew, the team out on the field were finished with running some plays, a player was walking towards Arthur. Taking off his helmet it was Daniel, the two had spent the last few days; since the weekend, working on his new look to be part of the team. His hair was shorter, almost a medium length arguably with curtains, with one side somewhat swept towards his ear and the other flopped over just aside his eye. His clothes when out of the football kit were gradually turning into fresher, more updated looks rather than band t-shirts that unsurprisingly most had holes in. Anyway, with just the hair sorted he looked great, miles better and he seemed to be beaming with happiness more often than his usual self.

It seemed Arthur had made a good friend who trusted him with his appearance and with choices Daniel had a big passion for. The next step was to practice more football with Daniel, hoping to polish some of his throwing and catching skills.

"Ey man, think you're gonna be up shortly." Daniel said preparing to take a breather next to Arthur on the bench.

The two sat there for a minute, "Here we go again." Arthur stretched his arms outwards. He sat up and flipped his helmet right side up ready to wear, a fist bump to pass by Daniel and he was off, ready for some practice in this new hobby.

Arthur was thankful for a few days of normality, without any mention of that kiss and nothing had become out of place at Pennyview.

As practice had ended and the team were all heading towards the locker room. Just as it were time for the showers.

Arthur was feeling brave enough to shower for the first time, his scars had faded enough to get away with it under the running water.

Arthur rummaged through his bag looking for his toiletries. Accidentally catching his phone, the screen lit up.

He noticed something that was startling to see.

There were five missed calls from Hannah and to match with that many messages, something must be urgent. Reading the few messages from Hannah, still holding his phone inside his bag. Ignoring the voicemails, all that could be summarised was an emergency and to get back to Pennyview *now*.

Picking back up his shirt, having to wear it whilst sweaty from practice, Arthur would just have to deal with being dirty for the time being. He had to get home quick, and his only option was to ask Daniel's mother for a lift sooner, he would have to shower later.

"Dan, can you give us a lift right now please? The house has called me to get back for some urgent reason. Is your Mum outside now at all?" Arthur quickly requested, hoping she was already there.

"Oh yea, she's already out there. We can head out if you like." Daniel kindly agreed with an unusual grin.

As they scrambled all their belongings into their bags. The two sped out of the locker room, walking around the side of the school to the car park, sighting out the pickup truck, getting closer. Arthur noticed that the driver's seat was empty, there was no one in the truck.

Confused, Arthur asked, "Where's your Mum? Daniel?"

Daniel's grin returned, "It's my truck, my Mom had to borrow it last time."

"You… can drive?" Arthur was amazed at that revelation.

Arthur knew how to drive but only on the other side of the road, only back home. The pickup truck was a bizarre choice of a vehicle to drive, but for Daniel it seemed to be quirky enough for it to make sense.

Arthur listened to the voicemails along the drive home, a lot of the voicemails were Hannah demanding him to head back immediately, as ordered by Ethel. Arthur lied to Daniel where to drop him off, a street away from Pennyview just in case there was something serious or weird and couldn't let Daniel see. Thanking him, he hopped out of the truck onto the sidewalk below. Luckily Daniel didn't pick up on the different drop off location.

Arthur stepped in large strides towards the street where Pennyview Boarding House was, keeping an inconspicuous pace, slowing down just before he was a few houses away to walk in alert and observant for anything unusual. Walking across the iron fencing on the outside, it all looked normal, the house looked like it always did. Opening the gate and leading on the main path, he hurried up and stepped onto the first step. He noticed the welcome mat had been thrown aside, there was some charcoal scrawled symbols on the stone floor.

Thinking the witches had drawn some protective symbol at the front door, he had a hunch to avoid stepping on it, for the sake of supernatural witch paranoia. Stretching his leg over to twist the door handle to get in.

It was locked.

"What? Why?" Arthur spoke out loud, everything seemed perfectly fine on the outside.

He rang the doorbell which the chime echoed throughout the inside of Pennyview. He stood there, one foot stretched behind the symbol and one foot over it, hand on the frame of the door. It took a while, there was some shuffling inside and a face appeared through the window netting. It was Hannah, sliding the door chain, opening the lock, twisting the door handle to allow Arthur inside. Only holding it barely open enough for him to smoothly get inside.

As Arthur stepped through into the foyer, it was bright, all the lights that could be on, were on.

Weird, he thought. It didn't seem like the house was lit up like that on the outside, at least he didn't remember that seconds ago. Hannah grabbed Arthur's arm and pulled him into the dining room where all the members of the house were sat around the table.

Both heads of the house were sat at either end of the table, it was interesting as Myra and Ethel always sat and stood next to each other at one side. Arthur knew it was a strange but serious situation just from the sight of that. Hannah guided him to the seat next to hers, taking her seat, Arthur took his.

"Finally joining us Arthur, there's been a curse placed upon this house." Myra issued without haste.

"What does that mean? It sounded serious from the messages. It all seems too calm around here?" Arthur questioned whilst looking at the many faces of residents around the table trying to gauge any further understanding.

"Something is going to happen soon; I can sense it." Myra continued to explain. "It may be the same threat that put upon that wretched creature at our house a while ago."

"Do we know from the markings around the doors what it may be?" Ethel asked her.

Arthur soon realised that the markings at the front door wasn't any of the Pennyview witches' doing.

Myra replied, "I'm unsure, it's magic that we haven't crafted before, we know little of it." she didn't sound confident at all which was slightly worrying.

Arthur understood from his time at Pennyview, that there were other beings of magical spells and power, and they're not all friendly from experience so far. Arthur thought what he could have to offer to help the house, as they have kept their promise to his somewhat normal life. Unsure of what is going to attack the house or those in it, Arthur stayed silent on how to help as he began to try and work out the situation to understand it in better detail.

He interrupted. "Wait did you say doors? Not door?"

Ethel rolled her eyes, "The markings drawn from some charcoal on the floor, outside every doorway into the house. You must've seen it on the way in." she clarified.

Soon realising that these markings are around every door entering into the house, Arthur took a split second to be thankful for not standing on the one at the front as he came in. Witchy paranoia paid off, for his sake.

He soon thought what he could do to help, whilst the table began to discuss options on how to research more.

"What's that smell? Like sweat and dirt." Kimberly asked over the table, halting any further discussion.

Arthur's eyes suspiciously darted around the room. This was clearly him being denied a shower, Arthur owned up to being the smelly one after football practice, where he excused himself to have a quick shower.

"Let me know if you need me for anything? After you've figured out the next steps." Arthur offered as he left the dining room.

As he entered his room, shutting the door behind himself. He began to empty his sports bag out onto his bed, organising what was dirty and what was clean. His phone vibrated where a message had pinged up, it was from Laura.

Arthur still didn't know what to do with Laura, he understood that she liked him in some sort of way, it was clear from school. She was cute, but she was a couple years younger than Arthur. She would be sixteen or seventeen, him nineteen, but it was more complicated than lying about his age. Arthur responded to her message returning the question on how her day had been, tossing his phone onto the bed. He would worry about that later. There was a more pending issue that Arthur wanted to sort out first, a shower. He walked into the bathroom where he began to turn the shower tap on.

It was warming up, the steam felt glorious as it shrouded the bathroom. Arthur began to undress, starting with taking his top off, anticipating the excitement of a well-deserved shower from practice.

He continued to undress, taking off his jeans.

There was a sound over the noise of the running water.

He stopped for a second, pausing, staring into the bathroom mirror, waiting to hear it again. It was a knocking sound followed by the bathroom door opening. Arthur froze, stood there in his underwear; head turned at the door.

Hannah appeared around the door, stopping to stare for a moment before speaking, "Oh hey, hey, look at you there in your underwear." she joked tightening her lips.

Arthur's privacy felt somewhat invaded, slightly being embarrassed. "What do you want?" he loudly questioned with an attitude.

"Oh right, yeah. We need you to try something out with these markings, Myra's requested you immediately." she insisted. "Come on!" as she pushed the bathroom door further open and disappeared into Arthur's bedroom.

Arthur walked over to the shower and turned the tap to the off position, halting the running warm water.

With a hint of sadness in his face, the shower wasn't meant to be. Not yet, at least for now.

After dressing back up in fresh clothes, grabbing some deodorant to mask his smelliness, it was the best that he could do for the time being.

He followed Hannah down the staircase.

Everything seemed normal still which presumably was good news. There she led Arthur towards the conservatory, the orangery as he discovered. Myra, Ethel, and Charelle were all waiting around the bar, Peter sat on the sofa in the middle of the room where Kimberly was resting with her eyes closed.

Arthur barely spent any time in this room, seeing a bar, laid out with spirits and mixtures all in its glory; Arthur would've spent more time in here sooner to unwind. Tall glass double doors were open facing the endless back garden letting in the shallow breeze, similar black charcoal markings were scrawled outside.

Myra was wiping her hands together with some charcoal powder on the bar, "It's a curse alright, to keep us in the house." she aimed at everyone in the room as Hannah and Arthur walked in, "Who knows what it'll do if we try to pass through it."

Ethel was perched on one of the stools sat by the bar, flipping page by page through an old book adding in some more knowledge of the curse, "From what I can put together in this old grimoire, it's an encasing spell used to trap in and haunt whatever it encompasses in an area." she flicked back and forth between two pages, "That's all I can understand from this old tattered thing." she added in slight frustration.

"Kimberly tried to walk through it, and she was pushed back into the house, but it made her pass out. Is she going to be okay?!" Peter pointed out as he sat with Kimberly's head on his lap, looking at Myra for assurance.

Ethel tutted at his question, "Of course Peter. I've told you already! She will be fine, just let her rest and stop bothering her."

Understanding to Arthur that there was clearly magic used to affect Kimberly, he could guess straight away why he was summoned to them with most magic being ineffective to him.

Arthur decided to beat them to the question. "And you want me to walk through it?" he presumed.

Myra looked at Arthur and nodded, "Correct. Magic didn't seem to affect you from experiments we have tried. This time I am curious to see what would happen to you, it's too dangerous for us to try again. But I know you can come back to life."

An inner sigh played through Arthur's mind. Yes, he could come back to life, but only the once after the undead intruder killed him. Deep down he didn't know if it was a sure thing and could work again. He was dubious and wasn't keen at the thought of being the dying test dummy. Another factor wasn't about him coming back to life, but he could still feel pain and that pain for this very moment could be real and excruciating. He had already passed the front door that had the markings, but what would happen if he tried to leave the house, or if the magic had settled to become more potent in any way.

After a few minutes of discussion, back and forth expressing his worries and understanding the reasoning of why those in the room wanted him to try, Arthur agreed to give it ago.

His heart pounded fast as he stood before the threshold of the double doors. He felt the breeze slowly tickle the hair on his arms, wondering if that was going to be the last feeling he will feel. Unsure if he will ever come back from dying again.

He took a mental leap of confidence, followed by the physical one, extending his leg and intentionally stepping on the marking. Slowly he applied his foot and leaned on the marking purposely pressing his foot flat. His guard lowered mentally; he was fine, for now. Now to bring the other foot forward and step through. Arthur closed his eyes and followed through his next movement.

He was fine.

He opened his eyes.

Arthur was on the other side of the markings; he was outside in the back garden staring off into the distance. There was no effect.

"You made it? Did you feel anything Arthur?" Ethel sounded surprised.

Arthur turned around to face the rest of the residents stuck in the orangery, he didn't feel a thing and nothing else happened but clearly this has an effect on the others. A selfish thought did pass Arthur's mind to jest and run the other way, leave the house for whatever haunting may come. But they may not have seen the humour in that. It was time to walk back in, he took a short breath and repeated the steps back into the orangery, backed now with confidence.

"We need something that can cleanse magical markings, something anti-magic, that may break the spell." Ethel concluded, "Something that can at least stop magic for a short time. We could then cast a counter spell."

Myra turned to Ethel, "We may have an idol or some vials of something we could work with somewhere in the attic." she suggested.

After that suggestion, Myra and Ethel left the orangery to find trinkets within the attic or basement that may help with a counter spell.

Those already in the orangery stayed there, all taking seats on the sofas around where Peter and Kimberly were.

Trying to relax in the moments of unease. The group waited patiently for the return of Myra and Ethel, hopefully with a solution to a counter spell or disenchantment.

"Huh?! What!" Kimberly whispered in her sleep, before bolting upright and letting out a short scream. She had come to, looking around the room at a group of startled faces. "Is everyone okay?" she asked.

"Are you okay?" Charelle asked in return, the colour returning to her face.

Kimberly seemed slow as she thought, "Yes of course? Why?" she wondered.

Peter's body entirely turned to face her, "You just got knocked flat out by some magic, woof, onto the floor." he explained, slapping his hands together.

Kimberly was slowly thinking again, "I did?" was all she replied, looking down into her lap.

Charelle made a disapproving noise, "Mmmhuh, okay, somethings wrong there. We need to keep an eye on her." she pointed out, aiming the caretaking responsibilities all to Peter with her eyes.

The group discussed possible options on what they could do for Kimberly, before she cut in.

"I should probably rest for a little bit longer." she suggested.

Everyone agreed in unison, no one opposed the idea of her sleeping for a little longer. Until Myra had returned, to check if she was okay.

The group waited for some time longer, it was becoming tedious as they were unsure to stay or leave the room, in case anything was to happen. Arthur sat there, swiping through messages of the guys from school, trying to keep himself occupied.

Hannah stood up, "Right, if we're going to be trapped in here, let's use what we've got." finding it the time to make a good use of the bar. She propped herself behind the bar and started to search through whatever was stocked, applying some recipe together in her head, placing the bottles and mixtures on the bar.

"Anyone else wanna help?" she asked, pausing with a bottle of some possible spirit to mix, staring at them around her in the room.

Everyone looked up, focused on Hannah. Arthur tapped his feet repeatedly, he was bored. "Okay yup, screw it. I'm down." lifting himself up off the sofa and walking over to the bar.

"Finally! Thinking on the same wavelength as me. Took you long enough." Hannah announced, before continuing to search through the bottles.

Arthur began to prowl through the cabinets at his side of the bar to find bottles of liquor, he might as well give it a go mixing some sort of concoction. Hannah began to mix a cocktail starting with various different spirits.

"Aha! Nice!" Arthur let out a slightly heightened scream of excitement.

A good bottle of Glenfiddich whisky was discovered which made Arthur's sad, boring and showerless evening that bit better. "Myra and Ethel know how to stock this bar nicely." he said to himself in approval.

Continuing to open the bottle, cracking the unopened seal. Arthur poured a more-than modest amount in his glass. "Dang." Arthur then followed with, "Need ice." It's fine, he can make his way into the kitchen to grab some in a moment he planned.

"Are you guys sure you should be drinking right now?" Charelle had suddenly become the oldest one in the room, the grown up one of them all.

Hannah and Arthur both looked at each other, Arthur shrugged.

"That's rich coming from you." Hannah laughed out, "Takes the edge off, right? What's one to hurt in a time like this." trying to justify her reasoning.

"But... it's just us in this room and anything could happen at any moment." Charelle continued her concern.

"Remember the rules, the oldest witch is in charge of the situation. Me, being the oldest here in this room makes me in charge. That's the rules!" Hannah reminded them, "That's witch hierarchy for you."

It was an interesting rule Arthur thought, but it made sense for many situations, having the oldest and most experienced witch in charge.

Arthur butted in with his reason, "I mean... I just had to be put through a near death experience?" he pointed out, "I think I deserve a little drink."

Hannah put on a pathetic voice, "Oh boohoo, I nearly died, waaa! Magic doesn't affect you." she laughed, tasting her drink.

Arthur placed his finger in the air and pointed at Hannah, "It could have..." he said softly, "It could have."

"It's a zoning spell, right? So, whatever it is, it will come to us eventually?" Peter asked, looking hastily between the witches of the room desperate for an answer, any answer.

"Everything's fine, nothing will happen until it's later in the night. Where it's darker and we're more tired and it's harder to see." Hannah was confident in her prediction that everything was fine, and nothing was going to happen, at least for now.

That sounded like good common sense for Arthur, investing his confidence in her prediction. Nothing was going to happen in this moment for now, at least that was an excuse for him to grab some ice from the kitchen.

Hannah also agreed, joining in with getting some ice as a great decision. The two, both ventured down the hallway and off to the kitchen together.

"We'll be back in a minute." she echoed back down the hall as they walked away out of the orangery.

Arthur walked into the kitchen followed by Hannah. Hannah began to fumble at the fridge taking Arthur's glass off him to fill it with the ice dispenser.

Arthur lost track of his attention looking out the kitchen window. It was starting to get dark outside rather quickly, he had forgotten how long they were waiting in the orangery for. Arthur continued to stare through the glass as though he was trying to imagine something were about to finally happen.

But nothing.

The clunk of the ice dropped from the fridge breaking his imagination, "Here, yours." Hannah said raising the glass of whisky outwards by her side whilst focusing on dispensing ice for her own drink.

"Who attacks a house like this? Why?" Arthur thought out loud.

"Hmm, some other witch coven that maybe doesn't like how we do things here... or that we are here on this territory, and they want it." she started. "Witches have a lot of power in the areas they live, a lot of erm... magical influence let's say. Some groups just don't like how others run things and try to take over. Witches do really suck to each other." she finished with.

Hannah turned towards Arthur, leaning her back on the front of the fridge. She took a sip of her drink, as so did Arthur, both satisfied at the efforts of getting a drink.

Suddenly, the kitchen door slammed shut, the attention span of both instantly snapped towards that door.

"Funny!" she shouted, "Good one guys." thinking the others were playing along, the other side of the door.

It was just silence after, not even a snigger, or a scuffle of feet escaping down the hallway in hilarity of trying to startle them. A strange feeling pulled Arthur to glance his head back to the kitchen window, that strange feeling overcame him, it was pitch black out there. Arthur walked closer in curiosity to the kitchen window, concentrating his eyes into the depths of what should be the garden, discovering that no outdoor lights had lit up out there. There was no light from the moon, neither any stars could be seen upwards into the sky and none of the garden lamps were on; it was thick with blackness beyond the kitchen window.

Hannah walked towards the door that had slammed shut. She grasped the doorknob firmly in her hand and prepared herself with courage; She inhaled deeply, twisting it and opened the door to an inch-wide gap. She paused, finding the next mental step of courage to either look through the small gap, or pull the door open even further. The lingering fact that the door slamming shut, and silence followed was possibly not a prank at all. Hannah decided to pull the door open, hoping that one of the others are on the other side. There was a struggle, clutching at the doorknob as she pulled, the door seemed to rattle as it held firmly in place ever so slightly open. An overwhelming shriek was heard quickly pulling the door out of Hannah's clutch, slamming itself shut, to then silence which filled the kitchen. The door handle began to rattle wildly, Hannah grabbed at the handle to stop it from rattling.

She grasped the handle firmly, twisting it to open the door once more.

It didn't budge at all. Something must be holding it from the other side, preventing her from being able to open the door to get out of the kitchen.

Arthur watched the whole thing, unknown what to expect or even say, he was silently observing. The thought of the others screaming for a prank would've been okay, but the force pulling back the door sent chills through him. Suddenly a prank of some sort may not be the case entirely.

Hannah looked at Arthur.

Arthur looked back at Hannah.

"Arthur give me a hand here." she asked, composing herself as she ran her fingers through her hair, trying to stop a hint of panic from breaking through.

Arthur walked over with a small feeling of vulnerability within him, he was strong there was no doubt about that. It was more of, he didn't know what was behind that door or what was even going to happen if it were to open. He's no expert in the field of curses and what had even been placed upon the house, he had no clue.

Arthur stood firmly aside Hannah, placing his hands on the doorknob as Hannah moved hers away.

"You pull it, you're stronger." Hannah ordered.

Arthur's heart pounced back and forth nervously, gripping the doorknob. He twisted it with some of his might, not trying to rip the door off the hinges or break the handle, he pulled it to anticipate a force to pull it out of his grasp.

It opened, like a normal door.

Puzzled looks were exchanged.

Hannah angled herself at the side of the wall by the doorframe, avoiding any eye contact with anything that could be on the other side through the gap. Her back flat against the wall.

The door passed Arthur's eyesight, he looked baffled. "That's not right." he stated loudly, whilst staring straight out of the kitchen.

Hannah edged over the door's frame from the side to just about see what it was.

It was a hallway but not the one they had just came through, it was similar like the hallway upstairs. The same tall white doors on either side matching in parallel and a singular door at the very bottom of the hallway. The haunt had finally begun, they waited before the entry into the hallway, inspecting every estranged corner of it as they looked in.

A short discussion between the two concluded a decision. Deciding not to go through the door that had just opened to some strange-familiar place, the two thought they should try another door, the other side of the kitchen leading to another part of the house.

Taking their chances with another route.

It was decided Arthur should open the other door in the kitchen first with Hannah on standby for any spells that were needed just in case.

Arthur gripped the doorknob of the different door, "This should lead to the dining room." he muttered under his breath.

Twisting the door, it opened with no fuss just like the other, how the door normally should. It was the same estranged hallway that had presented itself previously through the other doorway.

Hannah and Arthur discussed for a while on what they should do. There was no escape out of this kitchen besides going through one of the doors, but now they had a choice of two routes. There was the door to the basement, they both agreed that wasn't the best choice in any situation to go that way. The first idea was to scream and shout, which entertained them for a while, it did nothing, no one could hear them.

After some time, Hannah became tired with discussing any option the two could do, "Maybe it's a false choice, it doesn't matter which way we take it'll be the same anyway." Hannah tried to justify after being lost in thought staring out through the kitchen window.

Arthur added to Hannah's statement, "And anyway, the door might shut typically as we go through? So, we might as well just go through as we're getting nowhere here."

Hannah turned away from the kitchen window, resting her back on the counter, "Exactly, we should just go through it and prepare for the best. The others might be in danger."

The two were daring together, daring to go through the hallway and try some of the doors. Arthur could see in Hannah's eyes that she wasn't all that keen to go first. Bravely offering himself, Arthur prepared himself to walk through that door into this hallway of some design. Accepting the fact that the door will slam shut as soon as he stepped into the hallway, or he may get hurt, his chances were better considering he had no affect with magic.

He placed his left hand on the frame of the doorway and then lifted his right leg to pass through, firmly planting his foot onto the floor, he was fine. Hannah kept close by to Arthur, worried at the possibility of the door slamming shut and separating both of them. Tailgating closely behind Arthur, bumping into his back, she grabbed onto his shirt as she followed.

As they were both through the door looking downwards the hallway, they began to slowly step through it trying each of the doors. None of the doorknobs budged, not even with the strength of Arthur and Hannah put together. They were seemingly fake doors that led to nowhere, or so they believed. Understanding that the singular door at the end of this pristine, white hallway was the obvious one they needed to pass through this curse.

"Arthur, it's gone." Hannah said, paused in place, looking behind.

Arthur turned his head and followed her direction looking behind, "Oh yeah." he replied surprised.

The door which they came from the kitchen had disappeared, it was just a plain white wall. The unopenable doors that sat opposite each other at the start of the hallway began to leak through the gap at the bottom, it began to flow freely. It was like something was flooding from the other side and the liquid was red, a dark red.

An ominous scream began to echo down the hallway that got louder and louder. The two flinched from the sharping cut of the scream, forced through their ears. The red pool of what could only be presumed blood began to flow from the other gaps under the doors, releasing closer and closer to them. The scream began to cause a displacement in Arthur's ears. He looked at Hannah, this must've been worse for her, she was trying to block her ears completely with both of her hands. The two sped up their actions and started pacing faster towards the final door, reaching the end it took no time for the two to clutch at the doorknob in synchronisation.

As soon as they touched the doorknob the scream reverberated forcefully, Hannah began to drop to her knees becoming faint, losing a lot of colour in her already pale face.

Arthur seemed to be less effected from it, there must be some magical cause that seemed to hurt Hannah more. He could see she was in pain; he knew that he had to get her through that door no matter what.

Deciding to present the strength he held back Arthur twisted the doorknob and closed his eyes. He was in a rush, barging the door shoulder first as he twisted the doorknob. As he pushed with his strength the door opened ahead of him, stepping into the next room with his eyes closed.

A cold feeling overcame Arthur, pain began to crawl upwards through his stomach. Opening his eyes a small handle stemmed from his abdomen, he'd been stabbed by something, something that was staring right at him. Arthur joined in eye contact, there was nothing at the centre in its eyes, it was just black. The skin of the creature, rotten, barely covered in whatever drapes it had, it was something similar to the intruder some time ago. The creature grasped the handle of the item that had penetrated Arthur's abdomen, retracted it, and continued to repeat pushing the blade into Arthur.

Arthur gripped his hands on the creature's arms and began to hold it back, avoiding any more attempts of being stabbed. He could feel his blood begin to trickle down his leg, the wetness of it travelling downwards. The creature fought Arthur, pushing him back into the hallway, pinning him to one of the fake doors at the side.

Its strength was unexpected. Arthur attempted to hold the creature's wrist to stop it and take control over the power struggle between the two. They struggled back and forth to each side of the hallway. Arthur, trying to step around Hannah who still kneeled there in pain, barely keeping her eyes open to watch what was happening. The creature pushed him into the wall on the other side of the hallway, trying to claw at Arthur's face with the other arm that was free, as Arthur tried to force it off him.

Arthur didn't feel strong enough to overcome the creature as it gained an advantage against him pinned, with its unexpected strength.

It clawed at his face, scraping away over his brow and past his cheek. Something took over Arthur as he felt the creature's fingernails cut through the skin of his face. The instinct came back, Arthur felt it creep in, allowing it.

Finally, was all he thought as he began to lose control over his actions.

The rage ignited within him, rippling through every nerve in his body.

The two struggled back and forth, this thing was a strong match for Arthur physically. He needed an advantage to take over the situation, as they continued to wrestle for power. Arthur found himself firmly pinned again with his back to the wall. Hannah passed through Arthur's mind; she must be in serious pain. He could see Hannah at the side, he wanted to look at her, to know she was still hanging on.

His eyes moved to focus on her, she was kneeling and hunched tightly, still hanging in there.

"Did my body just do what I thought?" he thought to himself.

If only the instinct that took over his body listened to what he thought all of the time. Rather than being a passenger within his own body he knew he could help.

Something gave way in his mind, a mental resistance seemed to fall away between him and the instinct.

Raising his leg, firmly planting it on the wall behind him. He pushed from it, forcing the creature to fall backwards onto the floor. There was no hesitation, Arthur positioned himself on top of it.

His instinct had finally listened alongside his body.

In that moment as Arthur sat over the creature. The creature's hand was free, piercing the dagger into Arthur's side, at his ribcage multiple times.

Arthur let out a scream in pain, like a roar, feeling a strange rushing sensation that had ridden throughout his body. He grew some newfound strength. Arthur closed his fist and raised it in the air, he began to strike at the creature's face, repeatedly without hesitation as the creature stabbed freely at him. This instinct had put him in a trance to repeat hitting the creature critically. Breaking the repetition when Arthur's fist had reached the floor of the hallway.

There was blood everywhere, who's blood? Who knew at this point.

The creature lay limp, no signs of moving at all. Arthur sat there, gazed upon the caved in skull. He was still kneeling over the creature that he punched to its end. He didn't move, stuck through tunnel vision, and trapped in a trance.

The blood flowing from the end of the corridor had trickled its way down to where Arthur was, the flow meeting the tip of his knee and foot causing him to snap back to having a bit more control.

The scream began to curl back into his hearing, it hadn't stopped. Looking back over his shoulder he could see Hannah looking up at him somewhat conscious on her side, with her hands still covering her ears. Arthur stood up and the scream reverberated down the hallway feeling it through the hairs all over his body, the scream continued to get louder and dominate the hallway. The far end of the hallway began to sink into darkness that seemed to chase them, getting closer.

Rushing over to Hannah, Arthur looped his arm around her waist pulling her into the next room, her hands firmly clasping at her ears as she clambered to her feet. As the two dove through the threshold of the doorway, they both fell to the floor as Hannah laid there by his side. It looked like the scream had sucked out all the strength within her, an effect of this curse.

Arthur looked up, looking around it seemed as though they were in the house, everything seemed to be in the right place. The two were on the floor in the hallway by the kitchen door entrance, looking back the kitchen door slammed shut. From what Arthur had gathered they'd only stepped through the door that led them into the kitchen in the first place.

Was that whole hallway just a part of the curse, was it even real he questioned.

Arthur pushed himself up from the floor onto his knee, he slipped, holding himself up on all fours. Arthur was weak, he had lost a lot of blood and had become drained of energy.

There wasn't time to breathe. There was yelling heard down the hallway back towards the orangery, it was Peter's voice. Jolting up to his legs, Arthur gritted his teeth through the pain. Lifting Hannah off the floor and propping her up against him. She could just about walk, leading her to the orangery. The expression and colour in her face was dull.

It was an alarming sight in the orangery. Peter was restraining Kimberly's wrists, she was trying to stab him with some glass, gripped in her hand. Charelle was on the floor facedown not moving at all, from what seems to be the remains of a bottle next to her.

It was chaos.

Peter managed to push Kimberly away from him, from whatever manic state she was in. She stumbled backwards losing her balance and falling to the floor knocking her head. She laid there still, she wasn't getting up, at least for now.

Peter turned to Arthur and Hannah in distress, "What's happening here bro? She just went crazy!" he yelled, stopping halfway as he concentrated on Arthur a little closer. "Your eyes... Arthur... they're black and red. Are you, you?" Peter was cautious.

Arthur looked at him dead into his eyes. He thought about speaking, but nothing could come out of his open mouth. He was still a passenger inside his own body, but he could feel himself dying from the loss of blood. Whatever this instinct was, it controlled him and was not letting go whilst he was in such a fragile state.

An overwhelming gust flew through the room. A figure gracefully walked in through the doors from the garden outside, a middle-aged lady, dark skin, and black platted hair, with a black leather jacket, and some acid denim skinny jeans. A face that meant business, that held no room for joy.

"Well, well, well, what do we have here? Two warlocks? But you don't seem to have gone insane like the witches, hmm something else?" the stranger narrated out loud.

Without answering she raised her hand, open palmed at Peter, flicking him effortlessly to the corner behind. Peter collided with the wall, crashing hard onto the floor.

Her gaze then fixes on Arthur, the same hand gesture, open palmed and flicked her wrist.

Nothing happened.

Her face scrunched, slightly confused she chants a small spell.

Nothing.

"What are *you* then?" she curiously spoke, slightly tilting her head. "I can't seem to cast spells on you. Almost like… magic doesn't work."

Still keeping Hannah up, Arthur strenuously hobbled towards the armchair next to the sofa in the centre of the room and calmly placed her down.

Hannah clutched at his forearm as he lowers her into the chair, "Don't die…" was all she could say with her remaining strength.

Arthur knew that dying was already in the works for him, with the amount of blood he was losing. His wounds weren't healing fast enough.

Something spoke for Arthur, out loud. "I will make sure you're safe, before I go." A weak smile pulled across his face. Arthur was unsure if that was him or whatever had taken over him making a promise.

He knew his time was limited; he could feel it shorten.

Arthur stood up straight and turned towards the stranger taking a slow step forward, trying to hang on to his balance.

The stranger was clearly bad news and the one who was in charge of whatever was going on. Her eyes fixated on him carefully trying to analyse what he was before allowing him to get too close, as she walked the opposite way around the orangery. Keeping her distance, her eyes followed his every movement.

"Maybe I can't cast anything on you, but hell. I can on things around you." she announced with some disgust.

Her arm stretched out to the side; Arthur looked at her hand as it flicked away. Pulling the bar stool up off the floor right beside her, hurling it through the air. Knocking Arthur with such force to the floor, landing by the double doors as the stool broke in pieces on impact, collaterally hitting the glass window and smashing it behind him.

Some glass shattered to the floor in smaller pieces.

Arthur made a promise, shaking to his feet as he struggled with the small ounce of strength that remained. He prepared to pounce at her with whatever he had left.

Arthur took a leap.

Crash! Back onto the floor with the other bar stool used as a magic projectile.

He had nothing left.

He was on the floor, powerless, weak, bleeding out, and barely mobile.

The stranger walked over to Arthur laughing, cackling hysterically louder, "Well, it seems you don't have much longer left for this world, look at you." she smirked. "Pathetically painting the floor with your dirty blood."

"Hey, just stop it! Just leave us all alone!" Peter shouted trying to stand up from the corner of the room, grabbing the back of the armchair to help himself back up.

An expression of displeasure covered the strangers face. She turned away from Arthur and began to walk towards Peter.

Arthur lay there, dying ever so slowly, his eyes shutting uncontrollably. He could still listen to what was going on around him.

He had to do something that could help the others in the house. Even if it was his last living action.

The stranger walked closer to Peter, passing Hannah at an arms distance by the armchair. Hannah weakly grabbed the stranger trying to pull her down with what little strength she had to stop her. The stranger was firmly stood, raising her hand in the air. Giving Hannah a backhand to the side of her face, she fell back into the chair. "You will have no chance to live with this haunt." the stranger directed towards Peter as he gained his stance. "If it doesn't kill you. Then I will, then I'll finish off this bitch here."

Arthur screamed internally; they were both about to die. He thought as hard as he could, what could he do to stop this and save them. With all his focus he could just about open his eyes, he stared at the markings which were just a few feet in front of him.

The markings! There must be something he can do. If somehow, he could weaken the curse, hopefully freeing Myra, and Ethel if they were trapped in some similar hallway or room to how him and Hannah were. The back of his mind ticked, he remembered some of those words mentioned earlier.

"Something anti-magic?" weakly Arthur muttered, through the blood in his mouth. Something that could cleanse magic, something that could stop something magical from taking place.

Arthur *was* anti-magic.

He had an idea.

A disgusting idea.

He crawled and pulled himself towards the outside marking by the double doors, but it was no use, he didn't have the strength to pull his own body. He stretched his arm to reach out for some broken glass that had dropped next to him from the broken bar stool hitting the window. If Arthur was resistant to magic, his blood must be something of the sort? He thought.

Gripping the broken glass firmly in his hand, he began to squeeze, pushing it into the palm of his other hand. He forced the glass through his hand as best as he could with what little power he had left, to draw what blood that remained within his body. Blood drew and began to drip down his wrist, to his elbow. Arthur frantically shuffled closer to the markings and began to smear his blood over them just on the outside, rubbing his palm roughly over the area, the charcoal began to distort and mix away with the blood. The markings began to smear away.

Breathing heavily, it was almost time to let himself go into the darkness.

Something invisible dropped in the air, this magical smothering atmosphere had disappeared in an instant. Arthur could barely open his eyes, but he was still there, alive enough for that moment to hear the following.

"What have you done! How?" the stranger's voice pierced through his dying ears. Completely thrown off as a shrieking howl seemed to echo through the house, exiting it as it hit every corner of the rooms within it.

Arthur blacked out. Laying there in a deadly amount of his own blood. He was losing consciousness and fading into the darkness. Fear clouded his mind, worrying if he would ever come back from dying. He wouldn't even know how to come back if he tried. The feeling of fear overwhelmed him as this could be the end.

Darkness. Once more. The darkness continued.

There was nothing, but then a blur of the colour white, a small horizontal glimpse of it. Focusing on the white, Arthur wasn't sure if this was somewhere else this time around or if he were even alive. He focused hard glimpsing at the white blur. Some moments passed as he focused harder on it, where it seemed to get wider, worried if he didn't, he would slip away.

This is it, he thought, I'm almost over to the next side. The afterlife?

There were some subtle bumpy patterns within the white as it became ever so slightly clearer. What was it?

Arthur felt if he were to take his mind off it now, he might be pulled back into the eternal darkness. His existence depended on it.

The patterns became clear, there was a circular shade appearing at the bottom of this vision. This was his eyes opening, he could see a ceiling.

This was… his ceiling.

That was his lampshade. A muffled sound emerged dully through his ears; it wasn't clear what that sound was.

Arthur could sense the direction from where the sound came from, his eyes moved towards the direction. He could see a figure, the figure moved into his vision and his eyes began to focus sharply, it was Peter.

An immense sense of relief overwhelmed Arthur's mind, a familiar face. He was alive.

He felt something flowing through himself, like pins and needles travelling within each cell of his body, it was the return of his nerves. Slowly moving through his arms, on towards his legs and toes, Arthur began to struggle to sit up.

Peter spoke a few muffled words and leaned over to help Arthur sit upright in his bed.

Peter's mouth moved, the words could just be understood, "You okay? Can you talk?" he asked.

It was now becoming clearer to Arthur.

Arthur's eyes moved around the room, examining who was around. There was only Peter and Myra, she was stood at the threshold of his room.

Arthur began to exercise his jaw, moving it side to side, "Yeeaahh, I think so…" clearing his throat. "What happened? The others?" Arthur asked, sounding much clearer.

Myra stepped closer from the middle of the bedroom towards Arthur's bed, "Everyone's safe, thanks to you. The girls are fine, a little scratched or bruised, but will be fine. Ethel and I had enough time to get to them." Myra softly spoke.

"Any later, then I think we would've been seriously unlucky." Peter added. "You should've seen it bro, Myra and Ethel came in the room, all magic-blazing. The woman feared them and ran for her own life."

"Okay, thank you Peter." Myra modestly cut him off.

Arthur let out a sigh of relief, smiling to himself he managed it. He saved the house in some absolute bizarre way, but he did it.

Myra sat on the edge of the bed next to Arthur, "Look, Ethel and I will look after the house for now and enchant it to pick up anything like this in future, for now you need to rest, but thank you Arthur." placing her hand on Arthur's in gratitude, she smiled at him. "Come on Peter, let him rest." she added, nodding towards the door, gesturing Peter it was time to leave.

Arthur interrupted them leaving, "Who was the woman?" he curiously asked.

Myra paused, "Don't worry, we now know who is to blame for everything that has happened. We will get to the end of it. Don't you worry."

The door shut behind the two, Arthur lay there just about being able to move. He didn't want to rest. Managing to push himself up to sit, hanging his legs over the bed. Placing his feet firmly on the floorboards, Arthur looked down at his feet. He could feel his body returning to its strange normal self, he smiled to himself, pleased. It seemed to all be coming back to him, quicker this time.

He tapped at his phone by the bedside table, there was another message from Laura. It was her asking to hang out over the weekend at the mall, Arthur slid his phone off the bedside table and replied, "Great idea, we can talk about what we can get up to tomorrow." he certainly deserved a nice day out after that.

He stood up and stared out his bedroom window. All Arthur knew he wanted in that very moment was a shower.

A god damn, shower.

He hesitated no longer, no threats, no distractions he could finally have the shower he longed for.

Top off, taps on.

The steam started to fog the bathroom.

Arthur stared at himself in the mirror as the water began to warm up, a long hard look into his eyes. Life isn't going to be normal, not at all, he thought. He'd died a few times now and had come back to life. Arthur cracked a grin, the thought of being able to do that again filled him with a surreal feeling of existence. Whatever was inside of him, he felt closer to it, in control of it more. He could begin to embrace his new surroundings a bit more willingly, knowing he could make some deathly mistakes.

Taking the rest of his clothes off to be completely naked, he stepped into the shower drawing the shower curtain to a close.

Enjoying the heat of the running water over his face, he looked up at the shower head with his eyes closed, fulfilling the need he had wanted many hours ago.

He heard a bang.

Arthur let out a massive sigh "Oh come on... what now... I've gotten this far. Please! I've just gotten in the water this time" he muttered, waiting to hear another noise to confirm he had to just forget about showering for the night.

Nothing, so far. Arthur looked around the curtain, he became startled at the sight he saw. Hannah was getting undressed out of her nightwear.

"Hey! Whoa, what are you doing?" Arthur let out hiding, clutching at the curtain to keep it in place, from the neck down.

"It's alright, stay there." Hannah ordered.

Arthur didn't know what to do or think, he just stood there clutching at the shower curtain.

Hannah began to take her underwear off.

He let go of the shower curtain covering any sight of her and stood there staring at the pattern on the inside of the shower curtain.

"I'm naked in here." he echoed from behind the curtain.

"I know, that's the point." Hannah's voice came from the other side.

Her hand came around the curtain and her leg stepped through into the shower. Arthur faced her, keeping his eye contact level with hers, she stood there for a short while staring back into his. She had a look, a determined look. She raised her arms, placing them on both of his collarbones, sliding them up his neck and holding his cheeks. Hannah leaned in closer for a second and paused, she kissed him.

It felt great, Arthur embraced the kiss, momentarily losing himself.

He stopped, pulling away and stepping back in the shower to look at her.

Hannah reaffirmed him, "It's okay, we both need to unwind." ending with a short laugh.

He was still concerned, "Are you back to your normal self? You don't have to you know?"

Hannah just stared at his eyes, "I'm fine, I want to." she replied.

The words echoed through his mind; he wanted her. Arthur's eyes couldn't resist no more, he looked down, her body wet from the water falling from the shower.

The sight of her excited him.

Arthur reached his arm out and placed it round the back of her hip, feeling every inch of her skin slowly. Pulling her closer, Hannah placed her hands on his shoulders, pulling him closer for another kiss. He felt her body close to his, kissing passionately, she ran her hands up his back grasping his body. Arthur ran his hand up her body whilst the other tightly gripped her thigh. Wrapping her leg around Arthur, tightening it in place as her back leant onto the back wall of the shower.

This was a moment Arthur never had expected, Hannah had never seen him in this light, nor him to her. Arthur soon figured his strength had returned, picking up her other leg and lifting her up against the wall. Wrapping her legs around him, Arthur felt her closely to him as she moaned.

This was certainly a new boundary to be explored for their friendship.

After one of the best showers Arthur ever had, the two dressed up with a look of smugness between them. It was something that they would both definitely remember.

Hannah walked out of Arthur's bathroom as he continued to dress up in his nightwear. He was curious of what had taken over her, causing them to be intimate. He walked out of his bathroom, wondering if she had already left. She was in his bed, Arthur looked at her and decided not to question it. He didn't want to ruin anything in this moment.

Climbing into bed himself, he laid there. They both were quiet, the realisation of the intense sex they both had, sunk in. Smiling at each other, they both let out a chuckle.

Hannah closed her eyes and turned facing away from Arthur and began to fall asleep. Arthur laid there, unable to sleep at all. Wondering if their moment was just a gesture of thanks, or there was something more beyond it.

A date?

The sun brilliantly shone through the window, as Arthur laid facing it, the light causing his eyes to open. It was the morning, checking his phone on the bedside table, he realised that it wasn't long before his alarm would activate. He eagerly turned over to look inwards to the bed, it was empty, Hannah had already left from spending the night.

Collecting his thoughts from yesterday, it took Arthur a moment to realise what had happened with Hannah wasn't just something he'd imagined. She had left at some point during the morning, she would've stayed if it were anything more serious. Arthur lay there, stretching out and coming to terms with the sex was just an action of mutual gratitude. He basked in the thoughts of yesterday, he felt great. The basking shortly cut short, broken by the alarm on his phone, it was time to get up and ready for class. Even though he had died yesterday, he quickly recovered this time, of course he was going to go into school just like nothing had happened.

After the normal morning routine of preparing his clothes and spending some time in the bathroom. Arthur led himself downstairs towards the kitchen, for a short bite of something easy before heading off to school. That's if Hannah were still going in, as Arthur would have to find another method on getting to Lakebrook High. Walking into the kitchen the girls and Peter were all sat or leaning around the kitchen counter in the middle, everything seemed fine. They must be going into school if they're up this early and Peter to his day job.

A few of them greeting morning to Arthur as he leaned on the counter, swiping a slice of toast from the plate. There was a tension of awkwardness, well at least that's what Arthur felt, barely being able to keep eye contact with Hannah. She seemed perfectly fine with the events that had taken place.

Peter let out a satisfactory groan, "Ahh, what a day, yesterday huh?" he stood up, placing his plate into the dishwasher. "Right, I'm gonna head up and get ready for my day. Have a good day at school, kids." excusing himself out of the kitchen.

"Ready to go?" Hannah asked over the top of the counter, looking between Kimberly and Arthur

"I'm ready!" Kimberly chirped up.

Arthur tilted his head at Kimberly, trying to understand, "Are you sure? Because yesterday you were not okay?" he asked. Looking at her he was confused; Kimberly was dressed over-smartly than usual to go to school with them.

"I have a meeting this morning with the principal about my grades, that I can't miss." she began to explain. She had not been getting the best grades in most of her classes and it had become that serious, the principal had arranged a meeting with her.

Throughout the car journey, Arthur couldn't ask Hannah about last night, even though he was dying inside to ask. They came to understand on the car ride that Kimberly had been falling asleep in class, her days of school and practicing with magic seemed to be taking a toll on her. It sounded exhausting just listening to her. At least that was what she excused her poor efforts on.

The car parked up in the student parking lot, the three stepped out of the car.

"I need to go to the main desk and tell the receptionist that I'm here to meet Mrs Aster." Kimberly said out loud, as though she were preparing herself verbally.

Hannah slammed the car door shut and locked it with her car key, "Yeah, okay, we will walk you over there anyway." she offered on behalf of herself and Arthur.

Arthur thought it was strange for Hannah to offer as she knew he would normally meet his friends about now, but this could be a moment to clear up some questions from last night before the start of the day. Arthur would have to meet his friends in class later instead of out front by the fountain. The three walked up from the main path past the fountain, the school grounds weren't as busy. It was still slightly early before many had arrived.

As the two stepped inside the main entrance of the school, they stood there in the foyer awaiting Kimberly to make her move.

Kimberly stood there for a still moment, she took a deep breath, "All right, catch you guys later." she said, wandering off towards the front desk to check in with the receptionist.

"She'll be fine, she can always use a spell to get out of trouble anyway." Hannah pointed out. "That's if she knows the spell."

As they watched her disappear through the door of the principal's office. Now was the time and probably the only time Arthur could ask to stop it from playing on his mind the entire day.

"Us... last night?" was all that he managed to spit out.

Hannah smirked and faced Arthur, "It was great, but don't think much of it. It was a thank you, and I think you needed it as much as I did." she then giggled. "Don't think too much into it at all."

Arthur placed his hands in his pockets, he felt somewhat disappointed but also relieved at the same time. His question had been answered. "Gotcha." he nodded, taking his eyes up off the floor.

"Alright! I'm going to head in, I'll catch you after-school for the ride home, no doubt Kimberly will want to go out for a hot drink or something and tell us about her day." Hannah announced, before slapping Arthur's behind as she walked away, laughing. "Be prepared for that!" she shouted as she got further down the corridor into the school.

That *was* strange, Arthur felt like the two had gotten closer and seemed to be on a similar level more frequently, especially now.

As Arthur watched Hannah walk away there was a sense of abandonment, as silly as it seemed, he felt lonely. He continued to stare in the direction of where she had walked to, already out of view.

A voice came from the side. "You alright there kid?"

Arthur turned towards the voice, there was a middle-aged man standing there. He hadn't seen him before, presumably a teacher that taught outside his year group.

"Lost or something?" he stood there with a grin and didn't break eye contact.

"Oh no, I'm all good thanks, gotta find the rest of the guys. Erm it's just early, see ya." Arthur responded, turning away, and heading to his classroom before the first period of the day.

He glanced back at the teacher, who was firmly concentrating at something in the palm of his hand.

What a weird guy he thought, as he walked down the corridor to his class, keeping his head forwards.

Entering the classroom, he realised it was empty, it was still a little early for the start of class. Still, he made his way to his seat, sitting down to enjoy the silence before the day had begun.

A figure appeared through the classroom door, "Where were you man?" Daniel asked at the door, before walking over to him.

"Oh yeah, Kimberly, erm… another girl from the house had to have a meeting with the principal, so we walked her through to the front." Arthur explained, as some more of the class walked in.

The bell rang for first period to begin, it was math class. Arthur was quiet for a fair bit of the lesson, quietly sat at this desk answering mathematics questions. Mathematics was something he hadn't needed to do for years; he had forgotten so much.

Jade who sat over in the seat to Arthur's right, glanced over a few times. Double checking him, "Are you okay?" she asked in a quieter tone. It must've been obvious that he seemed out of place. The aftermath of Hannah staying in his bed had really put him out of sorts.

His name didn't register, Arthur wasn't really listening at all, he was in his own world as he stared at the questions on his paper.

"Arthur? *Woohoo?*" Jade sung in a slightly higher pitch.

Arthur broke his concentration and looked at her, "Huh. Oh yeah, yeah! I'm all fine." he replied, backtracking to remember what she had just asked prior.

"Are you sure, you seem pretty quiet this morning?" she began to pry, edging her chair closer and placing her hand on Arthur's forearm.

Arthur looked down at her hand touching him, it was probably normal how she acted. She didn't remember kissing him, right? He questioned internally.

Arthur looked back up, "I'm all good, just having a quiet start really." he added, retracting his arm away from underneath hers.

"Okay, if you're sure." Jade said dismissively before leaning back to her space and carrying on writing in her book.

Arthur widened his eyes before looking around, he saw Daniel looking over at Arthur. Daniel was giving a strange look of confusion with a very minimal nod, then raising his eyebrows a handful of times.

Arthur shook his head slowly, mouthing in silence "No." before looking back down and getting on with his mathematic questions in his book.

The morning proceeded slowly for Arthur; he was quiet right up until he noticed it was lunch. Sat in the cafeteria, watching the others laugh and joke as he ate his lunch.

His attention focused behind him.

"Hey Arthur!" A high-pitched greeting came across the cafeteria as a group were walking past, it was Kimberly, who prompted him with a thumbs up as she walked past with her friends. Presumably the meeting went well from how happy she looked.

Finally, it was the last class of the day. Arthur had been waiting for the day to come to its slow close, he wanted to be alone back at the house in his room.

Geography, researching on the school's library computers, it was a painful but simple end to the day. Arthur slumped, sinking in his chair still with the unshakeable feeling of loneliness. His mind began to trail, off task from the work he needed to complete. Dangerous thoughts started to wander. What had actually happened back home, what happened after he was claimed dead and in the morgue. Do they think that Arthur had just been buried and that was it?

He became dangerously curious, opening a new tab on the computer's browser he typed in a few searches and began to read. There was a range of headlines that dealt with the aftermath of the crash, it seems he was not the only unlucky one to die in the crash. Remembering there was a car in front of him which he came to a stop behind, with only a few inches of space. A chill crept throughout his body giving him goosebumps, that car was another victim of the crash.

Arthur began to lean forward in his seat, getting closer to the screen as he read further into the different news articles.

He began to be lost, deep in curiosity. A pit grew in his stomach the more he read, and the more he read, the more he fed the pit. He discovered the car in front was a family travelling through the night on that slippery road, it was a horrendous thought to know that they weren't lucky enough to wake up, like he had.

A voice from behind startled Arthur, making him jump with a hand on each shoulder of his. "Hey, this is boring don't ya think?" it was Laura, questioning and lowering her head over his shoulder.

"Uh yeah, I'm bored so I'm just searching up stuff." Arthur shared, before realising he forgot to close the article that was named 'Family tragically killed in a car incident'.

Obviously, it wasn't his family, they were fine. It was the family in the car in front, but he could only imagine that it didn't look good. She knew that he lived at the boarding house with none of his immediate family. Arthur couldn't explain, he didn't want that thought to last any longer, he quickly fired a question back after closing the tab. "School today has been boring, don't you think?"

Laura slowly sat down in the seat next to his, glossing over that question. "Is everything alright Arthur?" she asked, looking closely at any expression that would expose something. "You have seemed pretty quiet most of the day." she pointed out.

Arthur was quick to answer, "Yup, all fine, just feeling like a quiet day. How's your research going for erm… sedimentary rocks, was it?" he tried to move on the direction of the conversation.

Laura was silent for a moment; she didn't even answer that question, staring at Arthur's computer screen which now held a research page on some geographical study on his topic, metamorphic rocks. "So how about meeting up after-school today for a drink?" she asked, turning her head back towards Arthur and growing a slight, small smile.

"Oh yeah, the message you sent yesterday." Arthur had forgotten from all of the action that cursed the house after he'd received the message. "Uhm I might be busy after-school today, but did you want to over the weekend? If that's okay?" Arthur returned, knowing that he may have to endure Kimberly's update of how her meeting had gone with Principal Aster in great detail.

"I should be free, yeah you know, that sounds better actually. We can get more of a day out of it." Laura replied happily at the thought.

Arthur cracked his first true smile of the day, it would be great to hang out, just the two of them for a long part of the day.

Jade overheard and leaned in, "Are you hanging out on the weekend?" she asked. "Chad and I will be heading to the mall that weekend! We could all hang out?"

That was the last thing on Arthur's mind, "Oh yeah, we're not sure what we're gonna do yet. But we can message you if we do." he said, quick to think, putting that offer off for a while longer.

There was a sense of awkwardness in the air, Jade's face scrunched, "Okay well let me know!" before disappearing back down to her research.

Arthur placed his hand on Laura's arm and leaned into her ear, "No way, we're just going to hang out the two of us, right?" he whispered, wanting confirmation of just being the two of them.

Laura smiled and nodded, "Message later." she whispered in return. Placing her hand on his and paused for a second. "Alright, I'm gonna head back to researching, if you need to talk about anything, even if it's *family*. I'm here for you." she offered. Subtly dropping the family topic.

Arthur looked up at her, smiling, "It's okay, I'm all good I promise." he reassured her.

It was a nice offer, but it wasn't as much of a big deal as she may have thought it were. His family were certainly alive. He just felt alone, separated from his everything and everyone in his past life, he missed them. Arthur hoped that Laura didn't think his family were the ones in the news article, it would be weird to talk about and try to explain, but deep down he knew she would have thought it. He couldn't tell her the full truth that he'd died, and he was the named one at the bottom of the article.

Luckily, she didn't catch that part. Arthur didn't know how to really respond if she were to ask him directly what he was searching all about. Laura and the rest of the group knew that Arthur was brought over from England and was staying at a house where none of the residents were related to him in any way.

The weekend came, it couldn't come soon enough. Arthur had been looking forward to meeting Laura, more and more as Friday night came to an end. He was excited getting to know her and find out more about who she was, when it would be just the two of them.

He was slightly early sat down waiting at the coffee shop, the Starbucks at the mall. Laura had messaged the night before mentioning how excited she was to hang out with just the two of them. That message played on Arthur's mind anticipating the topics they could talk about, preparing them in the back of his mind to save any dull moment, it almost felt like a date.

Arthur looked out of the window as he waited, the mall was busy as others walked past about their day. He watched them walk from one side of the view to the other, carrying their shopping and disappearing behind the tall planters and stalls that sat throughout.

His eyes stopped, his eyes caught Laura, walking towards the door. She looked amazing, unexpected with how much this took him back. Her hair was tied back, with a fringe flicked over one side of her face, wearing a denim jacket and a pink top sitting above her waistline. Black skinny chino jeans that made Arthur take a second look as she came across to the entrance. She looked beautiful, Arthur was still taken back by surprise, lost for words.

She saw Arthur and she gleamed brightly with a massive smile.

Arthur had been looking forward to a calm weekend where they could just hang out and take it easy, this had been exactly what he wanted. The sight of Laura hit him differently inside, taking away any unwanted thought from all the supernatural nonsense, as though it had disappeared completely from his life.

Once the two sat down after purchasing their drinks, Arthur had a flat white whilst Laura smelled the aroma of her orange hot chocolate, holding it firmly with both hands. They began to talk, starting off slowly. It seemed to be a lot easier to talk to her now that they weren't in school, it felt like they had the time and no distractions from any others in the group.

Arthur began to understand a lot about Laura. He noticed that she would ask him all about his friends back in England, what activities or hobbies he would do in his spare time. Arthur bravely bought up the topic of family, asking how she got on with Ellie growing up, her non-identical twin sister. Arthur thought they were the same age, but soon discovered that they were months apart but still made it into the same school year. He could see how Laura and Ellie got on as sisters, by the way she spoke about her. They were best friends but entirely different compared to each other as sisters. Ellie is more outgoing and that was clear through the times Arthur spent around her in the group at school. Ellie seemed to join clubs throughout her youth whereas Laura was from more of a chosen, quiet upbringing. She kept to herself a lot more and seemed to be reserved with her actions and words. Her mother and father both worked in difficult jobs, her mother a realtor to the local area and her father worked in accounting, looking after a business's finance. Understandably it was picked up that Laura's family were well off.

There was a topic she avoided asking him about, which was anything to do with his family or siblings. Arthur thought she would ask him the same question in return after he'd asked about Ellie, but she never dared to ask. Arthur knew this was from the research on the news articles he had done the other day on the school computers. He could sense that this was something getting in the way between the two of them. He had to think of something as the two sat there in a moment of awkward silence.

Arthur's eyes looked back out of the window, following the shoppers passing by.

Laura swirled her hot chocolate in her mug, "So, what have you liked the most about being here in this new place?" she asked, looking up at him. "Lakebrook isn't exactly the most exciting place to be."

Arthur looked back at her, he tried to think. Many exciting things had happened, but he knew if he spoke about them, he would look insane. "Oh erm, there's been many things actually." he stalled for a brief moment, picking something normal to say. "I think it's been great how welcoming everyone has been, but it's all so different. I think I like that it's all just new and refreshing from what I was used to." he tried to string together as a suitable answer.

Arthur had enjoyed his time here so far, it has been extremely strange but the moments of even the supernatural events that have occurred, have been fun. He was now more open and accepting to the supernatural side after knowing he can come back to life; almost certain he can do that every time. That was one of the things he couldn't tell her, but the normal-ish side of this new life has been great also with meeting new people, getting a second chance to choose what he would like to study again and even finding that new hobby with American football. Among other things.

He leapt onto that topic that crept into his mind, just to avoid any silence, "Football has been great actually, I never had a chance to get into it from where I used to live." he started off.

Laura interrupted, "So, were you one of those sporty lovers in your previous school?" she asked.

That was the last thing Arthur wanted her to think, he wasn't just some stereotypical jock. "No, no, no, not at all. I didn't really like sports as much back in my old school, kind of hated sports really." he quickly rejected any link towards that stereotype.

"That's good." she responded, contempt with his answer. Before sitting quietly, sinking back into her chair for a moment.

The silence between the two began to creep in again.

Arthur could still feel something was holding both of them back, he knew he had to address it. Head on, it was the only way to sort it out.

"Look, I know you saw me searching up something on the school computer the other day. That wasn't anything to do with my family, it was a friend that had happened to, before I had to leave." Arthur lied, clearing that up and hoping it would end the strange awkwardness.

Laura stopped for a moment, looked down at her lap processing her presumption, then back up to Arthur. "Oh, I see. Sorry. You never speak much about your family though? I thought it was yours." she tried to explain, sounding withdrawn with embarrassment.

"My family is fine. I don't talk to them much and that's just how it is. But I'm happy with all that and how it has all turned out." Arthur continued to add to his lie, "Honestly, ask me anything you want to know about them." he offered.

This electrified the flow of conversation between the two, the awkwardness vanished instantly. Laura began to ask questions all about his family. Spending some time talking about them, it did make Arthur realise that this was where the loneliness had stemmed from. Spending the next better half of an hour, Arthur explained every member of his family. His mother and father, and his brother and sister. Laura sat there holding her head in her hands, fixed on Arthur as he went into detail of all the things they did and who they were, smiling longingly at him.

She was mesmerised watching Arthur talk.

They continued to talk for another hour or so, coming to the topic of Halloween, of course. Arthur had been a Lakebrook High student for over a month, getting close to two by now, Halloween was not far away. Time had unbelievably gone fast since Arthur had moved in at Pennyview.

The conversation between the two was cut abruptly, when a knock at the glass interrupted them, it was Jade and Chad. It immediately got uncomfortable as the two avoided messaging them to say they would be at the mall, and here they were. Jade seemed to be excited at the sight of them, even though Arthur wouldn't place Laura or himself as a close friend to Jade. Chad, as usual looked as cheerful as he always did being dragged around the mall; not at all happy. Most likely wishing he could push some weights, drink, or practice football no doubt.

The two walked around the glass into Starbucks, Jade pulling Chad along holding his hand, guiding him as though he were a toddler.

"Hey you two. On a little coffee date, are we?" Jade suggested, with a motive to cause friction between the two.

Arthur could see how nervous and withdrawn that comment made Laura feel, she became quiet. Thinking quick to answer like the two were hanging out, as no big deal, "Yeah something like a date, we're just hanging out you know?" Arthur responded bravely on behalf of both of them.

Laura's gleaming smile had returned, hiding some giddiness to herself. Jade didn't look too impressed at all for the matter, it was clear her mood had changed from hearing that response.

Chad grins at Arthur and nods in approval. "Alright babe, let's leave them to it anyway." Chad sliced the unnoticeable tension in the air, saving them.

Jade turned towards Chad, "But I wanna get a drink and chat." she demanded, putting on a voice of some pathetic manner.

Chad sighed loudly.

"I mean you guys could always get one to go?" Arthur suggested, "Don't let us keep you in the way of your day." alternatively hinting the option of avoiding them joining.

"You know what babe, that's a great idea. Let's just get some drinks to go." Chad ordered, with the final say.

Arthur and Laura continued to talk as the other two ordered their drinks, keeping a subtle eye on them, waiting for them to leave before they could fully relax.

"Thank you Chad, never thought I would say that out loud." Arthur expressed as they left.

Laura took a deep breath in relief and laughed, "How do you find Jade and Chad?" fixing her eyes back at Arthur.

Arthur shuffled in his seat, thinking how to answer, "I think they're a strange combo, but I don't really know Chad as a person besides what he's like at football practice. Jade, well. I'm not sure. She seems to speak to everyone and tries to please everyone at the same time." he thought about his response as soon as the words left his mouth, maybe it didn't sound great the way he put it. "I mean. She seems nice, but not the person I would hang out with back home. You know?" he added, trying to save himself.

Laura laughed, "I know what you mean. Jade is great, when you get *Jade,* and not when she's putting on a show for the others around her. But it's Jade and we'll love her for being her."

Arthur smiled to himself, at his own thoughts. Laura was truly someone who saw the positives in anyone, it was an attractive trait for sure.

Laura looked at her phone, "I need to go." she said hastily. Time had quickly passed since the two got there. It was almost time for her to be picked up.

Accompanying Laura to the car parking where she was to be picked up, the two waited outside for Laura's mother to pick her up, "Thank you for a nice time, Arthur. It was fun." she mentioned gripping at her phone with both hands happily.

It had been great; it had been very different to what Arthur had gotten up to so far living here. He felt as though the two of them had entered this new level of friendship or possibly something more that could last.

Laura could see her mother parking up, turning towards Arthur she said goodbye and offered him a lift home.

"Oh no, it's alright thanks. I'll get home by myself." Arthur stated, he didn't want anyone else finding out where he exactly lived because it wasn't... exactly normal from the recent events that had occurred.

Laura looked at Arthur for a second, there was a moment of awkwardness in the air. Arthur bravely went in to offer a hug goodbye, something he wouldn't have done meeting a girl like this for the first time. Laura placed her arms around him, delicately squeezing back. Stepping away from a hug, she barely kept a straight face. Normally to Arthur a hug would mean that they were just friends, but she felt different, something unexpected and no doubt this would play on his mind.

Laura disappeared into her mother's car, before heading off out of the parking lot.

It was Arthur's turn to get a ride home, opening the app on his phone, he summoned a taxi to pick him up. During the drive home Arthur's concentration on remembering what was for dinner tonight was interrupted, his phone vibrated. It was a message from Laura, so soon. "Thanks for today, it was great to hang out with you. Did you mean it when Jade mentioned it was a date? Xx" was what the message stated.

Arthur knew his next reply would lead their friendship in two different paths. He hadn't come here looking for a relationship but it's not like he wasn't going to have one, just not as sudden as he would've expected.

His lifestyle was difficult, among the things of living with witches who cast spells, he was a boy who could die and come back to life. That held its own problems, including having more strength and speed than a normal human and his wounds would heal at a quicker rate.

Arthur placed his phone on the car seat next to him in the back and took a moment to ponder out of the window of what is response could be. This was his new life, he shouldn't be bound with any difficulties, surely, he thought. It's not like anything was ever set in stone and if anything were discovered, the thought of asking the witches of the house to help Laura forget passed through his mind. Arthur smiled to himself, maybe he could build on this friendship, so it could grow into something more.

"I mean, I wouldn't mind it if it were, I enjoy spending time with you Xx" Arthur returned the message.

"Sent!" he said to himself, affirming his own confidence that his message was the right one to return with.

Arthur placed his phone back face down on the car seat, nervous for what the response from Laura would include. A few more streets passed as Arthur waited for his ride to arrive outside Pennyview, his phone vibrated again. He placed his hand over it, taking a deep breath in anticipation before he revealed the screen, it was a message from Laura.

Arthur unlocked his phone.

His smile, turned into a grin.

Supernatural hunters

Weeks passed since Arthur met up with Laura outside of school for that first time, the air began to get crisp with the cold. The leaves of the trees had far beyond turned to a golden-brown and had begun to drop. Winter was a foot; time had passed since Arthur had been getting into his new life here at Lakebrook. Meaning the winter holidays were just around the corner, but more importantly the school's American football league championship was getting closer.

Hannah parked up in the school car park, hesitating for a moment to get out of the car to embrace the cold. Turning her face to Arthur she said, "We're halfway to Christmas break, it actually might be nice to have some time off. I forgot how boring the junior year really is." she had already experienced high school; the affect of the new school had already worn off for her.

Arthur soon figured, with her being eighteen and only one year younger than him.

Kimberly moved forwards in her seat. "I'm having fun, I forgot how great it was to be at school, could you imagine Ethel trying to teach me half of the things at school, in the boarding house? Ugh. Kill me please." before slumping back into the car seat, double checking she had her bag.

Arthur agreed with Kimberly's statement of being in the boarding house, he had been enjoying this new experience of school even though some areas were repetitive to his own experience. But being able to choose a new path, that was lucky, everyone wished for a second chance at their school years.

The three got out of the car to take in the cold air, weaving through the cars parked throughout the lot, finding their way to the main path leading up to the entrance. Arthur's friends were awaiting by the fountain, where he would stop to join up with them in the mornings. Almost everyone was there.

"See you later!" both Hannah and Kimberly said to Arthur as they left him, off to find their friends deeper into the school grounds.

There was the new and improved Daniel Bayer, the two had been training and working out using the school gym after-school most days, the change of Daniel had been fast and forthcoming with Arthur's help.

Arthur took a deep breath to embrace the coldness in the air, he approached closer to the fountain towards his friends, "Hey all!" Arthur exclaimed energetically.

Abel hopped off the fountain's side, where he leaned. "Yo! Yo! You seem cheerful Art?" he spoke loudly, offering a high-five to Arthur.

Returning the high-five Arthur replied, "I dunno, I guess I just woke up feeling good today? The fresh air and all." he had felt more positive, nothing strange had happened in the weeks that had passed. Not even at Pennyview, which was a miracle.

Arthur walked closer to Laura and placed his arm around her waist and gave her a kiss on a cheek. The two had met each other outside of school over the past few weeks and had gotten closer, it all seemed to work out well with Laura. They decided to take some steps seriously and began to see each other exclusively.

Arthur had thought about the age difference, Laura had turned seventeen meaning there was only a two-year gap between them. That was fine, the only real issue was that Laura believed Arthur was seventeen also.

Jade tried to glare inconspicuously, keeping a close eye on the two, she had a hint of jealousy. She'd never been team Arthur and Laura, at all, possibly because of the little issues they have compared to her own relationship with Chad.

Some of the group began to pick up their bags, anticipating the school bell as they started to walk towards the main entrance. It was just another ordinary day at Lakebrook High and ordinary was exactly what Arthur wanted.

He longed for these days.

A few lessons of the morning had passed as normal. But when it came to English class, the students were sat at their desks waiting for the appearance of their new English teacher. There were rumours of the old English teacher being sacked for drinking on the job or going completely insane at a student. There was chatter amongst the students of the classroom until the door swung open, Principal Aster and a new face appeared through it.

The room of students fell immediately silent at the sight of the principal. As the two walked into the classroom, taking a stand in front of the whiteboard, the principal began to announce the new English teacher.

Arthur wasn't clearly listening; he was trying to think. Closely examining the new English teacher, he'd seen that face before, searching through his memory it couldn't have been any further back than when Arthur had gotten to Lakebrook.

It clicked; he'd remembered, "Ahh!" Arthur let out loudly, pleased he had worked it out.

The principal stopped talking and stared intensely at Arthur. "Sorry! Continue!" Arthur apologised, trying to bring an end to the intense stare of Aster.

The principal paused, holding that stare for a moment longer. Then continued.

It was the middle-aged man that Arthur bumped into many weeks back in the school's main foyer. He must've been applying for a job rather than being a current teacher. Arthur realised then and there that he hadn't seen him around after the only time he bumped into him.

The man's voice continued; it had a bit of a different twang than it did to some of the locals here in this state.

The stranger introduced himself, "Nice to meet you, I'm Mr Callahan, your new English teacher."

The class continued to be silent, Mr Callahan wasn't your typical nerdy, tight-dressed teacher like the old guy before. He seemed more... modern. He began to give a brief explanation of his background and understood what the class exactly needed to continue their studies. The class were taken back by the strategy and how efficient this new teacher seemed. This was a strange experience for Arthur as most of the teachers he had for English never seemed to be prepared at all.

Principal Aster left and some time had passed to start the lesson Mr Callahan had planned.

As Mr Callahan wrote away verses of some text on the whiteboard, a scrunched paper ball hit a foot away from where the teacher was writing. One of the boys were sniggering away a couple seats across from Arthur, it looked like one of them from the basketball team. That was daring.

Slowly Callahan turned around, he strangely seemed to know exactly where it came from. "Okay, okay. Test the new teacher. I get it, funny. *Funny!*" he raised his voice a tone louder. "Was that meant to be a good throw?" he added, looking at the boy who threw it.

The boy let out a bit of a laugh, with a menacing grin, "Yeah." he shrugged carelessly.

Callahan stood up straight and placed one hand in his pocket and the other rubbed his short beard, "Basketball team am I right?" he guessed.

"Correct." the student replied, taken back.

"You mean, correct Sir!" Callahan sternly shouted, filling the room.

The boy's expression turned from a grin to a very unsettled look. "Correct, sir." the student replied compliantly.

Callahan bent down and picked up the paper ball and scrunched it in his hand firmly. "Now," Callahan started, tossing the paper ball ever so slightly higher to catch it again. "If you were a good member of the basketball team, you would have either hit me or are you just a bad shot. Which means the basketball team isn't winning this season? Am I correct?"

The student sat there with an opened-mouth expression. Nothing to say, he was right. The basketball team weren't doing great at all, he began to sink into his seat slowly.

Everyone in the class just watched everything unfold, as though it were some captivating drama.

"So anyway, if you hit me, I suppose I'd have to give you a detention, which means no lunch or after-school basketball… Which means you won't improve, which means the school will still suck. *More*." he emphasised, raising the scrunched paper ball in his hand analysing it. "Luckily, you're a bad shot which means you've still got that free time to get better." Callahan turned the paper ball slowly in his hand, then switched his eye contact to the basketball student. Keeping eye contact, he raised his arm back with the paper ball in his hand, he released throwing a clean shot landing perfectly into the waste bin by the door.

There were a few gasps from the students, it was impressive, he barely even looked at where it would need to go.

That was brave Arthur thought, it was like he knew he would make the shot, before even attempting it.

Callahan turned towards the board and continued writing up some verses. That's it, from that point on he had captivated the class to his teaching will.

Forty minutes in, the class was silent, all writing away on some lined paper. Mr Callahan had set an assignment which titled, "How did the American recession affect the economy." occasionally he would patrol down the lines of the class, checking the time every few paces in his hand.

Arthur stared at the title on his paper, he'd written a paragraph. Peering over at Daniel's table who sat a few desks over from him, he'd done a lot. Daniel was from a nerdy background, of course he had written that much.

"Okay." Arthur let out ever so slightly exhaling to himself.

Trying not to be obvious, Arthur tried to look behind him seeing what Ellie had written. Now, Ellie wasn't smart, but she wasn't dim, if Arthur were to class her by intelligence. She would be in the middle, which is where he would exactly place himself.

A quick glance over.

Ellie had written a lot; Arthur returned his head forwards to face down at his paper. He knew *nothing* at all about the American recession.

"Something the matter?" the voice called from the front.

Arthur looked up. Mr Callahan was calling out to him. "Umm, I know nothing about the American recession, sir." Arthur answered back, conforming to Callahan's classroom ways. "I recently moved here. I know nothing about how this country is ran." he added.

Mr Callahan leaned forward from his desk, placing his chin in his hands. "Hmm, how much have you written, it was Arthur? Right?" Mr Callahan questioned.

How did he know his name? This man must have a good memory, which made sense for how efficient he seemed to be.

"Yea, it's Arthur sir, I've written 6 lines?" Arthur answered politely.

Mr Callahan slowly stood up from his desk and walked over to Arthur at a gentle pace. Placing his two fingers on his paper, dragging it to the edge of Arthur's desk to have a look. He stopped and opened his other hand and looked down at it, checking the time. Pausing for a moment, then to sniff up through his nose whilst pursing his lips. "So, 6 lines, in forty minutes, just about one paragraph. That doesn't look great, does it?"

Arthur took a second to think, he seemed strict. He needed to be compliant, "Erm no sir, it doesn't at all. Could I get a different topic?" Arthur offered.

"With about ten minutes left? Think of a topic. Come back at lunch, tell me what you've got, and we'll talk." Mr Callahan replied as a rhetoric.

Arthur nodded slowly, he wasn't too sure if Callahan was annoyed or if it was for the whole of lunch. It was clear from that moment; he was a hard man to read.

Lost in thought, trying to think of a worthy topic for the remainder of English class, the bell rang for next period.

The next class went quickly as it became closer to lunch, Arthur's topic of choosing was the only thing that played on his mind, he'd never been in trouble so far at Lakebrook. Arthur had no idea of what it could be. Saying goodbye to the few friends he had in his last class, informing them that he might not be about for lunch and to let Laura know. Arthur made his way to the other side of the school to find the new English teacher, Mr Callahan. Walking up towards the English classroom door, he knocked a few times.

"Come in." a voice was heard.

Opening the door Arthur walked into the classroom, "Hello sir, you wanted to see me about an essay topic?" Arthur started off. "I was thinking about doing it on something to do with sports or…"

Mr Callahan quickly cut him off, "Look Arthur, I get it, you're new here and I know being new to an entirely new system isn't easy. Trust me." Callahan stated, whilst prying himself off his chair and perching himself on the side of his desk. "Think about something that you possibly don't know much about already, look it up and get lost into learning something new. Write me something good, don't give me a half-arsed essay, this will go towards you passing this topic. Okay? he glanced at the time in his hand again.

Arthur looked down at Callahan's hand. He noticed a pocket watch of some design; Callahan must be a very punctual person who kept on top of this time keeping.

"What about England? Something that happened financially over there that involved a massive change?" Callahan questioned Arthur, raising an eyebrow.

Arthur stood for a moment, what had really happened in England.

Wait.

Arthur had begun a year of university learning about business management, the first year involved all about the foundations and failures of businesses. It was a great idea to reuse that knowledge from essays he had completed in that first year at university.

"I was thinking about doing it on the fall of smaller businesses in Britain within the past few decades?" Arthur offered as a genius topic.

Mr Callahan stood there and folded his arms, looking up as though he were thinking, nodding gently. A pleased readable expression seemed to appear on his face. "Sounds great, sounds like it would have a lot of educational promise you can write about. Hand in by Friday after-school? See me midweek to check in after-school to see the direction it's going in?" he instructed.

The support threw Arthur off, "Yeah that sounds good actually." he replied getting the impression that he didn't need to stay for the whole of lunch.

Mr Callahan gestured opening his hand and flapping it away as a sign for Arthur to leave.

"Erm, thank you…" Arthur said before leaving, "Sir." he remembered to add.

Arthur turned around and began to walk out the classroom door.

"Oh Arthur, I take it the basketball team aren't doing great at all?" Callahan questioned.

"Oh, nope, they are kind of sucking from what I've seen and heard." Arthur answered, holding his hand on the door handle, looking back at Mr Callahan.

Callahan added another question, "You're playing what sports?" postponing Arthur's departure.

"American football, sir." Arthur answered.

"And are they doing alright? Better than the basketball team?" Callahan questioned further.

"Erm, Coach Decker said we will actually have a chance this year with us new members in the squad. So, I'd say so, yes." Arthur briefly explained with some belief of his performance within the team.

"That's great, I'm sure it's going good with you in the team. Alright have a good lunch." he finalised, nodding as he walked back around to his chair. Finally allowing Arthur to leave.

Arthur left the classroom shutting the door behind him, confused about his new English teacher. He seemed harsh in class, but at a closer look, he seemed really supportive, friendly, and fair. Maybe that was his charm on how he won over students to work.

The last few lessons of the day passed, Arthur met the girls back at Hannah's car in the parking lot, ready for the drive home.

Hannah bought up the topic of the new English teacher, Mr Callahan during the drive home. She had been taught by him in the afternoon for her class. "The new English teachers a bit odd, isn't he?" Hannah started the conversation, openly to the others in the car.

"I don't think he teaches my year?" Kimberly added, of course being a sophomore, she had different teachers to Hannah and Arthur.

"Arthur? You've had him already today, right?" she redirected the question to him, glancing at the rear-view mirror a second before looking back at the road ahead.

Arthur thought about his response, he wanted to be fair as clearly, he may have seen a different side to him. "He seemed fine, quite a nice guy when you get talking to him for a minute." Arthur stated somewhat protectively. "I mean, he seemed harsh at first but, I don't blame him. No one wants to be new and a walkover." he continued to add to his opinion.

"Hmmm," Hannah let out a laugh, "We've got a teacher's pet right here, haven't we?"

Arthur was definitely not a teacher's pet, detesting that fact he turned the question back on Hannah. "Okay, tell me, what do you think then Hannah?" he fired.

"Strict yes, but there's something odd about him, something I don't like." she stated like she had some unspoken evidence to judge him.

There was silence in the car for a moment. "He also keeps looking at that watch or something in his pocket as he looked over my shoulder." Hannah further then stated.

Admittedly that was weird Arthur thought, maybe he had a problem checking the time and just had to know what time it frequently was. "I did notice that to, maybe he just has a thing with time keeping?" Arthur agreed, settling the topic of Mr Callahan moving it to another for the journey home.

Over the next day and a half, the weather began to drop, it was a lot colder, and snow began to fall from the sky. This didn't stop football practice; it went well and was certainly interesting practicing in the snow. Arthur's focus drifted off towards thoughts about his essay when he had a moment to spare from the football tactics, making sure it was going in the right direction. Somewhat scared that Mr Callahan would tell him to start again, he didn't want to write too much for it to be scrapped.

Lunchtime came around and Arthur was sat down with Daniel and Cheng in the cafeteria as they tucked into their food.

Daniel and Arthur were both in a trance listening to Cheng about how his date with Kay had gone. Cheng was busy explaining all the things that they spoke about and where they went after seeing a film at the cinema. The two listening, not being able to get a word in due to the excitement and rate Cheng verbally reeled off his story. Daniel and Arthur were jointly amazed that someone like Cheng, who would be a great contender for a shy valedictorian, had managed to ask a girl out for a date. Suspiciously, Daniel and Arthur, both thought it was Kay who did the asking, as she seemed more of the outgoing type, but they let Cheng own the bravery in his interpretation of how the evening went.

A hand slapped onto Arthur's shoulder, snapping him out of the trance. It was Hannah, as she pulled a chair out and sat next to Arthur. Edging it closer and closer, purposely pretending to take her time.

"Hey loser," she started off with. "I'm going to the mall after class today with the girls. Are you alright getting Kimberly and yourself home?" Hannah asked.

Arthur over exaggerated a massive sigh as a joke, Hannah grinned already knowing what his answer would be.

"I suppose I can, but you gotta bring back something from the mall for me." Arthur counter offered, whilst knowing he would have to pay for a ride on his phone.

"The cheek of you! Fine!" Hannah replied with an attitude to match Arthur's sigh. "Thanks." she said letting go of Arthur's shoulder and getting out of the seat.

"You better buy me something nice!" Arthur pointed out.

Hannah suggested, "A scarf or something. That'll keep you warm." she said in a sarcastic tone, "Oh and also, thanks for this." Hannah reached out to steal a few chips from Arthur's lunch tray before skipping back off to her friends.

Arthur looked down at the spot where the missing chips were "Hey!" Arthur shouted, slowly looking up from his tray towards Hannah as she proudly walked off.

It took Arthur a second to notice, but Mr Callahan was looking in the direction of where he was, watching Hannah walking away himself. He thought about bothering Mr Callahan right now about his essay, but then again, he saw him take a bite of some sandwich. No one wants to be bothered during lunch.

"Hey, I'll take you and Kimberly home Arthur?" Daniel offered.

"Yeah, thanks? That would be great, we all live at the same place anyway, so that should be easier to drop us off. If you don't mind?" Arthur clarified to make it seem easier for Daniel.

"It's all good man, wait I forgot, you all live together? Hannah *and* Kimberly?" Daniel asked with absolute shock, coming to terms that Arthur lived with two other girls.

"Uhh, yeah, I do, it sounds weird out loud. But it's pretty neat." Arthur replied.

Daniel was quick to ask again, "How do you guys not get sick of each other? And how is it not complicated between you and Hannah?"

"Well, we don't really hang out during the day and sometimes in the evening we do? Mostly we do our own things." Arthur answered, there were set evenings for the witches to practice magic, which did give Arthur some space. "We're just good friends, I guess. We seem to get on really well." he avoided answering the whole truth of what had happened between him and Hannah.

Hannah and Arthur had become great friends as time had passed, they seemed to be on a similar level of understanding to each other. The more Arthur would think about it, the more complicated it would become. The two were great friends and that was it, nothing more and that was clear anyway. Arthur had a new relationship with Laura which was going well, he would just have to keep that secret from her... and everyone else.

The bell rung for class, Arthur mentioned to Daniel that he had to see Mr Callahan after-school, which shouldn't take too long. Quickly messaging Kimberly on his phone to meet out in the student parking at Daniel's pickup.

As it came to the end of the day Arthur found himself sat in Mr Callahan's classroom at a student desk, awaiting him to return.

"Ah hey! Thanks for waiting, sorry I just grabbed a coffee." Callahan explained as he came into the classroom where Arthur was waiting by himself. "So, how's the paper going? Let's have a look?" Callahan held out his hand, being passed over the paper from Arthur.

He began to flick through the paper and nod to himself whilst Arthur stood there just awaiting some feedback. He hoped that Mr Callahan would not ask for him to restart it or stay any longer than needed.

"It's pretty good, do some of these businesses ever make any appearances again? Smaller stores, buyouts, or return to an online store?" Callahan offered as an idea.

Arthur jumped at that suggestion, "Yeah that's a good point I can add that in actually, I'm pretty sure there's a few that did that."

Mr Callahan handed the essay back to Arthur, he seemed to be happy with where the paper was going. He quickly changed the topic, "Are you and Hannah, friends? Saw her steal your food at lunch. Didn't know if it was a friendly thing, or if you're just getting bullied." he asked.

It was an odd question Arthur thought letting out a short laugh, "Yes we are friends, why?" he needed to know.

"Well. She's slacking in English, it's clear that English is not her favourite subject. You might want to give her a heads up or she might find herself sitting a detention, probably this Friday and many others after that catching up to rewrite her paper to pass this topic." Callahan explained with some sternness at the end of his sentence.

Arthur nodded, "Oh all right, yeah I will try to remind her when I see her." it was still an odd moment to bring up.

After collecting his paper back, Arthur began to make his way to the door.

"Oh Arthur, is it okay to go through that essay Friday after class? So, I can get it marked and done with, and I'll be caught up with your entire class." Mr Callahan asked, even though it felt like there was only one answer Arthur could reply with.

"Yeah of course, thanks sir. Have a good evening." politely Arthur had to agree.

Arthur left the classroom slightly annoyed recalling he the plans that the group were meeting that day to hang out at Laura and Ellie's house. Arthur would just have to turn up later, which would make getting a lift there slightly more costly. Then again, Callahan was doing him a favour, it's the least he could do.

Daniel and Kimberly were waiting out in the parking lot where Daniel drove the two back to their home at Pennyview. Arthur and Daniel began speaking about the football practice they've had in the current week, discussing actions of the other teammates and tactics that Coach Decker had gotten them to run.

Snow began to batter at the windshield of the pickup, where it came in strong flurries, building up as the window wipers shoved it aside.

"It's really starting to get cold out here, isn't it? Kimberly?" Daniel pointed out, making small talk in the car to involve Kimberly. "I've never really learned to drive in the snow." he finished with. Filling Arthur and Kimberly with a little doubt.

"Excuse me?" Kimberly leaned forward, "I'm sure you'll be fine in this monster of a truck anyway." as she continued to sit back into her seat and continue to tap away on her phone.

It was the street away from Pennyview, where Arthur got Daniel to drop him off ever since the events that occurred at

Pennyview. Daniel arrived at the point where he would normally drop Arthur off and parked up at the side.

"Why here? We don't live here?" Kimberly pointed out as she looked away at her phone, confused.

"Wait what! I knew my mom dropped you off at a different place that one time?" Daniel questioned, looking back between both, Arthur, and Kimberly.

Arthur had to think quick for a response, "Yeah the lady who is like, in charge of the house gets funny with anything, so it's easier to walk from here." Arthur weakly excused.

Kimberly slowly turned her head towards Arthur with a confused look on her face.

"I've always dropped you off here though?" Daniel questioned, "I thought it was different, compared to months ago." looking a bit more confused this time.

"To be fair, Ethel does get a bit weird meeting new people… and first impressions are never her strong suit. So, I'm not surprised you drop Arthur off here." Kimberly finally caught on, saving Arthur from sounding completely odd.

"Your house is so weird, Arthur." Daniel stated.

The two got out of Daniel's pickup thanking him and began to walk down the sidewalk to Pennyview. The snow had momentarily stopped but the temperature had certainly dropped to near freezing. The two walked side by side, Kimberly looked up to Arthur and shook her head.

"What? I couldn't risk anything." Arthur replied. It made sense to try and keep the life within those walls separate from the normal world, it was what Ethel and Myra wanted and Arthur had to keep that promise as best as he could.

It was later that evening after dinner Arthur was in his room, the many papers of his essay all laid out on his desk that sat by the bedroom window. Books stacked aside about vague businesses, loaned out from the school library. He was at the point where he was unsure if he'd overdone the essay. His focus switched off the essay, it had been taken away by something outside of his bedroom window. It began to snow again, lightly this time, Arthur gazed outside at the small drops of snow that floated down from the dark sky above.

As he watched the snow fall, calm filled throughout him, he felt at peace. He never had the time for anything like this before the accident. His daily life back then was busy from start to finish, there was never a full chance to slow down.

A knock at Arthur's door broke his peaceful gaze out of the bedroom window, he turned in his chair towards the door. It was Hannah opening the door, it looks like she had just returned from her evening at the mall.

"How'd it all go?" Arthur asked her.

"It was great, we went out for a meal at a restaurant outside the mall, some Mexican place. The food was nice, but the waitress was such a real bitch to us for the entire evening." Hannah informed him with such passion and a lingering sense of bitterness. "She was so stuck up, rude and just annoyed at whatever we wanted to order. So! Anyway! Don't tell Ethel or Myra this, I've been dying to tell someone! I made her trip up with a teensy bit of magic. The drinks went everywhere, it was hilarious!" she explained whispering, with such smugness, still standing in the doorway.

She clearly seemed happy with what she had achieved with her evening.

"Poor girl, that sounds brutal." Arthur replied, unsure if that was something he would do himself. "Well, if she was rude for no real reason. Anyway, I have this essay to do! Where's my present for making sure I got Kim home?" Arthur asked, rushing her to continue his attention back at the desk.

Hannah bent down to the side, lowering her arm behind the wall by the doorway and pulled up a shopping bag.

Walking into his room she dumped the bag on his bed, "Fine. Here you go! Don't say I don't get you anything nice." she added as she walked out of Arthur's room, closing the door behind her.

Arthur, still sat there in his chair, curious to what she would've bought him. Placing his phone on the table, he rose out of the chair and walked over to the bed. He stood a foot away from the edge of the bed, analysing the bag that sat there mysteriously. With his fingers stretched, he pulled at the side of the bag and peered in. It was something with a woolly texture. Arthur took a step closer, standing over the bag. Clutching at it gently, Arthur pulled the gift out of the bag, and it unravelled as he raised it in the air. It was a scarf which coincidently was the colours of the Lakebrook Titans and the school, a dark red and yellow. It was exactly what she suggested, it was a thoughtful gift, considering it came from Hannah. She had put some thought into the colours at least. Perfect timing for a scarf now that the snow just had begun to fall, and the temperature had dropped.
    Arthur wrapped the scarf around his neck, just to try it on for a minute. Turning around he stepped towards his desk, facing out of the window.
    Recollecting his eyesight to the snowflakes outside, following them as they pass down.
    Everything did seem peaceful.
    Hannah crept into his thoughts as he stared outside, she was different when they'd first met, she was now more open and friendly towards him. Arthur couldn't seem to forget about the two sharing an intimate moment together, that was most definitely the reason they seemed to be on the same wavelength.
    The more Arthur thought about it, the more he began to doubt his own feelings for Laura although Hannah made it clear that they were only friends. He was with Laura, and everything was going well with her, the two were good together. They were moving at a sensible and normal pace.
    Arthur shook his head, shaking away any thoughts that clouded his mind. Taking off the scarf, he gently wrapped it up and placed it aside on his desk.

He looked at his essay, from page to page, there's nothing more he could do. It was time to prepare himself for bed, knowing that it was going to be a normal day, but for sure it was going to be a cold one. He looked forward to waking up and it was a Friday, knowing the weekend would be ahead.

The next day, it was the last lesson before the bell marking the end of the day. Arthur caught himself staring out of the window in class, his attention was snatched away, it was still snowing, and it didn't stop since last night. This time, it was gradually becoming thicker and fiercer as it fell. It hadn't snowed like this since way back when Arthur could barely remember.

Arthur messaged the group mentioning that he would join them later in the evening at Laura's house, also letting Hannah know that he was going to head straight to Laura and Ellie's house straight after his essay with Mr Callahan.

Arthur did have a class led by Mr Callahan between the last few days of this week at school, but never spoke to him about his essay during class time. However, he did pick up more frequently now that Hannah had mentioned it, Mr Callahan would look at the watch in his hand. He would walk up and down the rows of classes and investigate the watch which he held, lowered by the side of him. It seemed he didn't do this as frequently as he did from the first few lessons when he joined as the new teacher.

As it came to the end of the lesson in Art class, the snow had set thick on the ground, there was an announcement for caution of the students and staff of the school trying to get home.

Arthur walked the opposite way of many students, all leaving and cheering that it was Friday and school was out the way and done with for the week. Arthur followed his way to his English classroom to finally hand in the essay that had played on his mind over the past week. He wasn't always good at English, but he felt like he needed to make sure he did his best. Especially now, knowing that this was his second chance at getting through education at this level. Arthur walked into Mr Callahan's classroom, the door was open, and it was empty, standing in the middle of the classroom he waited.

Mr Callahan walked in, "Just yourself?" he questioned Arthur.

Arthur didn't realise he was expecting anyone else, "Yes, was someone else handing in their essay to?" he asked curiously.

Arthur's eyes watched him closely awaiting an answer.

Mr Callahan walked across to his desk and placed down his coffee mug. "I was expecting Hannah, she didn't impress me at all over the past few days, so I had given her a detention after-school today." he stated.

Hannah hadn't mentioned a thing, she'd kept that very quiet, or knowing Hannah, she simply didn't care for detentions and would use a spell to inevitably get out of it anyway. Clearly, she hadn't been able to see Mr Callahan to use a spell to get out of this detention as he had just mentioned it.

"I'm not sure, she hasn't said a thing at all about it to me." Arthur stated, "Where should I sit anyway?" quickly moving on to get through this after-school as quick as possible.

Callahan gestured to any desk within the front row, walking over he dragged a chair from another one of the empty student's desks and placed it by the side of the desk Arthur had chosen. Proceeding to place his essay onto the desk with some confidence, Callahan took the first page before it settled flat on the desk.

There was a moment of silence, where Arthur sat there looking back and forth at Callahan reading. Trying to read the unreadable expression in his face to know if there were any contempt he'd needed to prepare for. He watched Callahan carefully as he picked up his next page and nodded ever so slightly to himself. This could only be good if he hadn't mentioned anything about the first page.

"This isn't half bad, there are key facts that you've extended on with the benefits and there are counter arguments for how harming those key facts were. It's good that you listened to how those businesses returned from being bankrupt in a capacity." Callahan mentioned as he placed his finger on the line he was reading, guiding it across the page as he spoke. "The only thing I would mention is to be specific, talk about a business you knew in particular if possible and how this affected the local population."

Mr Callahan stood up and took the essay to his desk and placed it flat, "Yeah, I think this will do nicely, if I say your feedback for this is to pick a business specifically and to expand into that one, I think that would be fair." Callahan stated to Arthur, looking up over the paper.

Arthur seemed to have gotten off easy, or maybe he'd just overthought this entire essay after all, but if it got him a pass. That was fine, at least this wasn't a fail.

Callahan began to pat away at the essay before placing it neatly into a teaching folder of some sort. He began to make casual conversation with Arthur, asking about what England was actually like, comparing it to France from where Callahan had been in the past. That was the closest he had gotten to England. Mentioning about visiting historical museums in France and had a keen interest in the peculiar history of the country.

"Apparently, they used to burn witches in France, that's what one museum told, but that wouldn't be the end. The soul of a witch lived on and could haunt those who sent her to her death if unjustified. Weird huh?" Callahan questioned whilst raising an eyebrow, "Witches. I've heard they can grant you spells... I mean I would ask for a nicer car and maybe a better paying job." Mr Callahan laughed off.

That was an odd fact for him to point out, from nowhere.

There was a moment of awkwardness and silence, Arthur looked at the time on his phone, it was nearing to five in the evening, it was dark out and the snow was still dropping.

"I don't know any witches I'm afraid." Arthur joked, lying. "It's getting late I should probably call for a ride home you know." the evening had come quickly before he could've noticed. He had gotten lost in the feedback and conversation of the stories of Mr Callahan had explained in France.

Mr Callahan looked outside and then glanced at the watch on his wrist this time. "Ah yeah, wow is that the time, it's Friday. I should be at the bar by now." he laughed, "Where do you live? I can drop you off?" he offered kindly.

Arthur thought that was generous, but he didn't want to impose. "It's okay I'm pretty sure I live probably in the opposite direction."

Mr Callahan pulled out his car keys from his pocket, "Where abouts? It's no problem. I've kept you here a little longer than I planned to, and you've listened to my tourist stories, it's the least I can do." Callahan proceeded.

Arthur looked out of the window, the snow was dropping quickly at quite a big rate, maybe he could've got Callahan to drop him off at the Laura's house.

"Go on, I insist. It's not a problem at all Arthur." he urged once more. No wasn't going to be an answer.

"Uhm okay sure, I need to get somewhere in the northeast of Upper Hills I think?" Arthur did remember, but he didn't want to give Laura and Ellie's exact address away, "I know the way more than I can say where the street names actually are if that makes sense?" he excused for the lack of direction.

Mr Callahan let out a laugh, "Alright one sec, let me grab my stuff."

The two made their way to the parking lot where the section for teachers would park, Callahan's car sat covered in snow. Mr Callahan began to clear some of the snow off the car, whilst Arthur sat in the passenger seat waiting in the still coldness of the car.

It was a slow and slippery drive to the Upper Hills, expectedly for how quickly the thick snow had already set. Callahan's car tried to keep up with the incline as they began to get through the climbing streets of the area. Mr Callahan kept glancing at the rear-view mirror as Arthur would direct which streets to pass through before making it a few streets away from Laura's home.

Arthur tried to make short conversation to Mr Callahan along the way, to make the drive seem less quiet. Mr Callahan always responded with a short answer and then check his surroundings. Arthur presumed that he barely knew the area, as much as he barely knew it himself being new here.

They were on the right street, the one away from Laura's house anyway. At least this way he could meet the group at hers and hangout with them for some of the evening that was left.

"Alright this is it, thanks Mr Callahan." Arthur mentioned turning towards him, as he slowed down to the side of the curb.

"No problem." Callahan replied.

As the car stopped, Arthur turned towards the door lever and began to tug at it, trying to open the door.

The door didn't open.

He was confused.

Something wasn't right.

An arm came across his shoulder holding him back, the other holding an object that was being pushed into his arm, it was a syringe at a glance. Arthur looked up to his right at Mr Callahan, he had a cold determined look over him.

Holding him back whilst injecting some liquid into Arthur's arm. Arthur began to feel sluggish very quickly, he couldn't react quick enough from whatever had just been injected.

"Whaa..." was all that Arthur could let out before his eyes forcefully closed on him.

The sound of a seatbelt clipped back around him; Arthur could still hear the muffled sounds of what was going on. The engine started to fire as the car began to move, he could feel the motion of the car. He was there, behind his closed eyes. Arthur could sense what was around him, it seemed to be a long drive which was followed by the engine halting. Arthur felt another sharp prick poke into his arm again.

His senses became duller than they were, it was another dose of whatever it was. There was movement, the car door his side opened, and he felt himself being dragged out of his seat.

Mr Callahan muttered as he dropped Arthur to the floor, being dragged through the cold snow, feeling the prick of the twigs and shrubbery scratch against him.

Arthur felt himself lift in the air, ever so slightly and dropped carelessly into some earth. It was cold and damp, he could just about feel the snow set on his paralysed body.

There were a few words, "Sorry buddy, but this is better for the normal living world." which could only be Mr Callahan's voice.

Intense pain coarsely ran through Arthur's body.

Something had pierced his chest. A sharp object slowly being pushed making its way through his insides, piercing his lung and heart. It felt like an intense fire that burned, spreading outwards from his heart. The pain was excruciating.

What had happened?

He soon began to feel blunt sounds of dirt being shovelled over him, before drifting out of what little consciousness he had.

There was another splash of dirt, the object that caused him pain from his chest seemed to give way loosely. Like it had been knocked out of place causing the immense pain to dull.

The dirt continued to be shovelled.

It felt like hours stuck in the cold, a covering pressure pushed against Arthur's body. There were moments of clarity where he felt he could move his hand, but the moment passed shortly. Coldness and then nothingness seeped back in.

More time would pass.

Arthur could still feel he was there.

Another moment came, finally, Arthur could feel between his fingers. It was damp, it was cold, and it crumbled. It was the earth. Arthur figured out he'd been buried; his fingers began to wiggle away at the earth that became loose around his hand. Clawing away at any earth around him, his hand became free, he felt the chill of the winter air.

The short moment of clarity had passed, and Arthur began to desperately gasp for air, there was no air under the amount of earth above him. Darkness turned into suffocating nothingness.

The cold began to settle into the freezing night. His loose hand jerked, followed by his fingers, he knew he was back.

Arthur had no time to waste knowing that this moment of clarity would again be brief. He began to claw at the ground once more, loosening the earth around the area above him with the same hand. The hand became free, he could just about feel the cold air; allowing him to claw away the earth above where is face would be.

He was close, he was almost there.

Arthur… was… free.

A loud gasp of air, inhaling in the crisp, cold chill. Arthur had gained a sense of mental willpower. He could hold on without losing consciousness once more.

Arthur continued to claw away and free his other arm, he grasped both sides of the earth above him and began to pull. He rose out of the earth, like a zombie rising from the grave from an old horror movie. Arthur opened his eyes and began to adjust to his surroundings; it was already dark. From what he could make out, it was a forest, somewhere deep into one with no signs of civilisation nearby.

The sudden realisation hit. Looking down at himself, Mr Callahan had killed him with a wooden stake which was still impaled into his chest. Unsure of how he was still alive. As he sat there, slowly raising his arm he pulled the stake out of his heart, every inch removing it was painful. The pain subsided as the stake was fully pulled from his chest and thrown to the side.

Slowly Arthur came out of his quickly made grave, stretching his limbs to regain some mobility. His return to life felt slightly different this time, it felt slower. This may have been because of the cold, or damage to the heart. Either way, he was unsure and needed to get help.

Reaching into his pocket, his phone had been switched off and the screen was broken. Arthur switched the phone on, it made a chime from the notifications he had missed, but he couldn't make out any from the broken screen. Looking around it seemed like a heavy snowfall had fell and the forest was completely covered. With no clue of what was nearby Arthur had a choice to choose a direction and begin to walk. There were no tyre tracks or footsteps at all to give a clue, Mr Callahan must've dragged him considerably far from his car and all those tracks would be covered by now.

As Arthur began to walk, it started with a stiff hobble, dragging his leg alone. He physically felt like he was a zombie back from the dead, pulling his leg along. As Arthur walked more through the forest in his chosen direction, he began to regain the full use of his legs, he began to move with ease.

Who was Mr Callahan? What was his purpose? He seemed to know something and that something meant danger linking it to Hannah, which could possibly lead onto the residents at

Pennyview. Arthur began to cough repeatedly, the cold choking away at him as he inhaled.

Spluttering away the first words for Arthur were, "A stake, vampire? Did he think I was a vampire?" he managed to say gently under his breath without straining his throat.

He continued for a little longer placing one foot in front of the other, with no idea how much time had passed. Arthur stopped in his tracks. "Wait… vampires are real then?"

He shook his head and continued to walk forwards, it felt like he had walked for an hour, tired mentally and physically, it was freezing out. He began to hear some noise.

Traffic in the distance.

The echo of tyres clawing across a bitter freeway in the night. Arthur followed the sound, his phone vibrated for a message. It was no use he couldn't see anything at all on that broken screen.

Arthur got closer to the sound of traffic passing, peeking through the tree line, it was a freeway with two lanes a small countryside road at best. Following it in one direction. He could see a gas station not far off down the road and approached it, remembering to keep out of sight behind the tree line.

He looked rough, his clothes were soaked, dried, and frozen with blood. He was in not fit state for unwelcome eyes.

Arthur's phone rang, he wasn't sure who it was, scrambling and scratching to get the phone back out of his pocket. He looked at the screen, it was no use. Arthur began tapping at it furiously and swiping to answer the call blindly multiple times.

The ringing stopped prematurely, Arthur gasped in anticipation and placed the phone to his ear. "Where the hell have you been?" a familiar voice shouted through the speaker; it was Hannah.

Thank God! Arthur had little energy in him, the only words he could muster up were, "Callahan killed… me. Chevron gas, freeway." the short sentence that Arthur spoke was relayed to someone in the background. Presumably the others.

"We will be on our way, hold tight and keep an eye out for us." Hannah responded.

The relief in Arthur hit overwhelmingly, spending some time sat aside by the gas station trying to keep an eye out for any recognisable cars but also to keep out of sight from the public, who stopped by.

Mr Callahan

It was a hazy drive back to Pennyview Boarding house after Arthur was picked up in the cold by the gas station. Arthur just recalled Peter helping him up and into the car, propping him upright next to him in the back seat. He had managed to get Arthur all the way up the stairs into his room, undressed him and left him on his bed.

Arthur was tired, he was drained of any energy entirely, this must've been an aftereffect for a new way of dying or trudging through the cold and the snow. Being struck in the heart is a new level of immortality as that sort of damage would stop pretty much anything in its tracks and now knowing, vampires possibly exist.

Flowing in and out of consciousness, or rather the heavy pull of needing to rest. Arthur could see that figures swapped and changed from the corner of his bed; the house was keeping an eye on him in rotations. Certain whispers and conversations could be heard, guessing what had happened to Arthur. They were eagerly awaiting to know what had happened first hand and managed to go through all that effort to kill him. Callahan was whispered a handful of times.

A stream of thoughts rushed through Arthur, replaying of what happened up to moments before his death, it was vivid and much clearer this time. His eyes opened wide in the darkness staring at what was the corner of his room and began to search around. Someone had tucked him in, propping himself up ever so slightly in his bed, leaning to the back of the headboard.

Peter half-asleep in Arthur's desk chair had awoken, rushing over to Arthur, and almost losing his footing. "Arthur, are you okay dude?" Peter exclaimed loudly with his voice, "He's awake, he's awake." he started to shout.

There was a distant thumping of footsteps, as the others began to scuttle through the upstairs corridor of the house to his room.

The majority of the house had gathered at his awakening.

"What happened to you?! Do you know how lucky you are?!" Myra gained the room's silence with those two questions.

Arthur began to explain what had happened and how he had come to being picked up, hidden out of sight at the gas station.

As he began to explain how it all began. Hannah cut in, "Mr Callahan!" she declared. Arthur's room fell with silence... "We need to kill him; he's a threat and he was after me to sit that detention also."

As the declaration settled and others glanced between each other, Arthur continued with his story. He had been pierced through the heart with a stake, mistakenly for a vampire he could only predict. Uncertain eyes searched the room for the confirmation that vampires exist, Ethel and Myra's eyes were still, focused, they already knew the answer.

Who knew what Mr Callahan knew, but it was clear that he was after Hannah also, meaning she may be at risk alongside the rest of the coven here at Pennyview.

The room began to bicker how they would need to kill him.

"Wait, if we plan to kill him, we need to do it out the way and as soon as possible." Arthur mentioned, we now know he's suspicious of us.

Many creative ideas of how to dismember, bury alive and also possess with magic came to light. Ethel was quiet as she watched the room of teenagers become experts in murdering. They started to bicker at which method should be used to kill Callahan.

"Quiet!" shouted Myra silencing the room, a few of them jumped. She had enough.

Silence proceeded.

Kimberly was the first one to break the silence, "Wait. Callahan isn't a normal type of guy; he is going to be hard to kill, isn't he? Why not simply threaten him? Get him on our side." Kimberly asked everyone, flipping her idea from brutally suffocating him with magic.

"That's true, he is smart…" Arthur came to terms with that fact, "He most likely will be prepared."

Kimberly's questions set the room silent, again. All lost in thought.

Ethel stood forward. "He could know a lot, considering that he was suspicious of Arthur being a vampire. We could make good use of his knowledge and talents." Ethel suggested.

The room. Still quiet.

To Arthur, it was a bitter idea to keep him alive, he wanted some revenge on the entire murder, but deep down he knew it made sense. Mr Callahan may have a fantastic knowledge of the supernatural.

It was getting late into the dark hours of the morning; it was a Saturday. The house had decided to plan away during the day, after a good rest.

As they all left, Arthur shifted his way out of the bedsheets and walked over to his belongings folded neatly on the desk by the window. One by one he picked up his belongings, his phone's screen was destroyed and now out of battery. He then placed the broken phone aside on the desk and placed his hand onto the next thing, the scarf, amazed to still have kept hold of that whilst being buried and dragged through the ground. It was covered in dried blood, the yellow musty with the stains of blood; Arthur gripped the scarf in his hand and squeezed firmly in anger. It was a new gift, and now it was ruined.

Hannah turned around as she stood in the bedroom doorway, "Are you okay?" she questioned standing there after the others had left.

"I'm annoyed, my phone and clothes have been ruined, especially the scarf." Arthur replied to her turning around with the scarf still gripped in his hand, feeling sensitive, as he clutched at it tightly.

Hannah drew a sly smile, "All objects, I'm sure we can replace the clothes and phone and I'll just buy you a new scarf if it really matters to you that much." Hannah offered.

He looked down at the scarf, it was clear to Hannah by his face that he had a lot going on emotionally.

She walked closer to him "Or we can look and see if we can get something strong to clean the blood out, but it might ruin the colours." she offered doubtfully.

Arthur slowly looked up as Hannah approached him, directly standing in front of him, smiling as though nothing in the world was a problem. His eyes were watering, the events of everything had suddenly caught up. Being murdered by a living human was different from the undead being previously. There was an intention to kill him this time.

Hannah placed her hands around Arthur giving him a hug, squeezing lightly to console him. Returning the gesture Arthur needily wrapped his arms around here.

Arthur sniffed up, "I don't know if I was going to come back alive from dying like that." he whispered, whilst his teary face was buried into Hannah's neck. "I felt everything as I got closer to losing consciousness, and the pain didn't stop."

Hannah inhaled, preparing herself on what to say. "Well, you did come back from that, and it's great that you're still here. It goes to show that you are something truly different in this supernatural world. *And...* I'm glad you're still here I suppose." she revealed, feeling proud as though she delivered that comforting statement perfectly.

Arthur's eyes opened from the touch of shock that came out of Hannah's mouth, he let go of her. "Wow that was nice coming from you." he pointed out, "I wasn't expecting that."

Hannah lowered her arms and stepped back, "I guess so, how weird of me." she paused for a moment, thinking of what else to say, "Does it hurt every time you die?" she questioned.

"Every. Single. Time." Arthur answered taking a pause in between each word. Placing the scarf back on his desk.

Hannah looked at him with a grin, "Sucks to be you huh?" she joked as she made her exit out of his room. "Catch you in the morning, I need to sleep."

That was the Hannah, Arthur knew.

The weekend passed with the house coming up with multiple ways of trying to trap, trick and persuade Mr Callahan. Kimberly had been out during that last day of the weekend to buy Arthur a new phone, leaving Arthur at home with the rest where Peter stayed to keep an eye on him. It was agreed that he should stay out of sight and contact from his friends, so there was no suspicion that Arthur was still alive.

They had a plan.

Monday morning came around for school, Arthur stayed at home prepared, ready for his moment when called upon. It was Hannah's English class with Mr Callahan, and she shared that class with Laura. As she walked into the room she was greeted by a slightly aggravated Mr Callahan.

"Where were you Friday after-school? You missed detention." Callahan demanded an answer.

"I forgot." Hannah shrugged, "I'll have to make it back up tonight, I have some plans, but I can push them forwards." she continued with a slight attitude to provoke him.

Mr Callahan's face showed a slight expression of frustration. His face crumbled for a moment, "After-school, tonight it is then." he said with a forceful smile through his teeth, hoping to interrupt any plans she had.

Mr Callahan had taken the bait from Hannah's attitude. Hannah had perfectly set the timing. Throughout the English class Hannah bothered Laura frequently with conversation, hoping that she would ask about Arthur. Hannah never normally spoke to Laura, it was unusual, but she had to inadvertently bring up the topic of Arthur.

He eventually came up, "Hey, have you heard from Arthur at all this weekend?" Laura whispered turning around slightly to make it less obvious.

"Arthur?" Hannah repeated a little bit louder to trap some attention.

She could almost notice Mr Callahan's ear twitch at the name, he was listening, that was for sure.

"Nope I haven't heard of him at all this weekend actually. I don't think he's even in today, I wonder where he is?" she continued.

An interrupting cough was heard from Mr Callahan at the front, cutting any further conversation off. Laura turned back around to focus on her work, taking the cough as a warning.

Hannah messaged Kimberly and Arthur once she had left her classroom for that period. It was time to get them ready for the plan.

It was the end of the school day and ten minutes had passed; Hannah was intentionally late to her detention just to create aggravation. She opened Mr Callahan's classroom door with elegance, "*Sorry* I'm late." Hannah purposely whined as she walked through.

Mr Callahan stood up from his desk and folded his arms, "Sit there at the front row." he ordered.

Hannah noticed that the blinds to his classroom were all closed, it was a suspicious sight giving off the feeling that he had planned a trap for her.

Another ten minutes passed, whilst Hannah sat there on edge, staying alert in case Mr Callahan moved against her before the plan had started.

The school intercom buzzed, "Could Mr Callahan make his way to the front desk, there is a message for you." it announced, it was the receptionist's voice.

Mr Callahan looked over at Hannah from his textbook and rolled his eyes, "Stay here, I'll be back in a minute." he ordered, slightly confused walking out of the classroom door.

Shutting the classroom door behind him, leaving Hannah alone. He swiftly made his way through the corridor towards the front desk.

"What's the message for me Clara?" he asked, putting on his usual charming personality, hiding that murderous secret underneath.

The receptionist looked at him in utter confusion, "I don't recall mentioning a message for you Mr Callahan?" she replied, unsure, looking over her glasses.

Mr Callahan stood there, "But, I just heard it?" he questioned. Seconds passed; it clicked in his mind.

Something was happening back in the classroom he thought, and it could be Hannah's escape.

Walking at a faster pace than usual he veered towards his classroom door, trying not to gain any unwanted attention.

He barged at the door twisting and opening the handle with such force, only the lights at the front were turned on. His attention was directed straight forward towards his teaching desk. Hannah was sat on his desk, her leg over the other with a smirk looking at her nails. His attention focused solely on her as he carefully walked a few steps closer. The classroom door slammed shut and Callahan's desk chair turned around, revealing Kimberly.

Mr Callahan clutched at his jacket pocket and began to fumble around for something; Hannah raised her hand and began to slowly lock her fingers into a fist.

Callahan fell to his knees with his head in his hands clenching in agony, it sounded intense from how he grunted.

"Can you feel the pain growing, sir?" Hannah sneered in smugness.

Mr Callahan's face began to go red with a tight-wrenched expression of pain, staring intensely at Hannah in outrage.

He tried to fight through the pain reaching for his pocket, Hannah twisted her fist further extending the pain immensely.

His hands dropped to his sides uncontrollably.

"That's enough Hannah," Kimberly stood up "hands where we can see them, and it'll stop." she added.

An exhale of relief came from Callahan as he dropped his hands to the floor.

"Sounds like you're a magical killer of some sort, Mr Callahan?" Hannah questioned the obvious.

Mr Callahan kneeled up and looked between the two girls in front of him. Reluctant to answer, "Something like that, a supernatural hunter, if you like." he added. "Keeping the balance for the living, and to keep the humans out of danger."

Hannah let out a deep laugh, so did Kimberly.

"Well, it seems we're missing one of ours and we know he was last seen with you. So, we need to figure out what to do with you." Hannah mentioned referring to Arthur.

"He was a part of your coven? A vampire? Even they're a threat to witches. What are you doing with a vampire?" silence fell in return of an answer from the girls, and it was clear Mr Callahan began to sweat, wondering if he were going to leave his classroom alive.

"I'm not a vampire. I was never a threat, but I certainly can be… a nasty one." A recognisable British accent came from the darkness in the back of the classroom. Arthur walked forwards, out of the darkness not breaking eye contact with Mr Callahan.

Callahan visibly began to shake "Impossible." he mumbled, slowly shaking his head. "Oh god, but I…"

Instantly he was cut off from speaking.

"Killed me? Killed me!" Arthur began to say louder, rushing towards Callahan. He pulled at his shirt dragging him up off his knees. "I meant you no harm!"

His strength forced him into the whiteboard, being this close to Callahan and looking at him triggered anger inside of him. Arthur's eyes had noticeably changed to black and red as he glared into Mr Callahan's eyes.

"I'm... I'm sorry, please don't..." Callahan began to beg, visibly shaking.

"I thought you were a decent guy, *sir*." Arthur stated fiercely gritting his teeth, the bitterness of keeping him alive was balancing thinly in his mind.

The girls could sense this was going to get out of hand, as they looked at each other unsure of what Arthur would do next.

"Hey, hey, hey there, *whoa* there." Hannah calmly walked over to Arthur, slowly placing her hands on his shoulders.

His senses and the anger within him dissipated, at the touch of Hannah, calming him down. Bringing him back to reality, regaining control over himself

"Remember we want to keep him alive." Kimberly reminded Arthur.

Arthur looked over to the left of his shoulder as Kimberly spoke. Turning back to Callahan and locking eye contact again, Arthur's eyes closed for a moment settling the control of his emotions. He exhaled slowly and focused, opening his eyes again, they were back to normal. Letting go of Callahan, he took a step back.

"They're not vampire's eyes..." Callahan quietly mentioned, "T-th-thank you, why are you not going to kill me?" he further questioned.

Hannah cleared her throat, "Okay. To the point Mr Callahan. We don't want to kill you, don't get me wrong, we could and hide you better than the job you did with Arthur. But we're no harm to the city, we have the same vision as you to keep things all in *balance*." she quoted in the air with her fingers, "We want us to be *allies*."

"You're lucky our friend Arthur here can come back to life, if not, well you wouldn't be alive right now." Kimberly added, walking towards Arthur, and patting him heavily on the back, "Right Arthur?"

Arthur's eyes were still locked on Mr Callahan, "I'm willing to forget and move on," he began, putting his hands into his pockets, "But... if you ever were to try that again, I won't hesitate and I'll be ready." he lightly threatened, ending with a half-smile.

Mr Callahan nodded, "Okay, just how many of you are there?" he questioned curiously.

"There are loads of us, you don't need to know who and how many. All happy, peaceful, in plain sight doing nothing harmful." Hannah replied.

"Alright, let's go, we're done here. It's getting late." Kimberly announced, making her exit to the classroom door.

Hannah and Arthur began to follow Kimberly to leave.

"Arthur?" Callahan questioned.

Arthur stopped and turned to face him. "I'm sorry." he just about managed to mutter, looking at him.

"I'll accept that apology when I know I can trust you." Arthur stated, nodding after he'd finished.

Mr Callahan nodded mutually in that response.

The three walked through and out of the school into the car park, to get into Hannah's car. There was some silence to start with on the ride home, noticeably Kimberly was cheerful with a grin on her face.

She couldn't hold what she had to say in, "Aren't you all happy we didn't need to kill and clean a mess up?" she pointed out.

Arthur was engrossed in his phone, finally being able to message his friends, excusing himself that he was out of town and had broken his phone.

"It's just Arthur's mess we need to pick up every time he dies. I wonder when the next time will be?" Hannah joked insinuating that there *will* be another time; the girls broke out in laughter.

Arthur looked up from his phone, his attention was pulled away from it, smiling as he caught up on the joke. He felt satisfied at the plan, it was great knowing he had some supernatural friends who had his back when he needed it this time around.

But deep down, a moment back there niggled at him, he lost control for just a split second in that classroom. The anger within him triggered, it was ready to kill Mr Callahan where he stood without any afterthought.

Lone Mountain

Winter break out of school had come and gone. Christmas was a surreal experience at Pennyview Boarding house, it was cheerfully and heavily embraced from the residents, especially at the fact they were all witches. Although it was strange being at another house for Christmas full well knowing he was missing out on one back home, tragically being classified as dead. It had been enjoyable.

Arthur had been spending time with Daniel and the others throughout winter break, they had continued training and hanging out at Daniel's house listening to all sorts of music he enjoyed and playing on his games console.

Arthur had seen Laura a few times over the winter break, there was a moment where she had stepped foot inside Pennyview as Ethel had asked Arthur to purchase some groceries for the house and to drop them off throughout their day together. The short stop inside Pennyview was brief, with the members being on their best behaviour as they came and went.

Now, school was back in session and Arthur had been waiting for it eagerly; the air was still cold, and the snow was still settling on the ground beneath them. It was certainly a lingering winter.

It was just another day back in school where Arthur, Daniel, and Abel were walking down the corridor to the lunch hall, "It's going to be a great birthday coming up this year." Daniel mentioned.

"Oh, yea? Why's that Dan?" Abel questioned.

Arthur continued walking along, listening, trying to work out how old these guys would be in their junior year.

Daniel began to elaborate, "Well it's the social studies trip to Montana in a few weeks and my birthday is going to be during it. Going to be a blast to start off the new year in the mountains."

"Oh yeah, I signed up to that already." Abel mentioned, "It'll be sick in the snow on your birthday, right?!"

Arthur couldn't remember the last time he had been on a school trip; it would've been a very long time ago. He interrupted the conversation, "I forgot to sign up! How do I sign up for this?" Arthur began to ask in a slight panic, he didn't want to miss out on an experience like that.

Daniel stopped walking, the other two stopped alongside him. He placed his hand on Arthur's shoulder with a smirk, "It's alright, I already signed you up without asking weeks ago." Daniel said proudly. "I wanted all of us guys to be there! Not sure how you paid for the trip though, they must've missed that out and just booked you on it."

The three walked into the cafeteria trying to seek out where the rest were sat as they scoured the area.

Abel looked over to the table where a small group of teachers were eating, "I heard there's a few teachers joining us on the trip. I heard that in total we will have Mr Roxham, Mr Callahan and also Miss Abigail." he listed, keeping his voice low.

Interesting that Callahan volunteered to be on the trip, considering he had no link to the social studies subject. He could only guess that Hannah must've signed up also if Callahan were involved, it was slightly suspicious. But then, everything seemed okay between the residents of Pennyview and Mr Callahan, he was still a touch distant ever since Arthur and the witches had put him in his place.

"Ah! There they are!" Daniel exclaimed, pointing out to the far side of the cafeteria, "Over there."

The three walked over to the table where the rest of the group were sitting. Ellie was already discussing the trip, "Did you see the list of who's going to the Montana trip that was finally posted this morning? It's going to be a great trip!" she giggled with excitement.

The entire time of lunch, the conversation was all about the trip to this mountain. From what Arthur could understand was, the list had gone up this morning of who was going on the trip. How long it will take by aeroplane to get there, the cold weather, activities, and finally the cost. He was signed up, somehow.

None of the above seemed to bother Arthur, the biggest thing that he needed to worry about was permission from the house. This meant that he would be out of the house alongside Hannah, for a handful of days at once. Wondering where that would leave the house, if two of them were out on this trip.

It was the last class of the day, art class. Arthur spent the rest of his entire day thinking up excuses of how he could go on the trip. Arthur was taping some paper to the easel to set it up, in front of the vaguely related objects that were in the centre of the room, trying to get the best angle. He didn't know what a stringless violin, a plastic fruit arrangement, an empty bottle, and a random armless action figure had to do with each other. All he knew was it was art, and that he had to draw it in some way.

There was a loud clunk next to Arthur, which had broken his focus on thinking up an excuse to go on the trip as he reeled off the tape.

It was Laura, setting up her easel next to his, "Hey you," she whispered as she nudged Arthur purposely. "The trip will be fun don't you think? It can be like our first getaway together." there was an intense level of excitement from her.

She was right; it would be to think of it. Things have been getting more serious between them as the more time they spent together, in and outside of school. Arthur was happy, but it still felt strange, he couldn't quite put his finger on it. Even though Laura was only a couple years younger, which was a small enough gap not to be creepy. It just may have been the fact that he was lying about his age in school, come to think of it when Arthur graduates from high school at the end of his senior year, he would be twenty.

Or it simply may be the fact that he is a part of the supernatural world, he still couldn't figure it out.

As the two were chatting and poking at each other with paint, Arthur looked over to Hannah across the room, this was one of the few classes the two had together. Hannah was in a similar boat; she was eighteen pretending to be seventeen and would be nineteen when graduating, which doesn't sound as bad as his situation. Hannah's name was on the list for Montana, Arthur needed to find out her excuse for getting on the trip.

"Laura, I'll be right back, I just need to ask Hannah something." Arthur excused himself, as he neatly slotted his paintbrush into the easel's shelf. "And actually, do your work." Arthur winked before he walked around the corners of the classroom, keeping out of everyone's view.

Hannah's eyes broke from the concentration of her easel, she took out one of her headphones. "Can I help you?" she asked.

"Actually yes, you can." Arthur replied. "What excuse have you said to Myra that you're going off on this trip coming up?" he waited eagerly for her reason.

Hannah's eyebrows lowered a little, "Is that it? You've come over here to bother me with that?" she laughed lightly, "Tell me. How long has that been bothering you?"

Arthur's eyes darted from left to right, "Well, most of the day, Daniel signed me up for the trip. So, I need to think of a good, educational excuse for it." he explained.

Hannah let out another laugh, slightly louder than the last. "He signed your name also? I did too." she began to smirk.

After knowing Hannah did also, it suddenly made sense that there was no request for Arthur to pay at all, knowing she was involved.

"Oh..." Arthur looked at Hannah's artwork; noticing it was awful. He looked back at Hannah. "Why is everyone signing me up for stuff?" he asked innocently.

"I think it's cause you're new here, my reason was that you haven't been on a school trip, and you didn't know how to sign up. It'll be a good growing experience." Hannah's eyes went back to painting a couple of strokes, "Anyway can't you just say it'll be fun?"

Fun? Is that it, that was one of Arthur's first excuses hours ago. "You really think they'll go for *fun?*" he asked, unimpressed.

"Well, we will just have to find out, won't we?" Hannah questioned in a mysterious tone, quickly changing the topic, "You and Laura seem to be getting on well?"

Arthur glanced back over at Laura who was painting away, "Yeah, it's going great actually, that's why I need to get on this trip also. She's going and it'll be an interesting memory for us to make." he explained.

Hannah sniggered abruptly, "That's cute." she leaned in closer to Arthur, pausing for suspense before whispering, "Gonna share a bed huh?"

Arthur wasn't prepared to talk about that with anyone at all, not even Hannah either. It's more than likely, he would have to be put with one of the guys anyway. Cutting any more conversation with Hannah short, "Alright! Well. I'll catch you later for the ride home. Good chatting to you." he said dismissing himself, walking back around towards his easel.

It was the drive home after art class where tension began to build up. Hannah's car pulled up towards the driveway of Pennyview, Arthur had his reason for wanting to go on the trip and had prepared himself mentally. Practicing those crucial persuasive lines over and over in his head. Pulling his bag out of the car and walking to the front door, Arthur aimed for the kitchen straightaway. Hannah followed behind as Kimberly leapt up the stairs to her room, leaving them.

Arthur walked into the kitchen and found Ethel and Myra, one relaxing with a coffee, reading a magazine and the other working with some herbs on the island counter scrunching them in her fingers.

"Good day at school?" Ethel questioned the two, briefly looking up from her mixture of herbs.

Arthur stopped just in front of the kitchen doorway, standing firmly, preparing his response. Hannah barged past him, making her way to the fridge, opening it to grab a drink.

"Yeah, it was great." Hannah answered before him, "The list for the school trip came out today. Arthur wanted to ask you something." she dropped him right in, with a grin from ear to ear as she observed his next response.

Ethel looked up from her workspace on the counter again, her expression on her face was waiting for Arthur to spit it out.

Hannah leaned against the fridge, drink in hand, tilting her head, directing it towards the two and raising her eyebrows to give the go ahead for Arthur to start his persuasive excuse.

Arthur had to trap them first in a question, offering him a space to reason why he should. "Uhm hey, yeah I have a question to ask." Arthur began. "The school trip to Montana is coming up and I got on the list, I was wondering if I could go on it? It's all paid for."

Arthur set the question, prepared with his perfect reasoning, waiting for the return of being challenged why he should go on it in the first place.

Myra looked up from her magazine, she had a confused look upon her face. "We know you're going on it. Hannah has already spoken to us about it." Myra placed her cup down onto the counter, "She explained it would be a good experience for you, not being on a school trip before."

Ethel jumped in her response, "And also, it'll be fun for you to go. It's only for a few days."

Arthur felt himself heat up, turning red with embarrassment, however a weight inside Arthur had lifted away. Hannah had set him up to feel like a clown. Looking over to Hannah, she was besides herself with laughter, holding it in as best as she could.

"Thank you for letting me go. I'm going to unpack now." Arthur expressed, before making his way out of the kitchen avoiding any moment longer lingering in the embarrassment.

Hannah strode after him, as Arthur made his retreat up the stairs. "That was great, ahhh, thank you for that." she giggled at his expense.

"Well done." Arthur responded, "You've pulled a good one there, watching me sweat about it knowing I didn't have to the entire time."

"It was great to watch, you seemed to be worrying about so much, so I thought I'd enjoy it. Your face *and* Myra's face when she said she knew about it." she continued to explain as she followed Arthur to the door of his room, gloating, proudly.

"Right, thank you for your help, Hannah." Arthur said in a bold tone. Stood, blocking his bedroom doorway, "Good one." before closing the door on her, leaving her outside his room in the hallway where he could hear her cackling down the hallway.

A few weeks passed and it was the day to departing for Lone Mountain, Montana. It was informed that the students had to be at the school parking for six in the morning. Arthur had found it hard to sleep the night before, he'd spent the last few days preparing what thermal clothing he needed for snow, sun, and heights.

The group had been excited for this trip more and more with every day passing closer with suggestions of what they could get up to.

"Hey, wake up! We're here!" Laura shook Arthur.

Arthur woke up, his eyes opened slowly, he had fallen asleep on the coach drive from the airport after landing.

Members of the class were already making their way off the coach with their rucksacks. Abel and Daniel were just seen heading down the stairs out of the coach. Arthur began to get out of his seat, reaching to the top luggage holder to pull down Laura's bag first, then his. Making their way off down coach he could see all the groups gathering around the cargo hold of the coach.

"Over here!" Laura said excitedly, making her way ahead of Arthur towards the group which consisted of Daniel, Ellie, Laura, and Jade; these were the few that had signed up for the trip.

Arthur gripped both of his rucksack straps, watching Laura rush off to the others as he stood there.

Mr Callahan stepped off the coach and stood next to Arthur, "Should be a nice trip, here's hoping the hotel has a bar." Callahan mentioned, looking towards Arthur and then the surroundings around him in the distance suspiciously.

Arthur turned to face Mr Callahan and asked, "Are you here to keep an eye on us?" he asked.

Mr Callahan laughed, "It's not all about you Arthur. I'm here on a free holiday paid by the school, snow, ski, and a bar, I hope." he paused for a moment. "If you were older, I'd buy you a drink. We can chat more about your supernatural self." he offered.

Arthur laughed this time, "I'm old enough to drink, just not in this country it seems. Which sucks ass." he revealed to Mr Callahan.

"Lying to school about our age are we, Arthur?" Callahan questioned in a sarcastic, unserious manner.

Arthur took a few steps forward and turned to Mr Callahan, "Secrets, secrets, secrets we all have secrets don't we." his eyes widened as he whispered sharply lining his index finger to his lips, to hush Mr Callahan.

Callahan shook his head with a smirk.

Arthur turned away from Callahan, approaching the group. As he got closer to the group, he could see the excitement on Daniel's face, his birthday was tomorrow. His present was in Arthur's suitcase which was currently being taken out of the hold from the bottom of the coach by the driver.

"Pick your twin! These are rooms of two here. No changing halfway through. Same sex only!" Mr Roxham shouted out to the class gathered around the coach.

Daniel was jumping up and down with each foot stomping away as he pointed towards Arthur who had just joined standing beside them.

"I got Arthur! I got Arthur! It's gonna rock man!" Daniel chanted, the excitement within him was through the roof.

"Awh man, that's all right. Don't worry! I guess I'll sleep alone." joked Abel.

Hannah walked over to Arthur's group; they all looked at her as she nudged her way into the circle they stood in.

"Right, girls! Clarissa and Ellen have a room together, which means I am a third wheel and at a need for a roommate." Hannah announced aiming towards the three girls.

Ellie, Laura, and Jade all exchanged nervous glances. Hannah never really spoke to them, if she did, it was only for a moment.

"Laura? We can get the gossip on Arthur?" Hannah offered.

What a terrible idea ran all through Arthur's mind, he felt a cold shiver run down his back. He couldn't let them two share a room with what Hannah was like and knowing what had happened between the two. Not like Hannah would mention anything... or would she?

"I've got Laura I'm afraid." Ellie said, possibly saving her sister from some sort of nightmare.

"Hmm okay, Jade it's you." Hannah directed towards her. Not the best option, but the better one of the two.

The coach driver called out the suitcases, they had all been taken out of the cargo hold and lined up in the gritty snow on the ground. The students began to grab their suitcases and head their way to reception where Miss Abigail was preparing room keys, announcing for the class to meet within the hour in the main foyer.

Daniel and Arthur followed the path leading up to the main entrance, where Miss Abigail waited by the reception desk. Collecting their keys and heading through the main foyer to find an elevator. After guessing which way they had needed to go on their floor, they had found their room number and began to unpack what they needed.

The rooms were pretty bland. Two twin beds stood aside the room with a parting of floor between them, they both shared a cupboard but had a small set of bedside drawers each. It wasn't luxury and the colours were nothing to get excited about, but then again, it's a ski resort. Who's going to be spending all the time in the bedroom for it.

"Tadaaa!" Daniel sung as he pulled out a clear bottle of an alcoholic labelled spirit from his bag. It was vodka. "I have the drink ready for the party tomorrow." he declared cheerfully. He preciously held the bottle out with both hands.

Arthur stared at Daniel for a second, with a small frown. "Just vodka, you haven't bought anything to mix it with?" Taking the bottle out of his hands to analyse it.

"I couldn't pack anything to mix it with as it would take up too much space in my suitcase." Daniel tried to excuse, "We can just buy standard coke or lemonade here, I'm sure."

He wasn't wrong.

"How did you get that anyway?" Arthur asked him, handing back the bottle.

"I snuck it out of my parent's liquor cabinet, they won't miss it. I've been eyeing it up for the past few weeks for this moment." Daniel justified his theft. "It had some dust on it anyway."

A smile grew over Arthur, "Have you ever thought that they would drink it when they've gotten you out of the house for a few days?" he joked, winking at Daniel.

Daniel's face turned to horror and disgust, before opening the seal on the bottle to take a sniff, "Ow, that's sharp." he blurted out.

The two agreed to take a swig, before heading out to the foyer, it was clear that Daniel had barely drunk spirits. It was certainly clear he was a beer sort of guy with the face he wrenched as he ingested it.

They made their way down the elevator towards the foyer where the first activity of the day was to start a skiing or snowboarding introductory class, which would set them up for the main activity throughout the day.

The group all gathered back together, discussing what option they all wanted to pick. Daniel was persistent on wanting to take part in snowboarding, this was the same for Arthur. Abel wasn't keen on snowboarding with an excuse of not having enough control, even though he was certain about it until that very instant when having to choose, whereas skiing offered that option of not trapping both feet. Ellie approached the two, as they were the only two of the group doing snowboarding. She had asked if she could tag along as none of the other girls were interested in snowboard, it threw them off.

Picking the options, the student's split into their two activity groups, Arthur followed the snowboarding instructor who took his group towards a baby ramp area. The skiing group took off elsewhere which involved the others.

It started off with the basics of what parts of a snowboard were called, to clipping in the feet, and then standing upright. Daniel had no intention of taking it easy and wanted to try the ramps sooner than the others, asking Arthur and Ellie to come along for support.

It seemed Daniel was certainly feeling the bravery being out on this trip, with how confidence he seemed wanting to get out there. Arthur had been on a skateboard before, when he was much younger, this couldn't' be much different he thought. It must be easier being able to use his strength or speed he imagined for this.

Ellie and Arthur both watched as Daniel slide in on the baby ramp. He didn't hesitate and leaned straight in, making it look easy. It was Arthur's turn to drop in from the top of the baby ramp. Arthur prepared himself, he looked around to see if anybody was watching. He was nervous, but the fear of being hurt from the drop had been removed, it was the fear of looking like an embarrassment. The ramp wasn't even steep enough for him to topple forwards.

He looked over to Ellie and Daniel, they both were talking to each other, not paying attention at all towards Arthur. That was the opportunity for Arthur to drop in whilst he could. He leaned forward and put some weight into his forward foot which was clipped firmly into the top of the board. Tipping his weight forwards on to his foot, he leaned in and slid effortlessly down the ramp.

"Heh, that was pretty easy." Arthur said to himself as he cleared the ramp area. Unclipping himself from his board, he picked it up and began to walk towards Ellie and Daniel through the shallow snow.

Ellie was laughing at something Daniel had said. Daniel seemed different, he was more confident ever since he got into the team and now that him and Arthur had spent time together. It was great to see that Daniel had begun to change into this new person.

Ellie turned to Arthur and began to clap, Daniel joined in cluelessly. They had entirely forgotten that Arthur was there in the first place, dropping in.

It was Ellie's turn to drop into the baby ramp, if Ellie could do this, then the trio could make their way up the mountain alone following the beginner's route.

Ellie made her way up the stairs to the top of the ramp.

"She's quite cool, isn't she?" Daniel questioned out loud randomly to Arthur, as he watched her carefully.

"Who, Ellie?" Arthur asked in return for clarification.

It was clear that Daniel had taken a liking to Ellie in that moment. Daniel screamed some words of encouragement to her as she reached the top. Arthur didn't get this kind of support from Daniel; she must be special.

Ellie took a moment, it was clear she was nervous, just like Arthur was.

"Just tip the weight gently into your front foot!" Arthur shouted, "And push gently into it. Don't lean in too much!"

Ellie stuck her thumb up; she took a few seconds to compose herself and dropped elegantly into the ramp.

The advice seemed to work a treat.

She walked back towards the two with a smirk on her face. "I did it! Thanks for the advice, Arthur." she excitedly thanked him.

Arthur smiled, "It was Daniel's advice, I just shouted what he said next to me." Looking at Daniel who took an extra second to catch on.

"Oh, said yeah, that's what I was saying to Arthur." Daniel caught up, understanding that Arthur was sending him the praise.

This meant that the three could now venture up the mountain and follow the beginner's route, with the instructors blessing.

Daniel couldn't wait to go up into the mountain, the instructor agreed that they could go up using the ski lift but had to avoid the red flagged ramps and routes. It was clear that those ramps were for the hardcore paying members who visited regularly and were incredibly experienced.

On the way up in the ski lift, Daniel and Ellie were both locked in a deep conversation with each other, Arthur looked around enjoying the sights. He felt his phone vibrate, he unzipped his pocket and had a look. It was a message from Laura hoping that he was having fun.

Arthur tapped away a message in return, "It's great being a third wheel, joking aside. Your sister and Dan seem to be getting along nicely Xx" The message sent. Arthur flicked through his phone meaninglessly, realising he'd missed a message from Hannah earlier, he must've not felt it whilst he was out there. She had ordered to keep an eye on Mr Callahan in her message, as he personally signed up for this trip, insinuating he only did after seeing both of their names on the sign up.

Arthur sighed silently to himself, "Callahan isn't here to keep an eye on us. Stop being paranoid." he wrote in a message to reply. Mr Callahan was a smart man and wouldn't dare to plot against them once more, or so he presumed.

As soon as Arthur put his phone back in his pocket, it vibrated again.

"That was quick." Arthur whispered to himself. As he pulled his phone back out of his pocket to take another glance.

It was Hannah, "Are you kidding me! Check up on him later and find out more. Update me!" she responded in the message; Arthur could hear the tone her voice from that message alone.

Why couldn't she just check Arthur thought, but then again. He wouldn't want to put anyone in harm's way if he knew that Callahan could be dangerous, and it made sense for him to check. It was weird, Arthur knew everything was okay since they had offered to be allies with Mr Callahan. There was no need to be worried, but it seemed that it was still an issue for Hannah.

"Here we are! At the top, there's a board with a list of smaller ramps and paths that we can take." Ellie exclaimed to the two boys. Following the routes with her finger.

She pulled out a printed map which had a route highlighted from Mr Roxham, which she had received earlier at the main foyer earlier and matched the route with the board.

As Ellie lead the two out of the ski lift zone towards the correct path she had worked out. Daniel turned back towards Arthur and signed a thumbs up. All of a sudden it made Arthur realise that he was *actually* the unintentional third wheel in this situation, he began to feel out of place.

"I suggest we all go down the mountain once, slowly to learn the route and then back up again to really try it out?" Ellie advised, "That's what the instructor said we should do anyway."

"That sounds a great idea actually, it makes sense." Daniel replied, "What do you think Arthur?"

Arthur looked up and around, they were high up as he peered down into the distance. This was going to take most of the day it felt. "I agree, but I think I'll let you two go ahead, I'll catch up at the bottom or something. I just want to take a while to take in the view." Arthur offered, giving Daniel the chance to be alone with Ellie and give himself a way out of being a third wheel.

"Man, are you sure?" Daniel asked, half-meaningfully.

"Yeah, of course." Arthur was sure, he wanted Daniel and Ellie to have a good time, and this would give him time to deal with Hannah's concern.

Ellie and Daniel began to walk on from the starting point of the trail, slowly treading through the thick snow in the distance.

This was a good time to seek out Mr Callahan, presumably at the bar, Arthur thought. "Actually," he interrupted the two walking away, a little louder, "I'll meet you guys later with the rest of the group, I'm happy to do this alone, is that cool?" he planned to take his time.

"Are you sure you don't want to meet us up at the bottom for the second run?" Ellie questioned Arthur, confused at his request.

"Naw, I might try and bump into Laura and see how she's doing." Arthur replied, using her as an excuse to go alone.

Agreeing, Ellie, and Daniel continued to make their way towards the starting flag of their trail. Deciding to give it sometime before he left, Arthur sat a further bit higher and closer to the edge nearby, looking into the vastness of the surrounding land around him. He watched the two arrive at the starting point, Daniel turned to look back and seek out where Arthur was. Arthur raised his thumb in the air to give him a go ahead, he really hoped Daniel had found someone he liked.

Arthur sat there thinking to himself, England never offered a view as beautiful as this, but then again it never offered him to come back to life and have many of these supernatural abilities that he shouldn't have in the first place. This truly was a new life that Arthur had begun to sink his efforts in. It felt like for once things were going well in the correct direction. Twenty minutes had passed, where he had spent that time thinking hard about what had happened since the start of living at Pennyview, to where he was now.

It was time to head down the mountain and give Hannah some closure that Mr Callahan was up to nothing out of the ordinary.

Arthur stepped through the thick snow to the start of the trail that Ellie and Daniel had followed, he paused and looked at the red flags. Why couldn't he go on the red trail? What was stopping him? he thought to himself.

He looked down the red trail.

Then looked around, there was no one stopping him, who would even know if he was a beginner in the first place.

Yes, it may have higher ramps or steeper drops, but he was alone and could use some of his supernatural side to have fun. "Only here once, might as well enjoy it." he muttered to himself.

He began to walk towards the red trail and clip his feet into the snowboard. Arthur started to glide towards the trail's beginning. Catching some speed and discovered the turns were more narrow, easier for someone with skiing equipment for sure. Dodging between the trees and staying within the track which had plastic fencing at parts to keep Arthur in lane. A ramp was looming upon him, he was ready. He glided into the ramp and launched into the air rigidly.

The view was fantastic, Arthur could see the hotel all the way down the mountain, but also the wilderness of the trees and snow either side.

He landed after gaining some air, stabilising from lowering to his knees as he continued to glide, continuing to follow the red trail further. The next ramp appeared which looked to be steeper, it aimed upwards into the clear blue sky. Arthur crouched, lower this time, to gain a bit more speed for this ramp, he was feeling a bit looser for this one.

What was the worst that would happen? A broken arm or leg, Arthur could fix that quickly, that's the least he could do, if he could recover from accidentally dying.

The ramp hastily approached, Arthur crouched lower and leapt from the bluff of the ramp. He reached in to grab his snowboard, twisting all the way round, before hitting the ground and rose from his knees. Arthur screamed involuntarily out loud in excitement, he had a knack for this... or his supernatural side did at least.

Arthur continued like this to the bottom of the slope, becoming less obvious as he got closer to the bottom, where he could still be sighted by his classmates or other members of the public. As he aimed towards the level area near the hotel lodging, he began to casually calm down to a simple descent. Arthur had stopped at the foot of the mountain, he checked his phone, it was an hour away until the class had to meet for food before the evening were to close on the first day.

This was a good time to find Mr Callahan and find out more. Arthur unclipped his feet from the snowboard and began to walk towards the hotel wading through the snow in search of him.

He dropped his snowboard at the rental hut, avoiding the sight of any students and teachers and began to make his way through the hotel and find the bar. Presuming that's where Mr Callahan would be hiding.

After asking a member of staff who worked at the resort where the bar was, who proceeded to give Arthur a strange and concerning look whilst pointing out the location of the bar. It wasn't far off from the main desk, but there were a few areas to relax and drink. Picking the first one, the closest obvious one from the main entrance. Through a great open archway there was a vast space, with an arrangement of tables dotted around the place. Neatly arranged with cutlery, napkins, and empty glasses upside down. Giant windows from floor to ceiling gave a wonderful view of the mountain side, allowing the clear blue sky to let the light into the space.

There he was, true to his word, he didn't travel far from the entrance at all. Mr Callahan were drinking at the bar sat upon a stool, hunched over with his drink in hand. Arthur walked over in the direction to Callahan, noticing he were engrossed in something, a book of some sort as he walked towards him at the side.

"Hello." was all that Arthur said, gaining the attention of him.

Callahan turned his head, took a moment, and then adjusted his posture sitting further back with a smile on his face looking more relaxed. He closed the book and gently slid it to the opposite side of him, flipping it cover face down, the back of it was blank giving nothing away.

Mr Callahan returned his greeting with a question, "Hey, how's it going Arthur? Enjoying the resort?"

He seemed normal; he seemed professional.

Arthur wasn't sure what Hannah was worried about, but maybe he should be direct with her concern and get to the end of it quickly.

Arthur thought how he could ask if Callahan were up to something, he couldn't start with off with that, holding off for a moment. "Great, I guess. What are you drinking?" he started with a short question, building up to it.

Callahan lifts his drinking glass in the air, held between his fingers from the top. He began to swirl it preciously "This here is a fine Hibiki, Japanese whisky." he stated proudly with a smile that grew.

Arthur knew that Hibiki was up there in the top list of whiskies, "I've only ever heard of it, never had some." he replied.

Callahan placed the glass down on the bar and slid it towards Arthur, slowly with two fingers pushing it. "Have a try, make sure none of the others are around first." he offered, his eyes also darting back and forth to the room to check.

Arthur looked around; he was confused. The look upon his face must've shown some distrust, unsure why the teacher would offer him a drink.

"It's not poisoned or anything Arthur. Who knows what would kill *you* anyway it seems." Callahan stated this time, his smile turned into a grin.

Arthur raised an eyebrow as he decided to sit down on the stool next to Callahan and picked up the glass with his left hand. He analysed it, tilting it ever so slightly watching the whisky tip to the edge of the glass.

"Why are you letting me have a drink?" Arthur asked, expecting a bit more of an answer to understand if he should try it.

"Well, you clearly aren't the age you're meant to be, and from England the drinking age is what? Eighteen?" Mr Callahan explained, "You're clearly older than the age of eighteen, from what I gathered earlier."

Arthur's concerning facial expression lowered, "Fair enough." raising the glass closer to his lips to take a sip, it tasted great. Arthur's expression changed to a surprising fulfilment; he felt his mood had changed.

Mr Callahan laughed, "Good right?" he stated as though it were a pure fact.

Arthur nodded agreeing wholeheartedly, sliding the drink back to Callahan's grasp. He knew he needed to ask the question that had been bugging Hannah, it was now or never getting around to it.

Arthur analysed Callahan on the spot, even he wasn't confident with his own trust in him, but he didn't feel he was a threat.

He had to get straight to the point, "Alright, I need to ask something, sir," starting formally, he paused to deeply inhale, "Hannah's worried that you're up to something on this trip."

Mr Callahan's expression froze, there was a pause of suspense, his brow furrowed for a second in a serious manner.

Callahan exploded into laughter and reached for his drink; he began to tap the rim of the glass with his finger. "I'm not here for you guys, well I mean I am." he stopped dramatically. Adjusting his focus to the glass, he tapped it and then back to look at Arthur. "If you knew half of the stuff that I did, you wouldn't let a class from your school go on a trip, to a place like this where kids can easily go missing. I can assure you and Hannah, I'm not a threat."

Arthur exhaled loudly in relief, he could finally message Hannah not to worry and settle that issue.

"Anyway, from what I understand, a stake to the heart didn't kill you. You're something else Arthur, something more sinister with dark magic." Callahan exposed with some disgruntlement. "I'm an expert in killing vampires and all sorts, but whatever you are I can only find out bits and even they're possibly rumours."

Arthur looked at him stunned, extremely curious.

"Hmm. You don't know what you are… do you? I mean I don't know a lot. But I have looked up bits." Callahan asked as he edged closer towards Arthur from his stool anticipating his answer. His eyes were closely examining Arthur's expression.

Mr Callahan stared at Arthur for a moment trying to figure if Arthur's expression of uncertainty was genuine, "You really don't have any clue, do you? Go get a seat over there, I think we both are gonna need a drink." Callahan instructed.

Arthur stood up from the stall and picked a table that was not in clear view of the large window within the room or in the doorway, one that was out of the way in a corner. Callahan returned moments later excitedly with two glasses of whisky, rattling with ice.

Callahan took a seat opposite and placed one of the glasses in front of Arthur. "How old are you really Arthur and what are you doing here? Here as in Lakebrook?" he fired the first few questions.

"Nineteen really." Arthur truthfully answered, then he proceeded to explain only few facts he knew. The facts that he had died and awoke at the beginning, to be then taken away by Hannah and to finish with explaining that he seems to come back to life no matter how he died. From what he had discovered so far throughout his experience.

"You've died that many times already? Wow, I sort of feel bad for staking you now." Callahan iterated again, "So why Lakebrook high?"

Arthur took a sip of his glass, it was a smooth whisky, nodding in approval as he placed it back on the table. "A second chance, I can't go back to England. So, if I get some grades over here, I guess I can live somewhat of a new normal life? Also, the witches that saved me live here anyway." Arthur returned the same question, "Mr Callahan, why are you here? In Lakebrook of all places?"

"I was hired to keep an eye here; this is my area to look after the supernatural balance." Callahan began to explain, moving onto that he had been hired by an anonymous organisation to kill any supernatural existence within Lakebrook and that's all he knew. He had come from a family lineage of supernatural hunters, who historically killed different types of supernatural beings.

"Aren't they going to come for you? Knowing you haven't done the job?" Arthur asked, a little feeling of worry began to creep in at the back of his mind.

"I told them that I had done the job, they aren't going to check, for a while at least. Until they hire someone new in my place. I like it here I'm going to take it slow in this nice town, it makes a big difference from Chicago. Where I used to live, by the way." Callahan added.

The question turned to what Arthur had wanted to know since he came back to life. "So, what am I, do you think?" he asked Callahan withholding himself in suspense.

Callahan took a drink and stared into the glass once more, tapping at the rim with his finger. "Everything supernatural derives from witches, casting spells to create other supernatural beings. With that, everything must be created within a balance. A weakness if you like. You're something that can't die, from what I've figured out so far as I tried to kill you like a vampire. Looking into it you don't abide by the normal supernatural balance."

Callahan took a sip of his drink. Arthur did the same whilst keeping eye contact with Mr Callahan, he was engrossed.

Was that all he knew? Arthur thought. A few words earlier came to mind. "What else? You said dark magic?" he asked further.

"Well, at some point in your life, or ancestors' life. You were spelled with some ancient dark magic so that you never die, never even age possibly. The confusing part is I don't really know what witch can do dark magic these days, in this century to that severity. So, *you* derive from something ancient, somehow. That's all I know." Callahan explained.

This answer still left Arthur with more questions and a daunting look of disappointment on his face, there wasn't much new from what Mr Callahan had said. Most of that was guesswork from what he had discovered since he had arrived at Lakebrook. Ageing was interesting, Arthur hadn't thought much about that at all, time hadn't passed enough for him to notice. Curiosity still lingered, the comment of ancient dark magic left him with more questions than answers.

"Look Arthur, that's as much as I know. I don't want to cause you anymore trouble, but you might want to ask whoever it was in your house who saved you... Did you ever think they may be holding onto some vital information?" Callahan suggested.

That was a good point, it couldn't harm in asking for a bit more information from Ethel or Myra, it would've been one of those who would've sent Hannah in the first place.

Arthur had one curious question left for Mr Callahan, "How did you know who's a witch and whatever? Now I know that vampires exist thanks to you."

Callahan reached into his pocket and pulled out the watch-like thing, the one he always looked at in his hand in class. He laid it on the table gently, facing upwards where the single hand in the middle kept spinning and stopping randomly at the same direction, it looked as though it was a compass of some sort.

"What is that?" Arthur was interested.

"An aura crystal compass, this detects supernatural beings and identifies what they are. Passed down from my father and from his." he explained as pointed to each section of the compass. "Witch, vampire, demon and a ghost."

"Demon? Ghost?" Arthur choked, inhaling; a few hairs tingled at the back of his neck. "And why does it spin around like that?" he pointed to the hand flicking away.

Mr Callahan let out a little chuckle, "That's because you're something else. Something else I'm not prepared for, or signed up to deal with."

Arthur let out a nervous laugh, he couldn't hold in asking about the other supernatural beings on the compass, he needed to know, "So, what is a ghost and demon?"

Mr Callahan points to the first icon, the ghost. "Okay, a ghost is almost like a witch, but back from the dead and they can possess people for a very long time. They can cast spells, but not to an intricate level as to a witch, as it would wipe out their ghostly existence using too much of their magic." Callahan proceeded to move his finger over to the demon section on the compass. "A demon, well they come in all sorts of ways, some can possess others while being in their own body. Some shapeshift to look like others, and some have unimaginable abilities, and they live forever, unless their spirit is cleansed in an exorcism. *They* are a pain to kill." explained Mr Callahan.

Arthur took a moment to digest the information he had just been delivered; it was somewhat scary to know there was other things out there that had so much power. "I have a few traits of a demon though? Abilities like strength and speed?" he questioned further.

"You're right, but the hand wouldn't spin round like that, like it's doing right now." Callahan corrected Arthur, tilting the face of compass to Arthur. "It would point to the demon section and stay there."

It was getting later in the hour, and it was time for Arthur to head back to the group. It was almost time for the class to get something to eat and settle down for the night. Arthur left Mr Callahan at the bar a while before they all had to regroup in the foyer, making it less obvious that they were at the bar together.

On his way back to the foyer to wait, Arthur messaged Hannah informing her that it was all fine. Mr Callahan seemed a decent guy from what Arthur had concluded from his drink with him.

The evening passed quickly, where the class ate and then had their own time for the evening. Most of the students headed to their rooms, tired from being up early in the morning, and from a day of intense activities.

Mr Roxham had mentioned to pack everything, reminding the class that they will be moving to a different location in the morning with some reasoning to make it easier to travel back home.

Montage

"Happy birthday!" a chant sung over Daniel in his bed. It was the morning of Daniel's birthday, everyone was there in the room early, Arthur was awake and had let the others in the room. They had all planned to wake Daniel up.

Daniel woke up in shock, slightly pale, then excitement filled his face. He began to cheer, "Seventeen, hell yeah! Thank you everyone! What a surprise!"

A few of the others had bought Daniel a little present, Arthur had bought him an American football team's jersey. He had no idea who the team was, but the green and white colour scheme seemed a good combination that suited him; Green seemed to be Daniel's colour of choice.

Laura and Ellie had bought him a gift voucher for shopping at TJ Maxx, maybe an insult to his fashion sense, which arguably had improved since.

Abel had bought the real present that seemed to hold the most value to Daniel, beers. Daniel seemed to be most excited for the beers more than anything.

Daniel worked his hand through his rucksack, "We can get a party started later." he said, proudly revealing the bottle of vodka.

"Nice!" Abel nodded in approval, snatching the bottle, and examining the label.

It was shortly time for the group to head downstairs and meet the teachers, ready for the day's plans, the girls left ahead to pack all their belongings in their room. Daniel scrambled to get dressed as Arthur packed what little he had unpacked in the first place.

"How was your day yesterday with Ellie anyway?" Arthur asked him whilst he waited for Daniel to finish up.

"Oh yea? Interested in Ellie, Dan?" Abel added.

Just the mention of Ellie's name brought a new kind of smile to Daniel's face. He stood there scratching the back of his head, smiling uncontrollably, "It was pretty great, I never really knew we got along so well, I've known her since kindergarten."

"Kindergarten?" Arthur asked.

"Small kid's school." Abel chipped in, "So is that a yes *or?*" he lingered verbally.

Daniel began to look awkward, on the spot. "Erm, I think so, she's really cool like." he was reservedly shy with his answer.

"It did seem you guys got along together really well, so I'd thought I should leave you to it yesterday." Arthur stated the obvious, showing support that the two together could be a good thing.

The three, all packed up with their belongings, carried them downstairs where some of the class had already gathered in the main foyer.

Mr Roxham, Miss Abigail, and a tired looking Mr Callahan were all waiting, checking student numbers.

"Pick up your itineraries here so you know what were up to today. It's a further a far trip today." Mr Roxham echoed over the class who were amid a chatter amongst themselves.

The three boys walked up to the girls where Arthur picked up one of the itinerary papers from Laura. It read southern hike, there was a picture printed of a map, which showed a line down from this hiking route to the Montage resort.

It looked like a dreadfully long hike.

"Alright split into partners, that will be the person you stick with during the hike." Mr Roxham ordered, "Meet us outside once you have picked, you have five minutes." he ordered, heading towards the doors to the outside.

There was a scramble of name calling as the students decided who to pick and who to betray. Arthur scratched his head, not really knowing who to pick, either his girlfriend, Daniel, or Abel.

Daniel leaned into Arthur and Abel and whispered, "Mind if I try and ask Ellie?" he asked.

This meant that Arthur should really pick Laura.

"Sure…" Abel let out a massive sigh in jest, "You're going with Laura also, Arthur?" he guessed.

Arthur nodded back with a shameless smile.

Arthur didn't mind at all; this solved his problem of choice for him. This meant he got to spend more time with Laura, to make up for yesterday dealing with other concerns.

All the class began to make their way outside in pairs, all lugging along their belongings in bags of all sorts. Outside the three teachers were waiting, who began to split into three hiking groups.

It was a brisk, chilly day for a walk, but that would be like every day in this place Arthur imagined. Arthur and Laura began to make their way down the snowy path following after their walking group, Laura looping her arm in between Arthur's arm, keeping close. This was a perfect time to get some gossip about Ellie, he wanted to know how she felt and he had the perfect person to find out.

"So, Ellie seemed to have a great time with Daniel yesterday, I even had to leave it got so awkward." Arthur humorously started off.

Laura laughed a little to herself, "She seemed to be really happy hanging out with him you know. You actually left them to it?" she asked.

Arthur keeping an eye on every step through the snow, nodded, "Yeah, I gave them a chance to get to know each other alone."

"Okay. What did you get up to leaving them to it?" Laura asked Arthur, she was curious.

"Oh, I went down another snowboarding route, took it easy and sat in the snow. Watching the mountain below around me." Arthur answered, not letting her know the full truth of what he had gotten up to.

Arthur wanted to pry more, turning the conversation back to finding out more about Ellie, "So do you think Ellie likes Daniel?" being blunt to the point.

"Erm, I think so, she wouldn't shut up at night talking about him and her day." Laura lightly joked, "She seemed to be smiling the entire time, she just wouldn't shut up."

"They do seem to get on well together, I think." Arthur had gotten his confirmation; he had the insight if ever Daniel was to ask. "Anyway! How was your day? I didn't ask."

Laura began to explain how yesterday was to Arthur, explaining all of the activities they got up to with the skiing group. The two kept walking and Arthur was listening to how Laura gradually got better at skiing yesterday.

The group had been walking for almost an hour and came to a stop, bundling the three groups together at a ski lift zone. A conversation could be heard between Mr Callahan and Mr Roxham.

"I just looked it up, this is a two hour walk, Gareth." Callahan called out Roxham informally. "It's only been an hour; these kids will be knackered by the time we even get down there."

Daniel overheard, wriggling his phone out of his pocket and began to look up the route to Montage.

"But it's the experience, Mr Callahan." Mr Roxham fired back in defence of his planned strenuous hike.

"Experience?! The kids walked for hours, in the cold. Without proper gear. Is that what you want them to say after they get home?" Callahan returned interjecting his comment.

The class were silent, Daniel nudged Arthur and showed him his phone with a map on it, it was one hell of a long walk.

"Someone has to say something?" Laura whispered leaning in to see Daniel's phone.

There was silence as the group looked between each other.

Abel nudged Arthur, "Art, you." was all he whispered looking at him.

Arthur had to chirp up now, if nobody else dared to, no one wanted to walk for another hour and desperately not even himself.

"I love your lessons Mr Roxham, but I think Mr Callahan is right. Another hour to walk isn't fun, especially with all our bags... And we want to enjoy this trip. Maybe the ski lift is a good choice?" trying to persuade him, slightly attempting to flatter.

Miss Abigail jumped at the offer, "We could leave it to a vote? Let the class decide." adding to the debate, full well knowing what the majority would want.

It was clear that none of the other teachers wanted to walk another hour, Mr Roxham was the only one.

Mr Roxham called for a vote, a show of hands to either walk the way or use the ski lift to get to Montage. The vote was called, and the majority of hands reached up in the favour of getting the ski lift. This meant that they had gotten more time to spend at the Montage resort at the expensive of a slightly grumpy Mr Roxham.

Groups began to herd into the ski lifts, trying to keep into their pairs as best as possible in each cart. Arthur managed to get into an elevator with his group of friends, sat squished next to Laura. The slow descend downwards to the bottom began. Arthur took a moment to take it all in, looking around the vast scenery around him. He hadn't seen anything like this in life, the mountain range, covered with snow and the trees that stretched on for miles, it was a breath-taking sight. Still thankful for not having to walk through it all in the cold.

His attention was directed to the friends around him, Jade, with Hannah and her two friends had made it into the elevator, Jade seemed to be fitting in with those girls easily.

Abel had clearly abandoned his partner, whoever that kid was earlier on this trip and was chatting to Daniel, Ellie, and Laura.

Arthur took a moment to look at all of those around him in the elevator, a giant wave of relief flowed through him. Watching all of them talk and laugh with each other was a great sight to see, Arthur enjoyed being a part of this group of friends, he felt lucky he had fallen into their social circle.

At that very moment he realised that things may have been very different if he hadn't been here, Hannah may have been dead, a few times over along with the rest of the house as he looked at her.

Moving his eyes along to the next person.

Daniel.

Daniel would still be his normal, reserved self. With an awful clothing sense, possibly still trying out for the Lakebrook Titans and *still* not qualify for the team. He may not have even been talking Ellie as a romantic interest.

Arthur looked towards Laura, who was chatting away with the other two. Arthur looked her up and down in thought. He wouldn't have been with Laura, and she may still be her quiet self, which hadn't changed much anyway since they had gotten serious. But the two had grown a connection that worked well, although they were still new to each other and at the early stages of their relationship.

It was strange how things have turned out so far and how very different things could dangerously be.

But.

It wasn't like that. Everything was great.

Arthur smiled to himself, looking like an idiot of his own internal joke staring at the others around him.

Hannah caught his silent expression and pulled a strange inquisitive face, raising her eyebrow. Arthur realised he was grinning, widely. Casually closing his mouth to a small smile and nodded in return to Hannah, breaking eye contact to return staring out of the window towards the mountainside.

"Finally! We're here!" roared Daniel, as the lift made it into the docking station at the foot of the slope.

There were a few cheers among the cabin.

Montage looked amazing as they stepped out the cart, it was a giant lodging resort, like a village, wooden cabins all littered the valley where snow had covered many of the roofs. Chimneys blew smoke throughout the view, lights hung throughout the main path towards the resort's entrance, all switched on even in the brightness of this sunny day.

Mr Roxham and some of the class had already begun to gather outside the lift hut, as the group got closer to the class, they could begin to hear what he had to say.

There was a sense of buzzing excitement in the air from the students.

"Five hours, go check in first with Miss Abigail. Then the resort is yours to discover. Don't forget to fill in your field reports, take a copy, take a copy!" Mr Roxham began to give them out frantically. "Five hours, check in, field report done then you are welcome to go on any ski routes or enjoy the resort." repeating himself partially.

Laura ran up to the teacher collecting multiple copies of the reports for the others, they would need to fill in for the social studies trip. Walking up towards the main entrance of Montage, Arthur noticed that Mr Callahan was checking the compass in his hand. Catching his glance, the classic Mr Callahan's face gave nothing away.

All of the students were based within the giant hotel at the centre of the resort, keeping them away from the lodgers who had rented a holiday cabin further out. After checking in their bags and getting their room keys, to dumping their bags in the rooms barely unpacking. Daniel and Arthur made their way to meet the others in one of the hotel's meeting rooms which had been allocated for their school. Lakebrook was scrawly drawn on a standing noticeboard outside the double doors.

The teachers were in the room already with some other students who were all sat, gathered round some desks hastily writing up their answers on the field report. It was clear some of the students were rushing the report to get out and enjoy their free time.

There was a discussion already at the top of the group as Daniel and Arthur arrived. Split between wanting to do the field report first for the trip and to view the resort after to have fun or the other way around. An agreement finalised to where they would spend one hour rushing the report and then explore the resort for the rest, Daniel made it clear throughout that he needed to buy soft drink for the get together later in the evening. The group had planned to eat at one of the restaurants first, then back to a room to drink a little bit in celebration of Daniel's birthday, out of sight of any concerning adults.

"Why don't we do the work in one of the seating areas where people relax and plan to work on different questions? Getting this report done quicker." Abel smartly offered to the group.

All of them agreed, leaving the meeting room to find their way towards any seating area around the resort where they could concentrate.

The group carried on where they found a seating area, it was open and light with glass windows surrounding it. A giant table near the middle of the room with empty metal food trays, a buffet table; it was the breakfast room of the resort. The view looked upwards to the mountain but this time through a dense forest, where some visitors could be seen skiing.

The five of them, Daniel, Abel, Ellie, Laura, and Arthur all scrambled to some seats, moving them to surround a table, they began to run through the report for the trip and share answers. Making the group efficient at completing the report as fast as possible.

Half an hour had passed, Mr Callahan walked into the room, compass in hand by his wayside. Noticing the group, he walks over stuffing the compass into his pocket. It was clear to

Arthur he was checking for something, but his face continued to give nothing away.

"How's the field report going?" he asked.

A few glances of who were to talk first were exchanged. "It's going great sir; we're getting through it." Laura voluntarily pointed out.

Mr Callahan nodded and peered over at each of the papers on the table, "Looks good, looks good. I'm sure Mr Roxham will be pleased. Make sure you don't wonder too far away from the resort after you've handed those in." Callahan began to turn and walk off.

That felt like a sly warning that only Arthur could interpret.

"Do we hand it to you, sir?" Daniel asked, interrupting Callahan from walking away.

Looking over his shoulder, "Nope, I don't want it. Find Roxham." Mr Callahan answered, "Or just leave it in your room…" he finished with quietly, continuing his departure out of the dining room.

Arthur thought that this were a good moment to catch him before he was out of sight. "One minute I need to ask him something." he said to his friends as he got out of his chair to catch him up before he left out of sight.

"Sir." Arthur stopped Mr Callahan.

"What is it, Arthur?" Mr Callahan replied, keeping that tone of authority.

Arthur somewhat lowered his voice, "You keep checking your compass? Need help with anything?" he offered.

Mr Callahan, gently shook his head with a smile, "No it's alright." matching the level of Arthur's voice, "I would just keep inside the hotel when it gets dark, if I were you."

"All right? Let us know if you need us." Arthur nodded as Mr Callahan continued to leave.

"Oh, don't bother with the field reports, Roxham isn't going to check them, he's one of the worst teachers in school. Just hand in a poor attempt and miss out your name, he probably won't even check them off by names if so many are missing." Callahan insighted before departing into the winding rooms of the resort.

Arthur laughed to himself slightly, making his way back to the table.

Sat back at the table, Laura turned towards Arthur and directed a question at him "Is he not weird?" she asked.

"Who Mr Callahan?" Arthur clarified, even though he knew who she was asking about.

"Yes." Daniel added.

"Naw, he's an alright guy, he's strict but actually he helped me pass the writing essay many weeks ago." Arthur stated, defending Mr Callahan.

"Hmm weird, I suppose that's just how he is from his previous school." Laura replied.

"Strict as a dictator?" Abel pitched in.

"Strict, just strict Abel." Laura corrected, before looking back down at her report to carry on.

The truth of the matter is that Mr Callahan did help Arthur with his English work, but also it cost him being staked in the heart, murdered, and dumped in the cold woods, but that was a thing of the past now.

All was well and is forgiven.

The group had finished their reports and made their way back to the meeting room, which was empty. There was a tray with some reports in it already on top of one of the tables. Presumably the teachers had given up waiting and had left to enjoy the resort themselves.

Arthur had barely filled in his report and looked through the few in the tray.

He saw Hannah's report, it looked great.

She had clearly not done this report herself and had gotten someone else to do it. Arthur looked over his shoulder to see where the others were, looking back he stretched over the table clutching at a rubber.

Rubbing out Hannah's name, Arthur wrote his own and switched the two reports over. He laughed to himself, "This'll get her back for the whole making me look like an idiot back home."

The next few hours of the day the group did a range of activities that involved shopping, drinking, and bowling. Daniel had enjoyed the daytime, especially when the group let him win at bowling, but it was the evening that he most looked forward to.

He was inseparable from Ellie since yesterday, something had clicked between the two and everyone had noticed it. It was clear they both had a thing for each other.

The evening was drawing in, and the group were dressing nicely to have dinner in one of the classier restaurants of the resort. The girls had emphasised on how they had to dress up smartly, it was an important factor for Daniel's birthday meal at the restaurant.

The three boys were all getting changed in Daniel and Arthur's room. Daniel and Abel were in front of the bathroom mirror, Arthur walked into the bathroom with a formal shirt on, with a tie he was just about to fasten around his neck.

Abel paused buttoning up his shirt, "Are you going to prom or something?" he asked Arthur with his eyes fixed on him, especially on the tie.

"Prom? This is smart wear, right?" Arthur asked. "This is what we would normally wear for something like this, where I'm from, I mean."

"It's fine, looks smart." Daniel complimented. "I'm sure the girls, and Laura will appreciate it."

Maybe ties weren't a big thing here, not having to wear one most days during school, like Arthur had to when he was their age. Still, Arthur kept the tie, he might as well look smart for a formal dinner.

Daniel began to muck around with his hair in front of the mirror, ruffling it and flopping it back before asking Arthur a question, "Do you mind if I can get the room alone tonight? Even just for a bit?"

Abel made a vomiting sound as he left the bathroom, into the bedroom.

Arthur grinned. "Yeah of course, I'll sort out where to go. Abel?" Thinking the only option was either Abel or Laura's floor.

"Yeah, sure thing," Abel called out from the other room. He popped his head back into the bathroom, looking at Daniel and Arthur through the mirror, he couldn't hold in the question, "Are you going to try something on with Ellie?" he screeched with high pitched excitement.

Arthur laughed out loud as he began to secure his tie, knotting it in front of the mirror.

"Shh!" Daniel hissed, like the girls would hear Abel's question from any room where they would be in this giant hotel. "Well, no. I'm not saying I am, but I'd like to see where this goes man and maybe ask her out." he sounded hopeful.

"I'll crash on your floor then Abel." Arthur demanded.

"I said yeah already, Art. That's cool. We gotta go shortly guys. We're going to be late." Abel reminded them all in the bathroom as he retracted his head back around the door.

There were different restaurants throughout the resort, all with typical themes. The three managed to remember the one they had needed; the girls were already sat at the table waiting.

As they got closer to the table, it was clear the girls had gotten ready and had paid a great effort in dressing up. His eyes magnetised to Laura, she looked great, wearing a purple fading to pink dress with her hair floating down over her collar to one side. Her fringe just flicked classically over her eye, like how she always wore it.

Arthur sat down opposite her. "You look nice." he complimented.

Laura smiled shyly, "Thank you, you look smart yourself."

"You look nice also, Ellie." Daniel, recycling Arthur's compliment.

Abel let out an exaggerated groan, "I know you've got a boyfriend, but you look nice Jade."

Jade laughed in response, "Why thank you Abel, you look erm… nice I suppose."

From ordering the food, to getting the meal on the table. Dinner at the restaurant had come and gone quickly, the evening drew into the night where it was time to hang out in one of their rooms.

Abel had offered to hold the get together at his room. Where a small arrangement of drinks was laid out on the dresser by the wall. Oddly sat around the small hotel room, either on one of the beds, the chair and on the floor, the group drank and socialised.

Later into the night, Daniel had gone to use the bathroom, the girls scrambled through a backpack one of them had carried around for the night. Which presumably had some soft drinks, snacks, and whatever else girls carried around with them. Ellie pulled out a small cake and began to frantically unpack it, pinning a candle in it that needed to be lit.

Laura rushed to the switch the light off within the room, preparing the darkness for the birthday cake surprise.

As the toilet door opened, the light switched off and the group began to chant happy birthday to Daniel. It was cute that the girls had prepared that for him, it was understood that they celebrated each other's birthdays like this in the group.

Daniel's face lit up vibrantly as he saw the cake and lit candle.

"Make a wish!" Laura insisted, stopping him from blowing out the candle prematurely by blocking it with her hand.

Daniel paused for a moment and a smile drew over his face, blowing the candle out with a lasting smile.

"What'ya wish for?" Jade asked after the small cheering had ended.

Daniel laughed, "You know I can't tell you. It won't come true."

The group continued to be cheerful and drink more of the vodka Daniel had bought, mixing it with whatever soft drinks they had purchased earlier in the day.

It began to get later into the night, and it was clear with a couple of exchanged yawns.

"Alright I think it's time for you all to head off, my weird roommate will be back soon." Abel explained to everyone.

Everyone began to get gather their belongings and gather outside Abel's hotel room quietly to not bring any unwanted attention, Daniel tapped Arthur on the shoulder as he waited.

He leaned in.

"I'm gonna go for a walk with Ellie man, I'll be back later. Might ask her you know." Daniel whispered.

Arthur raised his thumb up by his side out of sight, finally Daniel had prepared to make a move.

As all of them walked down the hallway, Daniel and Ellie announced that they were to split off to walk around the resort together.

"Alright I'll walk you girls to your rooms then." Arthur directed at Laura and Jade.

Arthur, Laura, and Jade all continued walking, it was silent now the other two had separated.

"How have you been getting on staying with Hannah? Jade." Arthur asked, breaking the silence, it's all he could come up with.

"It's been interesting, she does talk a lot, doesn't she?" Jade pointed out. "Oh, and she spends ages on her make up and I thought I did." she then laughed to herself.

Hannah did take care in her appearance, but Arthur had gotten used to that whenever he had to wait on her.

As the three got to the first door, Jade's door, she began to unlock it and head in. Arthur kept an ear out, there was no sign that Hannah was there. She must be out with the other girls or asleep by now. He hadn't really heard much from Hannah over the day.

After saying goodnight to Jade, the two continued further down to Laura's room, stopping outside her door.

There was a moment of silence.

"Well... Here I am." Laura said. "I... erm, never mind" she stopped.

Arthur scrunched his facial expression, "What's up?" he wondered.

"I want you to come in, but I'm nervous." she just about managed to say.

He really wanted to spend the night with Laura, but he didn't know what Daniel was up to with Ellie and this wasn't really the time to take any next step. "It's fine, Ellie might be back soon." he said with a smile, "Anyway. Maybe we can hang out overnight when we're not on a school trip without sharing rooms with others." Arthur added, smiling away.

Laura smiled and pulled herself closer to Arthur and kissed him, lasting for a moment before the two departed ways for the night.

Arthur decided it was now best to make his way back through the hallway to Abel's room, walking back he gleamed with a smile. It was nice knowing Laura was ready for the next step, but Arthur needed to be sure.

Sure of her, and sure of himself.

With one step in front of the other, the silence of the hotel was harrowing, it was surprising that there were no teachers patrolling to keep an eye out for the students.

Arthur knocked at Abel's room; Abel opened the door. "Cool to sleep on your floor?" he asked.

"Yeah, it's cool man, my roommate's back." Abel mentioned as he stepped aside for Arthur to come into the room. "Keep it down." he continued to whisper.

Arthur tried to make himself comfortable on the floor from the single pillow that Abel had given him, it was rough and uncomfortable. He laid there, wide awake wondering how much time had already passed, he couldn't fall asleep.

Through the unbearable struggle of trying to get comfortable, Arthur was saved. His phone lit up with a notification.

Unexpected, it was a message from Hannah, "Drink at the bar?" was all it read.

Checking the time at the top of the screen, it was just before midnight. It was a message out of the blue, but Arthur thought he should see if she was all fine. Anything to escape this uncomfortable floor. He replied that he would be down within a few minutes.

He sat up and began to sneakily shuffle out of the room, slowly turning the door handle to allow himself out. Preciously closing the door behind him stealing Abel's door key off the side, praying that he hadn't awoken Abel and his weird roommate.

As Arthur traced his way down to the hotel's bar, he could see her sat alone, whilst the bartender worked away behind the bar.

He walked up to Hannah. "Hey, everything okay?" Arthur asked.

Hannah looked at Arthur quietly for a moment, confused to why he was dressed up.

"Yeah, all fine, you actually look fit? I mean smart?" she complimented, brushing her previous comment away.

Arthur just realised the compliment was about the clothes he was still wearing from dinner. "Oh yeah, thanks. Dan's birthday meal." Arthur sat himself next to Hannah on the stool, "We all had to dress up nice for it."

"Looking good. Alright, what are you having? The bartender, erm, Dennis, was it? Is feeling generous tonight, with free drinks for us only." Hannah explained, she had clearly cast a spell on the poor guy. He was probably meant to go home by now.

"Yes," the bartender spoke, "what would you like buddy?" he continued in a monotoned voice.

"Fair enough." Arthur turned away from Hannah to face the bartender, proceeding to order his drink.

"This trip isn't so bad, but I can't wait to be back in my own bed." Hannah mentioned, whilst Arthur waited for his drink.

"I know what you mean, I just want to have my own bed again, without Daniel being there." Arthur agreed.

Hannah took a sip of her luminous green drink. "Oh! Jade!" she remembered, "She keeps trying to slide in questions about you, is she obsessed with you or anything?" Hannah said in an annoyed manner.

"Uhm, like what?" Arthur asked nervously, unsure of what she had said.

Hannah placed her glass down on the bar, "Like, what do you get up to at home? What it's like living with you? Ever seen you walk around topless or workout? I mean, topless is the least I've seen." Hannah laughed, slapping Arthur on the leg.

"How much have you drunk? That is a bit weird though I guess." Arthur said slowly, was that all she mentioned he wondered.

"I've not drank enough!" Hannah exclaimed cheerfully holding her glass out in front of her. It was clear she'd drank a few before Arthur had gotten there.

"Here's your drink sir." said the bartender, Dennis, as he slid over Arthur's drink.

Arthur placed his hand around the glass, "Thank you." he replied, turning back to Hannah, "Was that all? General stuff like that?"

Hannah seemed to hold back another piece of vital information, but only for a brief moment before being herself, unable to hold it in. "Well, she told me you kissed her, a while back." then letting out a bit more of a giggle. "You kept that one quiet, didn't you?!"

Arthur's eyes widened, "She kissed me! She kissed me!" he detested, lowering his voice, repeating himself. "She was drunk and basically kissed me! I remember clearly because I had to go back into the house to get Daniel's phone. I was fine."

"Whoa! Relax, you got a little defensive there. Like anyone cares anyway." Hannah added, "High school crap huh?" she questioned rhetorically.

They continued to enjoy more of their drinks and ordered another, reflecting how busy the school trip really was and what they had gotten up to.

A voice made them both jump, "Well, well, what are you two up to?" it came from behind them.

Arthur and Hannah simultaneously looked behind, somewhat startled, it was Mr Callahan.

There was a sense of relief, it wasn't any of the other two teachers. Being caught with alcoholic drinks in hand on a school trip would mean trouble, then again, Hannah could just spell away their memory.

"Up late, are we?" Callahan asked.

Hannah smirked, "Quick drink before bed." full well knowing Callahan couldn't and presumably wouldn't do a thing.

Mr Callahan placed his hands in his pockets and walked towards them, proceeding to take a seat at the bar next to the two. "One for me please, whisky on the rocks. Any of the good kind." Callahan placed his finger in the air ordering. He let out a massive sigh of relief, "Well, that's the vampire problem solved." he mentioned, particularly proud of himself.

Arthur and Hannah both looked at him, Hannah more so confused than Arthur. Arthur knew that Callahan was up to something the whole time, even though his face gave nothing away.

Lowering her voice, "There were vampires here?" Hannah asked as her eyes scoped the immediate area.

"Yup, not anymore though." Callahan answered, reaching out for Arthur's drink, then proceeding to take a sip without permission, impatiently waiting for his own.

Arthur glared at Mr Callahan as he placed Arthur's drink back on the bar, nodding at Arthur in gratitude. "Were they even a threat to us?" he asked.

"I'm not sure, but a school trip in the mountains. It would be an easy excuse for kids to go missing, so why let something happen if I can prevent it beforehand?" Callahan justified. "Vampires should all be killed, anyway."

Arthur just shook his head, "Can't argue with that logic I suppose." firmly grabbing his drink and returning it closer to his reach away from Callahan.

"They just want to feed and manipulate." Callahan added. "They're good for nothing, damn vampires." he sneered.

After Callahan received his drink the two left shortly after, saying goodnight noticing it was getting into the second hour after midnight. Leaving Mr Callahan to drink on his own at the bar, returning to their rooms in the resort. They were silent as they made their way stealthily through the halls towards the elevator. As Arthur and Hannah stepped into the elevator. Arthur pushed the floor number on the elevator's panel, "Thank you, by the way." feeling like he could speak in the elevator.

Hannah looked confused, turning towards him "For what?" she asked.

Arthur looked at Hannah, "For getting me onto this trip in the first place, it's been great. So, thank you."

Hannah stood there silently, with a glimmer of a smile.

He noticed her ego grow as though it were an act of greatness. "Oh! And thanks, by the way for the report." Arthur grinned, dragging her ego back down.

The soft smile from Hannah's face suddenly changed "The report?" she asked sharply in a serious tone.

"I saw your report on the pile in the meeting room, decided to swap our names over." Arthur gloated, absolutely proud of himself for pulling that move.

The reaction from Hannah was disappointing, Arthur was in fact expecting more of an outburst from her.

She was calm in her reply, "You're welcome, Roxham wasn't going to check them anyway?" she mentioned as she regained her complexion looking in the elevator mirror.

"How did you know that? Did Mr Callahan tell you?" Arthur sounded surprised.

"Callahan? Everyone knows that Mr Roxham doesn't really mark the student's work anyway. It's like a fact, anyway if he does give me a bad grade…" Hannah looked up to the ceiling of the elevator, "I'll just *witchy woo* a better grade." air quoting the words as she kept her eyes upwards.

Arthur just stared at Hannah, in amazement, she had not a care in the world. He let out a short laugh, keeping his eyes focused on her.

Typical Hannah.

Hannah looked back down from the ceiling and directly at Arthur, "I know, I'm great." she began to laugh at her self-proclaimed greatness.

She was unstoppable to her own standards.

"You're certainly something, alright." Arthur joked, as the elevator doors opened.

They were on the same level as the rest of the student's rooms, as they stepped out the elevator, they were quiet again. The only sound heard was each of the steps that they took.

The two stopped out front of Hannah's room, "Well this is me, thanks for meeting me for a drink." she whispered.

"Thank you to, we probably should have hung out more during this trip." Arthur whispered back, realising it had actually been pleasant.

Arthur pulled his hands out of his pockets and offered to hug Hannah goodnight.

Hannah looked puzzled, unexpecting a hug, "Why not?" she shrugged and placed her arms around him.

A calm feeling overwhelmed Arthur.

They held on to each other.

They both were lost in that short moment, it felt like it lasted longer than it should've, as Hannah reached around Arthur gripping tighter. He held her close as she rested her head under his chin.

The two let go of each other, Arthur could feel her hair tickle across his face as she moved away.

She looked at him as she stepped back, as though she had forgotten how she would normally act. They took a second to compose themselves, exchanging uncertain looks.

"Erm. Goodnight." Hannah quickly spoke, before abruptly retreating behind her door.

The door closed, leaving Arthur alone facing the door in the hallway. He turned slowly, trying to understand what he felt from that hug between the two of them. Quietly walking back to Abel's room, around the corner out of sight, he stopped. He stood there completely still in the hallway, taking in his surroundings. Still lost in thought of that hug, he took a deep breath and smiled to himself.

"Maybe it was nothing, not a bad trip at all." he spoke softly, nodding to himself, "I really want my own bed."

Falling out

Summer had begun, it was extremely hotter this side of the world, the heat continued throughout the day and all night long. The sun hung high in the clear blue sky, barely a cloud in sight for many of the days that passed. School was in session, and it was already halfway through the final semester.

Practice was in full swing at the Lakebrook High School playing field, the Titans were relentlessly practicing their skills and working together seamlessly as one. There was a massive improvement from the team's performance since the new players had joined.

The cheerleading squad were practicing at the side of the field, repeating routines and movements in preparation for the Gridiron school championship, that's if the Titans qualified.

Coach Decker was out in full force, calling out the players to *"pick it up"* and to *"push harder"* as his famous lines of motivational leadership.

The season of the high school championship will begin in September, during Arthur's senior year, but there was one more obstacle before Lakebrook could enter the championship. The team needed to pass a qualifying match against another school later this month to get on the championship's ladder.

As Arthur sat on the grass by the bench, taking a breather sipping some water, looking across the field he could see almost everyone was practicing hard. It was clear that this qualifier coming up meant a lot to the team, especially Coach Decker and the current seniors.

There was one player who stuck out the most as Arthur analysed the players further out on the field, left to right.

His attention halted at Daniel, who was practicing on the field, and it was clear he was the one with the least motivation of them all. Arthur sat there for a few minutes as he observed him throw the football poorly, back, and forth to another player.

Daniel had been seeing Ellie since the trip to the mountains, he seemed to have changed Arthur witnessed gradually, not in an entirely bad way. It seemed as though Daniel took his studies less seriously and his efforts within the Lakebrook Titans had simmered, he seemed disconnected from everything else since he began to see her. It was his first girlfriend from what was understood, Arthur was sat wondering if that was the factor that divided his attention away from other important matters.

A figure appeared the at the corner of Arthur's vision, trudging across the field. It was an angry Andrew Carver, paving his way towards Daniel, stomping furiously with every step he took. The quarterback looked certainly annoyed and began to grill him from what he could see way back over at the bench.

It must've been clear to others that Daniel's performance wasn't his best lately.

Arthur attentively rose up from his feet, preparing to walk over in a faster approach. He could see on Daniel's expression he was getting a telling off and it began to look furious from Andrew's hand gestures. He started to stride quicker, getting close enough he could just about hear what Andrew was saying.

"Less than a month away from qual! And you've been giving us this shitty performance the last month?!" he was screaming and pointing vigorously at Daniel's chest.

Uncontrollable testosterone seemed to be at a peak level for Andrew and like many others here at practice, he began to get physical by prodding at Daniel repeatedly, more and more aggressively.

Daniel's tolerance had enough, it was short lived, he leaned in aggressively and pushed Andrew back.

Arthur started to sprint towards the two.

Andrew, who stumbled backwards a few steps, managed to regain his balance, and lunged at Daniel, taking them both down towards the ground.

That push was all Andrew needed to turn over the testosterone in his body, fuelling his anger.

Andrew was seriously pissed, raising his fist in the air whilst pinning Daniel below in between his legs, preparing to indefinitely take a swing or two. Daniel raised his hands prematurely to cover his face, expecting to get a beating.

Daniel froze for a moment in fearful suspense to receive the first hit from Andrew, but nothing happened.

He opened his eyes.

Arthur stood above them both, standing up behind Andrew. Locking Andrew's arm back, with his arm woven through Andrew's bicep, keeping it immoveable. Arthur leaned back and stepped away, pulling Andrew off Daniel using his supernatural strength, dragging him up to his feet.

Arthur let go of Andrew. He quickly turned around to face who had effortlessly moved him off, with a face full of wrath.

"Enough!" Arthur shouted, pointing at Andrew.

At this moment a large collection of those on the field had stopped what they were doing, staring at the conflict that was unfolding.

"What?! You gotta problem to?!" Andrew leaned in close to Arthur's face, shouting with ferocity. Andrew slapped Arthur's finger out the way and tried to push him with both hands, Arthur didn't budge and just stared at him. Not letting the situation turn even uglier, thoughts began to bleed through his mind, the supernatural instinct inside him wanted to hurt Andrew.

Arthur stared intensely at Andrew, ignoring whatever the instinct in his mind wanted.

It was clear Andrew wasn't thinking clearly. "Enough! Stop!" Arthur shouted, repeating some more.

Daniel began to clamber to his feet, shaken from realising what had just happened.

Chad came running over, "Go cool off both of you!" he demanded forcefully using his authority as team captain.

Andrew looked Arthur dead in the eyes, rage fuelled within him. "You want to protect this pathetic excuse of a player?! He's going to let us down!" he announced out loud. Before storming away towards the locker room.

"You! Bleachers." Chad struck out his arm and pointed towards Daniel, then sharply directed it towards the bleachers.

Daniel began to wallow slowly towards the bleachers in his mud-stained football uniform, from being pinned to the ground.

"Nice work Arthur, you split that up making it look like it was easy. Andrew's ego must be hurt." Chad chuckled, then his tone changed to be more serious, "I'm going to ban them both from practice for the next week."

Arthur thought for a second, taking off his football helmet, "Let me sort Dan out and tell him, it'll be easier to talk to me, you can get Andrew." he offered, thinking the news would be better coming from him rather than Chad.

"Andrew will calm eventually. That's a good idea. Go talk to Daniel, you know how to talk to him, that's co-captain material right there." Chad agreed, jokingly.

Arthur had no intention of being co-captain, if anything it meant that he would be co-captain to Andrew at this rate when they graduate into their senior year. That would be some daily nightmare he would have to live through, that's even if Andrew would keep him as co-captain as soon as the succession of captain would be placed onto him.

Arthur began to walk over to Daniel, helmet in hand. A few students on the field were still watching Arthur, paused from their activities. Arthur noticed Hannah, who was mingled in with the cheerleading squad, she was watching him with folded arms. He wondered if that look on her face was a judgemental one against his actions stopping the scuffle.

Approaching the bleachers, Arthur thought how he could deliver the news, but mostly he wanted to find out what the whole lack of effort was all about; to address it. As he got closer, he could see Daniel clearly feeling sorry for himself, staring at his feet sat on the bleachers a few rows up from the bottom.

Arthur sat down next to Daniel and placed his helmet beside him on the seat, "Well, that was fun. Are you okay?" he began the conversation.

"Yeah..." Daniel spoke softly, still fixed downwards to his feet.

Arthur waited for a moment; he wasn't going to get any more out of him unless he continued to talk himself.

"Look, Chad said to take a week off from practice and come back with more energy." Arthur stated, "It's clear that something's up and not letting you put much effort into practice, even I can see it." he added.

Daniel raised his head from his hands and looked at Arthur, "You can? What's that supposed to mean?" his expression changed to appear agitated.

"Well..." Arthur paused, it seems like you don't have as much enthusiasm for the sport right now and to be fair, a lot of other subjects and other things." Arthur tried to begin explaining.

He was cut off.

"What's that all supposed to mean man?!" Daniel questioned, sounding as though he were becoming more ticked off by the second.

Arthur took a split second to decide if he should leave it or carry on trying to explain.

He chose the latter.

"I mean, since you've been involved with other things, you've been a little more distracted on stuff that matters?"

Arthur questioned, instantly regretting the words as soon as they left his mouth.

Daniel stood up with haste, "Other things? You mean ever since I got in a relationship with Ellie?" he was clearly annoyed.

Arthur looked upwards to Daniel, "Well, yeah. I think you need to still remember to put effort into other things?" again poorly choosing his words, with a second wave of regret.

"Oh, and you and Laura have the perfect relationship?" Daniel's voice became louder, "Does she know that you and Jade kissed?" he targeted him, still unable to keep the sound of his voice under control.

"Why would you bring that up?" Arthur asked, trying to keep the tone of his voice calm, not trying to catch anymore unwanted attention.

Arthur's questions had gotten under Daniel's skin, "I also heard from Jade that you were caught hanging out with Hannah late in the morning, thanking her for a drink." Daniel continued, "So yeah, you seem to be perfectly fine with Laura aren't you man. So! Screw you with your advice!" Daniel stormed off the bleachers towards the car parking lot, hiding his bright red face of frustration.

Stunned, Arthur spent a few more seconds sitting on the bleachers, processing what had just happened in silence.

He looked up, there were some faces still looking over in an earshot's distance. Some of those could've heard what inaccurate gossip had just been revealed.

Arthur instantly looked back down at his own feet, he felt slapped in the face, mentally from the overdramatic response of Daniel.

A blown-out proportion of events that weren't even true and more painfully, Daniel essentially his best friend had just fallen out with him. The anger inside Arthur was frothing to the brim, he tried to hold it in as he focused on his feet. The instinct inside him tickled at the back of his mind, coming back in to wrestle over his consciousness.

"Why now." he said to himself, trying to fight it off. Stopping it, only allowing a fraction to leak through.

He had to let out, it was a raging pressure building up inside of him. It needed to be released.

Arthur stood up, taking his helmet in his hand, gripping it ever so tightly. He raised the helmet in the air and swung it into the bleacher's rail.

As it collided with the metal bleacher post, parts broke off the helmet's sturdy exterior. "*Argh!*" Arthur shouted in frustration before walking off down the side of the pitch towards the locker room and calm himself down and out of sight.

Hannah jogged over to Arthur in a slight haste, catching him walking down the side of the playing field, "Everything okay Arthur?" she asked concerned.

Arthur blinded with his gaze locked onto the grass, looked up at Hannah and replied nastily out loud without thinking "I think you've done enough."

He continued to walk, looking around him he noticed that others were still watching around the field. His eyes stopped at Coach Decker, stood with a group of players, staring at Arthur. Decker, shaking his head slowly in disapproval gripping at his clipboard close to his chest.

Hannah stood there, confused. "What have I done?" she questioned quietly as she watched Arthur walk away.

Entering the locker room, Arthur was still full of anger mixed with embarrassment, he figured it would be best to just go home and cut practice short.

Andrew was sat on the bench in the locker room, feet up by his chest, leaning against the wall. Arthur began to take off his sports gear and get changed, slinging what gear he had on the dressing bench.

"Come to tell me off about hitting your boyfriend?" Andrew snidely commented.

It was a comment Arthur didn't need, already trying to keep whatever rage he had in control. A tingling chill rolled down his spine, "Why don't you get it out of your system, come take a swing." he grinned menacingly, the words involuntarily jumped out of his mouth.

Andrew sprung off the bench to his feet and walked up close to Arthur, leaning in *real* close to his face. The expression in Andrew seemed to change back to how he was on the field minutes ago, tapping back into the testosterone he almost had settled away.

"Go on, I dare you, thinking you're hot stuff." Arthur continued to provoke him. "Take a swing." he sneered.

Andrew took no more hesitation to accept that invitation, he brought back his arm, his hand clenched into a fist and swung at Arthur's face. Arthur closely watched Andrew's fist, leaning back to dodge the swing, clenching his fist in return, and swung back at Andrew. Contacting the side of Andrew's face, he stumbled backwards, hunched ever so slightly holding his face.

Blood showed through Andrew's teeth as he gritted them with rage, he ran at Arthur trying to clasp at his shirt. Arthur returned the grip to Andrew's shirt and reversed the power swinging him into the lockers behind himself with ease.

An ear catching bang was heard as Andrew collided with the lockers before falling onto the floor. It didn't take long for students to run from the outside into the locker room in search of the sound, shocked of what they had walked into.

Andrew was pushing himself up, facing downwards to the vinyl floor, droplets of blood from his nose dripping added colour to the musty yellow.

At this point Arthur knew he had gone too far with his anger. He looked around the room as more of the team had begun to fill the locker room, Arthur threw his belongings in his bag and swiftly walked out, half changed out of his sports gear.

"I'm done with this school, why am I even bothering to go through school again with all the rubbish that goes on." Arthur grunted to himself quietly as he began to walk down the street away from the school. Getting out of sight of any teachers, who could hold him accountable.

There was no chance Daniel would drive him home and waiting around for Hannah was out of the question. Ordering a ride from his phone, Arthur made it back to the boarding house, practice would've just ended by the time he arrived there.

He stepped outside the taxi, looking up at Pennyview, "Maybe no one will know what had happened..." he spoke to himself, in doubt.

He walked up the path to the house and opened the front door, there he was greeted by Ethel stood at the bottom of the stairs, "Well haven't you caused a special scene at school today?" Ethel spoke sternly.

Arthur began to open his mouth; he was cut off from whatever he was about to say.

"Don't even!" she erupted, "The principal called; it looks like I have been called to a meeting about your stupid fight... He was a human?!" it was now clear she was pissed.

"I know..." Arthur spoke softly.

"Know what?! You know better." Ethel shouted. "I suggest you think about what you're going to say tomorrow and pray you don't get expelled, because I'm not helping you with this one!" she pointed up the stairs, as though she were ordering her own child to their room.

Dismissed, Arthur began to make his way up the staircase towards his room, where he could sulk and be moody. He took a few steps and stopped, "Tell Hannah I'm sorry, I was just pissed." he asked Ethel.

Ethel didn't respond, Arthur looked back for confirmation. Ethel just glared; it was clear she had finished speaking to him for the time being.

"Thank you." Arthur said before continuing his way up the stairs, hoping that she would relay the apology.

Arthur sat in his room, reflecting on what had happened today during practice, it was an embarrassing moment of losing control. Ethel was right, he knew better, he was older. He had already gone through the phases of school and should've been the wiser. The wiser on what to say to Daniel and not to have struck or provoked Andrew.

He wrestled with his thoughts, blaming the supernatural side of him for what he had done to Andrew.

His thoughts were interrupted, Arthur's phone vibrated; it was a message from Laura, "I think we need to talk tomorrow." was all that it read.

He knew that this would be a break-up conversation, it was clear from experience and how cold that message read.

Sitting in the chair by the desk in his room Arthur stared outside his bedroom window deep in thought. Thinking what he really wanted out of high school and his new life, relationships were always difficult during school. Maybe a relationship wasn't what Arthur really needed in the first place and breaking up would be a sensible move. He needed a goal, a direction, something to aim for by the end of his senior year which could lead him beyond high school and set him up with a future.

For now, Arthur had no idea what that could be.

The silence filling the room was cut, there was a knock at the door, "Arthur?" it was Hannah's voice, as she opened the door without waiting a reply.

Arthur still sat in his chair, spun away from the window, and faced the doorway, where she stood at the threshold.

"Can I come in?" she asked.

Arthur nodded; Hannah then proceeded to take a few steps into his room.

"So, everything okay? Wanna talk about it?" she offered reservedly, whilst perching herself on Arthur's bed.

Arthur let out an overdramatic laugh, "Where to start?" he began, "So, I broke up a fight with Dan and Andrew, telling Dan, Ellie was a distraction for him. He currently dislikes me. I then provoked Andrew to fight in the locker room, but I didn't mean to, it was whatever it was inside of me. There are rumours that I kissed Jade, Daniel shouted out loud, even though it's the other way around. Loads of people heard that."

Arthur continued to tap away at the desk and avoid making eye contact with Hannah for the next point. "Oh, and Jade must've heard us talking in the morning, in Montana and that rumour presumes we were seeing each other after hours. That all seems to have gotten to Laura, magically, suddenly from like an hour ago. I'm pretty sure she's going to break up with me tomorrow." Arthur finally finished before taking a deep breath.

Hannah's face dropped; it was a lot to hear for anyone. She cleared her throat, unprepared to offer solutions for the heaps of issues Arthur had. "Well, Ethel will sort the whole fighting business out with you tomorrow. I'm sure it'll be sorted out with Daniel, but that'll take time. Laura isn't going to break up with you, how do you know? She might just want to talk about it." she reeled off in a short attempt to comfort all of his problems.

"Oh, nope, I've got the message." unlocking his phone, he held up and shook it by the side of his face, whilst wrinkling his forehead for a short moment. "It's the, we need to talk message. We know that means done. I mean, it's probably for the best, I have no idea where I'm even going with any of this." Arthur felt great saying that out loud for the first time, he then looked at Hannah, after getting all that off his chest.

"You're right, you can't be with someone like that, if you're not comfortable with who you are. Especially her being her, and you, being uhm, you." Hannah tried to explain, not sounding pessimistic with a short giggle.

Arthur looked down, staring blankly at the floor below Hannah. Nodding his head slowly, coming to terms with what Hannah had just pointed out. It was the truth he didn't want to hear.

The truth sucked.

"Well, whatever happens, you know you've got us in this house, we will always have your back. No matter what happens." she softly spoke in hopes of that remark would comfort Arthur.

Arthur took his eyes off the floor and looked back towards Hannah, it seemed to cheer him up. He felt better, "Thank you." he calmly said.

At that moment Hannah knew it was her cue to leave Arthur alone, after excusing herself goodnight she stood up from the bed.

"Uhm sorry again by the way, I don't know if Ethel passed that on." Arthur mentioned.

"Yup, she did. I don't know if she's going to help you tomorrow though. You'd better prepare what to say, she was *so* mad." Hannah warned before closing his bedroom door behind her.

Arthur sat there in the chair, he slowly spun back towards the window, where the late setting sun of the summer had begun to lower, the sky crawling with orange. He spent the next better half of an hour feeling sorry for himself, thinking of what he could say to the principal in the morning. That alone was going to play on his mind all night, instead of letting him try to sleep.

The morning arrived, Ethel and other residents of the house were in the kitchen with their normal breakfast routine, preparing for their day.

"Where is he?" Ethel stated with her hands flat on the counter in the middle, impatiently. "I've got other things I would like to do this morning."

"I'm here." Arthur announced, just outside the doorway of the kitchen, "I'm ready to go."

It was a nervous journey to Lakebrook high, the dread really sunk in when Arthur was in the car, the realisation that this could be his last day at Lakebrook High. It was a quiet drive from the beginning, Ethel seemed to focus what was a head of her on the road, rather than acknowledging Arthur in the car.

It was clear she was still annoyed with him.

"I'm sorry Ethel." Arthur had to say something, anything, that seemed the best option.

"Save it. Save it for the principal and that boy you brutalised, I don't need to hear it." Ethel sharply snapped back in return, ending any more discussion to be held inside the car.

They had arrived at the school; it was busy like always. Ethel parked in one of the visitor bays in the car parking lot.

As the two walked up the main path to the entrance of Lakebrook high, his usual friends were all gathering at the fountain, the usual meeting spot before school. A few other students around glanced at Arthur, the looks they gave, then to avert their eyes knowing what he had done. The event that happened within the locker room must've already spread.

As Ethel and Arthur walked past the fountain, Daniel stared at him with a blank expression, leaving their friendship hanging in an unreadable state.

Abel exchanged glances, with a subtle nod of support, he must've had an idea of what was coming next.

The next person to look at broke Arthur with any confidence he had built up. Laura, completely avoided eye contact, pretending he wasn't walking past and purposely turned her head. She wasn't ready to acknowledge him yet.

The sight of her threw his courage entirely off guard, Arthur felt vulnerable, causing him to look away from the group and continue forwards.

They walked in through the entrance straight to the reception desk. It was time to meet the principal, the old woman of a receptionist opened the door to the principal's office.

Uncertainty filled Arthur through and through, keeping him tense.

The door, now wide open.

It was empty.

His tension relieved temporarily.

"Take a seat, she'll be along shortly." the receptionist instructed, closing the door behind them after they had entered the principal's office.

Ethel began to pull a chair out to sit down, resting her bag on her lap, followed by her hands. Arthur did the same, sitting in the chair next to Ethel, school bag by the side of his chair.

Arthur looked around the room, Principal Aster's office seemed immaculate in its décor, his eyes focused on the nameplate proudly sat on the desk. It read "Principal E. Aster" Arthur never thought about the principal's first name until that moment, he guessed away. Anything to take his mind off the suspense in her arrival.

Moments of guessing passed whilst Ethel sat there patiently not making a sound.

The office door behind them opened, "Good morning, thank you for waiting. I'm Principal Aster." announcing herself as she entered the room, sitting down at her end of the desk.

As Principal Aster spoke, she aimed all her eye contact towards Ethel about the issue that had happened in the locker room.

Arthur seemed to dart his eyes back and forth between the two women speaking in the room. He felt like a young child between them.

Understanding from the conversation, he knew it was a severe situation. It became clear to Arthur that he could be expelled, something that he had expected the night before.

Arthur's stream of concentration broke, "Do you have any words to say for yourself Arthur?" Ethel turned towards him in her chair and asked.

That was the most she had said to him all morning.

Arthur sat there for a second, pretending to think on what he could say to save his place within the school. He already knew what to say, he had been practicing it over and over in his head all night.

It was time.

"I shouldn't have any reason that excuses my behaviour because my actions weren't acceptable in any situation." he stopped briefly, pausing for dramatic effect. "I had a lot of emotions and sadly Andrew and I don't have the best relationship, which seemed to trigger the final build-up of an outburst from these emotions. I will apologise to Andrew and see if there is anything I can do for him." Arthur stopped and his eyes sunk to the floor.

"Those are some fair words, Arthur." Principal Aster mentioned, raising her eyebrow in surprise. "Was that all?" it sounded from her voice that she may be doubting the decision she had prematurely made about his expulsion.

Arthur looked back up off the floor, "Actually, since I've gotten here, I've felt lost. Only in the past few months being here I've began to find my way. Please don't expel me. I've invested the only time I've had here and just started to find direction for myself. I'll do what it takes to make things right again." he quietly took a deep breath, trying to settle the thumping of his pounding heart.

This last sentence seemed to take both women by surprise. Ethel looked at Arthur hiding the shock in her face, her expression changing a little softer than usual, that was certainly something she wasn't expecting Arthur to say at all.

There was a moment of silence before Principal Aster spoke, "Arthur could you please wait outside." she asked politely.

Arthur stood up out of the chair, picked up his bag and left the office. Finding a seat to sit on outside the office to wait for whatever conclusion had been discussed.

It felt like ages.

The voices muffled from inside the office became louder, the door handle twisted and opened. Principal Aster held the door open for Ethel to walk out first, both were laughing at something earlier.

Arthur stood up attentively.

The two women stood in front of him.

"So, it seems your time at Lakebrook isn't over yet, Arthur. You've got redeeming properties about you. I don't see that in many kids at your age." Principal Aster began to explain.

Arthur drew out a long-held breath of relief.

"You will need to apologise to Andrew and Coach Decker and see if he will still have you in his team. Lunch and after-school detention for a solid week. Detention duties will follow. Class as normal, if Andrew is in your class, make your way to the library to work alone under the librarian. Okay?" Principal Aster finished explaining.

Arthur nodding obediently, confused at the outcome, "Yes. T-t-thank you." he remembered to spit out, he could easily take a detention all week if that meant he were to keep his place in the school.

"And thank you, Ethel, for coming in today." Principal Aster expressed her gratitude whilst shaking Ethel's hand, before disappearing back into her office after excusing herself.

Arthur walked alongside Ethel outside to the front of the school main entrance, "Thank you, Ethel" he mentioned.

"Thank you for what?" Ethel questioned Arthur.

"You must have done something because there would be no way I would still be allowed back in?" Arthur questioned back.

Ethel giggled to herself slightly, "I did nothing when you left the room, it seems your little speech did it all." she let out a small smile, before going back to her authoritative self.

"Well thanks anyway, for coming." Arthur smiled back at Ethel. That was one big hurdle back to sorting things out.

Arthur made his way back into the school, it was first period, English class. As he walked to class, he paused standing a foot away from the classroom door. He took a deep breath and knocked at the door, before opening it himself. As he appeared through the door the class was silent, Mr Callahan was writing something on the whiteboard. Everyone looked at Arthur as he stood there in the classroom doorway waiting to be acknowledged.

Mr Callahan stopped writing, with his hand still gripping the pen on the board he turned his head to the classroom door, "Take a seat Arthur." he said, looking him up and down.

Arthur began to weave his way through the desks to his seat, avoiding awkward glances from both, Daniel, and Ellie, who were in the same class. Whispers were heard as Arthur made his way to his seat, whispers which were confused to why he was still in the school.

Mr Callahan continued writing and speaking at the front, the class returned to being silent.

Arthur pulled his chair out and sat down, rummaging through his bag on his lap, to find a pen and textbook before dropping his bag under the desk. Arthur took a quick look around the room, catching a few of the student's glances at him, quickly averting their eyes.

The rest of the school morning continued to be the same theme, none of Arthur's friends spoke to him for longer than a few minutes in class. It was the morning break between lessons where Arthur caught any conversation, purposely staying away and sitting alone at a planter outside. It was the best decision to leave the group alone for a while.

A voice interrupted him as he sat there looking at his feet. It was Laura, interrupting Arthur who was sat alone on one of the planters outside.

"Hey Arthur, can I take a seat?" she reluctantly asked.

Arthur already knew what the conversation was going to be about, "Yeah go ahead." he offered, preparing himself for the heartbreak she would deliver.

Laura sat down, leaving a little gap of space between herself and Arthur.

She sat awkwardly for a moment in silence, with a look on her face as she was preparing what to say, "I've heard a few things that I wanted to ask you about." she began, sounding nervous.

"I know… I know what it's about." Arthur interrupted Laura. "Rumours that you've heard aren't true."

Laura made eye contact with Arthur, waiting for him to continue.

"The Jade one. I went back into the house to get Daniel's phone; she was drunk, and she kissed me. It was random. I never mentioned it because I was hoping she wouldn't remember even doing it, as it meant nothing at all." Arthur began to explain himself. "There's nothing going on between Jade and I." he explained, feeling as though he handled that well.

Laura sat there in silence, looking back at her hand fiddling with the bottom of her top.

He continued, "The Hannah thing I'm sure you've heard that one?" he questioned Laura.

Laura looked back sharply at Arthur, "Yes I have." her eyes fixated to his again, carefully watching his facial expression.

"She's like family to me, she asked to meet up and it was late on the trip. I thought something was up and well, she's like family. So, of course I would see if she was okay. It doesn't mean I was seeing her in that way." Arthur continued to defend himself.

There was another moment of silence where the two sat on the ledge of the planter passed. It was clear this was a difficult and new situation to Laura.

It wasn't an easy situation for either of them to be in.

Laura's eyes started to well up and she began to manage some words she could just about pull together, "Everyone is saying otherwise... I think... we should take a *break*?" she sounded uncertain.

Arthur could see that she was conflicted, he inched himself closer and placed his arm around her.

Laura didn't move, allowing him to comfort her. She laid into his chest, facing directly into him trying to hide her tears. He placed his other arm around her, hugging her.

Arthur knew deep down it was for the best, she would look silly if she stayed with him. Rumours were powerful at this age. "I know that's what you had in mind before you sat down and you're right. I think things for us aren't right, for right now at this time." Arthur held back the breaking in his voice as he whispered it. "I just wanted you to know that those rumours, aren't true. Please believe me?"

Laura, holding back some tears, nodded as she rubbed her eyes with her sleeves. "I do." she whispered back.

The bell rang for next period, Laura rose her head up and looked at Arthur, "I need to get to class." she quietly spoke.

Arthur took his arm away from her and nodded, "Yeah of course and I'll still see you around, I'll be here if you need me. And if it makes a difference, tell everyone you broke up with me." he offered, trying to force a false smile together as he watched her stand up and walk off further into the school building.

He sat there as the hustle of students walked past heading to their classrooms. A sinking feeling hollowed in him emotionally, emptiness left in the aftermath of that conversation. He'd broken up with others before in the past and had been on the receiving end of a breakup. This still hurt, more than he had expected.

The rest of the day passed quickly, it was quiet, and it was lonely. Only Abel would speak to Arthur during science class for a short while, but from what Arthur understood, it would be best to avoid the group for a while until things calm down.

It was during his detention where things became interesting. Arthur walked into the classroom where the detention would be held. Coach Decker sat in the chair at the front, legs up on the teacher's desk.

Arthur looked at him straight away.

He looked back at Arthur expectedly, "Take a seat and shut up." he ordered Arthur.

He deserved that, Arthur didn't linger, he walked to the second row and began to pull a chair out.

"Front row." Decker pointed out.

Tucking the chair back under the desk, Arthur stepped to the front row and began to pull another chair out to take a seat. He sat down and waited silently for the next order from Coach Decker, ready to comply with any instruction he gave.

A few minutes passed as Arthur waited, expecting Coach Decker to speak any moment. The detention room door opened once more, Andrew appeared and saw Arthur, an expression of dislike appeared all over Andrew's face.

"Front row. Sit." Decker ordered to Andrew.

Andrew purposely sat the opposite end over from Arthur on the front row.

Decker lifted his legs off the desk, getting up from his chair. He began to walk past them both, back and forth. The suspense grew as they waited for him to speak, following him with their eyes.

"So, you two idiots decided to pick a fight in *my* locker room?" he continued pacing.

"Coach! Arthur started it!" Andrew called out before being cut off by Decker.

"Rhetorical! Shut up! Never have I seen such actions between two members of the same team. It's an embarrassment to not just the team, but yourselves." he began his grilling.

Arthur needed to say something, Andrew was right, it was his fault. "Coach?" he interrupted.

"Quiet!" Decker snapped.

"Please? It's important?" Arthur calmy questioned Coach Decker.

Coach Decker raised an eyebrow, pulling a chair out to raise his foot on the seat. "What!" he asked fiercely, leaning on his raised knee.

It was time to solve another wrong, "Andrew's right, I started it. He shouldn't be here, I was just pissed from falling out with Daniel, after sticking up for him on the field. Andrew... Did nothing in the locker room. I provoked him and it was uncalled for." Arthur justified his actions, hoping the ownership of his pathetic actions would let Andrew off.

Andrew turned his head to face Arthur, tilting it in confusion.

"Is that true? Andrew?" Decker directed that question staring his attention on him.

Andrew seemed confused, "Uhm, yes. Coach." he started, "Arthur started it."

Arthur looked at Andrew nodding at him, before turning his head to the floor between his legs.

Decker was silent, as though he were thinking.

Arthur took his eyes off the floor, "Do we still get to play?" he asked, the most important question.

Coach Decker continued to walk back and forth past the two, he paused then nodded.

"Andrew, you have three days of detention instead, Arthur I know you've spoken to the principal. You both deserve to be here for being embarrassments and bringing disrespect to the team." Coach Decker stood firmly before heading towards the exit of the room, "Now let me go find the teacher who's meant to be here."

Arthur and Andrew both sat there, awaiting the return of whoever the detention duty teacher was.

Arthur turned to look at Andrew, he needed to look at him. Andrew barely looked away from his desk.

"Andrew?" Arthur tried to gain his attention. "I'm sorry for yesterday."

"You should be." quietly came out of Andrew's mouth as he sulked with his arms folded.

His response felt ignorant, slightly annoying him, Arthur had to add more. "I mean, you don't make it easy to be liked, being a bit of a dick most of the time. We're on the same team in the end." Arthur clarified further from Andrew's response to his apology.

Andrew didn't respond to Arthur's comment, surprisingly, he stewed sitting there with it. A few more minutes passed before the teacher of the detention duty walked in. Setting up and explaining the rules for detention, the two spent the hour sat, silent and obedient to writing an essay on perfect behaviour within the school.

The after-school session bell rang, also meaning it was the end of the detention. Picking up their belongings, Arthur and Andrew began to walk out of the classroom quietly together, walking to the front of the school towards the car park to be picked up. Both positioned metres away from each other, Andrew sat at the curb of the road.

Andrew was the first to speak after a long silent hour, "How long did you get?" he surprisingly asked.

"A week straight, including lunch." Arthur replied, with his hands in his pockets.

Andrew sniggered, "Deserved it." he said with a touch of humour as he looked upwards to the sky.

Arthur joined in with a short laugh. "Andrew, why do you need to be on edge all the time?" he took a risk asking.

It took a few seconds for Andrew to speak, "Well, I… Football is all I have." was all that he managed to say.

"Yeah, but you're good at it. You don't need to prove anything or do anything mean." Arthur pointed out, complimenting him, "That won't make you better or get us to respect you, you're going to be captain next year."

Andrew sat in silence, there was no response, clearly examining the thought of being captain next year.

Ethel's car turned into the car parking lot.

"Well, this is me." Arthur announced as the car approached closer. "Again… I'm sorry Andrew, at least we're both still on the team."

Andrew looked at Arthur, "Thanks… The team would sure suck if we weren't on it. Especially next year." a faint smile appeared on him.

The car rolled to a stop at the curb side where Arthur was waiting. Opening the passenger door to find Ethel, with a smile. Arthur sat in the passenger seat, leaning over to place his bag in the back.

Ethel began to drive off.

It was still quiet, just like it was in the morning as Ethel drove him in. Arthur didn't know how to entirely speak to Ethel, or maybe it was the other way around he second guessed.

He knew that this was a perfect time to ask Ethel a few questions that had been on his mind, since the trip to Montana from the conversation with Mr Callahan. Especially since the two were alone together in the car.

"Ethel, I have a question." Arthur started off, ridding the silence within the car.

Ethel looked at Arthur, before glancing back onto the road in front of her, "Mhm?" she let out, "Go on?"

"If I am immune to magic, how did you find me in the first place?" Arthur boldly began his first curious question.

"Ahh, I see. These types of questions." Ethel began to say, "I've been waiting on these sorts for a while now. You're not immune to all magic, there is a different type of magic that we don't use or particularly understand in this age."

"Dark magic?" Arthur cut in.

A stumped look appeared over Ethel's face, "Yes? How did you know?"

"It's been mentioned in the house. I've been doing a bit of research myself." Arthur replied, hiding the fact that Mr Callahan had informed him.

"I see..." Ethel said mysteriously. "Myra discovered the balance of magic was interrupted when your curse activated. She could feel it. Dark magic is rare and unusual, it's dangerously powerful and noticeable to those who have experienced it."

"Huh, powerful, so does that explain that's how I am right now?" he asked. Understanding Myra was the one who must know more about dark magic.

"Yes. You're not a miracle." Ethel didn't sugar coat her reply. "You were planned, and for whatever you were planned for, it would've been dangerous to anyone around you." she continued.

"What am *I*, to you?" Arthur asked, sounding vague.

"You are an immortal titan, Arthur." Ethel paused for a moment. "Something that is every supernatural being's nightmare. More powerful than even the nastiest of demons out there."

Arthur could feel the uncertainty within the car at that very moment, unsure of what his purpose was. "So, what is my purpose?" he questioned Ethel again. Wanting to know if he was a weapon of some kind.

"Your curse dates thousands of years back. Someone in your... condition. Would rule a settlement forever and defeat anything that threatens you or your people. Obviously that purpose is from an older, ancient time." Ethel did not stutter at all, "A side effect of that is, only dark magic can harm you, or by removing some vital organs."

"So, who am I to *you*?" Arthur repeated again, emphasising for closure, directly meaning the relationship between himself and the house.

"We didn't know your abilities when we found you, Arthur. We could just sense you were made up of dark magic, which we know is powerful. But luckily for us, you've became our friend. You've become somewhat of a protector or even a family member for us which we never expected in the first place." Ethel answered.

This answer placed Arthur at ease and give him a sense of relief, a better understanding of who he was and what he was to Pennyview. It was warming to know that Ethel, saw him as part of the family within the house.

He only had one question left which arose from the answers of Ethel.

Arthur knew he was pushing it, but he had to ask one more, "Who cursed me? Or activated me? Last question I promise."

It was clear the questions were becoming annoying to Ethel, she responded with a firmer voice this time, "I don't know who wanted or made you. That curse could have been potentially linked back to your bloodline centuries ago. Okay? We're almost home." bluntly putting an end to any further conversation in the car.

It was the next day, which repeated like the day before.

It was a quiet day at school for Arthur, sitting his classes as normal, no one continued to speak to him as expected and sitting alone during the breaks.

The only real socialisation that Arthur encountered for the days passing was during detention. Andrew and Arthur had been given jobs to clear up classrooms throughout the school. Arthur was wiping clean the whiteboard in a classroom, whilst Andrew was cleaning out the bin and replacing the bin bag within it. Tying it and chucking it at the doorway.

Andrew broke the concentration of Arthur rubbing away at the whiteboard with the spray and cloth, "You know Chad is after you right?" he said out loud.

"For his girlfriend kissing me?" Arthur questioned back to Andrew.

"Yup, he's going to come for you, but I don't know when." Andrew warned "He's pretty tough and patient about stuff like that. I'll have to be on his side when it happens, you know."

For a second there, Arthur thought Andrew cared, "Thanks for the warning, I think."

"No problem." Andrew replied, before continuing to clean up the other side of the classroom.

It was unexpected that Andrew would give him a warning, but it seems as though they had met a middle ground of understanding.

The next few days were dull, one after another and Arthur truly felt like he was alone during school, even after Andrew had finished his detentions sooner than his.

The days leading up to the qualifying match were quiet and practice was back on after the short ban had passed. There was no sight of any threats from Chad at all, he carried on as normal, as the team captain.

Arthur began to join up with his friends again after his detention had passed and what dust had settled, but interactions with a few of them were short. Daniel was civil having no interest in starting any topic with Arthur, as though he were still sore about the whole falling out.

It was a slow step towards progress.

More time needed to pass for things to get back to normal.

Resolutions

The flood lights illuminated the players on the field, drawing out their long shadows in multiple directions. The grass reflected an electrifying green. Everyone who was anyone from school was there. Roaring, cheering at their home team, The Lakebrook Titans. It was the last minute before the end of the game and the final chance to qualify for the Gridiron championship.

A voice in the air dominated the sound of the crowd, "The Lakebrook Titans need something of a miracle right now, with nineteen to twenty-three. Southdale high just need to hold that perfect defence."

It was deafening, constantly reminding the pressure that the Titans were facing.

The Titans were all huddled into a circle on the field, Coach Decker was shouting away observations he'd picked up from the side, pointing back and forth between players.

The circle's focus redirected their aim at Chad, "Titans on three, one-two-three!" he screamed.

Arthur quickly jogged over to his position, he had been ordered to play passively for the entire offensive of the match so far, as the tight end.

The whistle blew, the ball chipped back to Andrew, the quarterback who looked for a wide receiver. As he glanced to Daniel who was the wide receiver on the right, he had been tackled already to the ground. Andrew glanced to the left, unclear to spot the receiver on the right he began to run forwards, there was a thump, he was immediately sacked to the ground.

Not much distance had been made, to get the team any closer to scoring, things were getting tense in the stadium. The disappointment in the Lakebrook crowd was echoed at Andrew being tackled.

"A failed attempt from the Titans and time is running out!" the school commentator announced. "They will have to cook up something different to get through Southdale's defences."

The whistle blew again, the Titans were called to huddle again. The Coaches came running over.

All the noise in the stadium turned into a muffled sound for Arthur as he looked around the stadium, his focus turned to the cheerleaders where Hannah was, chanting away for their team.

Coach Decker began to snap his fingers furiously in front of Arthur's face, his eyes refocused towards to Coach Decker, the sound returned.

"Are you happy with that?" Decker shouted.

"Run it past me one more time!" Arthur ordered, covering up the fact he was never listening.

"Andrew suggested that we swap you over to wide receiver, fake to Daniel?" Coach Decker explained.

Arthur was surprised that Andrew suggested a swap that involved him, he looked at Andrew who nodded confidently.

"Right!" Arthur nodded to agree at Decker.

"Thirty seconds left! Let's make a miracle happen! Get us into that championship!" Decker shouted passionately.

The adrenaline was at an all-time high, the grunts and motivational cheers surrounded them as they broke up the huddle.

The players made their way onto the field in the newly amended formation, it was time for Arthur to take this play home and qualify.

"What's this? The Titans have switched a few players over on the offence." the voice echoed. "Will this change give them what they need?"

Arthur stood firmly in his position bending over, placing his right hand, a few fingers stretched on the ground. He looked right and left, catching Hannah's look as he stood in his new position; she was stood upright with her cheerleading pom-poms in her hand, paused in suspense. Arthur stared at her, wondering if she will move as the others were cheering, facing the opposite way towards the crowd.

She caught on that Arthur was looking at her, she nodded slowly, silently agreeing for Arthur to win this game.

That's all Arthur needed for confirmation.

He looked down at his right hand on the grass, as he prepared himself to get into the supernatural zone. Looking up at the defence that stood in his way, the feeling of excitement energetically burst through his limbs.

The whistle blew, the play by chants were made, the whistle blew for the final time. Arthur began to pace forwards whilst keeping an eye on the two defenders in front of him. Andrew drew the ball back over his shoulder, pretending to aim in the direction of Daniel. Daniel had been running afar as fast as he could to commit selling the play.

Andrew faked, he switched focus and direction, he threw. The defending player to Arthur's left, tackled to the ground by his teammate allowing him to keep running down the distance.

Arthur skipped in his stride to the side to receive the ball, he eyed it especially for the perfect capture, "Perfect!" he said under his intense breathing.

With only one defending player in front of him Arthur began to charge, placing one foot in front of the other, faster with every step tapping into his supernatural side. Arthur gained some momentum and began to run directly towards the player blocking in his way, they were juddering desperately, trying to predict where Arthur would go to stop him.

The commentator gasped, "It's-it's..." pausing in suspense.

The player was about to pounce, committing to jump at Arthur. Arthur hopped to left as soon as he saw the defending player leap, dodging him, missing by only a few inches.

The defending player flopped to the ground unsuccessful.

Arthur looked over his shoulder as he kept running, bounding with force with every stretched leap he took, fiercely chewing up the yards.

The end zone was creeping up quickly.

"Almost there!" Arthur exhaled. He leapt, placing his chest forwards to dive, sliding across the grass.

"Touch down!" screamed the school commentator in intense excitement.

The whistle blew from the official, "Touch down!" he shouted, blowing his whistle to finish off the game.

The noise in the stadium filled with astounding cheers and screaming, it was a prestigious moment for not only the team, but the school.

"Lakebrook Titans have done it! Twenty-five to twenty-three! Miracles happen! They've gotten into the championship!" the voice announced throughout the stadium, barely heard over the excitement of those watching on the bleachers and around the field.

Arthur bought himself back to his feet holding the football in his hand, smeared with grass and fresh dirt all over the front of him. He looked back at the field, the team and cheerleaders were running towards him, cheering and chanting.

Arthur raised his arms in the air in celebration, dropping the ball to the floor. The realisation of qualifying for the championship had hit, his fists squeezed tight in celebration repeatedly pumping up towards the air.

Chad was screaming repeatedly, as he ran towards Arthur, "We're in the championship!"

Arthur ran towards the Lakebrook mob, who all piled into Arthur, hugging, and patting him anywhere in congratulations. The only one who seemed to hold back was Daniel, with a weak smile clapping occasionally.

Into the locker room, the team were at a winner's high, getting changed celebrating with loud pop music.

The music paused; a confident Coach Decker stood in the centre of the locker room. He looked around the room as the players began to fall silent. "Congratulations! For the first time Lakebrook will be entered into the Gridiron championships. You all played great. It doesn't get easier, next year we will need to put in the double time." he glanced at a few of the seniors, "Thank you to the seniors, you've gotten us this far and I wish you the best next year. Wherever you have chosen to end up, know that you helped get Lakebrook into the tournament. It's now up to the juniors to lead the way. Now! Celebrate! You've earnt it!"

The entire locker room erupted with cheering as Coach Decker switched the music back on.

Arthur realised from his speech that the seniors won't be with them next year, this was their final year on the team, and it truly would be up to them being in the spotlight next year.

"Victory party by the lake!" Chad shouted out loud. "Bring your own!" he added, hinting to the team to bring their own drinks.

The senior years of the team cheered at the announcement of a victory party.

Arthur finished getting changed back into his casual clothes, a couple feet away from Daniel, who was in front of his own locker.

Arthur shut his locker and faced towards Daniel, "Dan, good game, you played great." he complimented, trying to start the process of rebuilding their friendship back. It had been a few weeks since they both had fallen out and barely spoken.

Daniel stopped for a split-second rummaging through his bag and turned to face Arthur. "T-thanks." he started to mumble, Daniel turned to face his bag, pausing again. "Great work to." he said sounding clearer, looking back at Arthur to show he was sincere.

As Arthur gathered his bag and had turned around ready to head back home leaving the locker room.

He stopped.

He turned around, "Catch you later at the victory party?" Arthur aimed at Daniel, hoping he would respond.

Surprise drew all over Daniel's face, "Uh. Yeah, see you there I guess." he replied with a hint of a smile.

Enough time had passed, Arthur had planned to finally resolve things between the two of them, now knowing he would be at the victory party by the lake.

It was later that evening back home at Pennyview, Arthur was waiting for the girls to get ready, sat at the bottom of the staircase. A white opaque plastic shopping bag of alcohol hid by the side of him, ready to be carried to the victory party. The grandfather clock ticked away in the hallway, constantly reminding Arthur that he was waiting on the girls for a while now.

Leaning to the side, he picked out his phone from his pocket, there was a message from Chad to all the team in a group chat, "Victory initiation drinks midnight." with a location pinned round the side of the lake, away from the main area of the party.

"*And* we're ready!" a voice sang, coming from atop of the stairs, it was Kimberly followed by Hannah.

Both Kimberly and Hannah had dressed up expectedly to look perfect, "You both look great." shouted Arthur up the stairs.

"Aww thank you." Hannah knew she did. That was one thing she was always sure of in herself.

"Took you long enough." Arthur laughed. Wiping the smug smile off her face.

The journey was short in the taxi, as the three appeared out of the car at a short stop away from the edge of the lake. There was an excitement in the air as the music was heard in the distance through the forest. A huge weight had been lifted knowing that the team had made it into the championship. The next year, Arthur's senior year would be challenging with what was to come, especially with the Gridiron school championship and the final exams of high school.

This would all be a new experience entirely, but now wasn't the time to worry, now was the time to celebrate.

The three continued to walk towards the lake weaving through the trees. There was a low pickup in the wind as it breezed in the night sky through the trees. As they walked closer it was clear that they were in the right direction, with the music becoming louder and other groups of students appearing ahead of them.

"What's the plan? Split up. Meet up at one, where we just got dropped off? Maybe two AM? And head home together?" Kimberly asked.

"Two, sounds great, what are you going to do Arthur?" Hannah asked, interested in his plans.

Arthur had one thing he needed to make sure he did tonight, and that was to make amends with Daniel, his best friend. "See Daniel first and try to sort things out, so it's like we're back to normal. Then some victory drinks with the team and I'll see what time we're at." Arthur replied preparing what he was about to say to Daniel, strange with the thought. "What about you?"

Hannah smirked, "Hang out with the girls, see which fit guy we can get drunk to make an ass of himself. Or that could be you, wanna join us for a drink later?" she joked.

Arthur laughed, "Well I have that team drink at midnight, but afterwards, yeah sure I'll message you." he mentioned, it might actually be nice to spend some time with Hannah for once at one of these school events.

As the group got closer, the smell of firewood smoke began to tease in the air alongside the voices of many who were having a great time. Appearing into a clearing which was full of students from the school and whoever else, a few campfires and tables filled with various alcohol were dotted around.

The three split up to find their own friends.

Arthur made his way through the groups of people, looking for Daniel and the others. Various students from Lakebrook greeted and congratulated him on the winning touchdown, as he walked past them. It took a few minutes as he scoped his way through the area to find them all sat by the edge of the lake. Arthur was nervous with his heart thumping and still no clue what to say to Daniel. He wasn't in the wrong with Daniel, it was the other way around, but something needed to be said that allowed them to rekindle their friendship.

The cracking footsteps of the pebbles caused silence over the group, where they sat circled further over, as they turned to face where the sound came from.

Their conversation had been paused, as the attention had focused on the steps Arthur took, walking over to the group. The wind picked up the gentle waves of the lake could be heard lapping at the pebbles that met the water.

Arthur looked at them all, "Hey." was the only word that came out of his mouth.

"Yo! Art! Great game today!" Abel responded starting off loudly, welcoming him.

"You played great earlier today, Arthur." Kay added which seemed to help break the awkwardness that still seemed to linger around the group.

Arthur nodded, "Thank you, it was a team effort which got us the win." he directed his look upon Daniel, "Dan, got a minute please, to have a word over here?" he asked. Still unsure of what he could say to sort out the issue between them both.

Daniel pushed himself up off his popup picnic chair and began to walk with Arthur further down the lake, Arthur still carrying his shopping bag of his beers in hand. The two walked for some seconds down the lake, before Arthur stopped, enough to be out of the way of the others.

Daniel stopped.

Arthur looked down at the ground and prepared himself with what he could string together, he inhaled through his nose, "Dan... you're my best friend and I'm sorry for whatever I've done." looking up directly at Daniel, to show the severity of his apology.

As Arthur looked at Daniel, he could see Daniel's eyes begin to well up. Maybe Daniel wasn't prepared for this at all.

Daniel opened his mouth to talk, but nothing came out.

He took a second to reply, "*I'm* sorry, everything got out of hand. I..." he paused to prepare his response. "I knew the rumours weren't true, but I didn't stand up for you. I was just angry at you for no real reason, but then I got angry at myself."

Daniel stopped for a moment preparing mentally for the next few lines he was about to say, scraping his foot in the ground, back and forth kicking up a few smaller pebbles. He then continued, "You tried to help me from being away from my studies and the team. I got angry because I couldn't see it, until everything had happened, and it was too late. Now you and Laura broke up and that was my fault."

Arthur looked at him with an expression of confusion, Daniel had honestly thought that he was the real reason that they had broken up.

"Dude," Arthur started, placing his hand on Daniel's shoulder looking directly at him as Daniel lowered his eyes. "We broke up because it just isn't the right time, right now, we spoke about it all and she believed me that the rumours weren't true. It's not your fault at all man." he said hoping that would comfort Daniel.

"You two don't really talk now though..." Daniel muttered; the regret was still heard in his voice.

Arthur laughed a little bit, "That's breaking up for you man, it always sucks. I'm sure Laura and I will soon get back to okay terms." he explained.

Arthur placed his shopping bag on the pebbled ground and kneeled, he began to fumble around with the packaging in the plastic bag.

Pulling out a beer, Arthur stood up and offered one to Daniel "So are you gonna have a drink with me?" he smiled, holding it out right in front of him offering it as a sign of resolution to Daniel.

Daniel sniffed up what guilt he felt and wiped his eyes and took the can out of Arthur's hand. "Are *we* all good?" he asked somewhat still unsure.

It was clear from that moment on, that the events had played a heavy toll towards Daniel's view on their friendship. Just as much Arthur's had been.

"We're all good man! Still best mates?" Arthur clarified for the first time, even though the two had never really pointed out being best friends.

A smile broke through Daniel's upset face, he nodded, "Yea we are man."

"Sweet, quick bro hug before we head back?" Arthur offered.

Daniel nodded, with an even wider smile, offering his arms out to hug Arthur. Arthur, placing his arms around Daniel. A short squeeze and pat on the back, the two stepped back.

Arthur nodded silently, happily accepting that the two's friendship had been resolved.

The two started to walk back to the others, "Thanks for having my back there with Andrew, weeks ago." Daniel commented, happily sipping his beer.

Arthur took a sip of his own, "Always got your back, Dan." he stated, before putting his arm around Daniel's shoulder as they got closer.

The group hadn't moved, they were all still sat in their chairs in the circle, "Alright, we're back!" Arthur announced, shaking his fist in the air in triumph.

The group cheered as Abel and Ellie clapped alongside the happy reunion.

"Hooray! Were almost back to normal again." Ellie announced out loud, happily welcoming a step to how things used to be.

Arthur took a seat in between Abel and Laura in the circle on the other popup chair that was empty, looking around there was no Jade or Cheng in sight, it must've been for one of them. The group began to chatter like normal, it was as though all of the friction between Daniel and Arthur had subsided and they could carry on. Things quickly went back to the way they should've been.

Laura and Arthur had managed to have small conversations between them, almost getting back to that level of being okay with each other.

Arthur was glad to be back, back with his group of friends.

"All right!" Abel grabbed the attention of the group, jumping up from his chair, raising his drink above in the air, "Almost our junior year over and the beginning of our senior year! Here's to the end of a good year!" he exclaimed, raising his drink further up in the air in celebration.

Everyone raised their drinks to celebrate and join in with the closing end to a successful year, there were still weeks left of school, but it was as good as over. Arthur thought what a great year it had been, close to the end of his junior year at Lakebrook High.

Arthur looked at his phone keeping an eye on the time, it was almost near midnight and time to go. "Dan, it's almost time for the team drink." Arthur pointed out from the message.

"Oh yea, Chad will probably do a speech or something I've heard." Daniel hinted, standing up brushing himself off, ready to head towards the meeting spot.

Arthur opened the pinned location on his phone preparing to track it, it wasn't too far away around the edge of the lake it showed.

Arthur and Daniel started to follow the edge of the lake around, unfinished drinks in hand to meet up with the rest of the team.

Heading through the trees familiar voices of the team could be heard where the location led the two on his phone, groups of the team were seen huddled in their pairs or more drinking away. The two joined up with some of the other players who were eagerly awaiting the arrival of Chad.

After moments of discussing the victory earlier, drinking, and excitement of looking forward to the championship game in the next school year. Members of the team began to fall silent and face outwards from the group. Chad, beer in hand, with some of the other seniors had arrived, two carrying a hefty keg between them.

Everyone was moving out the way and watching him as he walked through the centre of the crowd.

Chad prepared himself with a pumped up, striking expression, "Here we go! Alright! What's up Titans!" he was ecstatic as he high fived and patted members of the team as he passed through the centre of the crowd.

Chad stood in front of the team as they all gathered around, the keg was being connected up to a pump by some of the seniors behind him. He took a moment as the rest of the team stared on at him in sheer amazement, mostly quiet in awe awaiting his next word in the last moments of being the captain.

"Look at you all," he paused taking a sip of his beer, "Victors!" he then cheered clenching his fist in the air.

The crowd of Titan's cheer in union.

"We are here to celebrate a beginning of a championship dream, the Gridiron school championship. Now, this journey will only be for the juniors. It's time to say goodbye to us, the seniors. Their last game knowing they set the path for the new to follow on." Chad announced as he paused throughout. "For such an occasion. We've acquired this keg from Billy, where each of us will take a drink from, in joint celebration."

The team began to huddle closer towards the keg excited as they began to take a drink, some of the players howled, cheered, or let out a large burp in rush of the unifying event.

It was a means to an end for some of the seniors, as it were a cementing initiation to those younger within the team, ready to take place of those who stood before them.

Arthur and Daniel had lined up, it was their time to take a drink from the keg. Chad held up the pump and Arthur took a gracious chug.

"Arthur! Everybody! Taking us to victory in the final seconds against Southdale." Chad announced out loud to the team. The Titans began to cheer abruptly for the events that had taken place earlier today.

It was a great feeling for Arthur, being the one who took the Lakebrook Titans through to the championship.

He had finished his drink from the keg.

"Wait up after Arthur, I need a word with you bro." Chad whispered closely as he took the pump back away.

Arthur knew what this was going to be about, he turned to Daniel after the two had walked away to the outskirts of the crowd.

He informed Daniel what Andrew had told him during their time at detention.

"Are you actually gonna stick around?! He might be planning something." Daniel warned, pointing out the obvious.

Arthur knew Chad was planning something against him, "I know he is, but I have an answer that he clearly needs to hear, but he may not like it." Arthur looked over his shoulder to take another look at Chad, the queue had almost finished. "It's only if he will listen to that answer, is the thing."

Daniel paused for a second, looking concerned to what might happen. "He's had a few it seems already. Do you want me to stay?" Daniel offered in a lower, secretive voice.

"You don't have to for this." Arthur replied confidently.

Daniel looked a touch worried, "I will, I got your back man." he knew he couldn't leave Arthur alone; it was clear that Daniel felt this was one of the moments he needed so stay.

The crowd of players began to disperse back towards the party further back around the lake. Arthur, looking as relaxed as possible, with his hands tightly gripped in his pockets. Starting to walk closer to Chad, his heart began to pound away nervously. Chad was a year younger than him realistically, but it was clear he did work out physically compared to what Arthur had done.

A dumbfounded expression covered Arthur's face, he was powerful, he's an immortal. What did he have to worry about.

Chad broke from his group who were chatting away secretively and began to walk towards Arthur and Daniel. The rest of Chad's friends followed at his side.

Arthur leaned to Daniel wanting to reassure something, "Promise me you won't join in, whatever happens right now." he whispered to the side at him.

"Don't get involved?!" Daniel quickly, whispered back unexpectedly.

"Mmhmm, yeah." Arthur sounded back to confirm.

The few who remained met in the middle of the open area. It was Chad, a few other of the seniors, and Andrew. The rest had already left back to the main party.

Chad looked Arthur dead in the eyes, "So, Arthur. It seems we need to have a little *chat* that I've been waiting for." he explained in a threatening tone, squeezing his hand with the other anxiously.

At that moment Arthur knew that this was going to end with a fight of some sort, that was Chad's only plan. He quickly caught the look of Andrew; his expression was held tightly with a look of worry. The voices of Ethel and Myra went through his mind, he couldn't get into a fight. It's not what they would've wanted, Chad was human after all.

Arthur took his hands out of his pockets, he knew he had to take beating from Chad, he knew this was now not going to go down the way he had peacefully hoped for.

"Smart, waiting after the game. Well, it seems a rumour has been going around about something I had done." Arthur spoke up.

"So, tell me, what exactly happened between you and Jade?" Chad was stern, he wanted a straightforward answer. Not that it would matter, he had already decided the outcome.

Arthur sighed ever so slightly to himself; he knew that his reply wouldn't matter. "I went back into the house to get something. She was upset about the two of you. Asked if her she was okay, and she kissed me." he briefly explained keeping the events short to move on with his beating.

Chad took a step closer, trying to puff his presence out to intimidate Arthur, "She kissed *you*? I can't have anything like that happen and you get away with it. You know I gotta take you down? Don't you?" he finally threatened, getting to the point.

Arthur began to sturdy in his stance, "She kissed *me* though?" he tried to emphasise the truth.

"Doesn't matter! Can't kiss the captain's girl and expect nothing!" one of the senior players provoked.

"That's stupid." Arthur called out.

Chad began to jitter around in his steps, proceeding to take off his Lakebrook letterman jacket, "Don't worry, this won't take long." handing the jacket to one of the others at his side.

It was on, Arthur looked around and saw how excited, jumping up and down all of those who stood by Chad's side were getting.

Is this what high school was about? He thought. Glancing through each of them all, his glance stopped at again at Andrew. Andrew now had no expression; his body language seemed as though he became on edge. He wasn't jumping like the others.

Arthur could imagine that Andrew would be excited, ready to fight at Chad's side, if the two hadn't had detention together and found that middle ground.

Arthur's mind bounced back to taking a beating. It wasn't fair, he knew that he could easily take them all on here. But he was older and wiser, upholding the responsibility he had to in his position. He knew what was right and he would have to take this beating without putting up a fight.

A pointless beating over a fragile ego.

Arthur looked at Chad, dead in the eyes, he wanted to get through this as quick as possible. "You know what, have at it." he offered.

A look of confusion covered Chad's face; it wasn't a response he was expecting.

"Just you Chad, hit me. I won't move, or dodge. Go on. Have at it." Arthur confirmed, he knew he had to let this happen as he prepared himself mentally.

The offer seemed to suck the fun out of it from the face that Chad pulled. He took a step forward and drew his right arm in the air, he hesitated a second to look Arthur up and down, trying to work him out.

Their eyes met again; Arthur's expression was still.

The second passed and Chad swung.

The sound of a fist hitting his cheek bone, dimly echoed, some of the seniors and Andrew flinched standing behind. Arthur's face just took a punch from the captain of the team.

Arthur readjusted his gaze from the side and back straight to Chad. He stood still and firm, ready again.

Arthur was silent, he made no noise of pain.

Chad hesitated once more; it was clear that his testosterone was building on an all-time high, filling up and adding to his drunk self. He grabbed Arthur's shirt with his left hand and clutched it, raising his right arm again he prepared for another swing.

Arthur could smell the beer on his breath as he clutched.

He looked Arthur in the eyes again, and swung holding onto Arthur's shirt, not allowing him to stumble away. He paused looking back at Arthur waiting for any kind of response.

He gave no response.

Arthur looked back at him, still.

His eyes widened; he felt a kick inside of him. That instinct tickling in the back of his mind, trying to break out through the surface. Arthur couldn't let it break through, who knows what would happen if it did, he held it in using every ounce of mental willpower he had.

Chad raised his arm again and began to repeat hitting Arthur a few more times before stopping. "Are you not going to fight back?!" Chad shouted, pushing him back, letting go of his shirt.

It was clear Chad was disappointed from the little reaction Arthur gave away. Expectedly most others in his situation would have either fought back and lost or be on the floor whimpering away.

Arthur silently looked at Chad, as blood began to drip down the side of his face from the wounds.

"Stop it, that's enough!" Daniel shouted, pushing himself in between the two.

Chad was unsatisfied. "Grab him!" he ordered, pointing, as the seniors rushed to hold back Daniel over to the side.

"Are you done yet Chad?" Arthur finally broke his silence, smirking at him. Pushing him to get the rest of it out of his system.

Anger fuelled Chad, even more so now, the little satisfaction he was already getting from Arthur. He pounced forwards grabbing Arthur's shirt again and began to relentlessly punch him repeatedly.

Over, and over, again.

With every punch the instinct inside Arthur became louder, it wanted to murder Chad and it was clawing away behind Arthur's face. Screaming to let it out. This was the moment that Arthur needed to have control over it. The pain numbed to the side as he focused mentally holding it back, keeping it from letting loose.

Arthur fell to kneeling on the ground as Chad tried to continue in all his might, it was clear Chad had lost self-control.

The screams of Daniel being restrained became clear, bringing Arthur back to what was happening around him.

Hands appeared over Chad, pulling him off Arthur. "That's enough man!" it was Andrew, who just about managed to pull him back. "I think you've done enough Chad, look at him." Andrew gestured with an open hand at Arthur.

Chad seemed to claim some composure back and look at the work he'd done. Arthur looked up as he knelt on the ground, the entire side of his face covered in blood, dripping off the bottom of his jaw.

Arthur spat blood out on the ground through the side of his mouth.

Chad stared coming to terms with the brutality he had just done.

"Time to go, Chad, guys." one of the seniors announced that was currently holding Daniel back. Another ushering the rest to head off back towards the party back down the lake. One of the seniors began to pull away at Chad who began to follow along with them, slowly taking his focus away off Arthur.

As they began to leave, Andrew waited, he was the last to leave, "Daniel." he called to him.

Daniel looked at Andrew, "What!" he said sharply with some anger.

"Are you gonna be okay sorting Arthur out?" Andrew asked, showing some unexpected compassion.

Daniel didn't expect any kind of concern, especially not from Andrew. "Uh. Yeah." he replied.

Andrew nodded and stared at Arthur for a moment, before turning off and heading back to catch up with the others.

Daniel broke being frozen in place from the entire situation, he rushed down to his knee by the side of Arthur. "You okay?! Need me to get someone? Or something?" he urgently offered in a sense of emergency.

Arthur shook his head silently, as the relief flowed through him. It was over and he managed to hold back the beast within him, it was tough. He rose from his current kneeling position; Daniel wrapped his hand under Arthur's arm and the other around his waist. Helping him to his feet.

"I'm absolutely fine, I just need a minute." Arthur smirked. "That needed to happen, it's over now."

It was over and hopefully nothing more would come of it.

"You're f-fine?" Daniel stuttered, "You just took a beating from Chad?!"

Arthur did feel the pain, but it was only temporary as his supernatural state began to kick in. He began to wipe his dripping face with the bottom of his shirt, to soak up the blood. It had already spilled down and ruined his clothes.

"Give me five minutes Daniel, I just need to sort out myself before we head back." Arthur asked, pretending like he needed that time to seem somewhat human.

Daniel waited nervously, his eyes carefully watching Arthur, unsure if he would drop unconscious at any minute.

Arthur lowered himself down to his knees and spat onto the ground, clearing his throat. As they waited, Daniel was speechless, just watching in silence and observing as he crouched watching him intensely.

Arthur slowly stood back up, "Let's head back, but I'll need to take it slow." he excused.

They began to walk through the woods, towards the direction of the noise where the party was, after a few steps Daniel stopped. "How are you going to head back to the party looking like that man?"

Arthur realised that he didn't look in any fit state to return. "Oh, yeah. I should probably head home or something now you mention it. I can't really excuse tripping over, doing this to myself." Arthur joked, as they continued to proceed a few more steps. "I'll get a ride, but you don't need to come with or anything Dan."

"'I'll wait with you at least, until you get a ride man, you sure you don't need me to head back with you?" Daniel offered.

A peculiar noise clicked in the distance.

Arthur didn't reply, he suddenly stopped, frozen in the spot staring at the darkness in front of him. Daniel walked another few steps before realising Arthur had stopped.

He turned around "All good?" Daniel asked.

Arthur continued to stare into the darkness, figuring out what he was looking at as Daniel took a step closer to him.

"Bro? Arthur?" Daniel questioned looking for any sign of a response.

Arthur continued to stare, ignoring any sound from Daniel. He could almost make a shadow of a figure, of what was standing in front of him, a feeling of terror ran through his body. There was a sharp pinging noise, Arthur reacted fast, catching an object that was launched directly at him. He whipped the object out of the air and held it in front of him.

Daniel looked at Arthur's hand, as so did Arthur. It was a wooden stake.

Arthur quickly looked at Daniel and towards the direction where the stake had been fired. A different clicking sound was heard, followed by a short, pressured hiss.

Arthur was too late. Something else had been fired.

As he looked down at his lower abdomen there was a thin dart sticking out of him. The feeling in his body began to numb, it was a similar feeling to what Mr Callahan had used in his car a while back. Arthur began to feel lose feeling, limb to limb.

He turned to face Daniel, "Run." was the only word that came out of Arthur's mouth, before collapsing to his knees and being overwhelmed by his body shutting down.

Arthur's eyes forcefully closed as he fell to the ground, trying to use all his strength to avoid the dart's effect. There was no use, managing to open his eyes for a second and catch Daniel running deeper into the forest.

His eyes forcefully closed.

The next few moments for Arthur were vital trying to get information of what was happening, there were muffled sounds and the sense of being dragged somewhere through the forest. The dragging stopped after a few minutes, some more muffled voices were heard, there was more than one. He just about felt being slumped towards what could only be the base of a tree, feeling that he was left sat, upright against it.

Some of the voices began to get clearer, it seems the effects of the dart were wearing off sooner than he had expected. He felt something being wrapped around his neck, wrists, and legs.

"It doesn't seem to have any affect to keep him inflicted" a voice was heard, close to his face.

"Forget the rope, look he's beginning to move, just stake him." another voice ordered.

Arthur heard a higher pitched scream in detest, it was a girl's scream. As the footsteps seemed to get closer to him, Arthur forced his eyes open slightly for a brief second, his vision was foggy he could see a figure walking towards him and two others kneeling by a dim light of some sort.

As a figure strode closer pacing in haste, Arthur felt them place a hand on his collarbone, a sharp pain ran through Arthur's nerves. A stake ran through his heart, helplessly being able to react in anyway. The pain was sharp, it was like fire, spreading away from where his heart was. The darkness began to sink in, at the worst time possible.

The darkness surrounded his mind, losing the ability to hold onto his thoughts.

There was a bump and a sense of feeling returned through Arthur's nervous system, his body was coming alive with feeling again. A short burst of recalling what was happening around him, causing a rush of adrenaline which worked over Arthur's mind, as his eyes opened slightly.

The stake had been knocked out ever so slightly from being firmly planted his chest allowing his senses to return, he could just see one of the figures. It was Hannah who had bumped into him, she was loose from being tied up. One of the figures who were on their feet rushed to grab her, dragging her closer towards the dim light by her hair, she was screaming in pain.

"Her first, then the others, collect the check and get out of this shitty town." one of the hunters ordered, pointing to Hannah "She's the gobbiest and deserves to die first."

Arthur had to act. He pushed on to his senses, rushing mentally for them to return. He focused on the dim light at the centre of his vision, the light began to take shape. It was a camping lantern. Focusing on the light, the rest of the surrounding area began to take shape in his vision.

It was clear they were in a dangerous situation and these people were a threat, he could see three of them. A group of three supernatural hunters had gathered up Hannah and Kimberly, along with Arthur.

Arthur's eyes were now wide open. One of the hunters were standing behind Hannah, she was on her knees, he held up a strange, assembled crossbow with a metallic canister on it. Gripping it firmly towards the back of her head. This was the time to act immediately, these hunters weren't going to stick around any longer than they needed to.

He prayed on the thought that they must've mistaken him for a vampire, quite like Callahan had done earlier in the year.

It was time.

Arthur swiftly rose to his feet and pulled the stake out from his chest; he analysed the man holding the crossbow. Rapidly moving his hand to his chest and gripping the stake out with haste, he raised it to throw, releasing it from his fingers. The stake cut through the air with such velocity, impaling into the man.

The crossbow thumped to the floor, followed by the collapse of the man he had just impaled with such might.

His eyes fixated to the next hunter who gave the orders. Using his speed, Arthur leapt forwards and pushed him off his feet using his strength. The hunter flew shortly in the air before colliding into a thick tree behind.

The third and final member's face trembled with fear, he began to fumble at the strap of his crossbow. That powerful instinct that blinded Arthur had pushed its way in unexpectedly. Taking over his actions.

Slowly, he began to walk towards the final member of the group. The hopeless fool fumbled with his crossbow strap, finally freeing it from the belt clasp. He flicked it level in front of himself and fired at Arthur in a haste, striking into the side of his abdomen. Arthur didn't wince or stop walking, he continued to advance slowly to the man. Thinking clearly had gone out of the window for Arthur, the instinct inside him had completely taken over. It was in control now and all he could do was watch from the inside.

As Arthur became at a reaching distance, he pulled the stake from his abdomen with one hand and the other grabbing the man's clothes and pulling him closer. He drove the stake into the man pushing through his ribcage with ease, stopping when the stake had broken out through his back.

A brutal snapping sound ensued as his blood began to drop down Arthur's elbow.

The final hunter dropped to the floor, showing no signs of life. The beast within Arthur looked viciously to his surroundings, checking for any more threats.

His eyes stop and fix on something unusual, someone that he had not accounted for. There was a shaking young man, pale with the look of death in his face.

It was Daniel. He'd forgotten all about Daniel.

The familiar sight of Daniel pushed Arthur to fight to his controllable senses much more, trying his best to regain control of his body.

He took a few steps closer to Daniel, who was completely terrified. Every step was a struggle as Arthur tried to reclaim his mental and physical control.

Crouching down slowly, at eye level towards Daniel, Arthur wasn't clear of what he was going to do. The giant internal battle for him swayed, wrestling for his control.

Arthur reached his arm out slowly, placing his fingers on Daniel's cheek. He ripped quickly, pulling the tape off Daniel's mouth that had forced him to be quiet.

"Arth... Y-y-our, e-eyes." Daniel whimpered out, his hands and feet were still bound.

Those were the eyes of an immortal titan staring back into this human, emotionless, soulless and at worst, unpredictable. The redness that surrounded the outside of his eyes, keeping the hollow blackness within his pupil began to fade at the sound of Daniel's voice.

Arthur continued to stare, the look of fear, the call of his name, the resistance of keeping his instinct at the surface fell to the sides. He had reclaimed the control of his own self.

As Arthur's eyes returned to normal, his hand reached out in front of him, tugging and untying the rope that had been used to tie up Daniel's feet.

"You're safe now." Arthur whispered, making eye contact.

There was a rustling of branches, a crack cut the attention through the air, the hunter who had been pushed forcefully at the tree was running towards the two with his hunting knife drawn.

Arthur stopped to look behind at the footsteps of the approaching man.

Hannah was stood up, free from being bound. She gestured her hand flat in the air, out towards the man, pushing him off the ground and a few feet away from them. Preventing any more harm, she waved her hand and chanted a few words; he began to set ablaze momentarily whilst Hannah held out her hand. Screams of pain filled the air, as he was burning away on the ground as she stared into the flames.

"Burn." was all that she said in hatred. Before dropping her arm to her wayside, letting the fire instantly subside.

Arthur helped Daniel to his feet.

"W-what are you?" trembled Daniel. "W-who… are you?"

Arthur tossed at the thought of what to reply, checking with his wounds that had already began the healing process. Arthur looked at Daniel, "I'm still me, I'm… erm, not exactly human." he started off, before being interrupted.

It was Kimberly, "That's enough. We need to wipe his mind, now." she suggested.

Daniel's expression of fear had now also been mixed with the look of confusion. "Wipe my mind?" he questioned powerlessly.

"Hannah, don't you think? We can't have people knowing." Kimberly reinforced her suggestion.

"Yes, okay, let's get this over with and clean up this mess." Hannah had no objection to her idea.

Arthur continued to toss with his thoughts, he wanted to let Daniel know who he was and what he was. His first initial reaction was to ask, rather than run. Daniel may be okay if he knew the truth.

Whilst deep in thought, Hannah, and Kimberly both began walk closer towards Daniel, they held out their hands and began to chant another spell.

The spell to make him forget.

Daniel was confused, taking a few steps of caution backwards, before Kimberly cast her other hand bringing him to his knees forcefully.

"Arthur, what's happening man? I don't know what's going on." he worriedly called out for him, louder over the girl's chanting.

Arthur looked at him in distress.

"Stop! Wait. How much would he forget Hannah?" Arthur asked, halting her chanting.

The look of annoyance was clear over Hannah's face, "A whole day? Two? Give or take." she guessed.

If Daniel had forgiven Arthur, and had his mind wiped, Daniel wouldn't have any memory of the two becoming friends again.

Hannah looked closely at Arthur, from his silence Kimberly was still continuing the spell.

"Wait!" Arthur shouted.

Kimberly stopped chanting and looked at Arthur, still holding her hand out to keep Daniel at his knees.

"I don't want him to forget. We can trust Daniel, *I trust him.*" Arthur began to argue against the use of the spell.

"We can't have that; we can't have someone knowing who *we* are." Hannah emphasised, directing at the witches of the house.

A short burst of anger quickly swept over Arthur, he held it in, "Please!" shouting involuntarily in a mildly aggressive tone.

Hannah marched to him, placing herself firmly right in front of Arthur, "Why?" she asked, inches away looking at him closely, her eyes bounced between Arthurs left to right.

Arthur calmed the tone of his voice; Hannah was listening to his reason carefully. "You have your friends that you can talk to, I have no one and he's my one friend that I can trust. Kim has Peter?" he tried to excuse.

Hannah stared at Arthur, it was clear she was conflicted with the thought about letting Daniel remember, and the factor of allowing Arthur to have that one friend.

"Fine." she said bluntly. Turning back towards Kimberly and Daniel.

"What?!" Kimberly interjected.

Hannah looked at Kimberly, "It's fine." she said sternly.

"But?" Kimberly questioned.

"I've said so, let's sort this mess out." Hannah directed. Using her level of authority being the eldest witch in this current situation.

Arthur smiled and took Daniel aside, relief flowed over him, as the girls began to examine the hunters. He briefly explained to Daniel who he was, with no time for questions. As the pieces began to fall into place, Daniel's expression barely changed.

Daniel finally smiled, "That answers why you took the beating from Chad with ease earlier." Daniel chucked up a small laugh, understanding that Arthur could've beaten Chad. It was clear Daniel had many questions, but Arthur had one in mind, could he really trust Daniel to keep his secret. Let alone the others of the house.

He could, he knew he could.

The situation needed to be cleaned up, the more time they let pass, there could be a chance of someone discovering this murderous scene.

Arthur informed Daniel to head back as it would be easier to clean up, he could keep an eye out if anyone were coming their way. "Don't worry about all this, we will clean this up. Message me, look out for us if anyone is coming this way." he asked him, "Tell the others I went home from the incident with Chad."

As Daniel began to walk off, Arthur took a deep breath as he watched him disappear into the darkness of the forest. He joined in with the girls and began to look around the area where they were held.

Hannah stood above the leader of the hunter's body, the one giving the orders. "Well, I guess he isn't going to tell us anything now I suppose." Hannah shrugged off smirking.

"Well duh!" Kimberly stated the obvious. "Is he part of Mr Callahan's thing?" she then questioned to the two.

That began the ripple of accusation.

"I bet he is, it's strange that he knew who we were, and Mr Callahan probably tipped them off." Hannah began to add to her assumption.

Arthur turned towards both girls, "Wait. We're not going to go back and forth with this. I'm just going to call him and ask." Arthur stated, pulling out his phone from his pocket.

He dialled Callahan.

The phone rang for a long ten seconds, whilst Arthur, Hannah, and Kimberly were awaiting in anticipation for a voice to answer it.

After the fourth chime the phone stopped calling, "Arthur, what can I do for you?" a calm Mr Callahan answered.

Sharp whispers from Kimberly we heard, "Ask him! Ask him!" she repeated. As Arthur put a finger in his ear.

"Uhm, yeah hello. Three supernatural hunters here, all dead now, anything linked with you?" Arthur asked, holding back any hint of suspicion.

There was a moment of silence, before any response occurred. "What? Hunters? Where are you?" Callahan replied, sounding surprised.

Arthur thought he should be clearer with his words, "We're at a party, by the lake and we just had to kill three guys as they tried to capture us and what it seems, execute us. Do *you* have anything to do with that?" Arthur, sounding serious with his final question, before awaiting his answer.

"No, nothing to do with me, I promise. Are there others there? Not involved with any of that stuff?" Mr Callahan asked in what certainly sounded like urgency.

Hannah snatched the phone off Arthur, "Yes, there's a whole high school party going on not so far from here." she stated with irritation that she might be wrong thinking it had anything to do with Callahan.

Mr Callahan was quick to respond, "Send me your location, now!" he ordered. "I will head over, and we will clean this up before anyone sees. Let me have a look at these guys."

Hannah hung up Arthur's phone from the call, then proceeded to send the location of where they were to Mr Callahan. The three waited anxiously, whilst gathering the dead bodies and lining them up in row until Mr Callahan made an appearance.

It was certainly an hour or so past midnight by now, hopefully the party over the other side was dying down. Moments later footsteps were heard crunching, snapping through the branches in the dark distance. The canopy of the trees kept the moonlight out, allowing the figure to walk through the darkness unrecognised.

Out stepped Mr Callahan.

He walked closer towards the three and his eyes darting around the area, examining the crime scene that needed to be covered up.

Arthur greeted Mr Callahan, who proceeded to walk to the bodies and rummage through their belongings.

The girls observed Callahan closely, still not at ease with denying any of his involvement.

Kimberly pointed to one of the bodies, the burnt one. "He was the one giving orders." she pointed out.

Callahan looked back at the girls, not impressed with how burnt the body was. He rummaged through the burnt body's pockets, as best as he could. He found a remnant of a burnt-up wallet, which had no use for any information. The next thing found was a mobile phone, melted and inoperable to use. He began to look around the case of the phone, squeezing it between his two hands, pressuring the case. It snapped, giving way and the back separated from the screen.

Callahan turned around, there pinched between his fingers was the sim card, "Looks too burnt to be even used in another phone, what do you think Arthur?" Callahan questioned, as he tossed the sim card to him.

Arthur nodded, the sim card was damaged and there was no chance it would work in another phone.

Mr Callahan continued to rummage through the other two bodies. After some time, he stood up and folded his arms, "Right, as far as who these guys are, I don't know. They must've been hired to take my place as I stepped down from being the hunter here. Nothing to do with me." he paused for a moment deep in thought, looking between the three bodies. "The burnt one we can move elsewhere, far, it can be some strange cold case of him dying. The other two however, you've clearly killed with some object, so a devastating hiking fall through the hills isn't going to cut it for the cops. We will need to sink them both to the bottom of the lake." Callahan instructed.

"Can't we just leave him here?" Hannah asked slightly agitated at the effort that they will need to go through.

"If the police find any one of these, they will search the area and the lake." Callahan countered with fair consideration.

"CCTV, timings, reports, and that'll be a risk. Even with me, being here now."

He began to work through the belongings and items in the area, gathering up the rope, he tossed it to Hannah. "Tie something to both of those bodies, which will keep them underwater. Arthur can get the tarpaulin from my car, fast, to wrap this burnt one up and we will move it somewhere else." Mr Callahan seemed to be in his element, throwing his car keys at Arthur.

"Have you killed many people? You seem to be prepared and know what to do." Kimberly nervously questioned.

Mr Callahan looked at her and grinned, "Don't ask questions, if you already know the answer to it." he hinted, without wasting time and began to help tie up the other two bodies.

Arthur started running in the location of the car, he was quick with his pace. He found Callahan's car and opened the trunk, snatching the tarpaulin sheet out and running it back to them.

The bodies were ready, and the girls were ordered by Callahan to go back to the party, which would be nearly or completely over by now. They needed to show their face which made sense, they had been gone a while now and needed to be seen. Arthur had his cover story, if anything ever came to light, being beaten up by the team captain was enough to head home. Since Arthur was the one to be out of sight, it was up to him and Mr Callahan to dispose of the bodies.

Arthur was in charge of dragging two of the bodies to the centre of the lake, needing to sink them both to the bottom.

Mr Callahan waited by the edge of the lake, as Arthur began to undress some of his clothes, not wanting to be completely drenched in the rancid water of the lake. He waded deeper walking on the shallow bottom of the lake, dragging the bodies into the deep darkness out on the water. Callahan awaited on edge, keeping an eye out for any other visitors as he kept the final body nearby.

Arthur swam, dragging the two bodies out further, his surrounding vision became darker; closing in the further he made it to the centre of the lake. Remembering the direction in which he swam from, not wanting to get lost out here in the water.

It was time to let the first body sink as he tread in the water, letting it go, it began to disappear into the depths.

He swam further a smaller distance into the lake to drop the second body, it also sunk into the depths of the lake. Swallowed by the darkness of the water.

Returning to the direction he swam out from. Arthur saw the outline of a figure waiting at the lakeside, it was Callahan.

Everything still seemed fine.

Arthur and Callahan, picked up the body together as they began to escort it across the forest, trying to make as little noise as possible. After stuffing the wrapped body in the trunk of Callahan's car, they began to drive. The drive was quiet, Arthur didn't want to interrupt Callahan in his element, helping them solve this problem.

Arthur couldn't help feeling nervous, as the last time he was in this seat, things didn't end well.

The drive longed out, heading further away out of Lakebrook entirely seeing the signs noting, "You are leaving Lakebrook" the car journey lasted for a while.

Arthur turned to Mr Callahan, "Why are you helping us anyway?" he was curious.

Callahan smiled to himself for a second, "I couldn't leave you guys to clean up three dead bodies, close to my students, could I?" he laughed to himself, "By the sounds of it, Hannah would have just left them poorly hidden."

Arthur joined in with a joint laugh, he was right. "Why are we driving so far away anyway to ditch this guy?" Arthur asked.

"We need to get him out of our county, so it makes it harder to link him to Lakebrook if anything, his body is the most curious to solve and we don't want that anywhere near us. Especially how these guys are not exactly your normal working-class people." Callahan clarified.

The car turned off a main road, down a rocky, thin road which sat between high standing trees. A further amount of time passed, before Callahan pulled up to the side in this narrow opening of a stopping space. He switched off the lights of the car, he sat for a moment checking the rear-view mirror.

"It's all clear, we will get him out the trunk and just drop him off deep in the forest here." instructed Callahan.

The two raised the body out of the trunk of the car and repeated the same, both carrying the body without dragging it across the floor, making the least amount of noise possible to gain attention. Even though there were no signs of life around here entirely.

As the two shuffled with the body firmly grasped in their hands, Mr Callahan kept his voice low, "Have you ever killed a human before?" he asked.

Arthur had a sudden realisation, he hadn't. He hadn't even thought about it back there as he relentlessly killed them. "No." he replied, "I... I feel bad?" he questioned out loud.

Mr Callahan let out a quiet snigger, "Heh, I wouldn't let it weigh you down too much, you did the right thing saving your friends and yourself."

They continued transporting the body through the forest, where Arthur searched himself for any reasoning of consolation. He felt bad for killing a human, but then again, they had planned to kill them first.

Mr Callahan began to search around the area for a perfect spot to hide the body, dumping it at the foot of a steep hill.

The two were silent after leaving the body, covered in shrubs. It felt wrong, leaving it there, more than sinking the others in the lake.

They hurried back to the car, walking double the speed as normal. The car doors shut and the two sat quietly in the front seats, slowly allowing the calm in now that the last tough part of the cover up had been finished.

Arthur broke the silence, "Thank you Mr Callahan."

Mr Callahan didn't say a word as he leaned down to turn the keys in the ignition, the car started.

"You're welcome. If I need a super strong, fast immortal for anything next. I'll give you a call." he smiled, in a tone of relief.

The drive back felt like a long journey, it was quiet in the car. The time began to pass into the early morning, getting past 3AM, they began to see the outskirts of Lakebrook.

Arthur looked at his phone, there was a message earlier from Hannah he had missed, "Thank you for saving us tonight. Are you okay?"

Over an hour had passed since the whole attack by the lake, it must've been sinking in for both Hannah and Kimberly.

A second message had been sent to Arthur, "Hello?! Reply?! Are you safe?" again, from Hannah. It was sent only minutes ago.

She must still be up, worried about him being left alone with Mr Callahan.

Arthur replied confirming that they had hid what they needed to. He also replied that Mr Callahan hadn't tried to kill him... yet during the drive, as a joke.

They got closer to the suburbs of Pennyview, it was obvious the drive had played a tiresome toll on Mr Callahan, yawning repeatedly.

Arthur instructed Mr Callahan where to drop him off, the usual street away from Pennyview, still keeping everyone away from the house.

As the car came to a stop by the side of the road, "I remember the last time you offered to drop me off somewhere." Arthur joked.

A tired looking Callahan turned his head towards him, "How far we have come." he smiled. "Take care Arthur."

As Arthur climbed out of the car, he paused holding the door open, tapping on the door twice he leaned down. "Thanks again Sir."

Mr Callahan nodded in a silent approval before Arthur shut the car door. Arthur stopped and stood watching Mr Callahan drive off into the night, down the street. There was a moment of stillness in the air as the car's rear lights disappeared around the corner.

The street was silent.

Placing his hands in his pockets, Arthur hunched over a little, taking his time he began to walk down the sidewalk back to Pennyview. He had time to catch his thoughts, he started to reflect about how his life had been since his arrival, a significant amount of time had passed. It was May and summer was a few weeks away meaning the end of his junior year at Lakebrook High School. Arthur had discovered new, scary supernatural powers that he never knew existed. This year he had learned a lot, more so about his new supernatural self and only had begun to scratch at the capabilities he could do. He'd gotten close to others around him, in more ways than one, built friendships that were now in the balance of testing trust with not just his secret, but the witches who he now held close to him. He had developed a passion for American football, where the team had a chance next year for the Gridiron championship, of course with a little extra supernatural help.

Next year was going to be great, there was a lot for Arthur to decide and prepare for.

As Arthur's mind wandered off reflecting about his life as he walked closer to Pennyview, an interesting fact jumped in. "They thought that I was a vampire at the lake. Again... Still didn't meet any vampires, pfft! Maybe they don't really exist."

he said jokingly, keeping his voice down in case one would pop out from nowhere.

As Arthur found himself standing outside of Pennyview Boarding House, in front of the gates that lead upwards to the path of that red front door. He stared at the house for a moment, "I guess... this is really home now." he again, spoke to himself quietly.

He stared at every edge and window of the house.

In that very moment, Arthur finally realised he belonged here.

He was *now* home.

Walking up the path to the front door, the porch light lit up the way. Excitement filled Arthur. He was excited for what was to come next in his senior year, he grew a smile and felt a weight had been lifted off him as he finally accepted his place here. Even though there were unanswered questions and threats which would only be resolved in time.

Expecting an audience as he gradually opened his way through the front door, it was dark and empty. There was no one. He turned on the light that was on top of the stairs, placing his hand on the banister at the bottom of the stairs, he looked down the hallway.

It was all empty, everyone had gone to bed. He looked at the grandfather clock across from him, it was really late for anyone to be up.

Arthur quietly stepped up the staircase trying not to wake anyone in the house. Treading carefully through the hallway, he quietly grasped at the door handle to his room, twisting it slowly he opened the door ready to get some rest.

The early summer's sunrise stretched through the room, the curtains were left open, lighting up all of the furniture and space within it. Hannah was there, wrapped in Arthur's bedsheets kneeling up on his bed at his arrival.

Arthur stopped and his heart froze, looking at her and trying to understand what she was up to.

Hannah stared back at him with a look of enticement. "Are you going to close that door and join me, or what?" she asked gently, with a soft open smile on her face.

In that moment Arthur thought, forget next year.

It's going to be one hell of a summer first.

He gently closed the door behind him.

The end.

Acknowledgements

The thanks,
Thank you to my family, loved ones, and friends for being there for me and supporting me as I write away.

Thank you to all of those who have put up with me excitedly talking frequently about writing some vague supernatural book.

Thanks for those of you who supported me over social media, Instagram, and Facebook.

I can only imagine what the staff at my local coffee shop would think. Thanks for letting me be a gremlin in the corner writing away, and the absolute fortune I must've spent here.

And finally, thank you to myself. For all the projects I have left unfinished (sorry about those). But I finished one.

Printed in Great Britain
by Amazon